Bailey's Run

Ali Spooner

Affinity
eBook Press
NZ
2014

Bailey's Run
© Ali Spooner 2014

Affinity E-Book Press NZ LTD.
Canterbury, New Zealand

1st Edition

ISBN: 978-1-927282-33-5

Editor: Ruth Stanley
Cover Design: Irish Dragon Designs

Acknowledgments

I would like to thank Affinity eBook Press, my publisher, and staff for giving me the opportunity to publish this work. I would also like to thank a dedicated group of Beta Readers for their patience and guidance in making Bailey's Run a better story. So thank you, Erin, Donna, Nancy T., and Nancy K. for your time and commitment. I would also like to thank Terry Baker, whose wonderful reviews have inspired me to do more with my writing. To my readers, thank you for supporting me and providing feedback on my stories.

Dedication

To my wife, Rhonda. Thanks for believing in me. I hope we will have another great twenty years Baby Girl.

Table of Contents

Also by Ali Spooner

Epitaph

Prologue

A lone figure sat on the grassy hillside of Memorial Gardens next to a black marble headstone. She had tearstains on her face and her hands absentmindedly twirled the bouquet of pink carnations she held. They had been her favorites.

The deep shadows forming reminded her that the sun was rapidly disappearing and she knew the gardener would arrive soon to secure the cemetery for the night, so she stood, kissed the top of the headstone, and placed the bouquet on the soft grass. "Goodnight, my love," she whispered, and slowly walked away.

Chapter 1

A large mass of dark storm clouds roiled the skies west of Memphis, bringing a storm in from Arkansas. Bailey Chambers shifted gears and raced the clouds, hoping to be off duty and on her way home before the skies opened and rain pelted the city. She pulled her rig into the company parking lot, released her trailers, and took her logbook and keys inside. She tossed the keys to the warehouse supervisor and placed her logbook on the counter. "I will see you guys bright and early on Monday," she said as she headed for the door leading to the employee parking lot.

"Have a great weekend and be careful," he answered. Bailey waved as she strode to the door.

The sun was rapidly disappearing in the darkening skies as she made her way to the bright yellow Jeep for the short drive to Midtown. She needed a shower and a bite to eat before she made her way to her second job. During the week, Bailey drove a semi for the Memphis-based FedEx hub, her run taking her to Nashville and back every day. It paid the bills, with good money left over, but her weekend job bartending at a gay bar owned by her cousin, Louise, was the one she really enjoyed.

She looked forward to the weekends and her nights at the club. Her brother Tommy and his best friend Joe were the headliners for the Friday and Saturday night drag shows. The club, generally packed to the gills with men and women of all ages and ethnic groups, had become her second home.

The smile on her face grew ever wider as she pulled into the alleyway next to her brownstone and parked the Jeep as the first raindrops began to fall. Even the rain could not dampen her spirits tonight. It had been a long week and Bailey was ready for some fun.

Inside the house, she preheated the oven for dinner while she got her clothes ready for the evening. With her clothes freshly ironed and starched, she placed her dinner in the oven then headed to the shower. The hot water washed away the miles she had driven during the week and her body began to relax under the calming flow.

Once finished, she dried off, caressed some hair product into her shoulder-length hair, and slipped into a thick terry robe. She left the bathroom and turned on her stereo system as she passed through her living room, dancing to the beat of one of her favorite disco tunes on her way to the kitchen. Bailey smiled as she remembered growing up with Tommy sashaying through the house as he danced to Donna Summer and various other disco artists. She arrived in the kitchen with two minutes remaining on the oven timer and spent the time pouring a glass of iced tea and setting a place at the table.

Tommy was four years her senior and had been performing as the drag artist Marie Lepanto for nearly five years. He and his best friend Joe, aka Victoria Luxora, had spent years traveling the gay club circuit in the south and had spent over a year in San Francisco before returning home to Memphis. Except for Louise, Tommy was her only remaining family and Bailey had missed him terribly while he was away. She was ecstatic that he had settled back into life in Memphis.

The timer sounded on the oven and she pulled her dinner out to cool. Reaching inside the refrigerator for the leftover salad and a bottle of dressing, Bailey began singing along with the tune as she dished up the potpie and prepared her salad. She checked her watch and knew Joe and Tommy would be getting off work soon and going home to prepare for their evening at the club.

Bailey dug into her meal as the rain began to fall harder, pounding out a rhythm on the tin roof of her home. She usually joined the boys for dinner at least once a week. However, the fun they had on the weekends was what she looked forward to the most. Watching them perform their shows always brought a smile to her face.

Louise was a brilliant businessperson and had taken Club Fubar to the top of the dance and show clubs in Memphis. Cleverly, she refused to pay them a salary for their work at the club, which saved them a bundle in taxes. Instead, she had established investment funds for all three of them many years ago and the investments she managed continued to grow even in the bleak economy. Louise had purchased the best equipment for the club and spared no expense in continually improving the club for her patrons and her staff. Bailey never complained about not receiving a salary and knew that if she ever needed anything, Louise would provide the money she needed.

She finished her meal and placed her dishes in the dishwasher before walking back into the living room. Bailey reached for the remote to crank up the music, and her eyes fell on a photo of her and a beautiful cinnamon-skinned woman taken on the deck of a long-ago visited beach house on the Gulf of Mexico. Her fingers shook as she reached out to pick up the photo and caress the image of the woman in the photograph. Her heart ached with a longing that paralyzed her for several moments as tears flowed down her cheeks.

"I miss you so much, Nessa," she said as she wiped the tears from her face. It had been two years since she was murdered and Bailey still missed her with every beat of her heart. Tommy, Joe, and Louise had done everything they could to bring her out of the deep funk she had fallen into after Nessa's death, but there were moments when the heartbreak was almost too much for her to bear. She wiped a speck of dust from the top of the frame then placed the photograph back on the shelf, her excitement dulled by the painful memories.

Releasing a deep sigh, Bailey walked into her bedroom to dress for the club. She was not oblivious to her good looks or the women who came to Fubar with hopes of catching her eye. However, she was unsure if she was ready for any kind of emotional commitment.

Since Nessa's death, Bailey endlessly ran away from potential mates, much to Tommy and Joe's distress, and she felt their growing frustration with the failed attempts to hook her up with eligible women. Even though neither of them had a permanent partner, they knew how much Bailey needed a new love interest in her life, even if Bailey did not.

Slipping into a favorite pair of black Harley boots, Bailey looked at her image in the mirror. The handsome woman that looked back at her with haunted eyes was an image she almost did not recognize. The jeans that once fit snuggly were beginning to feel loose, even with the tail of her oxford tucked inside them. Bailey knew something in her life needed to change. The lust for life she had when Nessa was alive was gone and Bailey had no idea how she would light that spark again or even if she could.

Nessa had been the one she always dreamed she would spend her life with and without her Bailey felt empty. The boys and Louise did everything they could to lift her spirits, but Bailey finally realized change would have to begin with her.

†

Black leather bands circled her wrists and with a splash of cologne, Bailey was ready to go. She turned off the music on her way through the house and retrieved her keys from the kitchen before slipping out into the gentle Memphis rain. She pulled the Jeep onto the main street and carefully made her way to Fubar, luckily finding a spot close to the door.

The club was already crowded and noisy when she opened the door and stepped inside. The packed dance floor filled with a crowd of twenty-somethings, who would make the rounds of the dance clubs, was the first wave of customers for the night. Their gyrating dance moves created a heat wave and customers flooded to the bar for liquid refreshments. Bailey rolled up her sleeves and stepped into the fray, filling orders as quickly as she could. Louise caught her eye and smiled as she too rushed to fill orders.

When the rush died down, Louise approached. "I'm so glad you came in early tonight. It has been a wild night already," she said, brushing back the hair that had fallen into her face.

"I can see that," Bailey said with a huge grin. A thirsty crowd was good for business and good for tips. She glanced at her tip jar to find it was filling with bills after the rush of the crowd.

"How are you tonight?" Louise finally asked when she had caught her breath.

"I'm doing good, thanks. I was ready for this weekend," Bailey answered with a chuckle.

"Are you getting burnt out on your run?"

She took a rag and wiped down the bar as they chatted. "No, actually it is a pretty straight shot and not a difficult run at all. They offered me an overnight run, but I think I'll stick with Nashville for a while yet."

"It's okay to stay in your comfort zone," Louise said as she leaned against the bar.

Bailey flinched at Louise's comment but knew she was spot-on. Bailey was hesitant to step outside her comfort zone. Louise was the most aggressive of the three in pushing Bailey to move forward with her life, and even though Bailey knew her intentions were pure, she felt the growing pressure her cousin was putting on her.

"I know, I know," Bailey said. "One step at a time is all I can do."

Louise smiled at her younger cousin. "Just don't forget how to move those feet," she said with a wink.

Becca, a regular of the club and an avid admirer of Bailey, stepped up to the bar. "Is something wrong with Bailey's feet?"

"I'm not sure, Becca, why don't you take her for a spin on the dance floor to see if they still work," Louise suggested.

"Not a bad idea, Louise," she said as she stepped around a barstool. "Will you dance with me, Bailey?"

"Sure." Bailey walked around the bar and took Becca's hand then led her to the dance floor. It had been a while since she had danced with a partner, but she quickly caught the rhythm of the song and her body moved fluidly on the floor. Many sets of eyes watched Bailey's moves. She was a natural dancer and Louise smiled as the hormone level in the club skyrocketed when Bailey was in her element.

Bailey was breathing hard but wearing a smile when she finally escaped ten minutes later and made it back to the bar.

"Damn girl, you still got the moves," Louise said as she tossed her a bar towel.

"Not bad at all, huh?" she said with a grin as she stepped behind the bar. Dancing had felt wonderful, she thought as she approached Louise.

"Not at all," Louise said, happy to see a glimpse of the former Bailey.

"Do we have a full show on the menu tonight?"

"Yes, Tommy and Joe will be joined by a couple of queens they met who are up from New Orleans for the weekend," Louise answered. "Apparently Tony and Charles were in need of a short break from Bourbon Street."

"I can't imagine a queen getting tired of Bourbon Street," Bailey said. "Every time I have ever visited the clubs they have been packed from floor to ceiling."

Becca had returned to her barstool and had picked up their conversation. "Maybe you should join me for a weekend in New Orleans then," she told Bailey and flashed a wink at Louise.

"You do have vacation time to use," Louise reminded her.

"Yeah, I do. Do you think New Orleans is ready for you, Becca?"

"I only know of one way to find out," she answered.

"We will see how things go this summer," Bailey surprised them by saying.

Becca clutched her chest, and with flair of dramatics said, "Don't build my hopes up just to watch me crash back down to earth."

"You are such a goof," Bailey said with a smile and grabbed an empty tray as she moved past Becca to clear some empty bottles from the tables.

"Well, that wasn't an outright 'no' for an answer," Louise said with a grin.

"Nope, and she's going to find out how persistent I can be this summer," Becca said and took a long drink from a fresh beer Louise had placed in front of her.

Bailey returned with a tray full of empty beer bottles and took them to the storeroom to place them in empty case boxes for recycling. When she stepped behind the bar, she asked, "Do we need to restock anything?"

"No, I think we are good for now."

The door swung open and two of the most beautiful men she had ever seen walked over to the bar, carrying large bags similar to those Joe and Tommy used when they performed. The smaller of the two gave Bailey the once-over from head to toe and looked back at his friend. "This must be the place; Tommy said there would be a gorgeous bartender working tonight, and I do believe we have arrived."

Bailey could not help but grin at the pair. "You must be Tony and Charles, welcome to Club Fubar. Take a seat, and I'll get you both something to drink. The name is Bailey, by the way, and Tommy is my brother."

"I'm Tony," the smaller man said, "and this big lug is Charles," he said as they sat on barstools.

"The boys should be here in just a few minutes. What can I get you two to drink?"

"I would love a gin and tonic, darling," Tony said.

Bailey looked at Charles and waited for his order. "Surprise me," he said with a devilish grin.

She whipped up a gin and tonic quickly and handed it to Tony. They watched as she went to work blending several liquids into a tall glass with crushed iced. "A Smokey Blues," she said as she sat the drink in front of Charles.

Charles took a sip of the drink and began fanning himself. "My goodness, this is heavenly," he said. "I better be careful though, I still have to put my face on."

Bailey chuckled. "That is definitely a sipping drink," she agreed.

The door opened again and Bailey looked past the large man who was collecting the cover charge and checking IDs to see Tommy and Joe enter the club, carrying their bags. Tommy smiled brightly when he saw Bailey talking with his friends. "Hey, baby sister," he said and kissed her cheek. "I see you've met my friends."

"She is taking very good care of us," Charles said with a wink to Bailey as he hugged Tommy and then Joe.

"It looks like a good crowd so far," Joe said as his eyes surveyed the room.

"Good tippers too," she said, nodding toward her tip jar.

"Yeah, but you always get good tips, you hunk a hunk of burning love," Joe teased.

"Have you ever considered performing?" Tony asked.

"Who me? Heck no, Tommy and Joe have that market covered for this family," Bailey said as she nervously wiped down the bar.

"Honey, with your looks, you could make a fortune performing in New Orleans," Charles said.

Bailey blushed at their compliments. "Thanks, but I think I had better stick to bartending."

"If you ever change your mind, look me up and I will get you introduced to all the best clubs in Nawlins," Tony promised her.

"Thanks, I will," she said and turned as Louise returned from the restroom.

"This beautiful lady is the mastermind behind all this," Tommy said and introduced Tony and Charles.

"Thank you for having us this weekend," Charles said.

"You are welcome anytime," Louise said.

"Are you girls about ready to get dolled up?" Joe asked.

"Lead the way, handsome," Charles said and picked up his drink.

"I'll see you in a bit," Bailey said as they picked up their bags and headed for the dressing room. She watched as they disappeared through the crowd and when the current string of songs ended waited for the rush of thirsty patrons.

Some of the younger crowd began to thin out, moving on to make a circuit of the city's clubs, replaced by a slightly older crowd as the time for the first show approached. By the time the lights flickered to announce the show was about to begin, there was not an empty seat in the club.

Bailey wiped down the bar as Marie Lepanto stepped out on the stage and took a microphone from the DJ. "Welcome all to Club Fubar," she said. "Are you ready to have some fun?"

"Hell yes," came the response from the crowd.

"I can't hear you," Marie said as she placed a hand to her ear.

"Hell yes," came a louder response.

"Now that is what I was waiting to hear. Put your hands together for a warm Memphis welcome for the Fabulous Nikki Simone, visiting us from New Orleans," she said to a roar of applause.

The lights of the club went down and a spotlight glowed on the middle of the stage where Nikki, aka Tony, stood, head hanging low as the song began slowly. As the beat picked up, Nikki went into full gear and the crowd roared their approval, as her dance moves were incredible.

Dollar bills were waving in the air and Nikki slowed down long enough to accept the tips and give the owners a quick brush of a kiss on their cheeks as the performance continued. Tony was a beautiful man, but he was gorgeous as a woman, Bailey thought as she watched the performance.

"Isn't it a shame one of the most beautiful women in here is a man?" Louise said as she walked around the bar to stand next to Bailey.

"I was just thinking the same thing." Bailey returned her cousin's smile. "What is this world coming to?"

"I'll be damned if I know."

Becca returned to the bar. "May I get a fresh cold one?"

"You most certainly can," Bailey said and got a new beer for her friend. "What have you been up to these days?"

"Just working and chasing the occasional woman," Becca said.

"Have you caught any?" Louise asked.

"None worth keeping yet, but I'm still hopeful," Becca said with a wink to Bailey before heading back into the crowd.

Bailey watched her go and turned to find Louise watching her. "What?"

"You know she adores you."

"I know, but Becca is more like a sister to me," Bailey said. "She is a fantastic woman, but I feel no attraction to her."

"What about the other fifty or so women in here?"

Bailey had a pained look on her face. "I had what I wanted most and it was taken from me. I don't think I can ever replace that."

"You will never replace it, darling, but there are plenty of good women left in this world that would be lucky to have someone like you in their lives."

Bailey let Louise's words sink in. Deep down she knew her cousin was right. Nessa would not want her to go on like this. She would want her to be happy.

The number on stage ended and Marie came back out to introduce Charlise, aka Charles, and the show continued. People continued to crowd through the door and the bar was packed with drink orders most of the night, much to Bailey's delight. If she stayed busy behind the bar, her mind would not wander to places better left alone for now.

When the first of the two shows ended with roaring applause for all four performers, Bailey took a tray of drinks back into the dressing room. "That was quite a show," she said as she passed drinks to the heated performers.

"A good crowd for tips too," Charles said as he plucked dollar bills from his costume.

"Just don't spend it all in one place," Bailey teased. "Is there anything I can get you all?"

"No, baby sis, I think we're good for now. We have another hour or so before the next show, so once we touch up our makeup a bit we'll go socialize with our audience," Tommy said.

"Okay then, just give me a holler if you need anything."

"Thanks, love," he answered as she left.

Bailey collected empty bottles and glasses as she made her way back to the bar. Her tray was full before she made it halfway there. She set the tray on the counter and looked at Louise. "You know, we really should think about hiring another serving staff."

"I've been giving that some thought. Annette is great, but these weekend nights, she just cannot keep up with the crowd. Do you have anyone in mind?"

"I don't, but I bet Tommy could suggest someone who could use extra work on the weekends. It may help to have a little male eye candy in here."

"True, but it may make it difficult to keep him from flirting with the customers." Louise chuckled.

"That's always a risk, but I'm sure we could keep him under control."

"I will talk to Tommy about it later then," Louise said.

Bailey nodded her head and went back to work stocking the coolers. It was almost midnight when she finished and the lights flickered to let everyone know the last show of the evening was about to begin. The DJ let the song fade out and handed the microphone over to Marie as Bailey stepped outside for a breath of fresh air.

The rain had ended, at least for a time. The streets, washed clean by the rain, were shining under the moonlight and Bailey took a deep breath. The air had a freshness that only followed a good rain. She leaned back against the building and looked up into the sky. The heavy clouds were gone and the stars winked down on her as she breathed deeply, filling her lungs with fresh air. Off in the distance she could hear the blare of sirens, probably more of the senseless violence that plagued the city she had always called home.

The door to the club swung open as a young couple left and Bailey could hear the thumping bass of the dance music that would play for another hour after the show, before they announced "last call" for the evening. She watched the couple walk hand in hand to their car and then disappear into the shadows of the city. Her heart ached with the memory of holding Nessa's hand as they strolled together. Before complete melancholy could overcome her, she sighed deeply and walked back into the club.

The crowd began to thin out over the next hour. Tommy and his friends packed away their gear and sat in a booth together to enjoy a drink before Tony and Charles would head back to their hotel. Bailey took them drinks and pulled an empty chair to the end of the booth. She straddled the chair, propping her arms on the back, and grinned at her brother.

"That was a great show," she said.

"Not a bad performance for a Friday night," Joe said.

"Indeed," Tommy agreed. "The kids were out in force tonight."

"Didn't you say that Saturday night is even better?" Charles asked.

"Generally speaking, yes, they are," Tommy answered. "Especially when we have performers visiting from out of town. You'd be amazed how fast word spreads through this city."

Bailey glanced at the bar to see Louise swamped with thirsty customers. "I had better get back to help Louise. Is everyone good here?"

"Yes, ma'am," Tony said, and raised his glass to her.

Bailey was returning from the stockroom when the boys approached the bar. "Tony and I are going to go crash for the evening. Will we see you tomorrow night?" Charles asked.

"I'll be right here. You two be safe and don't get into any trouble," Bailey said.

"We would never even consider it," Tony said with a boyish grin.

"Come on then and I'll walk you out," Tommy said.

"Hand me that dishpan and I'll bus the tables for you," Joe told Bailey, who had begun washing up the glasses.

She handed him the pan and resumed washing as Louise prepared the cash register for the final money drop of the evening.

Five minutes later, Joe placed the pan on the counter, looked around and then back to Bailey. "Has Tommy not come back inside?" he asked.

Bailey had not seen Tommy return, but hadn't thought it strange. "Why don't you check to see if he is still outside chatting up the boys?" she asked.

With a smirk, Joe walked out the front door as Bailey dumped the last of the glasses into the dishwater. She was startled several seconds later when Joe flung the door wide and yelled for her.

"Bailey, come quick," he screamed. The horrified look on his face made her blood run cold.

On her way toward the door she reached under the bar and grabbed a Louisville Slugger she kept there in case of an emergency, and this sure felt like it was going to be serious. She hit the door with Louise hot on her tail. She looked in horror at the scene in front of her. Tommy was down on the ground in the parking lot and two men were pounding him with vicious blows. Tommy tried to curl up in a protective ball as they screamed and kicked at him.

Bailey turned to Louise. "Call nine-one-one," she said and took off at a full run.

Joe was screaming at the men to leave him alone but the men were in a frenzy of rage as their brutal attack continued.

"I can't believe you only have ten bucks, you stupid fag," one of them yelled as he kicked at Tommy.

Bailey, fueled with a rage of her own, rushed to Tommy's defense. She had not been there for Nessa, but by God, she would be there for Tommy. These men were not taking another of her loved ones from her without a fight. She swung the bat with all her might and landed a blow just above the closest man's right elbow. She felt the crunch of splintering bones as the man's pain-filled screams rang in her ears. She reared back for another swing, but the man had stumbled from the blow and started to run away. Bailey took aim at the other assailant and swung for the man's head. Lucky for him, the man ducked away at just the precise moment to prevent his head from sailing over the Mississippi River from the force of her swing. He stumbled backward but was able to regain his feet before Bailey could take further aim with her bat.

She chased him across the parking lot until she was sure they were both gone before turning back to find Joe kneeling over Tommy. She ran back to him and sank to her knees when she saw the blood covering his face. Her heart raced a mile a minute.

Louise ran back out with the tiny first-aid kit they kept at the bar, but there was so much blood covering Tommy they didn't know where to begin. He was still conscious and trying to speak as Joe cradled his head in his lap, tears streaking down his face.

Sirens wailed in the distance as the bat slipped from Bailey's grip and she took Tommy's hand. "Just hang in there, Tommy, help is on its way," she said through a throat so parched she feared it would come out as a croak.

Tommy looked up at her, his eyes glazing over with pain. "That was one hell of a swing you took at him. I always knew you had the best swing in the family," he said and when he managed a weak grin, Bailey saw that several of his teeth were broken.

"Those bastards," she said through gritted teeth. "I'd kill them if I could get my hands on them."

"Easy girl," Louise said as she dabbed at the blood on Tommy's face. "We don't need both of you going into the hospital tonight."

Bailey rocked back on her heels as she waited for the ambulance to arrive. The sirens seemed a hundred miles away and she feared they would never arrive before Tommy slipped away from them. Please God, let them hurry she prayed to herself as Tommy coughed and spit up blood.

She could hear a gurgling deep in his throat as panic overtook her. "Joe, you have to turn his head to the side before his lungs fill up with blood," she said and helped him ease Tommy onto his side. A large amount of blood ran from his mouth and pooled on the damp asphalt beside her. Bailey looked up when she heard the screeching of tires, happy to see the red lights of the ambulance approaching at a rapid pace. "Thank God," she breathed as the ambulance skidded to a halt and two paramedics grabbed their gear and rushed over to where Tommy lay.

"What happened here?" one of the men asked.

"My brother was jumped by two men who wanted to take his money," Bailey said as the rage boiled up inside her again.

"You all need to step back now and let us do our work," the other man said as he gently backed them away from Tommy.

Bailey watched through tear-filled eyes as the men hooked up several monitors to her only brother as he lay in a pool of his own blood in the parking lot. The men worked quickly to assess Tommy's injuries as Tommy tried to explain what had happened to him.

"You're going to be okay, buddy, just relax and let us take care of you," the man said.

Never one to miss a chance to flirt with a handsome man, Tommy said, "You can take care of me anytime, you sexy beast," and then promptly passed out.

If the situation had not been so dangerous, Bailey would have almost found his comment hilarious as the air leaving his lungs across the broken teeth made his comment sound like "you sexy feast," which is exactly what Tommy would make out of a man as handsome as the paramedic. Even in the dim lighting of the parking lot, she could see the blush on the man's cheeks and she couldn't help but grin when his partner looked to him and said, "Will you go get the gurney, you sexy beast."

The same man looked over to Bailey. "Is this your brother?"

"Yes, it is. His name is Tommy."

"Will you be going with him to the hospital?"

"Yes, I will," Bailey answered.

"I would suggest grabbing a coat if you have one, it can get cold in there. We'll put Tommy on the gurney and be ready to load him in just a few minutes," he said.

Bailey nodded her head and handed the bat to Louise. "Will you be okay closing down the club?"

"I'll stay and help her and then we'll come to the hospital," Joe said.

"Thanks. Joe will you grab my jacket from the Jeep?" Bailey asked as she handed him her keys with a hand shaking with fright.

Louise started back inside and Joe ran to her Jeep, returning with her jacket. "He's going to be all right," he said and kissed her on the cheek. "Louise and I will see you soon."

The paramedics had carefully placed Tommy on the gurney once they were sure he didn't have a back or neck injury and they were slowly pushing him to the back of the ambulance. "Do you want to ride in the back with your brother?" the driver asked.

"Yes, if I can," she answered.

"Don't worry. Stan will let you know if you are in his way," he said with a comforting smile.

"Is that the sexy beast?" Bailey asked and then snickered with nervous laughter.

"I'll admit, I have been called a lot of names on this job, but never a sexy beast," Stan answered.

"Well, Tommy never misses a chance to flirt with a good-looking man," Bailey said.

"It's a positive sign he still has a good sense of humor after what he's gone through. He's been beaten pretty badly, but he is going to be all right, so you relax, okay?"

Bailey nodded her head and allowed the driver to assist her in climbing into the back of the ambulance. "We are going to Methodist, is that okay?"

"Yes, that's great," Bailey managed to say as she pulled her arms through the jacket.

The driver closed the door and ran around to the driver's seat, and the ambulance pulled carefully out onto the street.

Chapter 2

Bailey must have gone into a mild case of shock, as she could not remember the ride to the hospital. She remembered climbing into the back of the ambulance, and then the next thing she knew she was sitting in the family waiting room at the hospital holding a cup of strong coffee.

When the door opened again, Louise and Joe came rushing to her side. "Have you heard anything yet?" Louise asked.

"No, not yet," Bailey said as she sank back down on the couch. Louise sat next to her and Joe took the chair to her left.

"He's a fighter and Tommy will be okay," Joe said, his voice trembling with emotion.

Bailey nodded at him and drank a sip of her rapidly cooling coffee.

"That looks good. Louise, would you like a cup?" Joe asked.

"Yeah, I think I could use one or ten," she said with a grin.

Joe brought them all a fresh cup and they began the vigil of waiting for news about Tommy. None of them really had the energy or courage to speak, so they sat huddled together and waited.

†

Detective Desi Dexter took the call from the lieutenant and stormed into the break room to find her partner. "Time to roll, Braxton, we have a new case."

"Please not another gang fight," he groaned as he crushed the Diet Coke can with his hands and tossed it into the recycling bin. He looked at Desi and saw the dark look of anger in her face.

"No, it's another gay bashing," she said with a growl in her voice. "Two skinheads beat up a young man as their Friday night entertainment. He's being transported to Methodist."

"Assholes," Braxton said as he grabbed his coat from the back of his chair. "Come on, I'll drive. You look like you could spit nails."

"I'm just so tired of seeing gays being beaten and harassed just because of their lifestyles," she said with her rage threatening to boil over.

"I understand, and agree with you, but you need to get a grip. We have a job to do."

Desi managed a weak smile. She knew her partner was right. She was a professional and no matter how angry she was, she had to be calm and collected once they arrived at the hospital. "You're right, thanks Braxton," she said and followed him out the door.

†

Twenty minutes later the door opened again and Bailey prayed it would be the doctor with news of Tommy, but she was disappointed when a man and a woman walked into the room.

The man was huge but the woman caught Bailey's eye. The gentle sway of her hips as she strode confidently into the room made Bailey sit up at full attention as they approached. The woman looked at her, and when she smiled, Bailey felt a swarm of butterflies in her stomach. Their eyes locked together briefly and Bailey swore there was a blush rising to the woman's cheeks as their gaze lingered. The man pulled back his suit jacket and pulled out a badge and Bailey's interest quickly faded.

"Damn," she said softly, not realizing she had spoken her thoughts aloud.

"Are you okay, Bailey?" Joe asked.

Bailey nodded and slumped back in her seat. She was certain the woman was gay and she was incredibly attractive, so why did she have to be a cop and ruin everything? Bailey asked herself.

"Are you the family of Tommy Chambers?" the man asked.

"Yes," Louise said. "I'm his cousin and this is his sister, Bailey, and his best friend, Joe. My name's Louise."

The couple approached. "I'm Detective Braxton," he said, "and this is my partner, Detective Dexter. We are here regarding Mr. Chambers. We hoped we could speak with you now. Do you have any word on how he is doing?" he asked.

Bailey fixed him with cold eyes. "No, we haven't heard yet."

The two detectives shared a look between them, and then took seats across from where they were sitting. The female took out a notepad as the man asked, "Can anyone tell us what happened to Tommy?"

Bailey exploded on the man. "Two motherfucking punks rolled and beat another fag in our fair city, for ten fucking dollars, that's what happened," she said and stormed out of the waiting room.

†

Desi looked at her partner, who was just as perplexed as she was, and then at the other startled people in the room. *What the fuck just happened here?*

Louise and Joe looked at each other in shock at Bailey's outburst, and then looked back at the detective with blank faces. Louise was the first to speak. "I'm sorry. Bailey is usually not like that at all."

"She has good reason to dislike cops," Joe said.

"Why is that?" Desi asked.

"Her lover was murdered two years ago and the police have not been able to solve the case. Bailey insists they didn't even try to find the killers," Louise explained. "She's had no closure and I'm sure tonight's activity has brought back many painful memories. Other than Tommy, I am the only family Bailey has left."

"I can empathize with the way she feels. It really is not all that uncommon for us to be treated harshly at the beginning of an investigation, so don't let it worry you," Desi said. "We will do everything in our power to bring the men that did this to her brother to justice, but we need your help."

Louise nodded her understanding. "Tommy had walked some friends out to the parking lot and when he hadn't returned after several minutes, Joe went out to check on him."

"I walked out the door and heard the men shouting at Tommy and kicking him when he was down on the asphalt. I ran back inside for Bailey to help," Joe explained.

"Did you get a good look at the men?" he asked.

"I know they were both white, young, skinheads," Joe said.

"What makes you think that?" he asked.

"They both had shaved heads and the bigger one had a swastika tattooed on his arm," he explained.

"Right or left arm?" Desi asked as she rapidly jotted down notes.

"His right; that will be the one that's broken," Joe said.

She looked up from her notepad and asked, "How did his arm get broken?"

Joe grinned at her. "Bailey keeps a Louisville Slugger behind the bar, and she got in a good hit just above his right elbow. I could hear the crunch of the bones from ten feet away," he said with pride.

The detective could not stifle her grin, so she quickly looked back down at her notepad.

"Bailey would have had a better look at him," Joe continued.

†

The door opened again and a female doctor approached. "Are you the Chambers family?" she asked.

"Yes, but wait just a minute until I can get his sister," Detective Dexter said.

The doctor nodded and sat beside Joe as Detective Dexter walked out of the waiting room. Bailey was nowhere in the hallway, so she stepped out a side door that led to a small patio.

Bailey was leaning against the building with tears running down her face. Desi wasn't sure how she knew it, but she would bet her paycheck that this woman did not shed tears easily. Her heart longed to go to her and wrap her arms around her in a comforting hug, even though the woman had made her distaste for cops perfectly clear.

"Ms. Chambers," she said. "The doctor has arrived to give a report on your brother," she said.

Bailey's head whipped around at the sound of her voice, the cold glare of anger still present in her eyes as she approached.

"I am not your enemy," Detective Dexter said. "I will find who did this."

"Yeah, I've heard that song and dance before, Detective," Bailey said as she stormed past the woman and through the door.

Detective Dexter shook her head and followed Bailey back inside the hospital. She could understand her mistrust, but Desi felt compelled to find a way of helping her resolve the grief that had a solid grip on her heart. Desi sighed when no answer came to mind and followed Bailey back inside.

†

The older female doctor smiled as Bailey approached and sat next to Louise, who wrapped a protective arm around her.

Desi returned to sit beside Braxton. She couldn't take her eyes off Bailey. It had been a long time since she had felt the pull of attraction to someone this strongly. She watched Bailey closely as the doctor began to speak.

"I'm Dr. Fields, your brother's ER physician, and I just wanted to let you know Tommy is going to be okay. He has regained consciousness and was asking about a sexy beast," she stated with a look of confusion as the others cracked up.

"I'm sorry for laughing," Louise said, "but you would have to know Tommy to understand the comment. He was flirting with one of the paramedics and called him a sexy beast before he passed out."

"Well, that certainly puts some things into perspective," she said with a grin. "It has taken several stitches to close up some of his wounds. He has several broken ribs, but all the tests we have run on him have been negative for any internal bleeding, brain trauma, or organ damage."

Bailey broke down and the tears began to fall once more. Louise pulled her close.

"He's going to be sore until those ribs heal, and he will need some dental work done, but in a couple of weeks he will be fine," she said. "I want to keep him overnight for observation and to get some fluids back into him, but there should be no reason he can't be discharged late tomorrow."

"Can we see him?" Bailey asked between gasps for air.

"Yes, one at a time, but please keep in mind he has not been completely cleaned up yet, so there is still a lot of blood and keep your visits short. Now that we are comfortable he has not suffered any brain trauma we have given him pain medications, so he may be in and out of consciousness." She stood to leave. "I will see about getting him a bed so they can get him upstairs and settled in," she said and left the room.

"You go first, Bailey," Louise said. Bailey jumped up and followed the doctor out of the room, brushing her tears away.

Louise noted with curiosity that Detective Dexter's eyes followed Bailey as she walked from the room. When the detective turned around, she noticed Louise smiling at her and the flush of embarrassment returned to her cheeks.

†

The doctor led her to the exam room where Tommy was still lying on the gurney, his eyes closed as he slept peacefully. She placed a comforting hand on Bailey's shoulder. "I will do my best to get him transferred to a room quickly," she said and left Bailey with Tommy. Bailey walked to the side of the gurney and took Tommy's hand in hers. She slumped in the chair beside the bed, finally realizing how mentally exhausted she was.

"I thought I was going to lose you, Tommy," she whispered as tears rolled down her cheeks.

"You won't be rid of me that easily, baby sis," Tommy slurred.

Bailey looked up to find his eyes open, but glazed from the medication. He attempted a smile, but the pain turned his face into a grimace.

"Hush now. The doctor says you are going to be fine, but you need your rest."

"Get my sock," he croaked out a whisper.

"Your sock, what sock?"

Bailey followed his eyes over to the counter where a bloodied stuffed sock lay. "I stuffed it down my pants," he said.

Bailey turned and picked up the sock and opened it to find money stuffed inside. She cocked her head at her brother. "Your tips?" she asked.

He grinned at her and nodded his head slowly. "I worked hard for those."

Bailey just shook her head as she stuffed the sock in her jacket pocket. "Next time just give them the damned sock," she said.

"I think I might," Tommy said and then dozed off.

Bailey stood, leaned over the gurney to kiss his forehead. "I love you," she whispered, then left the room so others could visit.

†

When she returned to the waiting room, both detectives were still asking questions. Joe looked at Louise, and she nodded. "Go ahead, I will see him after."

Bailey sat beside Louise, the tension still evident in her body language. Detective Dexter looked at Bailey with compassion. "I know this is a hard time for you, but we do need to interview you. Would you prefer we hold off until tomorrow?" she asked.

"No, if it has to be done, let's do it tonight and get it over with," Bailey answered, venom still in her voice.

Louise, totally shocked by Bailey's hostile tone said, "Relax, they are only trying to help."

"I know." Turning to the female detective, she said, "I'm sorry, but this has been a horrible night."

"I understand and we'll try to be brief," she said. "Joe told us that you may have gotten a good look at the men who attacked your brother and you may have injured one of them. Is this true?"

Bailey relaxed a bit. "Yeah, I got a good swing on the bigger of the two, and he will definitely be in need of medical attention. I heard and felt the bones breaking when I made contact."

"Joe said just above his right elbow, is that correct?" she asked.

"Yes, I was aiming for that damned swastika tattoo on his arm."

"Can you give us a description of the men?"

"Shaved heads, both pretty burly guys, maybe in their early- to mid-twenties. Both were white, around six-feet tall. They were wearing jeans, dark T-shirts, and boots, heavy boots."

Dexter rapidly took down notes of her descriptions and looked back up at Bailey. "Is there anything else you can think of," she asked.

"No, not at this moment," Bailey answered, forcing a weak smile.

Detective Dexter reached into her pocket and pulled out a business card. "Here is my card with my contact information, and I have written the case number on the back. If you think of anything else or have any questions, please don't hesitate to call." She offered a smile, but Bailey refused to look at her.

She and Braxton stood. "Thank you for your time. We will be back tomorrow to talk with Mr. Chambers," she said and left the room.

Bailey stuffed the card in the back pocket of her jeans and looked at Louise with tears threatening to fall.

Louise pulled her back on the couch and Bailey let her head come to rest on her cousin's shoulder. She stroked Bailey's hair and whispered, "He's going to be fine."

"They beat the crap out of him for ten lousy dollars," Bailey said. She pulled the bloody sock from her jacket. "He stashed his tips in here and stuffed them down his pants for safekeeping," she said as she handed the sock to Louise.

"What will those boys think of next," she chuckled and stuffed the sock in her purse.

†

Joe returned and looked even paler than usual as he sat next to them. "They will be moving him up to room 235. The nurse said to give them thirty minutes to get him moved and settled before we go upstairs to visit. She suggested we grab a bite in the snack bar while we wait."

"A little food in our stomachs would not be a bad idea," Louise said, unsure if she could convince Bailey to eat. "I imagine it will be a long night for all of us."

Bailey looked at her cousin. "I'm staying tonight, so you and Joe go home and get some rest."

"You aren't staying alone," Joe said.

"Fine, you stay, but Louise you need to go rest. You can relieve us tomorrow," Bailey said.

"Only after you get something in your stomach besides this battery acid they call coffee," she said.

"All right. I will eat something, then you go home," Bailey said.

†

"Well, that was certainly intense," Braxton said as he held the door open for Desi as they left the hospital. "That woman certainly has a chip on her shoulder."

Desi surprised herself by jumping to Bailey's defense. "From the sound of it she has good reason to be pissed off at cops in general."

Braxton grinned, never one to miss an opportunity to tease his partner. "If I didn't know better, I'd say you had the hots for her," he said with a wink and kept walking.

His comment caught Desi totally off guard and she stopped in her tracks. "Where did that come from?"

"Just an observation; I am a sharp detective you know," Braxton said and climbed into the car.

Desi shook her head and took her seat in the car to ponder his comment on the way back to the precinct.

†

They found the snack bar and ordered the cheeseburger specials announced on the menu board. Bailey was actually surprised at how good it tasted. The food and the sweet tea bolstered her blood sugar and Bailey found her energy returning.

When they finished eating she and Joe walked Louise to her car. "Do you still carry a pack of smokes in your car?" Bailey asked.

"Yes, but Bailey, you haven't smoked in years," Louise said.

"I know, but I could use one now."

Louise nodded her head and reached into the glove box for a lighter and package of cigarettes. Louise traveled throughout the city and made a habit of carrying a pack of cigarettes with her. She rarely gave the panhandlers on street corners money, but she would offer them cigarettes. One of the less fortunate she had befriended years earlier had told her that frequently homeless people traded smokes for other items, so she tried to keep them on hand. "I can't guarantee how fresh these are," she said as she offered them to Bailey.

"Hopefully it will taste awful, but I could use the nicotine to calm my nerves." She lit a cigarette and handed the pack to Louise. Bailey took a draw and let the smoke out quickly. "God, this is awful," she said and tried to keep from choking. She made another attempt with similar results and threw the cigarette on the ground and smashed it out with her foot. "Screw the nicotine. I will just have to put my big girl panties on and deal," she said, which made them all laugh.

Louise hugged her and climbed into her car. "Text me when you make it home, okay?" Bailey asked.

"I will, and call if you need anything tonight," she said as she started the engine.

Bailey nodded and then allowed Joe to take her hand and lead her back inside to find the elevator. They made it to the second floor and found Tommy's room. Thankfully, it was a private room and looked to have two relatively comfortable chairs on either side of the bed. A nurse was just finishing recording his vitals when they walked in. "Are you two staying the night?" They both nodded. "Let me get you a couple of blankets then. It gets rather cold in here," she said. When she returned a few minutes later, with blankets straight from the warmer, they thanked her for her kindness. "My name is Tammy and I'm your brother's nurse tonight. Call for me if you need anything at all."

Bailey sat back in the chair and placed the blanket over her legs before reaching out to hold Tommy's hand. It was cold and had an IV line taped to his wrist. She took a moment to look around the room at the various monitors attached to her brother, and the rhythmic beat coming from his heart monitor began to work its magic. Ten minutes later Bailey was sound asleep, and Joe followed closely behind her.

†

Two hours later Bailey awoke when she felt the air pressure change in the room as the heavy door swung open. Tammy had returned to check Tommy's vitals and give him more pain medicine. "Sorry, I didn't mean to wake you," she whispered as she recorded the measurements on his chart. "Can I get you anything?"

"No, thanks," Bailey answered and settled back in her chair. She watched Tommy sleeping peacefully and quickly sank back to her own dreams.

†

The detectives arrived back at the precinct and Braxton wrote a report for dispatch to send out to all units and the local hospitals to be on the lookout for a man needing medical attention for a broken arm. Desi, the faster and more efficient typist, went to work typing up the notes from their interviews.

When she had finished and they had signed off on the report, Desi stretched and looked at Braxton. "I'm ready for this shift to be over."

"I hear you. Do you want to go to the hospital for Mr. Chambers's statement before we clock out?" he asked.

Desi thought about the possibility of seeing Bailey again and she suddenly felt more alert. "He won't be released before the afternoon, so let's catch up with him later."

Chapter 3

A loud clanging of metal breakfast trays being delivered brought Bailey awake. She looked over at Tommy, who was still fast asleep, and then at the empty chair previously occupied by Joe, who was mysteriously absent. The mystery was solved moments later when Joe returned, carrying a bag of food and two very large cups of fragrant coffee that made sweet love to Bailey's nose as he walked by.

"How long have you been awake?" Bailey asked as she accepted the coffee he offered.

"Just long enough to hit the snack bar for coffee, breakfast, and a chance to chat up the cutest little Latino man I have seen in ages," Joe said with an impish grin.

"I swear you are such a hound," she teased. "Thanks for this wonderful coffee, though."

"My pleasure, darling. Louise made me promise to get you to eat some breakfast too," he said.

"When did you talk to her?"

"About twenty minutes ago. She was about ready to leave on her way here. So if you know what's good for you, you better start eating before she arrives," he warned.

"Good grief, I don't know which of you two is worse," she said as she took a breakfast sandwich out of the wrapper and took a large bite.

"Oh by far, Louise is," Joe said with a smile. "She has every intention of putting at least ten pounds back on you after seeing you last night. She remarked on how skinny you had gotten."

"I still have to be able to haul myself up into the rig," Bailey said.

"Oh, hush girl, you know any weight you put on is pure muscle, so don't give me that song and dance," Joe camped.

The door crept open and Louise stepped into the room. "Were your ears burning, love?"

"Should they have been?" she asked.

"Oh, yes, we were just discussing your plan to put some weight on this woman," Joe answered.

"Well, since that cat is out of the bag, I would like to see you eating more. You have gotten way too thin, in my opinion," her cousin said as she took a chair at the end of Tommy's bed.

"I wish someone would have told me we were having a party," Tommy said, surprising them.

All three heads whipped around to see him smiling at them. "Well, good morning. How are you feeling?" Bailey asked.

"Like you ran over me with your big truck," Tommy said with a painful grin.

Bailey threw her hands up in the air. "Wasn't me, I'm innocent," she pleaded.

"Innocent, I hardly believe, little sister, but you did come to my rescue from what I can remember from last night. Thank you."

"I just wish we could have been there earlier to prevent your attack," Bailey said. "No more being outside alone at the club for you."

"Amen to that," Joe said.

"Bailey, you know that is a fear we face every day; it's not just at night at a gay club," Tommy stated.

Joe placed a comforting hand on his friend's arm. "Careful, my friend, she may hire you a bodyguard," Joe said.

"Seriously, Bailey, we face that threat every day as gay men in this city. While we don't like it, it is reality here, dear sister," Tommy said.

"Regardless, we all need to be more careful to not place ourselves in danger, period," Louise said. "Leave in groups, and I think I will put in more lighting and a security camera too for the parking lot."

A soft knock interrupted them as a dietary worker stepped inside the room and stopped in her tracks when she saw the crowd around Tommy. "I'm sorry to interrupt, but here is your breakfast tray," she said and placed the tray on the portable bedside table.

Joe raised the head of the bed to as close to a seated position as Tommy could stand and placed the table in front of him. Joe lifted the lid and chuckled. "Not near as appetizing looking or smelling as ours, but doctor's orders."

Tommy looked down at the tray, which held soft scrambled eggs with extremely bland-looking grits and what appeared to be a canned biscuit with strawberry jelly. "I'm starved so I will give it a go. Can you see if you can doctor those eggs and grits a bit while I gnaw away on this biscuit?"

"Do you think you can handle this coffee?" Louise asked, switching to mother hen mode.

"I think so. The apple juice looks to be room temperature," he added, noting the lack of condensation on the container as he picked it up.

As Joe and Louise fussed over Tommy, Bailey looked closely at her brother and the wide array of colors across his skin, ranging from a deep angry purplish red to the already fading yellowish green of some of the smaller bruises. She could not help it as she started to chuckle.

"Bailey, what on earth do you find so funny?" Louise asked.

"I am so sorry for laughing, but I've always teased Tommy about being a silly fruit, but right now he actually looks like an overripe banana with all his colorful spots."

Her laughter was contagious and Tommy laughed, and then dropped his fork to make a grab for his sore ribs. "Are you trying to kill me making me laugh?" he asked.

Louise pointed a rather blunt-looking butter knife at her and simply stated, "You, outside until you can control yourself."

Bailey nodded her head and gladly obliged, stepping outside of the room while she tried to stifle her laughter. She leaned against the wall, horrified for finding anything in this situation funny, but in her exhausted state, she simply could not control herself. Several people passing by gave her rather strange looks, so Bailey took a deep breath and walked back inside, refusing to look directly at Tommy.

"I hope you can control yourself this time, young lady," Louise said gruffly. "We have planning to do."

Bailey nodded and slipped into a chair beside Tommy's bed and waited for Louise to speak.

"I want you and Joe to go to the club this morning, meet the guard for the bank deposit, and then go home for some rest. I will stay with Tommy until he is released, and then Sarah, my neighbor, has agreed to stay with him until Joe makes it home later tonight."

"But—" Bailey started to say, and was interrupted by Louise.

"That's simply the way it has to be," she said.

"The show must go on," Tommy said from his hospital bed. "I promise I won't do anything I shouldn't," he added.

"All right, if this is the way it has to be. I will stop by before going to the club to check on you myself," Bailey said. She looked over at Joe. "So much for planning. That sounded like more of a Louise mandate," she grumbled.

"Honey, you should know by now it doesn't do any good to argue with me, so just deal with it," Louise said. "Besides you two look a bit rough this morning, and I can still smell the smoke from the club on you."

"Yeah and we love you too, Louise," Joe said jokingly.

"You know what I mean. You both need some sleep and a good hot shower."

"What time do we meet the guard?" Joe asked.

Louise looked at her watch. "In twenty-five minutes, so you better get a move on. I will call if anything changes after the doctor makes his rounds," she promised.

Reluctantly, Bailey and Joe gave Tommy a kiss on each of his bruised and battered cheeks. "Love you, and I will see you later," Bailey said.

"I love you both," Tommy said and watched them file out of the room.

Bailey and Joe walked out into the hall. "I hope your car is here," she said.

"It is. I drove last night following Louise over here after we shut down the club. You can get your Jeep when we finish with the bank drop."

Bailey looked at him with a sheepish grin. "I hope I can shift gears. I am so stiff and sore," she said, rubbing her shoulder.

"Yeah, those chairs were not made for restful sleep. I look forward to a few hours' of sleep in my own bed."

"Will you let work know Tommy is going to be out for a while, and also bring Tony and Charles up to speed?"

"Yes, I'll take care of that. You just go get some rest when we leave the club, we really do look bad," he teased with a chuckle.

†

A little over an hour later, Bailey did manage to shift the gears in her Jeep and find her way back home. She was exhausted and decided to forego the hot shower until she had a few hours of sleep. Bailey peeled her clothes off and dropped them in her tracks as she made her way to the bedroom. She collapsed face-first onto the bed after barely gathering the strength to remove her boots. Bailey was asleep in minutes and slept soundly for several hours.

Her dreams, filled with memories of better days when Nessa was still alive and the good times they had shared, helped relieve her tension, as they often did when she felt stressed. She woke feeling refreshed, but her hand instinctively landed on the opposite side of the bed in search of Nessa. She longed for the comforting touch Nessa always used to relieve the tension or anxiety that sometimes plagued Bailey. Her heart ached knowing she would never feel that touch again.

She released the grip of self-pity and climbed from the bed to stumble to a much-needed shower. As she passed the mirror, she saw the tearstains that ran down her cheeks, leaving her to wonder if she had cried during her sleep as she sometimes did.

The shower magically relieved the soreness of her body, and she relished the feel of the hot water against her skin until the water began to cool. Bailey dried and moisturized her body then slipped into a thick robe. She was brushing her teeth when a knock on her front door interrupted her. She spat the toothpaste from her mouth and, with toothbrush still in hand and dressed only in her robe, she went to the door, thinking it was Joe or Louise.

To her surprise, there was a female figure standing with her back to the door as she waited to see if Bailey would answer. She could not tell who the person was, but opened the door and asked, "May I help you?"

Bailey was surprised to find Detective Dexter standing on her doorstep in much more casual attire than her cop business suit. She was wearing a dark Nike running suit with running shoes and a towel in her hands. The woman looked much more relaxed than she had appeared hours ago and Bailey regretted being rude to her. The smile she wore stunned Bailey for several seconds, until her wits returned.

"Let me guess, you were in the neighborhood and thought you would just drop by," she said sarcastically before even thinking.

The woman stiffened as the smile left her face. "Actually, Ms. Chambers," she said coolly, "I was in the neighborhood because I have lived three doors down from you for over a year. I thought I would drop by when I saw your Jeep in the drive to give you some good news, but I obviously erred in thinking it was okay to do that outside of my official police capacity." The woman paused before saying, "I will return tomorrow when I return to duty and am in an official capacity." The detective then spun on her heel to storm off the front porch.

Stunned by the woman's quick response Bailey called out, "Wait!"

The detective slowed her retreat, stopped, and turned to look at Bailey. Bailey could see the indecision on her face and was relieved when the woman started back to the house.

Noticing that she was still unsure, Bailey raised her hands in surrender. "Look, I'm sorry. I have had a rough twenty-four hours, and I don't know what has come over me. Please come inside and have a seat and let me get some clothes on."

Bailey took a step backward into the house and held the door open for the woman, who approached slowly. She stepped inside and Bailey closed the door behind her. "May I offer you something to drink," she asked as she pointed her guest to the couch with the toothbrush still in hand and walked toward the kitchen.

"Would you happen to have a cold bottle of water?"

Bailey smiled. "Yes, ma'am, I do." She carried two bottles of water back to the living room, handing one to her guest and placing another on a coaster on the table. When Bailey bent over to place the bottle on the table, the front of her robe loosened. Desi couldn't tear her eyes away as Bailey's upper body was exposed.

Bailey caught her stare and blushed as she pulled her robe tighter. "If you'll excuse me, I'll go get dressed."

The detective nodded and Bailey could feel eyes on her as she walked down the hall to her bedroom. She closed the door and quickly went to work dressing in jeans, boat shoes, and a T-shirt. Her hair still damp from the shower had a ruffled look to it and Bailey thought it would have to stay that way.

When she returned to the living room, the detective had finished half the bottle of water. Bailey sat in a chair across from the woman before she picked up her own bottle and took a sip. "I am very sorry for being rude."

"Apology accepted. We often are engaged by hostile witnesses, but I was not prepared to get that from you," she admitted.

"Oh, why is that?" Bailey asked, curious.

"You just don't look the type to me, but I guess my skills are slipping," the woman said with a glint of amusement in her eyes.

Bailey studied the woman for a minute. "I do have a rather strong distaste for the police of this city with good reason," she admitted.

"Your friends mentioned you did last night, but I would hope you don't stereotype us into one bunch of idiots. There are some good cops on the force, present company included, of course," she said with an adorable lopsided grin, which showed off a dimple in her cheek.

Bailey found she was staring at the dimple and had to shake herself mentally to return to reality. "Yes, I am certain you are not like the good ole boys that were just happy to see another woman of color murdered in our fair city, and even happier when they found out she was a lesbian," Bailey said with a snarl.

"Is that your lover?" the detective asked, pointing to the photograph of Bailey and Nessa.

Bailey's eyes looked at the photograph. "Yes, that was Nessa and I down at the Gulf. She was murdered two years ago during a carjacking," Bailey explained. "I hadn't heard one word from the detective since he came to inform me of my loss. For weeks afterward, I called almost daily to get updates and learned there was no new information on the case. When I finally realized there would be no real investigation, I tried going to the local media but they were just as aloof. Another murder in Memphis wasn't newsworthy and no one gave a damn about Nessa."

Desi heard her pain in her voice and it helped to understand Bailey's anger toward the authorities. "She was a beautiful woman. From the islands?" she asked.

Bailey found herself more comfortable talking to the detective. "Yes, her family came to the states from Jamaica when she was ten. She was an RN at Saint Jude's."

"How long were you two together?"

"Almost five years."

"That's a long time in this day and age. I can barely keep a lover for a year before the stress of being with a cop becomes too much," the woman openly admitted.

"That has to really suck."

"Comes with the occupation," she said. "Being a cop makes it hard to communicate with a loved one. There is so much despair and devastation heaped upon us day after day but we are unable to speak of our cases even with our spouses. It's no wonder the divorce rate is so high, not to mention burnout and suicide."

It was Bailey's turn to witness the pain and sadness in Desi's voice as she spoke. It gave her a new perspective of the burdens they experienced and carried alone. She couldn't imagine not being able to vent to her lover, to unload the frustrations and sadness she witnessed every day.

Turning back on her professional persona, the detective said, "I wanted to drop by and give you some good news."

"I could use some," Bailey answered.

"The swing from the Mighty Casey ended up putting one of our suspects in the hospital down in Jackson, Mississippi. He had to have emergency surgery to pin his right arm back together. After we left you at the hospital this morning, we contacted all local hospitals to be on the lookout for a potential suspect with the injury you described. It seems like our boy could only handle the pain a few hours before he showed up at a hospital in Jackson." She smiled warmly at Bailey. "Once he returned to his room from recovery a handcuff was placed on his wrist and attached to his bed with an armed officer outside his door. When he is ready for release from the hospital he will be transported here for interview and processing, but there is little doubt he's our attacker based on your description."

Bailey was beginning to feel terrible about the way she had treated Detective Dexter. They really had done what they promised her at the hospital. She looked up at Dexter with the flush of embarrassment on her face. "That was good work; and the other punk?"

"Not in custody yet, but we have good video of him dropping his friend off at the emergency room, so it's just a matter of time."

Bailey shook her head. "I feel like a real asshole now. You have done exactly what you promised."

She flashed Bailey one of her adorable smiles. "Just don't judge me before you know me," the detective said as she stood to leave. "I will keep in touch to let you know how the case is progressing, Ms. Chambers."

"Bailey, please call me Bailey, Detective Dexter," she said as she offered her hand.

The detective took the offered hand and shook it. "Desi, short for Desiree, my mother, a street artist in New Orleans, loved the name."

"That doesn't make for a tough street cop name, but a beautiful name all the same. Welcome to the neighborhood too, albeit a year late."

"Thanks. I've seen you around a few times, but always in passing and never long enough for a proper introduction."

"I run too, but I'd never seen you before last night," Bailey said.

"I run at varied times because of my workload, but most frequently in the early hours around sunrise," Desi said.

"I'm usually on my way to work by then. I run at night after work."

"What do you do?" she asked as they walked toward the door.

"I drive a big rig for FedEx during the day and tend bar for Louise on the weekends at the club. Come by sometime and let me buy you something stronger than water."

"I will," she said, smiling. "Are you working tonight?"

"Yes, as my dear brother Tommy stated, the show must go on."

"He is quite a character. He had us in stitches this morning when we interviewed him, and I don't think it was the medications." Desi let out a soft laugh that reminded Bailey of Nessa. "I'm off duty tonight or at least hope I don't get called, so I may just drop in and take you up on your offer."

Bailey smiled at her, feeling much more at ease. "If not tonight, any weekend night will do."

"Thanks," she said as they reached the door and Desi turned back to look at Bailey.

"Thanks for bringing me good news and forgiving my terrible behavior," Bailey said with a blush.

"I haven't said you were forgiven yet," Desi said, and with a wink she was out the door, leaving Bailey standing there with her mouth agape.

Chapter 4

Bailey finished preparing for work and made a run to Top's for a cheeseburger and fries. She normally didn't crave burgers, but the cheeseburger she had eaten at the hospital had tasted so good she wanted to try another.

Her fried food craving sated, Bailey drove over to Joe and Tommy's house. From the look of the driveway, half of the gay community had stopped in for a visit. She walked in through the kitchen to find Tommy in his favorite recliner surrounded by pillows and several of his friends. His eyes lit up when he spied her coming from the kitchen. "There is my favorite baby sister," he said with a grin.

"I am your only sister," Bailey reminded him as she leaned over to kiss his cheek. "How does it feel to be home?"

"Fantastic," he said. "I look forward to sleeping in my own bed tonight."

"Hey, handsome," Charles said as he walked up beside her. "Can I get you something to drink?"

"Thanks, but I'm good for now. I just wanted to stop by to give Tommy some good news."

"Okay, listen up everyone," Joe said and clapped his hands to get their attention and quiet the crowd.

Always the queen, Bailey thought, but his actions did quiet the crowd. She looked down at Tommy. "I had a visitor a little while ago. Desi, Detective Dexter, just happens to be one of my neighbors, and she stopped by to let me know one of the bruisers is in custody at a hospital in Jackson, Mississippi."

"I hope you messed him up good," Tony said as he hugged her neck.

Bailey grinned. "He needed surgery to pin his arm back together."

"Oh girl, I want you on our team if we play softball at the Pride Games," one of the men said from across the room.

"You would have been proud. She nailed that bastard good," Joe said. "What about the other thug?"

"Not in custody yet, but Desi said they got good video of him dropping his friend off at the ER."

"Desi, hmm. Since when are you on a first-name basis with a cop?" Tommy asked. The room full of men let out an assortment of moans and groans.

Bailey felt the blush rise to her cheeks and the men surrounding Tommy said, "Ohhhh," in unison.

"Okay, you can stop now. She was really nice, especially considering how nasty I was to her last night."

"You were pretty wicked," Joe said.

"She is a cutie though, and was very sweet when she came to interview me at the hospital this morning," Tommy said.

"Uh-huh, well…" Bailey said in hopes of dropping the subject. "I better get a move on. Give me a call if you need anything, and you do everything Sarah tells you or you know she will report you to Louise," she teased. "I will see you three later," she said to Joe, Tony, and Charles.

"I'll walk out with you," Joe said and followed her through the kitchen out to her Jeep.

"Is he really doing okay?"

"Yes, he is eating up all this attention," Joe said. "Once a queen…"

"Always a queen," Bailey added with a chuckle. "Last night scared the shit out of me, Joe."

"Me too. He doesn't look it, but he was lucky. He could have had much worse injuries the way they were whaling on him."

"I hope he can bounce back from this quickly and get back up on his feet."

"That's what I wanted to ask your opinion on," Joe said. "Tony and Charles are in no hurry to get back to New Orleans. Do you think Louise would be receptive to them performing the next few weekends?"

"I don't think she would have any problem with that, and the crowd loved them."

"Tommy and I discussed it and they could bunk with us and keep an eye on him while you and I are at work."

"That makes it even more attractive, and they do seem to be good for him."

"If you're okay with it, I thought I would ask Louise tonight."

"Yes, go for it, and I will be in support of it," Bailey said.

Joe grinned as she climbed into the Jeep and waved as she backed out of the drive.

†

It was still early but there were plenty of cars in the lot. When she walked inside, she found Louise behind the bar talking to a man seated across from her with a calculator and clipboard.

"Hey, Bailey," she said as Bailey made her way behind the bar. "Come here, I want you to meet someone."

Bailey walked over to her and the man looked up from his calculations. "This is John Dorn. He is going to be installing a security camera and more lighting outside in the parking area on Monday. John, this is my cousin, Bailey."

"Nice to meet you," Bailey said and shook his hand.

"Likewise, and I'm sorry to hear about your brother. How's he doing?"

Bailey smiled. "He is totally in his element, surrounded by gorgeous gay men treating him like the queen he is," she teased.

"What did you say that address was?" John asked with a grin.

"Ha, you would definitely get a rise out of Tommy, if you know what I mean," Bailey said as she joined Louise behind the bar.

John and Louise roared with laughter. "You finish up here and I'll handle the bar," Bailey said as she moved to greet a customer.

They finished making a deal and John waved to Bailey before leaving the club. Louise fell back into place beside Bailey. "Did you get some rest?"

"Yes, I did, and I got a visit from that female detective, who told me they had one of the thugs in custody at a hospital in Jackson, Mississippi."

"That is great news, and the other one?"

"Not yet, but Desi said they should be able to track him down quickly."

"Desi," Louise said with a raised brow.

"Yes, Detective Dexter—her name is Desi—and come to find out she lives three doors down from me."

"Hmm," Louise said. She let the conversation drop but ideas were running a mile a minute in her head.

†

Not long afterward, the boys arrived at the club. Tony and Charles went to the dressing room while Joe talked with Louise. She was delighted at the prospect of having Tony

45

and Charles around for a few weeks longer while Tommy healed. She especially liked the idea of having them watch over Tommy during the day to keep him out of trouble.

As the night wore on, Louise noticed Bailey would look to the door every time it opened, as if she was expecting someone. Finally, her curiosity got the better of her. "Who are you expecting?"

"What makes you think I am expecting someone?"

"Because every time that door opens your eyes check out who is coming through," Louise said.

Bailey smirked, thinking she had been less obvious. "I invited Desi to drop by for a drink and I thought she might come by tonight. She may have been called in to work though," she said with a note of disappointment in her voice.

Louise smiled, ecstatic that Bailey was finally showing signs of interest in someone, but did not make a big issue of it. "It's still early," she said with a great deal of hope in her voice. She offered up a silent prayer that the cute detective would walk through the door soon.

†

Bailey had taken a tray to bus some tables. She had her back to the door, giving driving instructions to a pair of customers, when the door opened and Desi walked into the club.

Louise smiled so broadly she thought her face would break when she saw Desi entering, recognizing the detective from her interview. She made eye contact with her as she came through the door and motioned her over to the bar.

Desi walked over and climbed onto a barstool as Louise welcomed her. "What can I get you to drink, Detective?"

"Please call me Desi. What do you have on tap?"

Louise called out the beers and Desi stopped her when she said Miller Lite.

"Miller Lite will do just fine," she said.

Louise placed the beer in front of her and noticed Desi looking around. "Bailey will be back in just a minute, she went out to bus some tables. Thank you for the great news today too, by the way."

Desi looked to her with a brilliant smile. "I had a promise to keep."

They both watched as Bailey stepped behind the bar carrying a tray full of empty bottles and glasses. She hadn't noticed Louise talking to Desi so when she turned around to place the tray on the counter, she came face-to-face with Desi.

"Hey," she managed to say, unable to form a more exciting response.

"Hey there yourself, how are you?" Desi asked.

"Good, thanks, and you?" Bailey said as she placed the cocktail glasses into the dishwashing sink.

"Let me have that tray and I will store the empty bottles," Louise said.

"Thanks," Bailey said as she handed her the tray then began washing the glasses. "I wasn't sure if you would come," she said as she smiled to Desi.

"I needed a night out on the town," Desi said as the lights in the club began to flicker. Desi seemed surprised. "Did you forget to pay the light bill?"

"No, that's a signal that the show is about to begin," Bailey explained.

"What kind of show?" Desi asked.

Bailey cocked her head to the side. "A drag show," she answered.

"Oh my goodness, I've always wanted to see one," Desi said, excitement lighting up her face.

"Seriously? You're from New Orleans and have never seen a drag show?" Bailey said with a puzzled expression.

"Never," Desi answered with a broad smile.

Bailey poured herself a beer. "Turn around then so you can get a good look," she said and walked around to sit next to her as Victoria came onstage.

"Good evening, people," Victoria called out. "Are we ready to have a good time?"

"Hell yes," the crowd answered.

"Excuse me?" she said and placed a hand to her ear.

"Hell yes," the crowd screamed louder.

"That is much better. Before we get the show started, I need your help tonight," she said. "Most of you don't know, but last night Marie Lepanto was attacked and beaten," she said, and the crowd groaned loudly. Victoria pointed to where a large sheet of rainbow cardboard hung on a wall. "I need you all to send a message to Marie to help her get better soon."

"Hell yeah," one of the customers called out and the crowd burst into laughter.

"Nikki and Charlise from New Orleans will also be staying a few extra weekends to help us out until Marie returns, so be sure to let them know how much we appreciate their kindness. Now, let's get this show on the road, so put your hands together for the beautiful Nikki," Victoria said and the lights went down.

"Joe is Victoria Luxora and Tommy is Marie Lepanto," Bailey explained.

"I kind of figured Tommy, but that was Joe?"

"Yes, ma'am, it is," she answered.

Desi's eyes stayed glued to the stage as she watched Nikki, Charlise, and Victoria perform the first show of the evening. Bailey did not interrupt her concentration and watched with a smile as Desi had her first drag show experience.

Louise returned to the bar and saw the smile on Bailey's face, which brought a smile of her own.

Victoria finished her number and stepped over to the end of the stage. "You know, I was just thinking," she said.

"Thinking of what?" someone shouted from the crowd on cue.

"Since Marie is not able to perform tonight, I was thinking another member of her family might grace us with a performance," she said.

"Oh, hell yeah," came a voice from the crowd that Bailey recognized as Becca's.

"Baaailey! Baaailey! Baaailey!" the crowd began to chant.

Desi turned on her stool. "Well, are you going to keep your fans waiting?"

"Come on, Bailey," Louise urged from behind the bar. "It's been forever."

It had been a long time since Bailey had performed, possibly since before Nessa was murdered, but people still remembered. Bailey stepped off the stool and began to weave her way through the crowd, much to the delight of the patrons.

"Many of you young'ns probably weren't even born yet when this song came out, but I bet you will remember it after tonight's performance. Put a big Fubar hand together for the one and only Bailey," she said. Victoria handed Bailey the microphone with a wink. "I thought "Lady" was appropriate for tonight."

"Lady," by The Little River Band, had always been one of her favorite songs. Bailey walked to the middle of the stage as the spotlight followed her. As the DJ cued up the song she looked over at the bar and saw Desi sitting on the edge of her seat waiting with Louise, now sitting next to her.

It had been a while since she performed on stage but her voice was as strong as ever from belting out the disco tunes on her stereo. She began the song and the audience, enthralled by her voice, sat frozen in their seats until she began to walk across the stage. As the crowd came to life, the tips began to appear from so many patrons. Desi temporarily lost sight of Bailey, and when she came back in sight, she was working her way through the crowd toward the bar.

She stopped, several feet in front of Desi, and sang the last chorus of the song, her sparkling eyes locked on Desi.

When Bailey sang the last note, the crowd erupted in a roar of applause. She handed the microphone back to a broadly smiling Victoria and took a final bow.

"I do believe many hearts have just broken in here tonight," Victoria said. "Thank you, Bailey, for giving us such a treat."

Bailey waved back to him as she walked back to the bar and stopped in front of Desi. "I guess you have to honor me with a dance now," she said.

"Just let me know when you're ready," Desi said, her eyes glistening with excitement. "What other hidden talents do you have, Ms. Bailey Chambers?" she asked.

"Only time will tell," Bailey said with a grin. She took a step backward and walked behind the bar for a cold beer. She needed the distance to escape the rush of desire that was screaming at her to lean in to kiss Desi at that moment. "Do you ladies need a fresh drink?"

"Yes, please," Desi and Louise answered.

Bailey drew up three fresh beers as Victoria announced another performance by Nikki to conclude the first show. She placed a fresh beer in front of the women and wiped her brow with a bar rag. "Damn, I forgot how hot those lights can get."

"Take a seat for a minute before the after-show rush," Louise said. Bailey joined them for a brief respite, sitting next to Desi. "You definitely got the ladies wound up now," Louise teased.

"Ha, it's good for business," Bailey said as she took a long drink. She was sitting close enough to Desi that when either of them moved slightly their legs touched and Bailey could feel the warmth of Desi's body.

"That it is," Louise said as she climbed down from the stool and made her way back to the bar to prepare for the rush. "It's going to get busy for a few minutes, but sit tight," Louise warned Desi.

Nikki finished her number on the stage and as the lights came back up the crowd rushed the bar. "Is there anything I can do to help?" Desi asked.

Bailey groaned as she stepped off the barstool and walked behind the bar, giving Desi a nice view of her backside. "Thanks, but we've got this," Bailey said as the first wave arrived.

Desi sat back and watched Bailey and Louise go to work serving the thirsty customers. She was amazed how many of the women flirted with Bailey, and she spoke to each of them kindly as she thanked them for their business. Bailey was a natural people person. Desi could hardly believe she was the same person that had attacked her less than twenty-fours ago with a wicked tongue.

The DJ cranked up the music and the crowd moved from the bar back to the dance floor with cold drinks in hand. When the last of the crowd returned to their seats, Bailey and Louise emptied out their overflowing tip jars. "Do you need some of this smaller stuff?"

"Sure, tell me what your total is on ones and fives," Louise said.

Bailey counted quickly and handed Louise a stack of bills and said, "One sixty."

Louise lifted the tray in the cash register and handed Bailey three fifties and a ten. "Don't spend it all in one place," she teased.

Bailey looked up at Desi. "May I treat you to an early breakfast?"

"That would be great," Desi said.

Louise grabbed a dishpan. "I'm going to bus some tables. Hold down the fort."

"Yes, ma'am," Bailey said as she leaned across the bar to talk with Desi. "So, Detective, what do you think of our little spot?"

"This is a great place, and the entertainment is fantastic."

"Was that really the first drag show you had ever seen?" Bailey asked, still in disbelief.

Desi smiled. "Yeah, it really was. Guess I live a sheltered life."

Bailey smirked. "I reckon so. I have been getting free shows from Tommy since he was about twelve."

"I bet it was fun growing up with him," Desi said, propping her chin on her hand as she watched Bailey.

Bailey nodded as she took a drink. "He was such a clown when he was a teen. Mom had her hands full with us."

"Are your folks still alive?"

Desi watched the excitement in Bailey's face turn to sadness.

"Mom died a few years ago, and our father took off when I was about five and we haven't seen him since. She raised the two of us on her own."

"She must have been a strong woman."

"She was incredible. She would work all day and then spend half the night cooking, cleaning, and helping us with our schoolwork."

Eager to change the topic away from the painful memories of her mother, she asked, "How about your folks, are they still alive?"

"Still very much alive and kicking in New Orleans. Dad is a retired teacher and Mom is an artist. She still goes down on the square to sell her paintings on the weekends."

"So how did a teacher's and painter's daughter turn to law enforcement?"

"I've been in love with guns since I got my first cowgirl hat and six-shooters at about five. I also loved the uniform," she said with a wink.

"So how long have you been a detective?"

"Three years this month," Desi said. "I did six years on the street in Nashville."

"I love that town so much I go there four times a week," Bailey said.

Desi looked at her puzzled for a moment. "Oh, for your truck route, I got it now."

"Nothing slow about you, Detective." She grinned.

Louise returned carrying a full pan of glasses, which Bailey washed as she continued talking with Desi. Louise took the empty bottles and placed them in the stockroom then took the dishtowel from Bailey when she returned. "Better let me take over for now."

"Why is that?"

"Because I have it from a very reliable source that there will be a slow song coming soon, and I will not tolerate you taking this gorgeous woman onto the dance floor with dishpan hands."

Both Desi and Bailey laughed. "You did promise me a dance," she reminded Desi.

"Oh, I had no intention of forgetting," Desi said. "I was just waiting for you to ask."

Right on cue, a slow song began to play. "Gorgeous woman, may I have this dance?"

Desi laughed and stepped down off her stool as Bailey came around the bar to lead her to the dance floor. Louise grinned as Bailey rubbed her hands on her jeans to make sure she did not have water on them and watched as they stepped onto the dance floor.

Bailey turned to face Desi and pulled her in close as they picked up the rhythm of the music. The alluring scent of the perfume Desi was wearing drew Bailey closer, and she found herself nuzzling Desi's neck as their bodies swayed together. Her hand was on the small of Desi's back and she could feel the warmth of her body through the thin material of her shirt. It felt good to have this woman in her arms. Bailey felt comforting warmth spread through her as Desi moved closer, and her body responded as her need for intimacy began to grow.

The song ended all too soon for Bailey's taste. She found herself staring into Desi's eyes for several long seconds after the music had stopped, a smile growing on her face. "Thank you for the dance," she said as she took Desi's hand.

"Thank you. I really enjoyed the dance. Maybe we can do it again sometime."

"I would like that," Bailey answered.

The night was flying by quickly and soon the lights were flickering to announce the final show of the evening. Victoria came onstage to perform a number followed by Nikki and Charlise, who also completed solo numbers. Finally, all three performers came onstage for a number together that brought the crowd to their feet with applause.

Bailey was preparing drinks for the performers backstage when she heard a disappointing sound—a ringtone—and looked up to find Desi staring at her phone with a disgruntled look on her face. When she looked up at Bailey, the look told her all she needed to know.

"So much for a night off," she said. "May I get a rain check on breakfast?"

Even though she was deeply disappointed, Bailey knew Desi had to go. "Sure. Just let me know when."

"I'm really sorry to ruin your plans."

"Don't be, I had a wonderful night having you here. Louise, I'm going to walk Desi out and I will be right back."

"Okay, be safe, and it was good to see you Desi. I hope you will be back soon."

"Count on it," Desi said and placed a twenty on the bar.

"Put that back into your pocket," Louise said with a wink and handed her the bill.

Desi stuffed the money in her pocket, met Bailey at the end of the bar, and they walked outside together. The air was crisp and cool as they walked out to Desi's car. "I had a nice time tonight and would like to see you again," Bailey said.

"I did too. I am supposed to have a real night off Monday, unless something really big comes up."

"May I cook you dinner then?"

"You can add cooking to your talents?" Desi teased.

"Well, I haven't killed anyone yet," she answered with a smirk.

"I would like that," Desi said. "What can I bring?"

"A bottle of wine," Bailey suggested.

"A nice red?"

"That would be perfect."

Bailey opened the door for Desi. "Be safe and I will see you Monday night around six?"

"I'll be there, thanks again for tonight."

"Goodnight," Bailey said as she closed the door and started back toward the club.

She strolled back inside the club with a smile growing on her face and went to the bar to get the tray of drinks for the boys. Louise caught her grin and asked, "Well, did you at least kiss her?"

"No, Louise, we've just barely met," Bailey said, taking the tray of drinks to the dressing room and leaving a grinning Louise in her wake.

She walked into the dressing room to a chorus of whistles and catcalls. "Girl, you knocked them dead out there with that voice of yours," Charles said. "Who was that sweet little number you were singing to?"

"That, my dears, was the lovely Detective Dexter. Isn't she hot?" Joe said.

"You would make an adorable couple, girlfriend," Tony said.

"Thanks for the vote of confidence, guys, but I'm taking this slow."

"No second date U-Haul?" Charles teased.

"Um, that would be a no, and we haven't even had our first date yet."

"She's here tonight isn't she?" Joe smirked.

"Was. She got called in to work."

"That sucks, and not in a good way," Joe said with a giggle and a wink.

"I'm sorry to hear that," Charles said. "Were you able to reschedule?"

"I'm cooking dinner for her Monday night," Bailey grinned.

"You go, girlfriend," Joe said and gave her a high-five.

"Enough about me. That was a great show tonight. The crowd really loved it."

"Great tips too," Tony said. "Nikki may get a new wig after tonight."

Bailey chuckled at his remark. "Let me get back out to help Louise. Holler if you need anything," she said and left the dressing room to enter the chaos of the main floor.

"So," Louise said when she returned to the bar.

"So what?" Bailey asked, playing dumb.

"So how did it go with Desi?"

"It was okay," Bailey answered, still playing her along.

"Damn, girl, are you going to make me have to drag it out of you?"

Bailey smiled at her cousin. "She's coming to my place for dinner Monday night."

"Now we're talking. Way to go, Bailey."

"It's just a dinner, Louise, so don't get all excited just yet."

"What are you planning to cook?"

"I thought I would make homemade chicken Alfredo, fresh garlic bread, and a nice salad."

"You will have her eating out of your hand after that meal. I love your Alfredo."

Bailey returned her smile and went to work stocking the beer cooler with the cases they had carried in earlier. The crowd began to thin out and by two they locked the doors behind the last customer. Joe and the boys volunteered to stay behind and help clean up so by two thirty they all went out the door together.

"You all please drive careful going home and I will see you tomorrow," Louise said as she climbed into her car.

"See you," Bailey said then climbed into her Jeep. "I will see you guys for our Sunday lunch at your place, okay?" she said to Joe.

"Yes, ma'am, be careful," he said.

As she drove home, Bailey contemplated her actions and wondered if things were moving too quickly. Self-doubt filled her mind the entire drive home. She was certain she was attracted to Desi, but worried the attraction was possibly simple lust. She didn't want to hurt Desi or any other woman by using them strictly to meet her physical needs, but the more she interacted with Desi the more her attraction increased. Bailey found Desi's self-confidence and her habit of reaching out to touch her during their conversations comforting and exciting at the same time. As she drove, she found herself smiling at how easily they had fallen into teasing one another.

Bailey pulled into her drive and shut off the engine, listening to the ticking as it cooled. What the hell, she finally decided, I am just going to let this happen, no thinking, just let it flow. She climbed from the Jeep and headed into the house.

Chapter 5

Bailey's grumbling stomach woke her at seven. She tried to ignore her hunger in hope of drifting back to sleep but her stomach was insistent. She climbed out of bed and pulled on a worn pair of sweatpants and a T-shirt before walking into the kitchen. Bailey opened the refrigerator door to stare at the contents and after a quick survey decided on an omelet. She pulled out several ingredients and placed them on the counter then made a pot of coffee.

Deciding to relieve her swollen bladder before cooking, Bailey was walking through the living room when she heard a knock on her front door. Who on earth is showing up at this hour, she wondered as she turned toward the door. She looked through the small window and swallowed a sharp intake of breath as her eyes landed on Desi standing on her front porch. She made a mad attempt of smoothing down her sleep-frazzled hair and opened the door.

Desi smiled when she opened the door sending Bailey's heart racing a mile a minute. "Good morning, I was in the area and saw your lights on. Is it too late for your breakfast offer?"

"It's always a good time for breakfast. Come on in and have a seat in the kitchen. I was just getting ready to cook omelets, if that suits you."

"That sounds wonderful."

Bailey placed her hand on Desi's arm and walked through the living room to the kitchen door. "Pour yourself a cup of coffee. I'll be back in a minute after a pit stop," Bailey said. "Coffee mugs are in the cupboard to the right of the sink."

Bailey stifled a shriek of panic when she saw her image in the bathroom mirror. Her hair was poking out in ten different directions and she had a drool stain on her left cheek. She relieved her bladder and went back to the sink to make her appearance more presentable. She washed her face, brushed her teeth, and made her best attempt to smooth her unruly hair. Desi had not screamed and run off when she opened the door, so maybe this one was a serious contender Bailey thought as she dried her face and hands.

Desi, sipping a mug of coffee, leaned against the kitchen counter when Bailey reentered the kitchen. She looked fresh and vibrant, especially considering she had been up for god only knew how many hours without sleep. "I'm glad you stopped by this morning, I hate eating alone."

"Is that the only reason?" Desi teased, causing a blush to cover Bailey's cheeks.

"No, but it sounded good at the moment. It's good to see you, even if you caught me straight out of bed."

"You look adorable," Desi said. "How do you take your coffee?"

"Light and sweet," Bailey answered.

"I will make you a mug if you promise to start cooking. I'm starved."

"You have a deal, ma'am," Bailey answered.

Desi chuckled and set her mug on the counter to prepare a mug for Bailey.

"Anything you don't like in your omelet?" Bailey asked as she began chopping vegetables.

"Just the kitchen sink," Desi answered with a grin.

"Okay, no kitchen sink."

"Is there anything I can help with?"

"You can make us some toast and pour some juice for us in a few minutes."

Desi handed her the mug of coffee then took her mug and leaned back against the counter to wait for Bailey to take a sip.

"This is perfect," Bailey said. Her reward was a brilliant smile from Desi that caused her stomach to fill with a swarm of butterflies.

Desi watched as Bailey chopped a variety of ingredients then got a carton of eggs and a jar of sliced Greek peppers out of the refrigerator. Bailey cracked four eggs into a bowl and began whipping them. She looked up to see Desi watching her and said, "You said you were hungry, right?"

"Yes, ma'am," Desi answered with another earth-shattering smile.

Bailey used a large drop of olive oil to coat the frying pan before pouring the eggs and carefully adding the ingredients for what was turning out to be a monster omelet. "Go ahead and drop your toast." Just before she was about to fold the eggs, she added a handful of pepper rings. "Will you hand me a plate?" she asked as she pointed to a cupboard.

Desi took two plates down and placed them next to the stove. "That looks delicious," she said, her mouth watering as Bailey slid the omelet onto a plate.

"Enjoy," Bailey said as she handed her the plate.

The toast popped up from the toaster and Desi placed the slices on her plate. She loaded two more for Bailey.

"There is apple and orange juice in the fridge. Do you want hot sauce or anything else?"

"Heavens no, this looks perfect," Desi said.

Bailey handed her a fork and butter knife. "Go ahead and get started while it's hot, and I will join you in a few minutes," Bailey said, beating another round of eggs.

"What kind of juice would you like?"

"Apple for me, please," she said as she added ingredients to her breakfast and dropped the lever on her toast. "There is jelly in the fridge if you want it for your toast."

"I'm good, thanks," Desi said as she cut a bite and began her feast. "Oh my Lord, you can definitely add cooking to your list of talents," Desi said with a moan as she took another bite. "This is just what I needed this morning."

"I'm glad you approve," Bailey said as she dished up her breakfast and joined Desi at the table. She picked up a bottle of hot sauce and dribbled a few drops across her omelet. "Like I said, I haven't killed anyone yet."

They enjoyed their breakfast in silence, sans the moans that escaped from Desi on occasion. Bailey stood and walked to the coffeepot for a refill. "What is on your schedule today?" she asked as she refilled their mugs.

"Some much-needed sleep before I have to be back on duty at two," she said.

"Damn, that doesn't give you much time for sleep."

"I know, but it happens like this sometimes. I wish these damned gang wars would get over soon. Every time we think they are cooling off another event happens that inflames them all over again."

"Is that what happened last night?"

"Yes, and it was a bloody mess. One would think with all the murders and the convictions the gangs would die off, but I swear they join up in droves."

"Is it the product of a lousy economy and the lure of easy money from selling drugs?"

Desi sighed. "I'm sure that plays a large part in it, especially with the lack of good-paying jobs available. It's just so tragic to see so many young lives lost so senselessly."

Bailey could read the sorrow in Desi's face as she spoke. "So what keeps you in law enforcement?"

"I ask myself the same question at least once a day. Maybe it's the hope that I can make a difference, and save just one of them."

Bailey swallowed the last bite of her breakfast. "You are a good woman, Desi. I would have fled the horrors years ago."

"Thanks, so what are you doing today?" she asked to change the subject.

"I'm going to visit Tommy and have a late lunch with the boys, and then hopefully come back for a short nap before going to the club later. We usually get together for a traditional Sunday dinner."

"When do you drive again?"

"Tuesday," Bailey answered.

"So you are off tomorrow?"

"Yes, ma'am, I have a dinner to prepare for a gorgeous woman."

Desi chuckled at her use of the term. "You're not going to let that one go are you?"

"No, ma'am, it fits you well. Does it bother you?"

"Heavens no, it's very flattering, especially coming from you."

"Well then, that's it."

Desi took a final drink from her mug and sighed as she noticed the time slipping away. "I hate to eat and run but I really need some sleep. Thanks for a great breakfast."

"Thank you for stopping by, it really made my day to share breakfast with you," Bailey answered, and stood to walk her out.

"May I at least help you with the dishes?"

"Absolutely not. You go get some sleep," she said and offered Desi her hand.

At the front door Desi stopped and turned to Bailey. Their eyes locked and Desi surprised her by leaning in to brush her lips softly across Bailey's.

"Thanks again for a wonderful meal and good company."

"My pleasure," Bailey said once the lump in her throat cleared to allow her to speak. "Be safe today and get some rest."

"I will. Have a great day."

A smiling Bailey stood in the door watching Desi back out of the drive. Then she stepped out on the porch to watch as Desi drove down the street to her home.

Desi smiled when she stepped from her car to see Bailey watching and waved before disappearing into the door of her home.

Bailey smiled to herself as walked into her house and closed the door behind her before lifting her fingertips to her lips. "Wow," was all she could think of to say. She returned to the kitchen to clean up with a smile so broad her cheeks ached.

Her spirits lifted and with energy to burn, she dressed for a run and was out in her yard stretching when Louise pulled in her drive.

"Someone is up awful early," she said, shifting the car into park. "You look like you are ready to go for a run too."

"I was just about to, yes; what are you doing up and about this morning?"

"It is such a beautiful morning I thought I would drive down to the farmers market for some fresh veggies and surprise you and the boys with a home-cooked lunch. I guess your surprise is out of the bag now, though," she said with a grin. "I was dropping by to see if you wanted to ride with me."

"That sounds like a great idea. I can go for a run any old day, but it's not every day my cousin asks me to go to the farmers market," Bailey teased. With a chuckle she turned back to her house. "Let me change into something more appropriate for the market. I'll be right back."

"No hurry, I will just enjoy the morning while you get ready."

"I might have a cup of coffee left if you would like one."

"Thanks, but I've already had a pot to myself."

Bailey nodded and returned inside to change clothes, deciding to run through a quick shower in the process. Ten minutes later, she was fresh and ready to ride as she locked the door behind her and slid into the seat next to Louise. "Are we going downtown by the river?"

"That is usually the best spot, in my opinion, unless you have another suggestion."

"No, ma'am, I agree that's the best spot for farm fresh fruits and vegetables," Bailey said as she put on her shades.

"I'm surprised to find you up this early," Louise said with a grin.

"I crashed when I got home last night and didn't eat anything so my stomach woke me at seven and would not let me go back to sleep. So I got up to cook breakfast. It was a good thing I was up too."

"Why is that?"

Bailey couldn't help smiling as she thought of Desi. "Because Desi was just dragging in from work and she was starved too, so when she stopped by I cooked breakfast for two."

"Good Lord, that child needs some sleep," Louise said with a frown.

"She left after breakfast to get a few hours before reporting back to work at two. Apparently they had another big gang war last night that will keep her busy for a while."

Louise shifted gears and looked over at Bailey. "I don't see how she does that kind of work on so little sleep."

"I guess she is used to the long hours."

When they pulled up to a stoplight Louise looked over at Bailey again. "You seem very relaxed and happy for a change. I am so glad to see you smiling."

"It feels good too," Bailey said. "Only one shade of green," she teased as the light had changed and it was their turn to go. "Better go before someone starts blowing a horn."

"Good grief," Louise said and gave the car gas to chug up one of the few hills in the area.

They found a parking spot not too far from the covered pavilions that housed the summertime farmers market. There was so much more than just produce and Bailey had grown to enjoy coming here every chance she got. Today a small quartet played down-home folk music while customers shopped, and Bailey slipped a ten in their tip jar as she and Louise made their way down the aisles. A bearded man with numerous missing teeth smiled and nodded his thanks for her generosity. Bailey smiled back at him, and stood listening for a moment until Louise grabbed her elbow and tugged her along.

They approached a table loaded with home-baked goods and Bailey refused to go any farther until she had bought and consumed an oatmeal and raisin cookie, from a bag of half a dozen cookies. Louise had brought a cloth shopping bag that Bailey carried as they bought shelled zipper peas, lima beans, okra, and a cantaloupe melon for Louise. Bailey grabbed Louise's arm when they approached a booth with homemade quilts, her eyes locked on a beautiful quilt. "Would you look at this?" Her hands softly stroked across the perfect stitches and she smiled at Louise. "I just have to have this." Bailey paid the vendor, thanking her for the beautifully crafted quilt. "This will be perfect on my bed," she said with an excited grin as she tucked the quilt under her arm as they strolled down the aisles.

They reached another stand and found fresh silver queen corn to boil. "I guess we will have to cut Tommy's off the cob for now," Bailey teased.

Louise poked her in the ribs with a stern finger. "That is not funny," she told Bailey, struggling to restrain a chuckle of her own.

Working hard to stifle her laughter, Bailey admitted, "Yes, of course Louise, you are right and I'm sorry."

Louise glared at her efforts to keep a straight face so Bailey stuffed another cookie in her mouth to prevent herself from saying anything further to warrant the wrath of Louise.

They came up to another fruit stand and found delicious strawberries. "This gives me an idea. Buy a gallon for tonight and two pints for tomorrow's dinner with Desi. I will be right back," Bailey said as she handed Louise a twenty and rushed off.

Louise shook her head and turned back to the vendor who was already packaging the order. "You heard the lady," Louise said.

Bailey rushed back to the baked goods stand where she had bought the cookies. The woman smiled when she saw Bailey return. "More cookies?" she asked.

"Yes, and I want to buy two of your pound cakes too."

"Does shopping always make you this hungry?"

"Only when things taste as good as your cookies. I'm betting your cakes are just as good."

"If you are not completely satisfied, please come back next weekend and I will return your money."

"Thanks, but if I come back next weekend it will only be to buy more of your goodies," Bailey said, paying the woman.

"Let me put these in a separate bag for you," the woman said, placing the two largest cakes in a bag and handing them to her. "Enjoy."

"Thanks, we will."

Bailey rushed back to find Louise. "What are we doing for some protein?"

"I thought we would stop off for some fresh cut pork steaks at the market that you could fry up while I prepare the rest of the meal."

"I can cook some rice and corn bread too."

"One last stop and we will be ready to roll," she said as they stopped to buy several large Vidalia onions and vine ripened tomatoes. "Damn, my mouth is watering already."

As they walked back to the car, Bailey said, "Would you look at that?"

Louise followed the direction of Bailey's gaze just in time to see a man in a pale yellow Cadillac roll through the parking lot. The car was exceptional but the man behind the wheel had caught Bailey's attention. The humidity was already soaring and he was dressed in a leather jumpsuit, the kind Elvis Presley wore in concert. They both noted the man had a striking resemblance to the King of Rock and Roll.

"Elvis isn't dead, he's at the farmers market," Bailey joked.

Louise shook her head at Bailey's comment. "Only in Memphis can you see something like that on a hot Sunday morning."

"Drop me off at the house, and I will take the Jeep to the market and you can take the rest to Tommy's and I'll meet you there."

"You have a deal," Louise said as they loaded their purchases and climbed into the car.

✝

When she pulled up in Tommy's driveway, she could hear the disco music from outside the house. She carefully cracked open the door to the kitchen and walked to the entrance of the living room to witness a drag show in progress, minus the costumes. Tommy was in his recliner roaring with laughter, holding a pillow to cushion his broken ribs, as Joe, Charles, and Tony were camping it up to "YMCA" for him. Louise was in the kitchen preparing the strawberries to go in the fridge.

"Have they been like this since you got here?"

"Pretty much, I think this is their fifth song."

Bailey walked in to kiss Tommy and sat on the arm of the recliner as they watched the boys.

When the number finally ended, Joe turned the volume down and the trio collapsed on the couch in laughter, fanning themselves wildly.

"You boys look like you are working up an appetite," she said.

"Oh, most definitely," Joe said. "I'm going to give you and Louise a hand in the kitchen while the boys keep Tommy out of trouble."

"That should be interesting."

Joe followed her back into the kitchen. "Where would you like us to start?"

"I have the beans and peas cooking already if one of you wants to shuck the corn."

"I'm all over that," Joe said.

"How about brewing us some tea?" she asked Bailey.

"Yes, ma'am."

Bailey moved around the kitchen with ease and found what she needed to brew the tea along with Joe and Tommy's tea jug. She dumped sugar into the jug while she waited for the tea to boil.

Louise finished cleaning and slicing the strawberries, and put them into the refrigerator to chill. She peeled the onions and sliced them onto a small plate then proceeded to wash and slice several of the tomatoes, and placed them in the refrigerator to chill as well. Her next task was to clean and slice the okra to soak in some buttermilk until she was ready to fry it.

Bailey watched her move around a kitchen with the same ease she had running the bar at the club. Louise was a born leader and people followed her instructions without question.

"We can relax for about a half hour to let the beans and peas cook before we start on the rest of the meal," she told them.

"Go check on the boys and as soon as I finish the tea, I will join you," Bailey said.

"Come on, hot mama," Joe said and led Louise into the living room.

Bailey leaned back on the counter and waited for the water to boil. Her thoughts wandered back to Desi leaning against her counter earlier that morning, she had looked so natural standing there. She could barely wait for tomorrow so she could see Desi again. Bailey remembered the way her lips felt as they brushed across hers during their first soft kiss and found she was longing for more. The hiss of a splash of water on the burner brought her back to the present, and she dropped the tea bags into the boiling water. She let them boil for several minutes then turned the burner off to allow the tea to steep.

When she walked into the living room she found the boys fawning over Louise. "I have heard so much about your cooking I can hardly wait to taste it," Charles was saying.

"You do have a treat in store for you," Bailey said as she scooted Joe over on the couch and plopped down beside them. "If she ever wanted to leave the club business she could easily open a restaurant."

Louise chuckled. "I think I will stick with the club. It's much easier to satisfy a bar customer."

From her vantage point, Bailey could see the rainbow poster board that had served as a get-well card for Marie. "Wow, you have a lot of adoring fans," she said, pointing to the massive card.

Tommy smiled broadly in spite of his broken front teeth. "The boys brought that home to me last night."

"Oh, that reminds me," Louise said. "You have an appointment with Dr. Barnes tomorrow to get those teeth fixed."

Tommy feigned hurt. "You don't like my jagged tooth look?"

"Um, no," she said with a chuckle. "I will be here at eight to take you myself."

"I really appreciate that."

Louise turned to Charles and Tony. "So what do you boys do in New Orleans beside perform?"

"That's pretty much it for now. My Mammaw died a few months ago and left me some money," Tony said. "She was an incredible woman and took me in when my father put me out of the house for being gay. Charles and I have lived with her since, and we took care of her for the last years of her life."

Charles smiled. "She was a Grand Lady and did not judge us for who we are, but she did tell us if we were going to dress like women, we would have to do it in good taste."

"She taught us everything she knew about makeup application and high fashion," Tony said proudly.

"Did she ever see you perform?" Joe asked.

"Oh, all the time before she got sick. She was and will always be our greatest fan." Charles nodded in agreement.

"Sometimes during the busy season, I work for one of my exes at a small kite shop on Jackson Square for some extra money, but our needs are simple and the tips are great," Tony said. "She left us her house and a relatively new car, so we just need to pay utilities and buy some groceries."

"Speaking of groceries," Louise said, "are we ready to get cooking?"

"Let's do it," Bailey said and returned to the kitchen to start heating the oil in the deep fryer for the steaks.

Joe walked in with Tony and asked what they could do. "You can mix up some corn bread, and Tony can set the table," Louise said and they boys went to work.

Bailey had filled a dish with flour and seasonings for the steaks. In a separate bowl, she beat some eggs and after rinsing the steaks, she dredged each one through the eggs and then coated them with the flour mixture. When the oil in the fryer reached the correct temperature, she placed the first two steaks in to cook. She dipped out a small amount of oil to coat the cast-iron skillet they would use to bake the corn bread and handed it to Joe.

"Pour the batter in here and pop it in the oven if you would please."

"You got it, boss," he said and placed the filled skillet inside the oven.

Louise walked to the pantry and took out four large bags of rice that she placed in the pot of boiling water on the stove and then dropped the ears of corn in to boil. "Did you buy pepper rings?"

"Is the Pope Catholic?" Bailey shot back.

"I will take that as a yes, smart-ass," Louise said as she wiped her hands on a dishtowel and popped Bailey on the hind end.

"Ouch," Bailey hollered. "That stung."

"It was meant to," Louise said.

"Hey, I heard you had a guest for breakfast," Tony said. "Congrats."

"Thanks, I was surprised, but very pleased she stopped by." A smile graced her face as she remembered Desi from their morning encounter.

"Is that a twinkle I see in your eyes?" Joe asked.

"Maybe," she answered and turned to check her steaks.

Bailey reached up into a cupboard and pulled down a large platter, which she covered with paper towels to drain the steaks. She removed the first batch and placed the next steaks into the cooker.

"Damn, those look good," Louise said as she peeked over Bailey's shoulder. "I can't wait to sink my teeth into one of those."

Tommy hobbled in to the kitchen in anticipation of a fine meal. "Something smells mighty good."

"Are you going to be able to chew this meat?"

"Baby sis, I will gnaw the hell out of it if I have to, but I'm sure it will be tender. Your steaks always are."

Bailey smiled at her brother's comment. "Joe, will you get that jar of pepper rings from the fridge, and make sure we have plenty of butter out for the corn bread?"

Louise busied herself coating the sliced okra with corn meal, and dropping in into a frying pan with a little oil to quick fry the okra. She knew it was one of Bailey's favorites, so when she started pulling out the cooked okra, she shielded it from Bailey's reach.

"You boys can grab a seat while we finish up here," Louise said.

Bailey carried the platter of steaks over to them and had them pass them around so she would have room for the next batch. The timer sounded and Louise took the heavy skillet of corn bread from the oven. "Let me get that for you," Joe said as he grabbed the hot pads and rushed to take the heavy skillet from her hands.

"If you will hand me one of the large round plates from the cupboard we can get this corn bread out and ready to go."

Louise pulled one of the plates down and handed it to Joe. "I will flip it and you can take the plate of corn bread to the table while I handle the skillet."

"Sounds good to me," Louise answered, and held her breath until Joe smiled, letting her know the bread had separated from the skillet intact.

"Go ahead and get started while it's hot, and I will be there in just a few minutes," Bailey said as she took the corn from the pot and carried it to the table.

The hungry men needed no further encouragement and the table turned into a flurry of activity. "This all looks so good, I'm not sure where to start," Charles said as he dribbled some pepper juice on his bed of rice and zipper peas.

Tommy was busy cutting his pork steak into small bites. When he placed the first piece in his mouth he chewed slowly and groaned loudly. "Bailey, if you weren't my sister, I'd ask you to marry me," he said. "This steak is off the chain, baby sis."

"I'm glad you like it," Bailey said with a proud grin.

"She ain't my baby sister," Charles said with a wink to Bailey.

"Lover boy, I don't think you could fight off that gorgeous detective that has her eyes on Bailey," Tony said.

"Whoa now, what makes you think she has her eyes on me?"

"Pu-lease, girl, who are you kidding? She practically drools every time she sees you," Joe said.

"Oh, she does not," Bailey said and looked at Tony and Charles for support but they were both nodding in agreement.

"You two really outdid yourselves today," Tommy said. "This is an awesome meal."

"The best I have had since Mammaw died," Tony said.

"Oh yeah, leave some room for dessert," Bailey said.

"Dear God, you have got be kidding," Tony said.

"If we keep eating like this I won't be able to get in any of my dresses," Charles said.

Tony snickered. "I could think of a few ways to work those calories off."

"Boys, not at the dinner table," Louise said and they both quickly went back to eating.

Bailey smiled as she looked around the table at her family and friends and realized there was only one thing missing, but she hoped to remedy that one day soon. She scanned the dishes and saw that the okra was going fast. "Would anyone mind if I finish off that okra?"

"Not at all," Louise said as she handed the dish to Bailey who eagerly scraped the remaining morsels onto her plate.

"I just love the summer for all the fresh vegetables," she said as she scooped a mouthful of the crispy fried okra.

Once everyone had eaten their fill, there were very few leftovers to store in the fridge. "Why don't we chill in the living room for a bit before we tackle dessert," Louise suggested.

A round of groans echoed through the room as chairs pushed back from the table. "You guys go crash and I will take care of the leftovers and picking up the kitchen," Joe said.

"I'll help," Bailey said.

"No, ma'am, you won't. After cooking that great meal the least we can do is clean up," Charles said as he ushered her out of the kitchen.

Bailey was so stuffed she did not have the energy to argue with him. Spotting an open recliner she sank into it and kicked back. "This is the life," she said as the footrest lifted her legs in the air.

The television was on and an old black-and-white musical was playing. Bailey tried her best to focus on the screen, but her eyes quickly grew too heavy to stay open and she drifted off to sleep.

†

Two hours later, Bailey awoke to the sound of laughter coming from the kitchen. She stood to stretch before she joined them. Louise and the boys had opted for dessert and had put the

73

cans of Dream Whip to good use, trying to see who could create the most lifelike male member on top of their strawberry shortcake. Bailey was surprised that Louise seemed to be winning the contest, which had the boys roaring with laughter.

Louise looked up when she entered the room. "Welcome back, sleeping beauty," she teased. "I'm not sure how much Dream Whip is left, but can I fix you a piece of cake?"

"It looks like you guys are having way too much fun with that," Bailey said, pointing to the sugary artwork as she took a seat at the table.

"As much as I hate to admit it, I think Louise has us all whipped. No pun intended," Joe said, which sent them all into a fit of laughter.

"I may not eat Dream Whip again," Bailey said with a chuckle. "How can an old-fashioned dyke know more about male anatomy than a room full of fags?"

"Makes you wonder huh, baby sis," Tommy said with his broken tooth lisp.

"I have seen a penis or two in my lifetime," Louise said with her hands on her hips.

"Sex toys do not count, sweets," Joe said.

"You all are incorrigible," she said with a grin and went to work preparing a large slice of the pound cake with crushed strawberries covering the top. She picked up the remaining can of Dream Whip and carried it with the cake to the table. "Eat at your own risk."

"I really will pass on the Dream Whip," Bailey said as she picked up a fork. "I'm afraid I will forever see snow-white dongs every time I see a can of the stuff now."

"Well, since Louise has whipped us all with her rendition, I think we should just eat our entries," Tony said.

The contest shifted from artwork to who could eat their creations in the most devious way. Bailey nearly choked on a strawberry when Louise deep-throated her creamy production to raucous whoops and hollers from the boys.

Bailey shook her head when Louise raised her head, the tip of her nose covered in the white cream. "I am SO revoking your butch card."

"C'mon, Bailey, don't be a spoilsport," Louise said, flicking some Dream Whip at her.

Bailey smiled and continued eating her cake. Louise was pleased to see her cousin smiling again. Since Nessa's death, a smile had been a rare sight on Bailey's face.

She finished her dessert and pushed the plate out of her reach. "You know we make a great team. I don't think we have eaten this good in a long time."

"We need to do it more often," Tommy said. "That was a fantastic meal."

Bailey checked her watch. "I think I will try to get a run in to work off some of these calories before it is time to head to the club."

"I'm sure that cute detective could work some of them off you," Tommy lisped.

Joe punched him on the arm, forgetting his injuries. "Ouch, that hurt," Tommy yelped.

"Don't rush the girls," Louise said as she began picking up the dishes off the table.

Bailey carried her plate to the sink and kissed Louise on the cheek. "Thanks for a great meal. I will see you all later," she said.

The oppressive Memphis heat wrapped around her as she stepped outside and she knew she would be working up a good sweat during her run. She drove back to her house, slowing again as she passed Desi's house to find her driveway empty, then entered her home to change clothes.

Chapter 6

Detective Braxton sat at his desk, ear pressed to the phone, in deep conversation. At her desk next to his, Desi's eyes scrolled down a page on her computer screen.

Braxton hung up the phone and turned toward her. "The Jackson boys have picked up the other thug that was involved in the beating," he said.

Desi was concentrating on the screen and did not hear his comment.

"Earth to Desi," he said a bit louder.

Desi spun in her chair toward him. "I'm sorry, what were you saying?"

"What are you so intent on finding?" he asked as he came over to sit on the edge of her desk.

"I was looking for the case file on the murder of Ms. Chambers's friend," she answered.

"Our current caseload isn't enough for you, so you want to look up a cold case from two years ago?"

"Just call it a curiosity," Desi said. "What were you saying?"

"The Jackson police have both of our suspects in custody and ready for extradition. Would you like to take a ride with me to go get them?"

"Why, Detective Braxton, that's the best offer I've had all afternoon," she teased. "Let's go before something else erupts."

"I hear that," he said.

Desi saved the file that had just popped up on her screen and took her blazer off the back of her chair. She would read the file once they returned from Jackson, if she had time.

When they reached their unmarked car and were seated inside he turned toward her and asked, "You in a hurry?"

"No, to be honest, I could use a nap," she answered.

"Kick back and relax then, and try to catch a few winks. The ride to Jackson is pretty boring," he said as he put the car in gear.

Desi smiled and nodded at him. She was lucky to have Braxton for a partner. They had grown to be close friends, and while he knew about her lifestyle, they never brought it up in conversation. Once paired, it was not long until they realized they complemented each other's style nicely, and they had earned one of the top case closure rates in the department.

Sleep came quickly for Desi, and she slept for two hours until the roughness of a construction zone jarred her awake. She smiled as she stretched. "That was just what I needed."

"You must be tired."

"What makes you think that?"

"Because you were snoring to beat the band," he teased.

Desi chuckled. "Sorry about that."

"No problem, the wife says I build a house every night."

"Maybe we are in the wrong business then," Desi teased him back.

"You have never seen me with a nail gun in my hands."

"Safer to have your sidearm?" she asked.

"Much, for everyone involved," he said with a wide smile. "How about a Starbucks?"

"You buying?" she asked.

"Yeah, you bought last time," he said as he turned on his blinker to exit the interstate. "I got a text from the patrolman who is in charge of canvassing the crime scene from last night. He has a list of witnesses for us to talk to later today."

"That's a lucky break. Usually the neighbors clam up."

"I think they are finally getting fed up with the killings on their front porch steps," Braxton said. "It's about damned time too."

"With the number of errant shots that went off last night we are lucky nobody in the houses got hurt," Desi said. "These kids with the high-powered autos end up spraying bullets everywhere."

"I know. When I was a kid we thought we were the shit with a revolver. I can only imagine the trouble we would have gotten into with the weapons today's teens have access to," Braxton said as he pulled into the drive-through to order their coffees.

Back on the road, he surprised Desi when he said, "I pulled up that file too, and the woman does have reason to be angry with the police."

Desi turned and looked into his eyes. "Why? What happened?"

"The lead detective on the case was Thomas Harvey, and he was less than stellar in his prime. Bailey was right, he did very little to try to solve the case. He opted into early retirement not long afterward, and the case went cold. No one else bothered to pick it up."

"Is there much to work with?" she asked.

"I didn't have a lot of time to look it over, but I certainly wouldn't be averse to digging a little deeper when we have time."

"I know it would be a shot in the dark, but I think we owe it to her loved ones," Desi said.

Braxton took a sip of the coffee and placed it in the cup holder. "I probably don't need to remind you, but you need to cool your jets until the case is over. I'd hate for these assholes to go free because you were involved with the main witness."

Desi felt a blush rise to her cheeks. "Is it that obvious?"

"Only to someone who spends half his life with you," he answered. He could not hold back a chuckle. "I have never seen anyone get under your skin the way Ms. Chambers did at the hospital. You both had sparks flying everywhere."

Desi knew he was right. If she were going to pursue a relationship with Bailey, it would have to wait until the trial was over and the sentences ordered. A good defense attorney would have a field day if he found out they were romantically involved. "She is an interesting woman; I appreciate your reminder."

"That's what partners are for," he said with a wink. "You think you can handle a woman that headstrong?" he teased.

"I don't know, but I sure would like to try."

"Ha, I'm not sure she is ready for you," he recanted.

"I just hope this whole process moves quickly and doesn't drag on forever."

"The case should move quickly. We have good evidence and witnesses. Maybe they will cop a plea, and we can forego a trial."

"I don't see these guys copping to anything, but we can hope," Desi said.

They were approaching Jackson as the sun was creeping below the horizon.

†

Bailey was finishing her third and final mile when a soft breeze began to blow. She slowed down to a walk to cool off, and found her feet had taken her to Desi's house. She stopped for a drink from her bottle and looked at the small house and well-kept yard. She wondered how she maintained the yard with the number of hours she put in at work. A passing car brought her attention back to reality and she began her cool-down walk.

The run had worked. She felt much better after a good sweat, but it did leave her hungry, so she decided she would stop in for a quick pulled pork sandwich at Top's before going to the club.

Feeling better than she had in months, Bailey showered and dressed in jeans and a black tank top that showed off the body she worked hard to maintain. She saw herself smiling at the image looking back at her from the mirror, and realized the strut that had turned so many heads in the past had returned as she brushed her teeth to finish her routine.

†

Desi and Braxton made record time processing the paperwork to extradite their prisoners, and Braxton wasted no time in getting them back to Memphis to begin the interrogation. Braxton had raised the plexiglass shield to separate the front and backseats, and had turned on the microphone in case their passengers wanted to share any information. Buster Doogan, the smaller of the two, attempted to talk with Harold Whitlock, the man Bailey got a good swing on, but he quickly told him to shut up. She smiled at Braxton. "That would have been too easy."

"I know, but I think once the little one realizes he will soon be someone's prison bitch, he will start singing like a canary," Braxton said with a satisfying grin.

"So how do you want to do the interviews? Separate or tag team them?"

"Let's start together with Buster, and then when he starts dishing details, I'd like for you to go in and have a chat with good old Harold. I'm sure he will detest a woman putting him through the wringer."

"I would love to go a few rounds with him," she sneered.

When they arrived back in Memphis, they booked the two men and placed them in separate interview rooms while they got fresh coffee and took a restroom break. They took great delight in watching Buster squirm in the room and jump at every little sound he heard. It was obvious that Harold was the dominant one of the pair and Buster followed him around like a puppy.

"I don't know about you, but I'm feeling just a little bit wicked tonight," Braxton said. "Let's take Buster back to one of the old rooms at the back of the precinct. Let him do his perp walk through general population." He grinned even wider. "It sounds like the natives are very restless back there and I bet he will come close to peeing himself."

"Detective Braxton, I do believe you have a truly evil sense of humor, but I love it," Desi said. "Do you want to take our boy and I will follow you in a minute or two?"

"Yeah, that way they will focus totally on him and not be distracted by you," he answered.

Desi watched as Braxton removed Buster from the quiet interview room and led him to the door of general population. She could hear the roar of shouts and obscenities targeting Buster as Braxton took his time walking him through. When the door closed to shut out the noise, she let out a chuckle and walked over to her desk to check for messages. The list of witnesses was on her desk so she took them and tucked them in her notepad. She walked down a back hallway to the interview room and opened the door.

Buster was in tears and whining through his hands to Braxton. "I ain't never been in jail or in trouble before," he was saying.

"Well, you better get used to being in jail," she said. "There are several men already taking bets on who will get to you first," Desi said, watching a hard swallow reveal Buster's shock and understanding of her statement.

"I bet Leon wins," Braxton said. "He's a big sum bitch and nobody messes with him. If I was a betting man, I'd put ten bucks on him."

Desi let out a dry laugh. "Too bad Harold will go up to county. I bet Leon would have a great time breaking him down to his knees."

"H…Harold won't be here?" Buster stammered.

"No, Harold will be in a separate unit, so you will be all on your own. These Memphis boys hate it when you boys from Mississippi come around to fuck with their turf. Oh yeah, they will be waiting on you, Mr. Doogan." She smiled when she realized how much she was enjoying tormenting him.

"You have to protect me," Buster whined. "I'm innocent, I ain't done nothing."

Braxton took a folder of pictures out from under his arm and started placing them on the table in front of Buster. They were pictures of Tommy taken at the hospital showing plenty of blood and pain. Buster turned white when he recognized Tommy, and turned away from the photographs.

"This isn't what I would call innocent. We have witnesses who will testify you and Harold did this to this unfortunate young man," he said as he tapped on the table to bring Harold's focus back to the photographs. "You two assholes beat him almost to death, and for what ten dollars? Was that right, Detective Dexter?" he asked as he loomed over the smaller man.

"That's right, for ten dollars. You probably spent more than that in gas to get up here," she said to Buster as she glared at him.

"I didn't do any of that. It was Harold, his idea, and he said it was easy money. We could just threaten the queers and they would give up their money and go running off, screaming like little girls," Buster said.

"I bet that's not what Harold is going to say. He's going to say it was your idea and leave you holding the bag—and having to deal with Leon and them other boys," Braxton taunted. He sat on the edge of the table and got real close to Buster, picking up the worst of the photographs. "Look at this," he said. "This is what you two did in a matter of minutes, and it is nothing compared to what they will do to you for hours, days, weeks, and years once you are convicted."

That was all Buster could take. His bladder gave way to his fear, his urine soaking the floor underneath the chair.

"Look at you, wetting yourself like a baby," Braxton taunted. "The boys are going to love that."

"It was all Harold's fault. I just drove him to Memphis for some fun," Buster said. "He was the one that did the beating, I just cheered him on."

"Detective Dexter, could you ask one of the guards to get Mr. Doogan some coveralls and flip-flops so he can get out of these soiled clothes?"

"Sure thing," Desi said and left the room. She gave instructions to one of the guards who went for the clothing and returned a few minutes later.

"Please have him change and bring him back up front through gen pop," Braxton said with a wink to the guard. "You can go ahead and toss his nasty clothes. He won't need them for a long, long, time," he added.

Buster was in tears when Desi and Braxton left the room. "Damn, but you are cruel," she told her partner.

"I will get him into a room and have him start writing out his statement if you want to have a go at Harold. I bet he will have the sense to lawyer up once you tell him what we have."

"I will see you soon," Desi said and took the envelope of photographs from him.

Desi walked down the hallway to the newer interview rooms and checked the camera and recorder to ensure they were on before she stepped inside the door. Harold was stretched back in his seat and looking confident as she entered the room.

"Mr. Whitlock, do you understand the charges against you?"

He leaned forward across the table in an attempt to intimidate Desi but she held her ground. "I didn't do anything," he said with a cocky grin.

"What happened to your arm, by the way, I forgot to ask earlier."

"I broke it playing football," he sneered.

"Playing football at three in the morning, isn't that just a little unusual, even for you Mississippi boys?"

"We was just out having some fun, reliving our glory days from high school until we got carried away and my arm got hurt."

"That's funny. The surgeon who operated on your arm said there was no way you broke this playing football. It was blunt force trauma from a very solid and forceful strike of a hard object. Now unless you boys got your sports mixed up and were playing baseball, your story isn't going to fly."

Desi watched with great satisfaction as the confidence started to fade from Harold's face. Harold had not anticipated the surgeon being able to determine the cause of the trauma, and the fact had him visibly shaken.

"So tell me, Mr. Whitlock, how did you really get hurt Friday night?"

"I already told you, bitch," he snarled. "We was playing some ball."

"That is not at all what Mr. Doogan told us. He said he had driven you up to Memphis so you could have some fun, and since you did not have money to party with, you suggested 'rolling some queers' for easy money. I think Buster said, 'they would give up their money and run off screaming like little girls,' to be exact."

Whitlock went white with shock as the blood drained from his face and then a deep red from anger when he realized Buster had sold him out. "I want a lawyer," he said and turned away from her.

"Do you have anyone in mind or want a court-appointed lawyer?" she asked with obvious contempt for the man.

"What do you think, bitch?"

"That would be the court-appointed kind," she said sweetly and left the room.

Braxton was outside the door watching through the monitor. "Very nicely done," he said.

"Thanks. How is Buster coming along?"

"I think he is on his third page already," he answered. "Will you go ahead and bring the DA's office up to speed?"

"Yes, I'll make the call and write up a quick report on both interviews while you wait for Buster to finish," Desi said. Her favorite young ADA was on call so she dialed his number and filled him in on the case. She promised to e-mail him the files and videos as soon as possible.

Desi, who was a much faster typist than Braxton, had already finished the report regarding Buster's interview and was nearly done with the much shorter report on Harold when Braxton returned with Buster's statement. "You can go ahead and sign that one, and this one will be ready in just a minute," she said as she pointed to the report lying on her printer. "ADA Bartlet is on call and I told him we would e-mail everything to him, so he can start the casework."

"Good job, partner," Braxton said and gave her a high-five.

"Will you start scanning the other information while I finish that report? Then we can send the file and go see some witnesses." Desi was smiling proudly as she knew the majority of their work on this case was over. The DA's office would take the information from them and start the prosecution. She and Braxton would meet with them several times before trial, but they were free to focus on other cases until that time was near.

✝

Sunday evening at the club was usually a more relaxed crowd, but tonight the full moon had the crowd in a partying mood, and it was nearly two before they could usher the last customers into a waiting cab. Bailey locked the door behind her as she returned and looked at Louise.

"Good Lord tonight was wild."

"Definitely not our typical Sunday night. You finish stocking while the boys and I bus the tables," Louise said. "I don't know about ya'll, but I'm ready for the bed tonight."

"I hear that," Joe and Bailey said in unison. It had been a long but productive day. Bailey was looking forward to her day off and sleeping in for a little while if her internal clock would allow it to happen. With the extra help from Tony and Charles, the work was finished in record time and they all started out for home.

Bailey had the top rolled back on the Jeep and welcomed the cool air against her skin as she drove home. She passed by Desi's house and saw her car in the drive, but there were no lights on in the house. Desi too was probably enjoying being at home in bed.

Chapter 7

The bright sunshine filtering through her window shades woke Bailey the next morning. She stretched and enjoyed a few more minutes of relaxation before climbing from the bed. Bailey walked into the kitchen to turn on the coffeepot and clicked the remote to her stereo system to add some music to her morning.

Today was the big day. She was excited about having Desi over for dinner and a little nervous. Bailey had not been on an actual date since Nessa was murdered. Bailey looked at the list of ingredients she would need to buy at the grocery and worried for a moment if she would remember how to cook the meal from scratch. She walked through the house, judging it decent enough for company and made her way back to the kitchen.

Bailey poured a mug of coffee and took the strawberries from the refrigerator to wash and slice them into a bowl. She would later use a potato masher to smash them into smaller bits, and add a spoonful or two of sugar to the juicy mixture.

When she placed the bowl back into the refrigerator, her eyes landed on the can of whipped cream and she let out a giggle as she remembered yesterday's contest. Her mind could think of many different imaginative uses for whipped cream other than building the perfect penis. She closed the door and took her coffee mug to the table to finish a grocery list. The Alfredo sauce was a given, so she added the ingredients she would need for that, but she had not made homemade pasta in years. After looking at the recipe, she added pasta ingredients, salad items, and a fresh loaf of Italian bread to the list. The bread would be the only non-homemade item on her menu, as baking bread had never been her specialty.

After finishing her list, Bailey poured another mug of coffee. She had put water on to boil to make a fresh pot of iced tea when her cell phone rang.

She saw Louise was the caller and answered on the third ring. "Good morning, Louise."

"Good morning, Bailey. Did you sleep well last night?"

"I can barely call it sleeping. I think I was comatose until about twenty minutes ago."

"I was calling to see if you could stop by the club in an hour so John can train us on the new security system," she asked. When Bailey hesitated, she continued, "I know this is a big day for you, so I promise it won't take long at all."

Bailey knew it was important for her to be there for the training, and she would not disappoint Louise. "Of course I'll be there. I need to shower and dress, but I can come by on my way to the grocery store."

"Thank you so much," Louise said with relief in her voice. "You know I am very low-tech and will screw things up on the first opportunity."

Bailey laughed at her cousin's remark. Louise still used an old-fashioned crank can opener because she never could master the art of the electric ones. "No problem, I will see you in an hour," Bailey answered.

"Are you excited about tonight?"

"Yes and a little scared."

"Relax, sweetheart, things will go just fine," Louise said in her most motherly voice.

"I sure hope you are right."

"I know I am. Now go get your cute butt in the shower," Louise said, ending the call.

Bailey dropped the tea bags in the pot to allow them to boil for several minutes and then turned the heat off to allow the tea a chance to steep while she showered.

Thirty minutes later she was dressed and on her way to the club to meet with Louise and John.

✝

Desi slept until noon and then took a quick shower before she dressed to run to the store for a bottle of wine. Desi was clueless as to what she was looking for other than a good wine, so she sent up a silent prayer for a kind person at the store to help her pick out something nice. She pulled out of her drive and rolled by Bailey's house. Even though her Jeep was gone, Desi felt a smile growing on her face. She had given thought to Braxton's reminder that she needed to refrain from becoming personally involved with Bailey until the case was over, and thought briefly about canceling their dinner. She couldn't do that to Bailey but would share the concern with her face-to-face.

✝

John was just finishing the install when Bailey arrived at the club. He expertly ran them through the benefits of the added lighting and the security cameras before showing them how to activate the new alarm panel he had installed. John said the system operated by one remote, making the system as Louise-proof as possible. Bailey smiled as Louise let out a sigh of relief. "See how simple this is?"

"I know I got myself worked up over nothing," Louise said to a smiling John.

"Here are a couple of extra remotes in case you want the boys to have one as well," he said as he handed her a small package. "Don't hesitate to give me a call if you have any questions, or any problems. Everything is set to automatic, so there is very little you will have to do. I will be by at least every two months to check the system and change out lightbulbs."

"Thanks for everything, John," Louise said as they walked him to the door.

"My pleasure, ladies, and thanks for the business. Call me if you want to set up a system at your homes and I will give you a good deal."

"I will be calling you," Louise said, closing the door behind him. "See, that didn't take long and I feel much more protected now. We should have done this sooner."

"Probably so," Bailey answered. "Are you going to stick around or head home for a nap?"

Louise chuckled. "You know me too well, a nap it is for me. You go on now, and get to the grocery store so you can start cooking for that lovely woman."

Bailey waited until Louise locked the door behind them, and they walked to their vehicles. "Call me and let me know how things go tomorrow when you get back on the road."

"I will," Bailey said and climbed into the Jeep. She pulled out into rush hour traffic, cursing her poor timing, but made good time to the grocery store. By one o'clock she was back at home and had her hands in flour as she began the process of making fresh pasta.

†

Desi hit the jackpot when she arrived at the liquor store to find one of the staff was well educated on the wine selection. He helped her pick out a bottle of pinot noir for dinner and gave her instructions on how to chill the wine before serving to get the best flavor. The smile on her face kept growing as she drove home with her prize and placed it in the refrigerator to chill.

Desi's smile quickly turned into a frown as she made her way to her bedroom closet in search of something to wear. She searched hanger after hanger filled with business suits and various other detective attire. She made a mental note to go shopping for some casual clothes. She breathed a sigh of relief when she found a decent-looking pair of jeans and a white three-quarter sleeved shirt. With some starch, and a hot steam iron they would be presentable enough she thought as she placed the clothes on the bed.

†

While Desi was busy ironing her clothes, Bailey was in her kitchen rolling out the pasta dough to prepare it for the pasta cutter. The Alfredo sauce was simmering along nicely, and the salads were in the refrigerator chilling. She looked at the clock and was amazed how much time she had spent on the fettuccine noodles. For a split second she wondered if she had made a mistake by not buying premade noodles. Then she remembered how much Nessa had enjoyed the taste and texture of her homemade pasta. Nessa had enjoyed every meal Bailey had ever cooked for her, and they had spent many memorable hours in the kitchen creating special meals together. Her heart sank with the memory, but she knew Louise was right. Nessa would want her to find someone to make her happy again. She wiped sweat from her brow with her forearm and hoped Desi would appreciate the loving care she used to make this meal.

Time was passing too quickly and Bailey had a moment of panic when she realized she had not cooked the chicken breast yet. Desi would be here in a half hour, and she was disappointed there would not be time for a quick shower and fresh clothes.

†

Desi had showered and dressed before taking the bottle of wine out of the refrigerator to breathe. She was thankful she could uncork the wine in the solitude of her home rather than trying to do it correctly when her nerves would be on edge trying to make a good impression on Bailey. She had very little history with wine and hoped she still had a corkscrew somewhere in the kitchen. After rummaging through two drawers, she spied the utensil and tried to remember the salesperson's advice for removing the cork. Desi held her breath as she turned the screw, driving it into what she prayed was the center of the cork as visions of cork fragments floating in the bottle crossed her mind. When she pulled the levers down each side of the bottle she smiled in relief as the cork slid smoothly from the neck of the bottle where it had snuggly rested for six years. She was rather proud of her accomplishment.

While the wine breathed, Desi paced the kitchen as she watched the clock tick ever so slowly until she could stand it no longer. Desi decided to walk to Bailey's house since she was so close. As she returned the cork to the bottle, she hoped Bailey would forgive her for arriving early.

†

Bailey had just finished pounding the chicken breasts flat when she heard a knock on her front door. Her panicked eyes flew to the clock to find that it was barely five thirty. She rinsed her hands at the kitchen sink and wiped them on a towel as she walked to the door. To her absolute horror, Desi was early and standing at her front door.

She opened the door to a nervous-looking Desi and smiled warmly. "Please forgive me for being early but I was wearing out my floor."

"No problem. Come on in. I am still working on dinner, so you can pour us a glass of wine and keep me company while I finish."

"Is there anything I can do to help?"

"No, ma'am, this meal is totally my doing," Bailey said as she closed the door behind her. They walked to the kitchen and Bailey pointed to a cabinet. "The wineglasses are there," she said and turned the burner on the stove to heat the olive oil in the pan. Bailey squeezed a package of Ritz crackers until they were fine crumbs and poured them into a bowl.

Desi poured their wine and arrived at the counter just as Bailey was dredging the first breast in beaten eggs. She watched as Bailey coated the breast with cracker crumbs and placed it in the frying pan with ease.

"That looks delicious," Desi said as Bailey repeated the process with the three remaining chicken breasts.

Bailey smiled and rinsed her hands then emptied the bowl of eggs into the sink before turning to pick up the glass of wine. She took a sip and smiled at Desi. "This is very good wine."

"I'm glad you like it. I don't know much about wine, but there was a nice young man who helped me pick this out."

"You both did a terrific job. A pinot noir?" she asked.

"Yes, he said it would be good with just about anything you cooked."

Desi relaxed against the counter now that she was certain the wine was satisfactory. She looked over to see the pasta machine. "Did you make the pasta from scratch?"

"The pasta and the Alfredo are both homemade. There is no comparison with the boxed and bottled meals, and I guarantee you will agree once you have tasted fresh."

"Please don't be disappointed when you look in my pantry then," Desi answered.

"I have the prepackaged stuff too for convenience, but when there is time to prepare, nothing beats the real thing."

"Have you been cooking all day?"

"No, just most of the afternoon, it takes a while to make the fresh pasta."

"I am very impressed, Ms. Chambers," she said. "You really are talented."

"I haven't cooked like this for some time," she admitted. Bailey turned the thin sliced breast in the pan to brown the other side before taking them out to cool and let the excess oil drain from the meat before she would slice them.

Desi sipped her wine and admired the way Bailey made every motion look effortless as she sliced the chicken and prepared the fresh bread for toasting with her own blend of special seasonings.

"I hope you are hungry," Bailey said. "I can never seem to get the portions right for just two people."

"I'm starving, but I bet this will be just as good as leftovers."

"Good, you will be the proud owner of lunch for tomorrow then," Bailey said.

Desi chuckled. "I may have to fight Braxton for it."

"No worries, I will send you away with enough for two," Bailey told her as she dropped the pasta into the boiling water and placed the bread in the oven. She lifted the lid on the Alfredo sauce and the air instantly filled with a pleasing aroma.

"As good as that smells, Braxton may not get any," she said as she peeked over Bailey's shoulder.

Bailey smiled at the compliment. "I'm a bit old-fashioned so I made a pot of tea if you would like some with your meal. We can finish the wine after dinner if you would like."

Desi smiled and cocked her head at Bailey. "I can't drink alcohol with a meal either. I was hoping you would be the great southern hostess and have some fresh sweet tea."

"I would never dream of disappointing you, ma'am," Bailey teased.

"Dinner will be ready in just a few if you would like to make us a glass of tea and take our salads to the table."

Bailey took a large serving platter down from a shelf and placed it on the counter. After draining the pasta, she spread it across the platter and garnished it with the slices of chicken. The timer went off for the bread and she rushed to remove it before it burned.

"Will you cut this into slices and put it on that plate?" she asked Desi while handing her a knife and pointing to the plate.

Desi sliced the bread and carried it to the table while Bailey finished the dish by pouring the Alfredo sauce over the bed of pasta and chicken. Bailey carried the dish to the table then sat down across from Desi and used the serving utensils to place a large portion on their plates to cool while they enjoyed the salad.

"This is so good," Desi said between bites of her salad.

"I'm glad you are enjoying it," she said with a smile.

They made quick work of the salads and moved on to the main dish. Bailey watched with anticipation for Desi to take a bite.

"Oh dear Lord, will you marry me?" she said. "This tastes fantastic." Desi took another bite.

Bailey flashed her crooked little grin and began eating. All it took was one comment from Desi to make all the hard work of the day worthwhile. She took a bite of the bread and stifled a moan. The seasoning for the bread had been a new recipe she was trying out and the result had turned out deliciously.

Desi took a break from chewing only to take a drink. Bailey watched her devour the first half of the serving like a woman possessed and appreciated her healthy appetite. "How long has it been since you ate?" she teased.

"I actually haven't had anything today, but this Alfredo is awesome."

That was the last bit of conversation Bailey managed to get out of Desi. She was content to watch her enjoy the meal. When she finished her serving, Bailey refilled their tea glasses and sat back to watch her new friend. Desi had taken another small serving so Bailey took her dishes to the sink and began working on dessert, away from Desi's view.

She placed two slices of the pound cake on each plate, and then smothered them with the crushed strawberries. She placed the bowl back into the refrigerator and smiled as she took the can of whipped cream from the shelf. Bailey decided not to add the whipped cream without asking Desi, so she carried the can of cream and the two plates to the table.

Desi's eyes grew large as Bailey approached. "What is that?"

"It's called dessert," she answered calmly and put a plate down next to her. "Would you like whipped cream?"

"You didn't mention dessert, but yes, whipped cream would be great."

"I will let you add that when you are ready," Bailey said and picked up her fork to begin eating her shortcake.

The juice from the crushed strawberries soaked into the already rich pound cake slices. Bailey contemplated adding whipped cream for a moment and decided against the extra topping. She watched with a huge grin as Desi popped the top off the can and added a pile of cream to the top of her dessert. Her mind rushed back to the competition Louise and the boys had the previous day and she debated whether to tell Desi about it.

Desi looked up to see the grin on Bailey's face. "What's so funny?"

"We had this for dessert yesterday at Tommy's. I woke up from a nap to roaring laughter and when I walked in to see what was going on in the kitchen, I found Louise and the boys competing to see who could create the most realistic penis with the whipped cream."

Desi stopped midbite to ask, "Who won?"

"Unbelievably, Louise did," Bailey said.

"That had to be hilarious. I wish I could have seen that."

"Stick around. I'm sure there will be several repeat performances this summer."

"Do you all eat together often?"

"I usually eat with Joe and Tommy once during the week, and Louise joins us when we get together on the weekends."

"Does Louise have a partner?"

"No, she's been single for several years now. I think has given up looking," Bailey said.

Desi sensed the sadness in Bailey's voice. "Hopefully, the right one will come along for her. She seems like a really nice person."

"She's been like a mom and older sister to Tommy and me."

"I guess I am very lucky to have a supportive family."

"Very much so, but I think we have done pretty well for ourselves," Bailey said.

"It would appear so," Desi answered.

Desi was quiet as she finished her dessert and Bailey sensed something was bothering her. "Is everything okay?"

"I have had a really good time tonight, but I need to tell you something and I don't want it to ruin our evening."

Bailey felt her heart sink to her stomach as a wave of anxiety turned into a swell. Here it comes, she thought, the truth. She has a girlfriend, or boyfriend, or both. She calmly placed her fork on her plate and looked at Desi, expecting devastating news. She steeled herself for the disappointment that was sure to come just when she had decided to open herself up to someone again.

"We have both of Tommy's attackers in custody," she said.

"That's great news."

"It is and it isn't."

"What do you mean?"

"It's great that they are in custody and Tommy will get some justice for what they did to him."

"So, what is the bad part?" Bailey asked, feeling somewhat relieved, but still confused.

"Until they have gone through trial and been sentenced I can't risk being seen associating with you. I want you to know I am very interested in a relationship with you, however, a decent defense attorney could get them off if they found out I was in a relationship with the victim's brother," she explained.

"Well, that sucks," Bailey said, a bit stunned.

"Yeah, it does, but I won't risk Tommy's attackers getting off so easy," she said. "So, I guess my question to you is can you wait a month or so until the case is settled?"

"I don't know a month…is a long time," Bailey said with a grin. "Do you think it will go that quickly?"

"We can only hope," Desi said.

Bailey reached across the table and covered Desi's hand with hers. "If I must wait, I will wait for you for as long as it takes. I am very interested in you too and look forward to the day Tommy gets his justice, and we can have our freedom."

Desi smiled with relief. "Thank you for being patient."

"Don't thank me yet," Bailey teased. "A month is a long time."

"It will be long for both of us," Desi said. "After tonight, we should only see each other in a professional capacity or in a large group until it is over."

"I understand. I don't like it, but I understand and agree with you."

They sat and looked at one another for several long seconds. "If you have had enough to eat would you like another glass of wine or some coffee?" Bailey asked.

"I think we both have early mornings, so why don't we have a glass of wine while we clean up here?"

"You pour, and I will work on the kitchen," Bailey said.

"I can help," Desi said.

"I know you can, but I'd rather you fix lunch for you and Detective Braxton for tomorrow and then you can help me put the leftovers away."

Bailey took the last of the dishes from the table, placed them on the counter and then located containers for Desi to fill for their lunches before she started to rinse the dishes for the dishwasher.

Desi filled the containers and found a smaller set that she filled with the remainder of the food for Bailey. "Will this be enough for your dinner tomorrow night?"

"Yes, with some salad that will be plenty."

"I don't know if Braxton will get any of this," she teased. "I may just keep it all for myself."

"I won't tell if you won't," Bailey told her.

They quickly finished cleaning the kitchen and sat at the table to finish their wine. "This is going to be hard you know," Bailey said.

"I know and just the fact we have to wait at all is killing me," Desi said.

Bailey looked surprised. "Do tell, Detective."

"From your first snarky remark at the hospital I knew I was interested in you," she admitted.

"I was rather nasty to both of you. I'm sorry for that."

"You had your reasons and your attitude only intrigued me more."

Bailey chuckled. "If there is one thing I have its attitude."

"Not to mention a great deal of passion for what you believe in too," Desi added.

Their wineglasses were nearly empty and Desi knew the evening was quickly reeling away. "Tomorrow should be very interesting and informative."

"Why is that?" Bailey asked.

"The thugs will go for their first appearance tomorrow, and we should have a better idea about how long this case will last."

"Are you confident about the case against them?"

"It is rock solid, and we have one of my favorite assistant district attorneys working the case. Doogan, the smaller of the two, sang like a bird when we started putting a squeeze on him, and I have no doubt we will get a conviction."

"What is the best-case scenario?"

"That they would both plead out and we could skip a trial. But I don't see that happening, even with the evidence against them. Harold knows he is going down and will delay the inevitable for as long as possible." She looked at Bailey and a lightbulb popped on in her head. "Oh, I almost forgot, I need to get your bat for evidence."

"Okay, well you can drop by the club or I can get Louise to drop it off here."

"Thanks for the offer, but we have to pick it up, to preserve the chain of evidence."

"Why do you need the bat?"

"Because I bet your initials are burnt into the Louisville Slugger label."

Bailey chuckled. "Yes, they are. It was a gift from Tommy years ago, but how do you know this?"

"Because the hospital took photographs of his injuries and there is a perfect image of the bat's label on his arm, including your initials. So we need it to add another nail to Harold's coffin."

"That's amazing," Bailey said. "I guess I did get a really good swing on him."

"I would say you did, my friend."

"Will I get it back?"

"Yes, I will make sure it is returned to you after the case is over."

Silence hung between them for several seconds before Desi said, "I guess I should be on my way. I will call you tomorrow night, if that's okay, to let you know how the arraignment goes."

"I would appreciate that," Bailey said as she picked up the bag with the leftovers. "I hope you enjoy lunch."

"That will be a bright spot to my day," Desi said as she took the bag she offered.

Bailey walked her to the door and Desi stood on her tiptoes to kiss her lightly on the cheek. "Thank you for a great evening." Desi desperately wanted to kiss Bailey's lips, but she knew that was dangerous territory and feared she would not be able to stop with a kiss.

"You are welcome. I really enjoyed having you here and cooking for you."

Desi looked up at her with excitement sparkling in her eyes. "Goodnight, Bailey, be safe tomorrow."

"You too. I look forward to hearing from you," she said and watched Desi walk through the door to disappear into the darkness.

✝

Desi walked the short distance to her home and slipped inside her back door. She placed the bag of leftovers in the refrigerator and looked at the clock. It was just after nine and her mind was too wound up for her to sleep, so she decided to drive over to the club to get the bat.

Desi heard the blaring music as the door opened and a young couple exited the bar as she approached. The bar was packed on a Monday night only proving that the club was truly a hotspot for Memphis nightlife. The man working the door recognized her from her previous visit and passed her through without issue. She walked toward the bar where Louise was busy serving customers.

Louise looked up to see her and smiled warmly as Desi took a seat at the end of the bar. "You are the last person I expected to see here tonight. Is everything okay?"

Desi chuckled at her comment. "Yes, everything is fine. I needed to come by and get Bailey's bat as evidence for the case," she explained.

"I thought you were having dinner with her tonight. Did I mix up my days again?"

"No, ma'am. Bailey cooked me a terrific meal and we had a lovely evening."

Louise was confused. "So you are here now instead of enjoying the evening?"

"We have both of the men in custody and they will go through a first appearance tomorrow. I can jeopardize the case against them if their lawyer finds out I am romantically involved with the main witness in the case. So Bailey and I are going to wait until the case is concluded before we initiate a relationship," Desi told her. "I am very interested and attracted to her, but it will have to wait a few more weeks."

"Oh. Okay that makes sense. So may I get you a beer?"

"No, thanks. We had some wine earlier. I would take a Diet Coke, though."

"Coming right up," Louise said with a smile of relief.

"The club is really hopping tonight," she said when Louise set her drink in front of her.

"Yes, business has been great lately."

"How do you manage this work all by yourself?"

"It's come to be my life. Bailey and the boys help out when they can."

"Have you considered hiring someone to help you during the week so you can get a break?"

Louise smiled. "We have been talking it over just recently. The boys are on the lookout for me."

"Good," Desi said and took a sip of her drink.

Louise reached beneath the counter and pulled out Bailey's bat, placing it on the bar in front of Desi. "Tommy bought this for her when they visited the factory in Louisville."

Desi looked at the bat's label clearly showing Bailey's initials. "The hospital in Jackson took several photographs of Harold's arm before they performed surgery and there was a perfect image of this label including Bailey's initials in the bruising on his arm," she explained.

"That's pretty damning evidence isn't it?"

"Yes, it is, and will be very useful if we have to go to trial."

"Do you think it will go to that?"

"Probably so, we have a rock-solid case against them, but Harold will do anything to delay his eventual arrival to prison, and he understands we have the evidence to put him there."

"Will they be released on bond?"

"Hopefully not considering the heinousness of his crime, but we will know more tomorrow."

"Will you keep us posted?"

"Of course I will," Desi said as Louise was pulled away to serve a customer.

Becca came up to the bar and took a seat beside Desi. "You are one lucky woman," she said with a slight slur.

"Why is that?"

"I have been chasing Bailey for over a year as well as a half dozen other women and all she has done is run from us. You swoop in and instantly steal her heart," she said as Louise returned.

"Some things are just meant to be," Desi said. "And yes, I do consider myself lucky for having met Bailey."

Louise smiled when she heard Desi's remark. "I guess you will have to find someone else to chase," she told Becca.

"Easier said than done," Becca said followed with a hiccup.

"I think you should probably head for home," Louise said.

"Yeah, you're right. Will you call me a cab?" she asked.

"Sure, I'll be right back," Louise said.

Becca looked at Desi with eyes starting to blur. "Just don't hurt Bailey; she's gone through enough heartache."

"I have no intention of hurting Bailey or anyone for that matter, but I appreciate your concern for her. You must be a very good friend to her."

"I try to be," Becca answered slowly.

"You okay here?" Desi asked Louise with a nod toward Becca.

"Yes, I'm good. Thanks for asking, though."

"I'm going to head out and get some sleep."

"Have a great night, and I look forward to hearing from you."

"Goodnight," Desi answered and walked out the door. The night was beautiful for Memphis this time of the year and she walked slowly to her car. A noise coming from the back of the club caught her attention so she walked to the back to investigate. She approached slowly as a small black blur moved in the shadows and she prayed it was not a skunk. Braxton would never let her live it down if she ended up sprayed by a skunk.

Inside, Louise watched Desi leave the club through the camera and was alarmed when she saw her turn toward the back of the club instead of walking to her car. She left the bar and went out to see what was happening.

Her footsteps caught the attention of the animal and Desi jumped in surprise when a tiny black kitten bounced out into the light. She was relieved to see the black ball of fur instead of a skunk and bent down to call the small animal to her.

Louise turned the corner just as Desi was picking up the small animal. "Good grief, what have you got there?" she asked when she saw the tiny animal.

"Apparently an abandoned little one who is looking for something to eat. It is skinny as a rail," she said as she walked to Louise carrying the now purring kitten.

She held up the kitten for Louise to look at and Louise sneezed. "I love cats, but I am highly allergic," she said, taking a step back.

"I guess I just got a pet then," Desi said. "There is no way I'm taking this cutie to the pound," she said as she held the kitten up to try to determine the sex. "Still too early to tell," she said.

"A cat would make a great pet for you with your work schedule. They are incredibly independent and low maintenance," Louise said.

"Fubar," Desi said as she looked into the kitten's deep green eyes.

"What's that?" Louise said unsure what Desi had said.

"The kitten's name. I will call him or her Fubar since we found it here."

Louise laughed aloud. "That's a great name."

"Well, little one, it looks like we have to make a store run now," Desi said as she and Louise walked back to the parking lot.

"You two have a great night," Louise said.

"Thanks," Desi said and carried the kitten to her car.

†

After a stop at a nearby store for kitten milk, food, litter, and a litter box, Desi and the kitten arrived at her new home. "First stop for you, little one, is a bath. You smell like the Dumpster," Desi said as she started the water to warm it up and went to the bathroom for some shampoo. "This will have to work for now," she said as they returned to the kitchen.

The kitten eyed the sink and then looked at Desi with total disbelief when she realized what Desi was planning. When Desi attempted to place her in the water, the kitten's feet splayed out in all directions. Fubar hissed loudly and began struggling to prevent Desi from lowering her into the water. Desi finally managed to dunk the kitten in the tepid water then reached for the bottle of shampoo. Fubar took advantage of Desi's momentary lapse in concentration to shake her body, spraying Desi with water from her coat. Desi squealed in shock and Fubar wiggled out of her grasp and bolted from the kitchen sink, tearing through the house. She ended up in the bedroom, hovering just out of Desi's reach under the center of the bed.

Desi crawled under the bed, banging her head on the bed frame and made a grab for the kitten. Fubar hissed and dashed out from under the bed and out of the room. Determined not be outsmarted by a kitten, Desi gave chase, closing doors to rooms as she passed by them to limit Fubar's escape route.

Finally, after racing around the living room furniture several times, Desi lunged and lifted the kitten by the scruff of her neck. "Oh, hell no, you aren't winning this round," Desi said as they returned to the kitchen to quickly finish a bath.

Five minutes later, a damp kitten was eagerly lapping at the warmed kitten milk as Desi collapsed in her recliner. After a few moments' rest, she set up the litter box and put out a small bowl of food and water. Desi sat down on the floor and watched as Fubar drank its fill of milk then strolled confidently over to her and climbed into her lap with a milk-swollen belly.

"You definitely smell better," she said as she stroked the kitten's soft fur. The kitten let out a soft burp. Desi showed her the litter box. The kitten instinctively adapted to the litter box and proudly did its business, covering it before climbing out to look up at Desi. "Good kitty," she said as she scooped up the kitten, stroking its head before placing it back on the floor.

"Okay, so it's time for me to hit the sack," she said and the kitten followed her into the bedroom. Desi got ready for bed while the kitten sat at the foot of the bed watching her. She set her alarm and looked down at the kitten, who was staring at her with large green eyes. "You aren't going to let me sleep unless I put you in the bed too are you?"

The kitten let out a soft meow in answer, so Desi scooped it up and placed it on a spare pillow on the bed, crawled in between the sheets and turned the light off. Seconds later, she felt the soft vibration of the kitten's purring as it snuggled next to her warm skin. Desi curled her arm around the kitten and fell asleep stroking its soft fur.

Chapter 8

Bailey awoke refreshed and eager to start her day. Sleep had taken her easily and after a good stretch she walked to the kitchen for coffee. The sun had not yet risen, but the morning sky was glowing as it anticipated the sun's arrival. There was no rain in sight today or for the remainder of the week, so she hoped her routes would go well. She poured her first cup then placed the remainder in her thermos for work before strolling back to the shower.

As she rolled out of her driveway, she looked to the right to Desi's house. The house was still dark with no evidence of movement inside. She turned left and drove to work, a smile growing on her face as her thoughts wandered back to last night's meal with Desi.

†

Desi felt a warm spot on her chest and opened her eyes to find the kitten's deep green eyes staring into hers. "Good morning, Fubar," she said as her fingers scratched the kitten's head. "Are you ready for some breakfast?"

She carefully lifted the kitten and walked to the kitchen to set her in the litter pan while she started the coffee and warmed some kitten milk. A trickle of urine in the litter pan let Desi know the kitten had learned quickly. She placed the bowl of warm milk on the floor and went to shower.

After her shower, she pulled on a robe and Fubar met her at the bathroom door. "Did you finish your milk already?" she asked as she went to the kitchen for a cup of coffee. The bowl was empty, but she hesitated on seconds, knowing she would drop the kitten at a veterinarian office close to the precinct on her way to work.

Fubar bounced along behind her, chasing the hem of her robe as she took her coffee and went to the bedroom to dress for work. "I guess I should have gotten a carrier last night," she said when she realized the kitten would be free to roam the car as she drove. Desi was pleased later when the kitten remained snuggled safely in her lap until she carried her inside the vet's office for a checkup.

"Good morning," the receptionist said as they walked through the door. "Who do we have here?"

"Good morning, this is Fubar Dexter," Desi said. "I found him or her around a Dumpster last night while I was working on a case."

"Let's see what we have here," an older female vet said as she entered the room and took Fubar from the receptionist. She lifted the kitten and gave it a brief exam. "You are the proud Mama of a baby girl," she said. "I'm Dr. Lynch."

"Desi Dexter," she said, extending her hand. "I work at the precinct just a few blocks down, and I hoped you could give her an exam and any treatments she needs."

"You found her at a Dumpster?"

"Yes, she's such a tiny thing, I almost didn't see her."

"She is only about six weeks old. What did you feed her?"

"I warmed some kitten milk for her."

"Good job. We will give her a good exam and test her for feline leukemia and worms. Those are the two most prevalent issues with feral kittens. Will you pick her up later today?"

"Yes, probably around five, if that's okay," she said.

"That will be fine. Susan will need to get some information from you, but we will have Miss Fubar ready for you this afternoon," the vet said and left the room.

"She is a cute little thing," Susan said.

"Yes she is," Desi said proudly and began filling out the paperwork Susan handed her. Ten minutes later she was at the office, putting the large bag of leftovers into the refrigerator in the break room.

"Good morning," Braxton said as he entered behind her to get fresh coffee. "What do you have there?"

"Lunch for us," Desi said. "The most incredible homemade chicken Alfredo I have ever eaten."

"Did last night go well then?"

"Yes it did, thanks. She was very understanding."

"That's good," Braxton said as he watched her place the containers in the refrigerator. "That seems like a lot for lunch."

"We also have fresh strawberry shortcake for dessert," she answered.

Braxton chuckled. "You better go get a padlock to lock the fridge then or we won't have lunch."

"Trust me, I plan to keep a sharp eye on it."

"Bartlet called."

"Yeah, any news yet?" she asked.

"Nope, but he promised to call as soon as he can."

Desi followed him back to their desks. "You need me for a bit?"

"No, I'm just reviewing notes from our interviews on the gang shooting. What's up?"

"I'd like to read over that file we discussed the other day."

Braxton smiled at her. "Go ahead. I'm hoping we can have a peaceful day today."

She went to work reading through the scanned documents and it did not take long for her disgust to surface from Harvey's lack of effort on the case. Desi quickly uncovered two potential leads he never bothered to follow up, or if so, he never documented them. Her first move was to run the fingerprints through the national identification system, while she continued to read. The prints could take hours or days to run through the entire system, so she went back to the witness list. Elma Jones was on the list as a potential witness but there was no further mention of her or any interview records. Desi jotted her name down and then searched to find her last known address.

"I'll be back shortly," she said. "Keep an eye on lunch," she teased.

Braxton threw up his hand to acknowledge her comment but never looked up from the record he was reviewing.

†

The thermos of coffee had Bailey's bladder begging for a stop so she pulled into a rest area and made her way to the facilities. She was washing her hands when a woman entered talking on her cell and continued talking as she used the facilities. Bailey thought it was hilarious, but it did remind her to call Louise. She returned to her truck and clicked a button on her Bluetooth earpiece. "Call Louise," she said as she started to roll out of the lot.

"Hey there," Louise said when she answered the phone. "How are you?"

"I'm doing great, thanks, and you?"

"Fine, fine, we had a great night at the club last night and I had the most interesting visitor."

"Did Desi stop by to get the bat?"

"Yes, she got that and so much more," she answered with a chuckle in her voice.

"You don't say. Do I have to drag it out of you? Speaking of drags, how did Tommy's dentist appointment go yesterday? I forgot to call him."

"His appointment went well, and his front teeth look as good as new. "That's good news. So, what else did Desi get?"

"When she left the club, she heard a noise in the alley by the Dumpster and went to investigate. She found an adorable black kitten that she named Fubar."

"Aww, that's too cute. I bet a cat will be the perfect pet for her."

"That is exactly what I said to her last night."

"She will have her hands full with the little one for a while then."

"So how did your dinner go?"

"You would have been proud. The meal turned out great and I was on my best behavior."

"Desi told me about having the two thugs in custody."

"Did she also tell you that we have to wait until after the trial before we can see each other romantically?"

"Yes, she did. Are you okay with that?"

"I have to be. I understand her reasoning, but I want so much to be with Desi. She makes me feel really good."

"Well, have you considered taking her away for a weekend?"

"That thought did cross my mind last night, but I think it would only make the waiting worse. I have waited two years for someone to come along, so a few more weeks should pass quickly."

"I hope they will and all this ugly mess will be behind us so you two can move on with your lives."

"Me too. So what plans do you have for this morning?"

"I thought I would do some shopping for you."

"For me, what do you mean?"

"I think a kitty package is in order."

"A kitty package," Bailey said.

"I thought I would drop by a pet store and buy a nice colorful collar, some kitten treats, and toys for Fubar and leave them on Desi's step from you. I know you won't be back in town in time to surprise her."

"You are an angel, Louise. Thank you for thinking of that. Just let me know how much you spend and I will reimburse you."

"Don't worry, I will just take it out of your salary."

"Well, okay then," Bailey said, knowing Louise would not take any money from her period. "Thanks again for helping me out."

"My pleasure," Louise said. "When I get done I will call and let you know what I got so you won't be surprised when Desi calls."

"You think of everything, don't you?"

"I try. Ciao for now," Louise said and ended the call.

Bailey pushed the button on her earpiece and continued her run to Nashville. The weather was gorgeous and she enjoyed the drive even when she had to slow for road construction. When she made it to Nashville for her turnaround, she grabbed a quick sandwich at a shop next door to the depot after she swapped out her trailers. She ate her sandwich outside to enjoy the sunshine, hoping Desi and Braxton would enjoy their lunch.

†

Desi followed the directions from her GPS and found herself in a subsidized housing project in south West Memphis. It was probably not the part of town for her to be in alone, but she was on a mission. She grabbed her notepad and made sure her holster was unlatched before she left her car. She locked the car and hoped it would still be there with all the parts still in place when she returned.

She verified the address on the dilapidated building and looked for an elevator. As expected, there wasn't one so Desi started up the stairs to the third floor. Once there, she went in search of unit 322, noting how eerily quiet the building was.

Desi located the apartment and stopped in front of the door cocking her head. She could hear the faint sound of a television or radio, but could not ascertain if it was coming from the unit or somewhere else down the hall. She knocked on the door and listened carefully for sounds of movement inside the apartment. Not hearing anything, she knocked again, louder this time.

"Hold your dang horses," a voice yelled from inside.

Desi waited patiently while she heard the sound of several dead bolts and locks unlocking. The doorknob turned and the door slowly opened as a pair of big eyes peeped around the door. "May I help you?" a tiny voice asked.

"Are you Miss Elma Jones?"

"Yes, I am, and who are you, young lady?"

"I am Detective Desi Dexter, from the Memphis PD," she answered as she fished out her badge and held it up in front of her.

"That's useless for me, honey. I can't see much past the end of my nose these days," she said and opened the door wider. "Please come in."

Desi stepped into a small, meticulously neat apartment and turned back to look at Miss Jones. "I am sorry to interrupt your morning, but I need to talk to you, if you have a few minutes."

"Honey, time is the only thing I have these days. Come have a seat at the table. I was just about to pour another cup of coffee when you knocked. Would you like one?"

"Yes, that would be great, thanks," Desi said as she took a seat at the table.

"I've got some of those Little Debbie cakes if you would like one," she offered.

"Oh, no thank you, but you go right ahead."

She watched as the woman tottered through the kitchen to the coffeepot and poured two cups of coffee. Miss Jones carried them to the table and pointed to sugar and cream. "Help yourself, young lady."

"Thank you, Miss Jones," she said as they added cream and sugar to their cups.

"Now, what can I help you with?" she asked and took a sip of coffee.

"I am looking into a case from two years ago that listed you as a possible witness. I hoped you could tell me anything you can remember."

"Oh, that poor beautiful Jamaican woman that was killed," she said. "Is that what you are talking about?"

"Yes, Nessa Williams," Desi said, her hopes skyrocketing.

"Back in those days, I worked in a kitchen at a local old folks' home and I was on my way to work that morning. It was early. I had to be there by four thirty to start on breakfast so I was at the bus stop for the four o'clock bus. It had been raining and I remember thinking how fresh the air smelled that morning." She paused to take a sip of coffee. "I remember seeing two young boys out on the street and wondering why they were out that late. They looked like they was up to no good, so I kept a close eye on them as they approached, and wrapped the straps of my purse around my arm several times."

Desi smiled at the entertaining way the woman described the events.

"I watched a car drive by slowly and come to a stop at the light about a block past the bus stop, and then all hell busted loose. Them boys pulled out a gun and started hollering at the driver to get out of the car. One of them stood in front of the car, confident the driver would not run him over, as the other busted the window and pulled the driver out." She shook her head at the painful memories. "When I saw it was a woman, I feared for her safety and prayed she wouldn't put up a fight and just let them have the damned car, but she didn't."

"What happened then?" Desi asked when Miss Jones paused.

"That poor woman tried to fight the boy and he whipped her across her face with that pistol. When she came at him again, he shot her. I do not think he meant to shoot her, but the gun went off and she was only a foot or so away from him. I can remember it seemed like it took forever for her to fall to the ground, kind of as if she was falling in slow motion. You know what I mean?"

"Yes, I know that feeling," Desi stated.

"The other boy, the one in front of the car, started screaming, 'man, what did you do' as he started to panic."

"Then what happened?" Desi asked, making notes of their conversation.

"The one with the scar, he's the one that did the shooting told the other one to get in the car, but he was frozen so he yelled at him again as he jumped into the car."

"What kind of scar?"

"The one that did the shooting had a long scar all the way down the right side of his face like he had been knifed."

"How old would you say these boys were?"

"Teens, maybe sixteen," she answered.

"Did you get a good look at the other boy?"

"He looked like a baby with a big round face with one of those red bandanas around his forehead like one of them gang boys," she answered.

"What else can you remember, Miss Jones?"

"When they shot her I ducked down hoping they had not seen me, and I watched as they drove away, hitting a parked car. Then I ran to a pay phone to call the police. Then I ran over to the woman, my Lord she was covered in blood. So much blood," she said with tears in her eyes. "That poor woman was gone, wasn't nothing anyone could do to save her. I found out later she was a nurse at one of the children's hospitals. Such a waste." She shook her head.

"Did anyone from the police talk to you?"

"I talked to a really nice officer when he arrived and he said a detective would come to see me, but nobody ever did, until now."

"You have been very helpful, Miss Jones," Desi said as she closed her notebook.

"Do you think you can find them boys after all this time?"

Desi smiled at the woman. "I am going to try my very best," she answered.

"I sure hope you do so that poor woman can get some justice."

"Thank you for talking to me and for the great coffee," Desi said.

"You are so welcome, child. I don't get too many visitors these days."

Desi felt sorry for the woman and wondered where her family was to leave her all alone in this hovel.

"I hope you have a great rest of your day, Miss Jones," Desi said as she began walking to the door.

"Good luck, young lady," Miss Jones said as she followed her.

Desi left the apartment and stood at the door until she was sure Miss Jones had locked it behind her, and then walked back to the stairs. She breathed a sigh of relief when she returned to find her car intact and jacked the air-conditioning to high as she drove back to the precinct.

†

In no hurry to return to the mayhem of the precinct, Desi took a few more minutes when she arrived to review the notes she had developed during her interview with Miss Jones and added a few more to her notebook. She was overwhelmed with disgust at Harvey for being so negligent of his duties on this case. A short visit with Miss Jones had proved to Desi that there could have been hope of solving Nessa's murder, if only he would have been a competent detective. She had no clue if she would be able to piece the case back together after two years, but she would give it her best effort. She felt she owed both Nessa and Bailey an honest attempt at justice. Desi closed her notebook and walked inside the precinct.

"There you are," Braxton said when he saw her approaching.

"What's up?"

"I'm starving, that's what's up. I thought I was going to have to put an APB out on you or risk potential starvation," he said with a grin.

She patted his belly as she walked by. "I think you are at low risk of starvation, but I will start reheating if you will buy us some drinks." Desi placed her notepad on her desk and walked into the small break room.

"Damn that smells good," he said as he placed two Diet Cokes on their table.

Desi looked at the drinks he bought and smiled.

"You said this was homemade right?"

"Yeah, so," she said.

"So it is probably loaded with calories if it tastes half as good as it smells."

Desi chuckled as she took the heated container out of the microwave and placed it on the counter, where she divided the dish, a little more than half going onto Braxton's plate. She remembered how great it was last night but feared the heaviness of the meal would make her sluggish this early in the day, and she needed to get some work done before she left for the day.

"Have you heard anything from Bartlet yet?" she asked as she carried a plate over to him.

"He called just a little while ago. No surprise both the boys pleaded not guilty. Bartlet is very impressed with the case we have put together for him and feels he can convince Doogan's public defender to make a deal."

"I just hope the case moves quickly," she said as she joined him at the table.

Braxton grinned and nodded in agreement.

Desi watched as Braxton took a bite of Bailey's cooking, and smiled when she heard him moan with pleasure. "If this is how she cooks, you better snatch this one up quick," he said with a wink. "This is fantastic."

"I will be sure to pass your compliments on to Bailey when I call tonight to give her an update."

When Desi finished eating, she went back to the fridge for dessert. She could not suppress a smile when she took out the can of whipped cream Bailey had put in the bag last night. She knew her partner well, placing a large portion of the canned cream on his cake before she carried it over to him.

"Dear Lord, that looks sinful," he said, but went right to work on the tasty dessert. He took a bite and before he had barely swallowed, he said, "If you don't marry her, I will."

"I'm not sure Mrs. Braxton would be too excited about that," Desi teased.

"I love her to death, but she never cooks like this," he said, taking another large bite.

Desi just shook her head and took her dessert to the table where Braxton eyed it closely.

"Let me know if you need any help with that."

"No worries, I can handle this just fine."

Braxton went on to ask her how her morning had gone as they finished dessert. Desi brought him up to speed on her interview with Miss Jones and remarked how badly Harvey had botched the case. "I think he would have had a good chance of solving the case had he given it any effort at all."

"By that time in his career, I don't think Harvey could even spell effort," Braxton said. "Do you think we have enough to pursue the case?"

"I would like to give it a shot," Desi answered.

"Why don't you spend some time on it until our next call. After all the facts have come in on the gang war, we only have one perp that wasn't killed in the fight and I have an APB out for him now." Braxton hated typing but he knew how important this case was to Desi. "I will work on the reports on this one, while you work the cold case."

"You have a deal," Desi said.

She rinsed out the containers and placed them into the cloth bag. She would take them home and wash them properly before returning them. Desi placed the bag beside her desk and returned to her computer. The fingerprint analysis was still running and she decided to begin searching for a perpetrator in the system that would fit the description Miss Jones had given her for the shooter. Desi knew it was a long shot. The prints were the only viable lead she had to work with.

The afternoon passed quickly. Desi decided to give her eyes a break from staring at the computer screen and walked to the vending area to buy another Diet Coke and a Snickers bar. She sat across from Braxton to eat her snack, laughing at his mumbling at the computer screen as he typed. "How is it coming with the reports?"

"Slow, but I'm getting there." He looked up to see her eating the candy bar. "Where's mine?" he asked with a pout.

Desi reached into her pocket, pulled out a second candy bar and tossed it to him.

"How is your search going?"

"I am sick of looking at mug shots, but I have identified a few possibilities." The irony she thought was that even if she could put together a viable list of suspects, she doubted Miss Jones with her limited eyesight would be able to identify the photograph. Still, Desi knew she had to exhaust every effort.

Desi had finished her candy bar and was about to ask Braxton a question when they heard a chime from her computer notifying them that the fingerprint analysis was complete. Braxton jumped to his feet and rushed over to her desk, Desi hot on his heels.

Desi sank into her chair as they watched the screen begin to blink with a positive match on the print. "Click on it," she told Braxton. He pushed the button and a mug shot filled half her screen.

Tyrone Butler was a nineteen-year-old serving time on death row at Riverbend Maximum Security Prison in Nashville for a gang-related killing that occurred two months after Nessa was murdered. Desi looked at the profile photos and did not see the scar Miss Jones had described, so Butler must have been the accomplice in the carjacking.

"He's not the shooter, but he could tell us who was," Braxton said. "I think it is time for us to go to the lieutenant to see if he will authorize a trip to Nashville. That is, if you are up for a ride."

"Oh, hell yes," Desi answered. "I think it would be best if you brought this up to him and tell him we stumbled across this case while working on a current one."

Braxton raised an eyebrow, "Even though you have done all the legwork?"

"It's not about the credit. I just want us to be able to close the case."

"I will go talk to him if you will print out the information you have found and start a new case file."

"You're that sure he will say yes?"

"On a chance we could close a cold case, heck yeah."

"I'm on it," Desi said and went back to her computer as Braxton left the office.

†

Bailey rolled down the interstate until she approached the Tennessee River and traffic in both westbound lanes was at a dead stop. She got on the radio to find out a fellow trucker had drifted off to sleep crossing the bridge and had jackknifed his rig just after crossing. The traffic already stalled for a half hour, was standing at a halt for five miles. An eastbound trucker said the authorities looked to be set to right the truck and get traffic moving again soon, so she prepared for a delay.

Louise chose to call at that moment, which was perfect to help Bailey pass the time. "Hey there," she said.

"Hi, how is your day going?"

"Was going good until I hit a traffic snarl from an accident right at the river bridge," Bailey said.

"Have you been stopped for long?"

"No, not yet, and another driver said it looked like traffic would be moving again soon," she reported.

"That's good news at least. Was anyone hurt?"

"It doesn't look like it, but I bet he has to change his clothes." Bailey chuckled.

"I was calling to report in that I had a great time shopping for Fubar."

"Oh yeah, what did I get?"

"A bright green collar, some toys, food bowls, a variety of treats, and a cat condo."

"A what?" Bailey asked.

"You know, one of those carpet-covered tiered perches they can climb and scratch on," Louise said.

"Oh, okay thanks. Sounds like you got the kitty set up well."

"And you got Mama a rose and a card for her new arrival," Louise said.

"Oh, my goodness Louise, you think of everything," Bailey said. "Thank you for that very nice touch."

"Anything I can do to help," she said. Bailey could imagine the wide smile that was on her cousin's face. "How late are you going to be?"

"Probably an hour or so. Why?" Bailey asked.

"Just curious. Would you be interested in stopping by the club to share some Chinese with me before you head home?"

"That sounds great," Bailey said. "Do you want me to bring it or are we getting delivery?"

"I'll order it and have it delivered about the time you should be arriving, so call me if anything changes."

"Yes ma'am," Bailey answered. "See you soon."

"Be careful," Louise said.

Bailey pushed the button to end the call with Louise, and pushed it a second time. "Call FedEx." She called the depot to let them know of her delay and then watched some boats on the river until traffic started moving again. She noticed the driver sitting by the side of the road on his cell phone. He had no obvious injuries, but Bailey knew he was probably quite shaken emotionally. She would have been if it had been her. It was slow going at first with traffic creeping by to gawk at the accident, but once that cleared, she was able to get back up to speed with no problem.

†

Braxton returned wearing a huge smile. "Be here and ready to leave by eight," he said and collected a high-five from her as he passed her desk.

"Good job, partner," she said with a glowing smile.

"Just as I thought. He jumped all over the chance to close a cold case. As long as all hell doesn't break loose tonight we are good to go."

"Thank you," Desi said. "I have our file all set."

"Let's call it a day then. Tomorrow could be a long one."

†

Desi drove to the vet's office eager to see Fubar. She found a parking spot and walked inside the office. Susan looked up to see her and smiled. "I just want to tell you that you have one sweetheart of a kitten on your hands. She has spent the afternoon curled up on my desk," she said with a grin as she pointed to the sleeping kitten. "We had a ball playing earlier so she decided on a nap."

"Is she healthy?"

"She had all the shots we could give her and was dewormed. Her feline leukemia test was negative and she weighs a whopping one-and-a-half pounds."

Bailey chuckled at the lightweight announcement and the kitten woke. "Are there any other recommendations?"

"A flea treatment you will put in the fur on her neck once a month, and then bring her back according to this schedule for the rest of her kitten checkups. Will you be declawing or spaying her?"

"Definitely spaying, but I'm not sure of declawing her just yet," Desi said as she handed Susan a credit card.

Fubar had climbed onto the counter after hearing Desi's voice and was rubbing up against her, loudly purring. Desi reached down to scratch under her neck as Susan ran her card and fixed her a kitty bag to go.

"You two have fun and we will see you again soon," Susan said as Desi picked up Fubar and her bag to walk out to the car.

She pulled out into rush hour traffic and made her way back to Midtown in less than an hour. Fubar took her spot lying across Desi's lap while she drove and sang to the radio. She had an oldies station playing and smiled when the song Bailey had sung to her came on air. She would never think of the song the same way after Bailey's performance. She found herself smiling so broadly her cheeks ached. She would get Fubar home and settled then give Bailey a call later in the evening.

When she pulled into her driveway she was startled to see items sitting on her side steps, especially since one of them was a vase with a single rose. "Let's go see what's going on," she said to Fubar as she parked and carried the kitten and her bags to the steps. She placed the bags on the steps and unlocked the door to carry Fubar inside while she went back to retrieve her bags and presents.

She carried the items to the small kitchen table and placed them all there. She looked inside the large bag to find it filled with all types of kitten products, and a card addressed to Desi and Fubar. She opened the card to read a sweet note from Louise:

Dear Fubar and Mama Desi,

Bailey asked me to do some shopping today in celebration of your new arrival, and to congratulate you on becoming a family. We hope you will enjoy these items as you grow together. There is one more item that requires assembling, which Bailey will deliver as soon as possible. Welcome home Fubar, and we hope you have many wonderful years together.

Sincerely,

Bailey and Louise

Desi smiled as she lifted the rose to smell its fragrance. "That was a very romantic thought by your Aunt Bailey and Aunt Louise," Desi said as she started unloading the presents for Fubar. The kitten instantly fell in love with a tiny stuffed bear and carried it in her mouth through the house as she followed Desi to the bedroom. The stuffed bear probably weighed as much as Fubar and it was comical to see her carrying it in her mouth.

†

Bailey breathed a sigh of relief when she reached her exit on the interstate. She could almost taste the sweet and sour chicken Louise was sure to be ordering just about now. She downshifted and left the interstate with only ten minutes to go.

†

Desi changed into some comfortable clothes then went to the kitchen to warm some kitten milk for Fubar. She placed the milk on the floor, climbed into her favorite recliner and dialed Bailey's number.

"Hello," Bailey said, not recognizing the number.

"Hey Bailey, it's me Desi."

"Well, hello there, Detective, how are you today?"

"I am spectacular," she said, "and you?"

"I got tied up on the interstate for a while so I'm running late, but otherwise I'm good."

"I promised I would call to give you an update but first I want to say thank you for the gifts for Fubar, and the rose and beautiful note Louise left for us with the gifts."

"You are more than welcome. I can hardly wait to meet your new addition. Louise sounded very excited when she told me about her this morning."

"She is adorable and has the biggest green eyes I have ever seen. I hope they stay that color. Oh and the choice of collars was perfect. She is strutting around here like a diva with a diamond necklace," she added with a chuckle.

"That's great. I know there is an item I need to assemble. Would you mind if I dropped it by later tonight? I promise to be quick."

"Yes, that would be perfect."

"Do I need to call first? I'm on my way to have dinner with Louise, but I promise it won't be late."

"No silly, you can drop by whenever. I also wanted to let you know that the first court appearance went as planned. Both men pleaded not guilty, but the ADA is positive he can get Doogan's lawyer to cut him a deal."

"So what happens next?"

"Basically, their attorneys will get with the ADA and it will proceed from there. If it goes to trial, I hope it will get on the docket quickly."

"So you are pleased with how it is going so far?"

"Yes, most definitely, and ADA Bartlet is very pleased with the case we built for him."

"That is great news. Thanks for the update."

"My pleasure," Desi said. "I'm glad you are stopping by."

Bailey smiled to herself. "I will see you later then."

"Be safe," Desi said to end the call.

†

Bailey arrived at the club and passed the delivery driver as he exited the club. As she had expected, Louise had ordered a bounty of food that she had set up on the end of the bar. The night was still young and there were few customers sitting at the bar so Louise could share the meal with Bailey with very few interruptions.

"Were you planning to feed an army?" Bailey said as she took a seat on a barstool.

"I was hungry and couldn't decide, so I ordered several things. Besides it makes good leftovers."

"That it does," Bailey said as she accepted a plate from Louise and started filling it with food.

"What do you want to drink?"

"How about Mountain Dew, I haven't had one in ages."

"One Dew coming up," Louise said.

She brought them drinks and sat beside Bailey. "Have you heard anything from Desi today?"

"Yes, I have. She called just a few minutes ago to thank us for the gifts and the rose. Very pleased too, I might add."

Bailey took a bite from an egg roll and chewed. "I told her I would bring the other item by tonight."

"I thought you might. The box is in my car. I ran out of time, so I figured you could assemble it and deliver it to her."

Louise took a bite of her egg foo young and smiled at Bailey. Bailey knew well that Louise was an instigator and would do everything in her power to ensure that she and Desi would see each other, if only briefly, as often as possible until the trial was over. She admired her cousin for that and would do her best not to disappoint either woman.

"This was a perfect choice," Bailey said as she took another bite of her sweet and sour chicken.

"I know it's one of your favorites," Louise said.

"That it is."

They ate in silence for a few minutes before Bailey asked, "Have you talked with Tommy today?"

"Yes, I stopped by before I went shopping this morning. He is looking good and is talking about going back to work."

"That may be the best medicine for him right now," Bailey admitted. She noticed a rather excited smile on Louise's face. "What else is going on, Louise? You are smiling like the Cheshire Cat."

"One of his neighborhood friends was there, a rather attractive single woman near my age, and Tommy told me she had just been laid off at work."

"Oh, do tell."

"She has experience tending bar so I asked her to come try the place out tomorrow night. If she is a good fit, she could be the help we have been looking for."

"There goes the gay boy eye candy," Bailey teased.

"She would be much less drama I'm sure," Louise said.

"So what is her name? Tell me more."

"Her name is Beth. She is forty-nine and has been in Memphis for about ten years. She was a manager for one of the chain sports bar outfits until they laid her off last week."

"Can we afford her if she was in management?"

"I think so and the tips we make here will be a nice supplement to her salary."

Bailey did not miss the sparkle of excitement in Louise's eyes as she talked about Beth. It would be fantastic if Beth turned into more than just a bartender she thought. Louise needed a good woman in her life. Bailey had to chuckle at herself for thinking the same way Louise had thought of her for the last two years.

"I know it's a weeknight, but could you stop by to meet her tomorrow night?"

"Of course I can," she answered. "What time would be good?"

"Around eight. That will give me time to orient her to everything behind the bar. I really would like your opinion."

"No problem at all. What did Tommy think of the idea?"

"Oh, he was all for it. He really likes Beth, and she has been coming over regularly to check on him too."

"Sounds like a win-win situation then."

"I agree," Louise said and took another bite of food.

A customer walked up and Bailey said, "Sit tight and I will get this." She filled the customer's order and then walked back to Louise.

"Thanks, I didn't realize how hungry I was," Louise said.

"Did you take time to eat anything today?" Bailey asked. "You were pretty busy."

Louise thought for a second. "No, you're right, I didn't have lunch."

"Well then, I'd say you have a right to be hungry. Eat up so you can maintain your strength," she teased.

Bailey finished eating and sat with Louise while she finished. She waited on two more customers to give Louise an opportunity to eat in peace. When she had finished, they placed the leftovers in the walk-in and returned to the end of the counter.

"Thanks for dinner and everything you bought today."

"My pleasure," Louise said. "I had a blast. Do you have my spare key on your ring?"

"Yes, I do. Is the box in the trunk?"

"Yes it is. Sorry I ran out of time."

"You did all the shopping. The least I can do is put it together and besides, it gives me an opportunity to see Desi tonight."

"I noticed I didn't have to twist your arm," Louise teased.

"No, ma'am, not in the least. I was trying to think of an excuse to stop by before you called." She gave Louise a big hug and kissed her cheek. "I will see you tomorrow night."

"Thanks, Bailey," Louise said. "Be safe."

†

Bailey walked out to Louise's car and opened the trunk to pull out a good-sized box. She looked at the picture on the front and hoped she could put it together quickly so she would not be keeping Desi up late. She carried the box to her Jeep and drove home. Bailey walked straight to her small garage with the box and found the tools she would need to build the kitty condominium.

She was relieved to find the assembly simple, and within ten minutes had it assembled and ready to carry over to Desi's house. She closed the garage and walked to Desi's, carrying the prized possession. Bailey knocked on the door and waited for Desi to answer.

When Desi opened the door, her smile took Bailey's breath. She was simply dressed in a pair of shorts and a T-shirt. Bailey's eyes started at Desi's legs and roamed over her body until they reached her face and she was sure her face had flushed by the time their eyes met.

"Come in," Desi said as she held the door open.

"Thanks," Bailey said and carried the kitty perch inside. She was barely inside the door when Fubar came scampering toward them. "She is adorable," Bailey said as she placed the perch on the floor and bent down to pick up the kitten, "Would you just look at those big green eyes."

"Bailey, this is Fubar," she said as she reached up to scratch under the kitten's chin.

"She is adorable," Bailey repeated. "I will never understand how people can abandon animals, but at least you have a good home now and a Mama that will love you," Bailey cooed to the kitten.

"She is smart too. Watch this," Desi said, taking the kitten and placing her on the floor. "Go get your baby, Fubar," she said. They watched as the kitten disappeared from the room and returned seconds later carrying the small teddy bear in her mouth.

"Oh, my goodness," Bailey said as she knelt down to the kitten. "How adorable is that?"

"That was the first toy she picked out of the bag and she has been carrying it around with her since," Desi explained.

"That is just too cute."

Fubar ran over to the three-tiered perch and climbed inside the lower level. "She is going to love that," Desi said.

"I hope so," Bailey said. She watched the kitten for a minute and then looked up at Desi. Damn, but she was beautiful she thought as she watched her following Fubar with her eyes.

When Desi realized Bailey was looking at her, she asked, "Can I get you something to drink?"

"No, thanks. I am stuffed to the gills. I just wanted to drop that off before it got too late."

"Thank you for everything," Desi said. "The rose was an especially nice thought."

"You are very welcome."

Bailey found herself staring into Desi's eyes, longing for a kiss. Desi must have been thinking the same thing, as she appeared to be leaning into her. Bailey reached out to pull Desi closer and kissed her softly on the lips. Desi opened to her and Bailey's tongue slipped inside the velvety warmth of Desi's mouth as her hand caressed the back of Desi's neck.

Bailey felt a surge of wetness rush from her body and soak her panties as the kiss deepened further. She broke the kiss and looked into Desi's eyes to find desire burning in them. She took a step back and dropped her hands to her side. "I think I had better go," she said, even though it was the last thing she wanted.

Desi only nodded, still breathless from the kiss. "Thanks for bringing the condo for Fubar."

"You're welcome," Bailey said as she turned to the door.

Desi grabbed her by the hand and spun her around for another kiss. Bailey's hand crept underneath the T-shirt to feel the smooth, firm skin on Desi's back as their tongues swirled together. Desi let out a soft whimper and Bailey felt her knees go weak. She wanted nothing more than to pick Desi up in her arms and carry her to a bed to ravish her body, but she knew this was not the time and broke the kiss.

"I'm sorry, but I have to stop if you plan on me leaving here tonight." Desi remained silent but nodded her head.

Bailey turned back to the door and rushed out into the night. She walked quickly, afraid if she turned around to see

Desi standing in the doorway that nothing would stop her from running back into her arms.

Desi watched Bailey rush away and when she disappeared into the night, closed the door behind her.

"Damn," Bailey said aloud as she made it inside her door and collapsed against it. Her fingers brushed her lips, still excited from the heated kisses they had shared and she smiled. That felt so right, she thought as she stripped out of her clothes and rinsed off in the shower before climbing into the bed.

Chapter 9

Bailey had feared sleep would be difficult for her, but she quickly fell into a deep sleep. Her dreams focused on her life with Nessa and the love they had shared. When Bailey woke the next morning, she could taste the last kiss Nessa had shared with her in her dreams. She could faintly remember the conversation they had shared in her dream, but she woke with the realization that Nessa was urging her to move on with her life. The memory of Nessa in the dream would linger with her all day as she drove to Nashville. Her heart felt lighter than it had in forever and she decided it was time to stop and visit with Nessa's mom.

She did not realize until then that it had been almost a year since she had last visited with her. After Nessa's death, Bailey visited Merita often as the fellowship of their grief kept them bound together, but after a year or so Bailey found it too painful and stopped visiting or calling. Now she realized how selfish she was to do that to Merita and a sense of guilt threatened to set in. Bailey made a plan to see Merita tonight as soon as she got off work to correct the error of her ways.

Bailey dressed for work after a quick shower and prepared her thermos before leaving the house walking out into a beautiful morning. She smiled as she passed Desi's home and felt her heart race as she remembered the sweet taste of the kisses they had shared last night. Would they be enough to carry them through until after the trial, when they would be free to begin a relationship?

†

Desi fed Fubar before going to shower. She was excited to go to Nashville to interview Tyrone Butler. He was already awaiting execution on death row and she hoped he had enough conscience left to come clean on the carjacking and help them close the case. She placed soft food and some treats in the food bowls for Fubar in case she was late returning home and walked out to her car.

Braxton was waiting for her when she walked into the precinct and the look on his face told her he had bad news to share.

"What's up?" she asked.

"We have to postpone our road trip for today. We caught a domestic this morning," he said with obvious disappointment.

"Well, at least we know Butler won't be going anywhere," she said, trying to mask her own disappointment. "Where?" she asked.

"The south side," he said. "Where else?"

"What do we have so far?"

"Let's get a cup of coffee and I'll bring you up to speed."

Desi followed him to the break room where he poured them coffee from a relatively fresh pot. Taking seats at the small table where they had shared lunch the previous day, Braxton opened a file and took out a preliminary report.

"Galaxy Truman, fifty-two, took a knife to his live-in girlfriend, Bonita Thomas, about five this morning, apparently after returning home from a long night of drinking. He cut her up badly and she bled out before the ambulance could arrive. A neighbor heard their argument and her screams as he sliced at her with the knife."

"I hate knifings," Desi said. "There is always so much blood."

"That's not the worst part," he said. "Thomas's twelve-year-old daughter was in the apartment and saw her mother killed."

"Oh, dear Lord, that poor child, where is she now?"

"Staying with an aunt near Midtown. If you don't mind, I'm going to let you interview her. I think she would react to you more positively than me right now."

"I agree. Where is Truman?"

"He was treated for minor cuts and then taken into custody. I will work on him if you will take the daughter."

"Was he the father of the child?"

"No, her father was killed a few years ago. Her aunt is the only surviving family that we know of," he answered.

"What is the child's name?"

Braxton looked through the report until he found the information. "Shelby Thomas." Braxton looked at Desi. "On your way back will you stop over at county and pick up the medical examiner's report and the crime scene photos?"

"Sure," Desi said as she drained her cup.

"I'm sorry our trip was delayed," Braxton said. "Hopefully we can go tomorrow."

"I hope so too," Desi said as she poured another cup and walked back to her desk. Braxton had given her the contact information for Shelby's aunt that she tucked in her notepad. She took out the file on Tyrone Butler and stored it in her desk drawer for safekeeping before she walked out to her car.

†

Desi entered the address into her GPS and started her car. "Damn," she said as she pulled out of the lot. She would much rather be on her way to Nashville than going to interview a traumatized child that had seen her mother brutally murdered. She turned onto the road and took her time, dreading the painful interview ahead with each block she passed.

†

Bailey pulled out of the lot with another beautiful day ahead of her. She was tempted to give Desi a call to see how her day was going, but she did not want to put her in a potentially difficult position at work, so she shifted gears and brought the rig up to speed as she entered the interstate.

Traffic was relatively light so she made good time to Nashville. If all worked out well, she would return to Memphis on time for a change. She would leave work and go directly to Merita's and take her to dinner if she did not already have plans. Just thinking about reuniting with Merita made her heart feel lighter and she found herself singing along with the radio as she drove.

†

When Desi reached her destination, she took a deep breath before leaving the car and walking up the sidewalk to a small house. There was an older man sitting in a rocking chair on the front porch, watching her as she approached.

"May I help you, miss?"

"I am Detective Dexter from Memphis PD. I'm here to talk with Shelby Thomas," she said.

"That poor child had no business seeing what that bastard did to her mama," he said, slowly shaking his head in disgust.

"I agree completely. How is she doing?"

140

"She's walking around like she's dead on her feet and she won't hardly speak a word to anyone." He let out a big sigh. "Anita, her aunt, tried to get her to eat and lay down, but I think the poor child is afraid to go to sleep."

"Do you think I could speak to Anita for a few minutes out here before I talk with Shelby?"

"I will go ask. Have a seat if you will, miss," he said with a warm smile and disappeared inside the house.

Desi took a seat in a rocker. Normally that type of chair would relax her, but this morning she dreaded the task that awaited her just inside these walls. There was little Desi could do to prevent hurting the child any further, but she had to try to get her statement. Desi looked up when she heard the door open again, and a small woman approached. "Miss Anita?" she asked.

"Yes, that's me," she said as she sat next to Desi.

"I am Detective Desi Dexter from Memphis PD, and I need to talk with Shelby for a few minutes," she explained. "I am so sorry for your loss."

"Thank you, Detective," Anita said. She nodded her head and said, "I understand, but I don't know if she will talk to you. Shelby has barely spoken since we got back from the hospital. The doctor said she was in shock, but otherwise she was physically fine."

"It was lucky that Truman did not hurt her as well."

"That bastard," Anita hissed. "I hope he burns in hell."

"We are going to do everything we can to make that happen," Desi said. "Do you have any idea what happened this morning?"

"All I can piece together from what little Shelby said was that he was very drunk and very angry when he came in around four thirty this morning from a night of drinking, but that's all."

"You have no idea what set him off?"

"None at all. I told her all along he was not a good man, but Bonita swore she loved him in spite of his faults."

"Love can truly be blind sometimes."

"Amen to that," Anita agreed.

"Would you stay with us while I talk to Shelby?" she asked. "I think she would be more comfortable with her family present, don't you?"

"Probably so. I think she is still in the bedroom, if you are ready."

Desi nodded, unable to state that she was ready for the job she had to perform.

She followed Anita down a narrow hallway, her heart pounding in her ears as anxiety built deep inside her. The darkness of the hallway filled her with an impending sense of doom that Desi struggled to ward off. *Deal with it,* she told herself, *you have done this sort of thing a hundred times.* They passed an empty bedroom, the only light coming from partially opened blinds. The room was barren except for a partially made bed. An overwhelming sense of depression ran through Desi's veins.

Desi almost sighed with relief when they arrived at a closed door and Anita knocked before they entered the room. A small, dark child sat in the middle of the bed, rocking with her arms wrapped tightly about her. She looked up at Desi with eyes that would be haunted with terrifying memories for a lifetime. Desi choked back tears.

"Shelby, honey, this is Detective Desi," Anita said. "She needs to talk to you."

Shelby rocked with no sign of recognition of what her aunt had just said. Desi looked at Anita who nodded to her and Desi took a seat on the edge of the bed.

"Hi, Shelby, I am very sorry about what happened to your mama," she said.

"He killed her. That bastard Truman killed her," she cried out and launched her body toward Desi, wrapping her arms tightly around her.

Desi was startled at first, then instinct took over and she wrapped her arms around the child and spoke to her softly to comfort her. "We will make sure he won't hurt anyone else," she whispered as she slowly rocked with Shelby in her arms. Desi's heart ached with the vibration of the child's sobs as they racked her body and she felt the fabric of her shirt soaking with tears. Desi was more surprised when she realized tears were flowing down her cheeks.

When Shelby began to quiet, she looked up to see Desi crying and reached to wipe away her tears. Desi's display of emotions touched the child and a weak smile formed on her face. "Did you know my mama?"

"No, I didn't," she answered.

"She is a great mama," she said and fought to choke back her tears.

Desi still held Shelby's hands. "Can you tell me what happened? I know it will be hard, but I need to know."

"Mama and I had finished supper and watched *Big Mama's House* after we ate. Mama tucked me into bed about ten and went to bed herself. She had to go to work the next morning at the café she worked at and would be up early." Shelby sniffed a few times, but did not start crying. Desi smiled, impressed by how brave the child had become.

"I heard the door slam and knew Truman had come home. He was loud and his voice was angry. He yelled for Mama, who was asleep in their bedroom." She winced as she remembered the anger in his voice. "I heard Mama say something to him, but I didn't know what it was. She didn't come out of the room though, and when he tried opening the door, he found it locked."

"What happened next?" she gently asked.

"I heard him banging on the door, shouting mean words at Mama, and then a loud boom when he kicked the bedroom door open. That was the first time I heard Mama scream. I pulled the covers up over my head."

"Did your mama and Truman argue a lot?"

Shelby nodded her head. "Not at first. He was very good to both of us for a time, until he lost his job. Then he started drinking and he became a bad man."

"Did he ever hurt you Shelby?"

"No, Mama always protected me from him."

"Do you know what he was angry about when he came home?"

Shelby nodded her head. "He was hungry and he told Mama to get her," she paused as she looked at her aunt who nodded, "he told her to get her ass out of bed and cook him breakfast."

"Mama told him she had to go to work and needed her sleep, and if he wanted something to eat he should cook it himself. That's when I heard him slap her."

Desi felt Shelby squeeze her hands tightly before she continued. "I heard loud noises coming from the bedroom and peeked out my door to see Truman dragging Mama to the kitchen. Mama was yelling back at him and Truman picked up a knife and started cutting and stabbing her as she screamed for him to stop. I remembered what Mama had told me about staying safe, so I closed and locked my door and climbed under my bed. I stayed there until the police arrived and took me to the hospital."

"You are a brave young lady," Desi told her. "Your mama would be proud."

Shelby lowered her gaze away from Desi's eyes, but nodded that she understood.

"Thank you for talking with me." She reached into her pocket and pulled out her card. "If you need anything, I want you to call me okay?"

Shelby took the card and with a voice barely above a whisper, said, "Thank you."

Desi leaned forward and kissed the child on top of her head then left the room after she nodded to Anita. Desi rushed down the hallway and back out into the sunshine as quickly as she could. The porch was empty when she walked back to her car. She took in a deep breath and held it to fight off the scream that she wanted desperately to let loose.

She climbed inside her car and drove three blocks away until she found a parking spot where she cried until she had no more tears. When she regained control of her emotions, Desi took out her notebook and wrote down the notes from her meeting with Shelby. The child had been so brave during the interview, but Desi knew all too well that Shelby had a difficult life ahead of her. The brutal killing of her mother would leave her emotionally scarred and forever distrustful of others. Desi mourned for the loss of childhood innocence taken from Shelby by the violence. Her aunt would be the best loving and nurturing substitute for her, but she would never again experience building memories with the woman who had given her life. Desi closed her notebook and placed her forehead on the steering wheel as the cold air from the air-conditioning bathed her face.

Interviewing children who witnessed violent crimes was Desi's least favorite part of her job and to say she dreaded the task would be a huge understatement. It was a necessary part of her job and she clearly understood Braxton just did not have the heart for it, especially when a young girl had witnessed a male commit the violence. Desi felt it was unfair for the task to fall on her shoulders, but Braxton would always find some way to make it up to her. She remembered the time he saved her from Dumpster diving to find a murder weapon in a Dumpster filled with maggots and spoiled food. The memory brought a temporary respite from the emotional trauma the interview had left her feeling. She put the car in gear and remembered Braxton's request for her to stop by the county morgue to pick up the report, crime scene, and autopsy photographs from the medical examiner's office.

†

She took her time driving through traffic and when she reached the morgue, she checked in and found her way to the medical examiner's office. When she walked into the sprawling office, an older woman looked up from her desk.

"Hello, Detective," she said with a warm smile.

"Hey, Ms. Ellen, how are you?"

"I'm well, thank you. Are you here for the Bonita Thomas case?"

"Yes, ma'am, if it is ready."

"I finished typing it up just a little while ago. That was a brutal attack," she said.

"Yes it was, and unfortunately her child was there to witness it," Desi said. "I just finished interviewing her."

"That must be very difficult for you," she said with a look of genuine concern.

"It is one of the few parts of my job I really dislike."

Ellen handed her the file. "Doc Burns had the case and said you could call her if you have any questions. The cause of death was pretty obvious and she said it was a shame, she was an otherwise very healthy woman."

"Thanks," Desi said and tucked the file in her notebook. "Have a great day."

"You too, Desi," she said and watched her leave.

Desi decided to wait until she got back to the precinct to view the file with Braxton. It was nearing lunchtime and she wished she had more of Bailey's leftovers for lunch, but she and Braxton would have to fend for themselves.

She walked back to her desk as Braxton was finishing a phone call. "Welcome back," he said.

"Thanks."

"How did it go?" he asked gently.

"It was horrible, but Shelby did pretty well. She said Truman was pissed because her mama wouldn't cook him breakfast."

"That's no reason to slice anyone up," Braxton said as he shook his head in disbelief.

"Some people don't need much to snap and I guess his day was today," Desi said as she took the file from her notepad. "Do we want to open this before or after lunch?"

"We might as well get it over with," he said.

Braxton opened the file and handed her the report as he sorted through the photos. Truman had been very thorough with his knife. Braxton tried to count the stab wounds and slices, but easily lost count.

"Sixteen stab wounds and at least two dozen slices including one that just barely missed her jugular," she said when she saw him squinting at the photographs. "Damn," Desi said, continuing to read the report.

"What?"

"He broke the knife blade off in her chest with the last blow," she answered.

"That doesn't surprise me. He's a big son of a bitch."

"How did your interview go?"

"He copped to the murder right away. He knew we had him dead to rights. Said he was hungry and just needed some food to soak up the alcohol he had consumed."

"Did he show any signs of remorse?"

"Actually he did. I don't think he meant to kill her, but he just snapped. He cried like a baby during the interview."

"We have one more witness to talk to, correct?"

"Yes, the neighbor who called nine-one-one," he said.

"Let's go talk to them, and then maybe grab some lunch," she suggested.

"Him, a Walter Goodson," Braxton said.

"Come on and I will even let you drive," she teased.

"You hate my driving," he said. "What are you up to, Desi?"

"You can drive and buy lunch," she said as she punched his shoulder.

"I knew there had to be a catch. Happy Meal here we come," he said as he grabbed his notepad and met her at the door.

†

Bailey's run was going extremely well and once she was on the interstate for the return to Memphis, she keyed her earpiece, and said, "Call Merita."

Two rings later, a woman answered the phone and Bailey's heart plunged to her stomach. Merita had the same beautiful accent Nessa had and the sound of it made her heart ache with longing. Bailey was speechless, completely unprepared for the painful reminder brought about by the sound of Merita's voice.

"Bailey, is that you, honey?" Merita asked.

Bailey's throat was dry as she croaked out an answer. "Yes, Merita, it is. How are you?"

"It is so good to hear from you. I am well and you?"

"I'm okay," Bailey said. "I'm on my way back from Nashville and I wanted to know if I could stop by and see you for a bit tonight?"

"That would be wonderful," Merita, answered. "Are you up for some jerk chicken?"

"Oh, hell yes," Bailey said. "What can I bring?"

"A good appetite," Merita said. "What time is good for you?"

"I can be there by six if all goes well," she answered.

"I will see you at six. Thank you for calling, Bailey. I think of you so often."

"I know, and I'm sorry for not calling sooner."

"No worries, we can catch up tonight."

"See you soon," Bailey said.

She lowered her sunglasses to shelter her eyes from the glaring sun as she drove hard for home.

†

Desi let Braxton handle the interview with the neighbor and then they decided on a barbecue plate from one of their favorite haunts for a late lunch. She knew there was no way Braxton would eat a Happy Meal, but he so often enjoyed teasing his partner.

"Keep your fingers crossed that we can make our trip to Nashville tomorrow," he said as he tucked his tie safely away from the sauce-laden sandwich he was preparing to dive into with his usual gusto.

"I will," she said as she picked at her sandwich.

"Are you okay, Desi?" he asked, his voice filled with concern.

"Yeah. The interview with Shelby Thomas was unusually hard for me this morning," she said.

Braxton knew how she felt. "Thank you for taking that."

"One for the team," she said with a weak smile and took a bite.

"I think we can both use a few hours out of the city," he said. "See what the rest of the world looks like and all that," he teased.

"I hope you won't be disappointed," she answered with a grin.

"I can't be disappointed with you sitting beside me," he said.

Desi knew that there was an ounce of truth to his comment. They had grown close as partners and even when he had opportunities to work with another male detective, Braxton had chosen to stay with her. Right from the start, she knew Braxton was the one meant to be her partner and even if offered a change she would pass.

They finished their meal and went back to the precinct to complete the reports before stopping for the day. Desi took out her file and looked at the mug shot of Tyrone Butler, then closed the file and slipped it back into her desk. She hoped tomorrow Tyrone could fill in some of the missing information on Nessa's death, and they could find the shooter and bring him to justice.

She closed her drawer and followed Braxton out to the parking lot. "Have a good night," he said when he split off to go to his car.

"You too," Desi said as she climbed inside her sun-heated car. She rolled down the windows as the AC roared at full strength to push the heated air from the car. She pulled out of the lot and started for home, eager to see Fubar and escape the memory of today with a hot bubble bath and a large glass of strong alcohol.

✝

Desi's car was in the drive as Bailey passed and, for a minute, she battled her desire to turn into the drive and take

150

Desi in her arms for a long, slow kiss. Then she remembered the agreement she had with Desi. Lord but weeks could last forever, she thought as she drove past the house for her dinner with Merita.

†

Desi had spent time with Fubar before deciding to draw a bubble bath. She started the water and poured bubble bath before returning to the kitchen to pour herself a strong drink. Desi did not drink alone often, but after the day she had just finished she felt she deserved a strong drink. She carried the glass into the bathroom with Fubar chasing along behind her. Desi undressed and sank beneath the luxurious bubbles in the tub. Her hand dangled along the side of the tub, and Fubar licked and nibbled on her fingers until she got Desi's attention.

"I feel you there, baby girl," she told the kitten who looked up at her with huge green eyes. "I promise to play with you when I get done taking a bath."

Fubar blinked at her and sat patiently, waiting for her to finish her bath. Desi picked up the mixed drink and took a sip, wincing as the strong liquor burned down her throat. She placed the glass on the edge of the tub and stretched out to relax. The warm water soothed her tired body and eased the weariness weighing down her soul. The room was so quiet Desi could hear the soft beating of her heart while she soaked. Today had been awful for her and she longed to be able to have someone to share her life. Even though she could not discuss details of her cases, it would be nice to have someone hold her and reassure her things would be right in the world once more. Her last two lovers had quickly grown tired of her moodiness when she had rough days and couldn't put her feelings into perspective for them, ultimately causing the relationships to end. She hoped Bailey would be different, and be the one perceptive enough to know when she needed holding by a pair of strong arms.

†

Merita opened the door and pulled Bailey into her arms with a warm smile. "It is so good to see you," she said as she led her inside the house and hugged her again.

"You look fantastic," Bailey said as she returned the hug and kiss.

"You do too, except you are way too skinny," Merita teased.

"Hey, I've been working hard to keep this body in shape."

"You look fine, but a few more pounds wouldn't hurt."

Bailey took her teasing in stride. Merita had said the same thing when Nessa was alive. "I still have to be able to haul myself up into the cab of my truck."

"Still driving, hey?"

"Yes, it suits me," Bailey said.

"Come, let's get you a drink," Merita said and took her hand as they walked to the kitchen. "I'm having a Red Stripe. Will you join me?"

"That sounds great." Bailey took the opportunity to look closely at Merita while she went to the refrigerator for a beer. "Retirement looks good on you."

"It's not all fun and games, but I'm enjoying it."

"Something smells really good," Bailey said as the aroma of the jerked chicken filled the room.

Merita handed her a beer and joined her at the small kitchen table. "I know how you love jerk and it was fun cooking for two again."

"It's not easy is it?"

"No, and I get tired of leftovers," Merita said with a chuckle.

"I usually don't have to worry about that. When I really cook I have Louise or the boys to feed, so there typically is not much left over."

"How are the boys and Louise?"

"Joe and Louise are well, but Tommy was attacked leaving the club the other night and is recuperating from his injuries."

"Oh, my goodness, is he okay?"

"He will be. He took a good beating from a pair of skinheads who thought he was an easy target for some spending money."

"Bastards," she said. "Did they catch them?"

"Unbelievably, yes," she said. Her thoughts turned to Desi for a moment.

"That's a relief," Merita said.

"The detectives working the case were really good," she said.

Merita smiled. "They have such a hard job in this crazy city."

"Yeah, they do," she agreed.

"I am so glad you came tonight. I really have missed you."

Bailey smiled. "I missed you too. But for a while I was just lost without Nessa, and seeing you just hurt too much."

"I can understand that," Merita said. "I'm glad that you are better."

Bailey took a long drink from the beer and sat it on the table. "I have been dreaming about Nessa a lot lately, and I think she is telling me to move on with life."

"You know she would expect that from you. She loved you more than life itself, and she would be pained to see you so sad." Merita reached across the table and covered her hand. "Nessa will always have a special place in your heart and that will never change, but you have too much to offer a good woman to stay alone any longer."

"Have you been conspiring with Louise?" Bailey teased. "She tells me the same thing all the time."

"Listen to us and open up your heart."

"I'm trying," Bailey admitted.

Merita's face lit up with a smile. "Have you found someone special?"

"I think so. She was one of the detectives working Tommy's case. I was such a jerk to her, but she stayed professional and was persistent with me until I finally realized she wasn't my enemy."

"Were you critical because the police never solved Nessa's case?"

"Yes, I was really nasty. Desi wasn't involved in the case at all, but I let my frustrations out on her and her partner."

Merita smiled warmly. "I'm sure she has probably dealt with that before in her profession."

"Yes, but it was very unfair of me to stereotype her, especially when they worked so quickly to handle Tommy's case."

"She must be very special. I would like to meet her sometime."

"I think we can arrange that."

A comfortable silence fell between them as they drank their beer. "Are you ready for some food?"

"I thought you would never ask," Bailey answered with a grin. "May I help?"

"I've got this," Merita said and began preparing a plate for each of them.

Merita made open-faced sandwiches with the jerked chicken and added generous portions of spicy slaw and slices of cold melon to the plates. "I have some chips if you would like some," she said as she carried their plates to the table.

"No, thanks, looks fantastic," Bailey said as she eyed the massive plate of food Merita placed in front of her.

"Are you ready for another beer?"

"Yes, please."

Merita brought them both a fresh beer and sat next to Bailey. "Enjoy."

Bailey had not realized how hungry she was and managed to consume the entire helping. "That was fantastic," she said when she pushed the plate away from her.

"Would you like more?"

"Oh, heaven's no, I could not eat another bite," Bailey answered.

Merita smiled, very pleased with how well Bailey had eaten. "You make my heart feel good when you eat like that."

"I will not have any problem sleeping tonight," Bailey said with a smile.

"Do you have to go soon?" Merita asked.

"I told Louise I would drop by the club around eight to discuss some business, but I promise I will not let a year pass before I see you again."

"You can always call if you get caught up with life, just to let me know you are doing fine," she said.

"I can certainly do that," Bailey said. "Let me help you with the dishes before I go."

"Stop being silly, I can handle these few dishes. You go on and take care of business."

Bailey stood to leave and took Merita in her arms, holding her tight. "I missed you."

Merita looked up at Bailey with tears shining in her dark eyes. "I'm glad to have you back."

"I will call you soon, I promise," Bailey said as they walked to the door.

"Be careful and I will look forward to hearing from you again," Merita said.

"Goodnight, Mom," Bailey said, and Merita smiled brightly.

"Goodnight, Baby Girl," Merita said, using Nessa's pet name for Bailey.

Bailey nodded and walked out the door to climb in her Jeep. The visit with Merita made her feel good. She shifted the Jeep into gear and headed off for the club.

†

Bailey walked into the club and instantly felt the electricity between Louise and Beth as they worked side by side at the bar. Bailey liked her immediately and felt Louise was making a good choice both professionally and personally—if she chose to enter into a relationship with Beth. They interacted easily and comfortably together, as if they had known each other longer than just one night.

Bailey smiled at the banter between the two and with a nod to Louise when Beth left to serve a customer she let Louise know she approved of her decision. "Good choice," she said to make sure. "I think you two have everything in hand, so I'm going to go home and crash."

"Is tomorrow your Friday?" Louise asked.

"Normally it would be, yes, but I'm going to pick up an extra shift this week," she said. "Did you need something?"

"No, just curious," Louise said.

Bailey thought if Louise and Beth were to make a go at a relationship, she would put in an extra night at the club when she could to give them some time away to enjoy themselves. Maybe she could even get the good detective or Merita to give her a hand, she thought as she hugged Louise goodnight and waved to Beth before leaving the club.

✝

Desi had finished her bath and poured the majority of the drink down the drain before preparing a light meal for herself. She kept her promise to play with Fubar until they were both tired and climbed into the bed together. Desi was drifting off to sleep when she thought she heard Bailey's Jeep drive by. A smile graced her face. "Goodnight, Bailey," she whispered and pulled the covers up to her chin.

Chapter 10

Bailey was well into her run when Desi arrived at the precinct. Braxton met her at her desk and said, "Let's get out of here before the phone rings. We can get coffee on the road."

Desi grabbed her notepad and her Tyrone Butler file and followed him quickly out the door. "Find a Starbucks and I will buy," she said with a huge grin.

They nearly ran to Braxton's car and within minutes were out of the parking lot headed to the closest coffee shop where she bought them both extra-large cups of the hot brew. Desi breathed a sigh of relief when they reached the interstate and were heading eastbound to Nashville.

"You know, we should buy a Starbucks franchise and build it near the precinct," Braxton said.

"That's not a bad idea," she agreed. "Maybe we could retire early."

"Wouldn't that be nice?"

They drove in silence until they got out of the city. It was a great day for a drive without a single cloud in the sky. Braxton set the car on cruise as Desi relaxed back in her seat and enjoyed her coffee. It had been a while since Desi had driven the I-40 corridor and she had forgotten how much commercial traffic it carried on a daily basis.

When they passed the second set of blacked out SUVs in the median, Desi looked at Braxton and said, "We should have a job like theirs," she said, pointing at the SUVs.

"Yeah, the ATF and DEA boys have it cushy out here. Sitting in plain sight and watching their heat-seeking equipment looking for hot bales of pot while they practice racial profiling when they do actually pull someone over," he said.

"You never see them at night or on the weekends either."

"Leads you to wonder if they ever catch anyone," Braxton said with a grin.

"I know one thing, if I ever run a load of drugs, I'm doing it on a weekend, especially if it's a UT football home game," she said.

Braxton roared with laughter, but agreed with her assessment.

They moved into the left lane to pass yet another FedEx truck. Desi found herself sneaking a peek into the cab of every FedEx truck they passed, hoping to catch a glimpse of Bailey.

Braxton caught the careful glances his partner sent out the passenger side window. Never one to miss a chance to tease his partner said, "Who would have thought there were so many FedEx trucks on the road?"

Desi chose to ignore his taunt. "It seems like every third truck you pass is from FedEx."

Braxton smiled at her comment. "I sure hope that case ends soon."

"Which case?"

"The Chambers case," he answered.

"Why is that?"

"I could get used to your woman's leftovers," he teased.

Desi burst out laughing. "She's not my woman yet."

"No, but it is just a matter of time. That woman can cook so you better grab her up as quick as you can," he teased.

"I will be sure to tell Bailey you are putting in a good word for me," Desi teased back.

"Look, another FedEx truck," Braxton said.

"You are so not right," Desi told him. "Can you pull into the rest area coming up?"

"Sure, my coffee has run straight through too."

†

Bailey crossed the Tennessee River a good hour ahead of Desi and Braxton. She too was enjoying the beautiful day and was singing along with the radio. Her thoughts kept wandering back to Desi, which brought a smile to her face. Louise had reminded her that she had a plethora of vacation time built up, and she thought maybe after the trial was over she would take some time off for a trip with Desi. It would be a great way for the two of them to get to know each other, and she believed they both would welcome some time out of Memphis.

She thought about the possibility of a trip to New Orleans, but she did not want Desi to feel pressured to introduce her to her family who lived there. Savannah or the Outer Banks could be options, or even the Gulf, she thought as she began downshifting when the traffic outside of Nashville started to slow her flow. Bailey could not help but chuckle at herself for planning a vacation together when they had only had one brief date. She knew in her heart though, that fate had brought her Desi.

†

"Have you ever been to Riverbend?" Desi asked when they returned to the car from their rest stop.

"No, I haven't. What is it like?"

"I made a lot of trips out there when I worked in Nashville. It is a state-of-the-art facility, but it has a reputation for being a tough place to do your time. A lot of gang activity as you would imagine." She smiled at a memory. "I wonder if King Willie is still there."

"Who is King Willie?"

"He is one of the higher ranking generals of the Mexican Mafia from LA. They sent him to Nashville in hopes of reducing his influence on the California prison gangs, but everyone inside knew King Willie ran the show," she explained.

"Did you ever meet him?"

"Face-to-face, no, but I did get a good look at him on one of my trips. He is not a physically imposing man, but he has the coldest black eyes I have ever seen. I could easily see why prisoners were intimidated by him."

"I assume he is a lifer," Braxton said.

"Oh yeah, I think he pulled down four consecutive life sentences for murders he and his crew committed. If he had been convicted here, he would have been given the death penalty."

"I hear the Mexican Mafia and the other Cali-based gangs are pretty ruthless. They would make our local boys look mild."

"I bet that's true. I hope we never get anyone with the influence like King Willie to organize the activity in Memphis."

"I think I might be tempted to move to the middle of nowhere if that ever happens," Braxton said. She knew from his tone he was serious.

Desi thought about his comment for a few minutes. "I think I'm just about there now."

"Where?" Braxton asked.

"Ready to move to the middle of nowhere," she answered. "I don't know how much more of Memphis my psyche can handle."

"Is it the job or the city itself?"

"Is there really any difference?" she asked, leaving Braxton to ponder her question. "Take the next exit and I will guide you through a shortcut."

†

After switching out her trailers, Bailey walked over to her favorite sandwich shop to grab a bite. She entered and approached the counter, studying the menu as she did.

"Someone looks very happy today," the young woman behind the counter said.

Bailey looked at her, flashing a smile. The young woman had worked at the shop for over a year, but Bailey didn't know her name. She had been so mired in her personal funk she had paid little attention to the people around her. She looked at the woman's nametag on her shirt. "It's a beautiful day outside, Riley, and life is good."

"You know in the year that you have been coming in here, I believe that is the most words you have ever spoken to me," she teased.

Bailey looked at her, surprised by her comment. "I apologize, but the last year has not been the best of my life."

The woman cocked her head at Bailey. "Well, I certainly hope whatever has changed, that it continues. You look good with a smile."

Bailey blushed at the obvious flirtation from the woman. "Thanks, I promise to do better."

"No problem at all, ma'am. So, what can I get for you today?"

"The usual, I guess," Bailey said to test the woman's memory.

"Six inch on honey wheat, turkey breast, pepper rings, honey mustard, with light lettuce. Plain baked Lays and a large sweet tea?"

"Damn you are good," Bailey said with a wink.

"You are pretty easy," she answered.

"Hey, don't let that news out or you will ruin my reputation," she said.

"I seriously doubt your reputation would be flawed," the woman said. This time it was her turn to blush.

Bailey watched as the woman made her sandwich and then walked to the register to pay for her purchase. "Thanks," she said, dropping several ones in the tip jar. "Have a great day and I will see you next week," she said, taking her meal outside to enjoy the beautiful day.

†

Braxton and Desi drove through the security gate after showing identification and found a spot in the visitors' parking lot. The Constantine wire, high above the tall fence, shone in the late morning sun as they left the car to walk inside the prison. They checked in showing identification and securing their weapons before passing through a metal detector then following an escort to an interview room.

"Inmate Butler will be brought to you in about five minutes. May I get you some coffee or another type of drink?" the correctional officer asked.

"No, thanks, I think we are good," Braxton said.

He and Desi took a seat at a table and waited for Butler to arrive. She flipped open the file and looked at the baby-faced mug shot of Butler and ran through his rap sheet one last time.

A moment later, a knock sounded on the door and a young man in shackles shuffled into the room, escorted by a large CO. Prison time had already taken its toll on Butler. He face was no longer the baby-faced youth of his mug shot. His face was hard and his eyes roamed over the room as he approached the table and sat across from them.

"What's this about, man?" he asked Braxton. Suspicious, he clearly had no idea what or who had brought him in from death row for an interview.

"I am Detective Braxton and this is Detective Dexter. We are from Memphis and wanted to talk to you about an event from a couple of years ago," he explained.

"What's in it for me?" he asked with a tone of bitterness.

"There is nothing we can do to get you off death row," Desi answered.

"So why should I help you?"

"To give a mourning family a little peace of mind. Is that too much to ask?"

Butler smirked. "Where is my peace of mind?"

"I hoped clearing your conscience and giving some answers to two families that were crushed by your violence might be something you would consider. It won't change your consequences one bit," she added honestly.

"I don't know what you're talking about."

Desi opened her file and pulled out the crime scene photographs that were still available and spread them across the table in front of Butler. "We know you are not the shooter in this crime, but we do have a positive ID that you were there when this murder occurred, a carjacking gone awry on an early morning in Memphis."

They watched as Butler's eyes scanned the photographs and the expression on his face made it clear that he knew exactly what crime they were looking into.

Butler looked straight into Desi's eyes. "You're right, I was there, but I wasn't the shooter."

"Can you tell us what happened and who did the shooting?" she implored.

Butler pushed back his chair and Desi was afraid he was going to leave the room without giving them any of the answers they sought. When he looked back up at Desi, she swore he had tears in his eyes.

"I guess it really don't matter now. I'm screwed and JT is dead," he said.

Desi sat on the edge of her chair waiting for him to continue. Seconds ticked by while Butler regained his composure and began speaking.

"We was just kids you know, trying to find our place in the world. Me and JT, we didn't have nothing. We had been expelled from school, and we were desperate to get into the Red Tails so we could make some money running drugs." He took a deep breath and continued. "We were told we had to jack a car as our first test for initiation, but it had to be one particular car. It had to be a Honda Accord. Me and JT had walked around town all night, smoking weed and looking for a Honda to jack." He looked up at Desi again. "We were so tired of walking and were walking back home when we saw a shiny new Honda Accord coming down the street. JT looked at me and smiled. "*This is it man*," he said. The light changed and the driver had to stop, so we rushed into action."

Desi felt the genuine pain in his voice as he talked, and looked at the photograph of Nessa.

"She was such a pretty lady," he said with a smile. "She had one of those island accents and the most beautiful caramel-colored skin," he said as he drifted back in his memories. "I stood in front of the car, so she couldn't go forward without hitting me, while JT approached her with the nine they had given us to jack with," he explained.

"She begged us to not take her car and offered JT her purse, which he tossed back into the car as he pulled her from behind the wheel. We was so stupid. The car was still in gear and was starting to roll forward as he pulled her from the car." He lifted his shackled hands in despair. "The door hit JT's hand and the gun went off. That poor woman was only a foot away from him and the bullet hit her right in the chest."

When he looked up at Desi again, tears were running down his cheeks. "I shouted, what did you do man," at JT, who just stood frozen as he watched the woman fall to the ground. I was trying to hold the car back from rolling over me and yelled get in the car, man, and he finally jumped into the car and hit the brake." He wiped at his eyes. "There was nothing we could do for her then, so we got in the car and drove off. JT was so scared he hit a parked car, but we eventually made it back to the park where the Red Tails hung out."

He paused and Desi pushed him on. "What happened then?"

"The dude who was the top dog at the time was crazy excited that JT had done a killing, but he knew they had to get rid of the car. So some of the boys drove it out of town and torched it, after they stripped what they could out of the car. They took me and JT with them from house to house for several days until they realized the heat was off the carjacking. They took JT back to the park to get his teardrop tattoo. After that, we ran drugs and other errands for the gang leaders."

"What was JT's last name?" Desi asked as she opened her notebook to look at mug shots.

"Boykins," he said.

Desi pulled out a photo of JT Boykins from her file. "Is this him?"

"Yeah, that's my boy JT. We was best friends since second grade."

"You said earlier that he was dead. What happened to JT?" Braxton asked.

The smile left Butler's face. "Once he got his teardrop, everyone thought JT was a tough guy and started taking him on drive-by runs and other hits. JT wasn't no tough guy; he was just a kid from the 'hood who accidentally shot a woman, but once he was inked, his innocence was gone forever. He was out with some chick one night when members from another gang ran into him and cut him and the girl down with AKs right on the sidewalk."

He looked up at Desi, meeting her eyes. "I know it don't mean much, but I'm sorry about that woman. If she hadn't drove up that night a lot of things might have turned out differently."

Desi closed her notebook after putting the photos back inside. They had gotten the information they had come for and while they would not be arresting a murderer, they could at least close the case and let Bailey and Nessa's mother know what happened. She stood and offered Butler her hand. "Thank you for telling us the truth," she said.

Butler looked surprised by the offer of her hand, but he reached out and gently shook it, then Braxton's hand, as they stood to leave.

Braxton followed her out of the room. "Great job," he said.

"Not quite the information we hoped for, but at least we have some answers and can close the case." The story Butler told differed slightly from the version Miss Jones had given her but the outcome was the same.

"You can write up the report while I drive," he said as they reached the desk to retrieve their weapons and drop off the visitor passes.

They realized time had passed quickly when they emerged from the prison. It was past two and they were both starving. "Let's get something to eat before we hit the road," Braxton said when they reached the car.

"Sounds good to me," Desi said as she climbed inside the car feeling emotionally deflated.

†

Bailey finished her route ahead of schedule and went home for a run before she showered, ate a salad, then dropped by to check on the boys. Tommy was in rare form. He was excited to start back to work the following day, stating sitting at home was driving him crazy. He still looked a bit rough, but work would help him heal.

Joe, Charles, and Tony were practicing their routines for the weekend shows while Tommy coached and judged their performances. Bailey used the additional workday for the week as an excuse to leave early. She drove past Desi's home only to find she had not returned from work. Disappointed she took advantage of an early evening to get a full night of sleep. Bailey would drive to St. Louis and back tomorrow, which was a longer route than her usual run, and she would barely make it back in time for her shift at the club.

†

When Braxton and Desi returned to the precinct, they were relieved to learn they had not picked up a new case while they were gone. Braxton left for home while Desi stayed behind to type up and print the final report on Nessa's murder that they would present to their lieutenant the following day. After his approval, she and Braxton would discuss arranging a meeting with Nessa's mother and Bailey to discuss the case. When she finished the report it was almost nine. She was exhausted as she drove home, fed Fubar, and collapsed into her bed.

Chapter 11

Bailey was glad to see Friday arrive even considering the early start to her morning for the run to St. Louis. It was not a run that was completely unfamiliar to her, although it had been months since she had filled in for Jimmy, the usual driver. Once she crossed over the Mississippi River on I-55, it was a smooth ride, good interstate driving all the way into Missouri.

She passed through West Memphis and soon found a grin growing on her face. She knew she would soon be passing two road signs that were the inspiration for Joe's and Tommy's drag personalities. First up was a sign that read Marie Lepanto, actually two small towns in Arkansas. Just a few more miles north would be the sign for Victoria Luxora. When they were in their mid-twenties, they had taken their mother to St. Louis to visit an old friend and when Tommy saw the signs, he knew his drag personality had been born. He called Joe later that night and they began performing together on a regular basis.

Thinking of those memories only added to her good mood as she motored down the interstate. The only thing that could make her day any better would be to see or hear from Desi. Bailey found herself thinking more and more about her and aching to see her again. She promised herself she would do a drop-in tomorrow if she did not see Desi today.

†

Desi had poured a cup of coffee and was sitting at her desk, reviewing her typed report when Braxton came strolling into the precinct.

"Good morning, partner," he said in an exceptionally good mood.

"Hey, Braxton, what's got you so happy this morning?"

"I just stopped by the travel agent to book a cruise for our wedding anniversary," he said. "In one more month I will be wearing Bermuda shorts, gaudy Hawaiian print shirts and drinking something with tiny umbrellas as we sail to the Virgin Islands."

Just the thought of Braxton in a Hawaiian print shirt was enough to put a smirk on Desi's face. "You're going to have to ask Donna to e-mail me a picture of that," she teased.

"It's a surprise, so don't let the cat out of the bag if you talk to her, okay?"

"That is quite romantic of you, Braxton. I wouldn't have thought you had that in you."

Holding his hands over his heart, Braxton feigned hurt. "Actually, Donna has been hinting about a cruise for years, so I can't take all the credit."

"Well, it at least proves you were listening to her."

"Oh believe me, she makes sure I hear her every word," he said with a boyish grin.

"How many years has she put up with you?"

"Next month will be fifteen years, why?"

"I was just wondering if she has met criteria to be nominated for sainthood yet," she teased.

"Very funny. Is that the report on the Williams' case?"

She handed him the three-page report she had typed up the previous night. "I thought you could run it past the boss for approval. Then we could arrange to meet with Bailey and Nessa's mother to let them know what we found out."

"You know what is going to happen don't you?" he asked.

"What?"

"He is going to see the great work you did and we are going to get more cold case assignments."

Desi thought about it for a minute. "Maybe that won't be a bad thing," she said. "I enjoyed working on the case even if it was a matter of personal pride."

"Lord knows there are a ton of cold cases that have gone unsolved for years," he said. "If he were to offer for us to work them full time, would you be interested?"

"To get us off the active case roster even for a while, heck yeah. Would you be interested?"

"Yes, I think I would. No more middle-of-the-night calls and some decent hours for a change, yeah I could handle that."

"Go work your good ole boy magic on the lieutenant then," she said with an excited grin.

†

"Hey, Bailey, I haven't seen you in ages," Ralph, the St. Louis depot manager, said when she entered the office to sign in her load. "Are you finally taking on our route?"

She smiled warmly at the man who had been trying for years to get her to drive his route. "No, Ralph, just filling in for Jimmy while he's on vacation," she answered.

"Well, damn, I got my hopes up when I saw you walking in."

"Sorry to disappoint you, Ralph, but I'll pick up some extra runs when I can so you can see my beautiful smiling face," she teased.

"What else could an old man hope for?" he teased back. "Just keep in mind, I'll have a spot open for you if you ever wanted to transfer."

"Thanks Ralph, I really appreciate that," she said with genuine appreciation.

"I'm not rushing you off, but we have bad weather moving in, so get back on the road south as soon as you can. I'd hate to see you snarled up in traffic when the weather hits."

"Thanks Ralph, I will head out as soon as the boys have me set and thanks for the heads up."

"My pleasure, Bailey," he said. "Drive safe on your run home."

She gave him a warm smile. "Always, Ralph. See you soon."

Bailey walked out of the depot office and looked to the west where clouds were beginning to form. She would definitely be lucky to be ahead of that weather before it hit the metro area. She would head south and stop around Hayti for a late lunch, if the weather permitted. Otherwise, she would drive straight on to Memphis.

†

Desi was concentrating on her computer screen and did not see Braxton as he returned. When she did finally glance up at him, he was smiling broadly.

"Well?"

"We have his blessing to meet with Bailey and Mrs. Williams," he said. "The boss was so impressed with the good work he jumped at the idea of us working cold cases. We have to finish out our last two cases, but we won't be in the rotation to catch new cases."

"That is the best news I've heard all day," Desi said. "I'll have the Truman report finished in a few minutes if you want to see if we can get an appointment at the DA's office later today to review that case and the gang case. I will also give Bailey a call to see when we can set up a meeting to discuss Nessa's case."

"Before you do that, I need you to come with me for a few minutes to see something."

"What?"

"Just follow me," he said and turned away.

Desi saved the file before leaving the computer. She would die if she lost the file to a flicker of power or some other crazy event. She followed Braxton down a long hallway to the storage areas in the precinct. He opened a door to a large room with two desks in the middle. Desi could not see the back wall of the room, hidden by box after box of files, from floor to ceiling.

"What's this?"

"Our new office and our new caseload," he said to a shocked Desi.

"All of these are cold cases?"

"Just from the last twenty years," he said.

"Holy shit," she said.

"Do you want to reconsider?"

"Heck no, I just don't know where we will want to begin," she said with a huge grin.

"The boss took care of that for us. He has kept a list of cases for the last ten years and he wants us to start with those."

"Let me go finish that report. You can make the call to the DA, and while we wait we can look up the top two on his list."

"You aren't excited or anything, are you?" he teased.

Desi's answer came in the form of a grin as she left the room.

"We have a three-thirty appointment at the DA's office," Braxton said, hanging up the phone.

Desi looked at her watch to find it was nearly eleven. "How about an early lunch and we can tackle the caseload when we get back," she suggested.

"Sounds good to me. Don't forget to call Bailey too," he reminded her.

"I'll call her after lunch. She will have made her drop and be on her way back by then."

"Italian then?" he asked.

"RG's downtown?" she said.

"Not as good as your woman's, but it will do in a pinch," he teased.

Desi just shook her head at his comment, but she was beginning to think that it was starting to sound good. She would love nothing more than to have Bailey as her woman. "Let's go," she said.

"You're going to have to drive," he said. "I need gas."

"Oh all right, come on then," Desi said to hurry him along.

†

Bailey made it safely out of St. Louis before the rains began to fall and made good time back to Hayti where she did manage to stop for lunch at a truck stop. She was eagerly attacking a chef salad when her phone rang. She looked at the screen to see the number for Memphis PD and hoped it was Desi calling and not more bad news.

"Hello," she said, still chewing a bite of salad. She was relieved to hear Desi's voice on the other end of the line.

"Hey, this is Desi. Where are you?"

"In the big city of Hayti," she said. "I stopped for some lunch."

"I'm sorry to interrupt your lunch."

"No problem at all. What's up?"

"I need you to do something for me."

"Sure, what can I do?"

"I need you to arrange a meeting for you, Nessa's mom, Braxton, and me. We have official police business to discuss."

"Okay," Bailey said. "When would you like this to occur?"

"As soon as we can get it arranged," Desi said, struggling to hide the excitement in her voice.

"Is six tonight okay with you?" Bailey asked. "If so, I will call Merita and get her to come to my place and we can meet there."

"Six would be good. Give me a call if we need to change times."

"I will," Bailey said. "You aren't going to give me a clue are you?"

"Sorry, but this has to be a face-to-face meeting," she said.

"Okay, well, I'll see you at six."

"Thanks, Bailey."

"No problem."

"Be careful on your drive home."

"I will, thanks."

Bailey ended the call and brought up Merita's number. Merita agreed to the meeting, so Bailey finished off her salad and raced for home. The trip passed quickly as she tried to figure out what Desi was up to. She made it to Memphis in good time and hoped she could shower and change clothes before their meeting.

†

Desi returned to their new office and found Braxton standing in front of the massive pile of boxes, staring at the overwhelming task ahead of them. "What are you waiting on?" she asked.

Braxton turned to look at her. "I was waiting for the muscle to arrive," he teased.

"Here I am," Desi said as she posed and flexed for his benefit.

Braxton broke out laughing. "Actually, I'm looking for box 232."

"You start on one end and I'll start on the other," she said as she walked to the farthest end to begin her search. Par for the course, the box was on the next to last row from the top and out of Desi's reach. "I've got muscles, but you have the reach we need," she said as she pointed to the box.

Braxton chuckled as he walked over to where she was standing to pull the box down and blow the dust off the lid. "Our first two files are in here," he said. "Take your pick."

Desi chose the file from the back of the box and carried it over to the desk to open it. She carefully opened the file and began sorting information across the desk. She placed reports in one stack and photographs in another and then organized the reports in chronological order to begin reviewing the file.

Braxton took his file and performed the same tasks as they began their reviews.

Jasmine Bryan, an exotic dancer at one of the airport area's seedy strip clubs, had been found murdered on December 24, 2005, and her body dumped on Highway 61, just south of Memphis. Desi stopped reading and picked up a stack of photos wanting to put a face to the name of the murdered woman.

Jasmine Bryan had been twenty-three when she was murdered. Desi found a photograph that was a professional shot. In the photograph, Bryan was a beautiful African American woman with an infectious smile. The remainder of the photographs, the crime scene photos, documented a young life cut short. There was evidence of bruising around her neck and Desi was certain once she read deeper in the reports there would be petechial hemorrhaging noted in her eyes from strangulation. The photos showed her fully clothed, but Desi would be surprised if she had not been sexually assaulted based on her experience from the streets. The killer had not merely dumped her body, but had taken the time to carefully pose her leaned against a tree with her hands crossed in her lap. Desi made a note on her pad. *Perp familiar enough with the area to know he had time to pose the victim versus just dumping the body.* She picked up the photo and examined it closely. Something was off about the sweater Bryan was wearing. Desi went to her desk to retrieve a magnifying glass.

Examining the photograph closely, particularly the sweater, Desi noted the light blue sweater fit the victim's body snuggly. Desi turned the photograph and studied it for several seconds at different angles before she realized what was off about the sweater. The small white manufacturer tag was visible on the front side of her body, further adding to her suspicion of a sexual assault. At the least, Bryan had been undressed and the killer placed the sweater on her backward. It was possibly a mistake by the killer or it could have been some type of signature. Desi picked up her pen to jot another note. *Sweater returned to the body backward.*

Desi placed the photograph back in the stack and returned to the reports. She flipped until she got to the medical examiner's report and confirmed the sexual assault and the cause of death as asphyxiation. The ME's report also listed several items of interest under the physical evidence section of the report. Possible carpet fibers were located at the crime scene and DNA samples were possible from semen stains and skin samples taken from underneath Bryan's fingernails of her right hand.

She picked up the close-up photographs of Bryan's hands. Several of the nails on her right hand had been smoothly cut by the ME staff to retrieve the evidence, but the remaining nails were jagged and broken. Bryan had not given up without a fight, which had probably led to the bruised left eye. *Check report for DNA analysis and carpet fiber analysis* she added to her notes.

Desi and Braxton had agreed upon a method to which they would review the cases they chose. They would each select a case and review it separately, making notes independent of each other. Then they would exchange files, and once they had finished reviewing both files, they would decide if either case warranted further investigation.

They had swapped files and had been reviewing them for several hours when Braxton checked the time. "Our meeting is at six, correct?" he asked.

Desi looked up from the file and stretched. "Yeah, what time is it?"

"Almost four thirty," he answered. "My eyes are starting to cross. Can we stop for the day and grab a quick bite?"

Desi was also hungry and quickly agreed to meet him at a nearby deli.

†

Desi and Braxton placed their orders and located a table to wait for the food. "Are you ready for the meeting?" he asked.

"I think so," she answered. "Why?"

"I'm just there for moral support. You did the legwork on the case, and I think you should be the one to share the news with them."

"Thanks," Desi answered. "I admit I am worried about how the news will be received."

Braxton smiled at his partner with true admiration. "You cannot control that, you can only deliver the facts as they are, and hopefully together we can answer any questions they may have."

His confident smile did little to bolster Desi. Deep down she was worried about telling them that Nessa's killer would escape conviction for his crime against her, but at least she could tell them why and what had happened.

The food arrived and Braxton ate with his usual gusto while Desi picked at her salad as her mind struggled with what words she would use in addressing Nessa's mother. She felt confident that Bailey would want the information straight up, but she would have to temper her presentation based on a brief introduction to Mrs. Williams.

When she had eaten all her stomach could tolerate, she looked up to see Braxton watching her. "What?" she asked.

"Are you sure you are ready for this?"

"I have to be. I cannot hold this information inside me any longer," she said with a weak smile.

"Let's roll then," he said.

✝

Bailey had showered and was just finishing dressing when someone knocked on her front door. It was a quarter to six as she flipped off her bedroom light.

"Hey there," she said as she opened the door and pulled Merita into her arms for a hug and a kiss.

"Did you have a good day?" Merita asked as they walked to the living room.

"Yes thanks, and you?"

"Busy, but good. I have been worried about this meeting ever since you called," Merita said. "Do you know what they want?"

"Honestly, I haven't a clue and I could not get any information from Desi, which I found odd."

"I guess we will know soon enough then," Merita said as they heard car doors closing.

"May I get you something to drink?"

"A bottle of water would be nice. I will get it if you will meet your guests at the door."

"Fair enough," Bailey said and walked to the door to greet Braxton and Desi.

Merita emerged from the kitchen with a bottle of water and they all sat in the living room as Bailey introduced Desi and Braxton.

Desi saw the resemblance immediately when her eyes landed on Merita. She walked over to sit beside her.

"Can I get you two a drink?"

"No, I believe we are good," Braxton said.

Bailey thought Desi looked nervous and she smiled at her to ease some of her discomfort.

Desi smiled warmly back at her. "Thank you both for agreeing to meet with us tonight on such short notice. We have some information we wanted to share with you about Nessa's case."

Bailey sat back in the chair, her body language indicating she was bracing for bad news.

Desi shifted nervously on the couch. "I did not know your daughter, but what happened to her was unforgivable," she said to Merita.

"She was a great daughter and woman," Merita said, her chin held high.

"We took the liberty to look into the case regarding your daughter's murder," Desi said as she turned to face Merita. "When we first met Bailey, she was very angry about the negligent way in which her case was handled. After reviewing the file I immediately realized she had cause to be angry."

Bailey was shocked. She had no idea Desi was looking into Nessa's murder.

"The detective assigned to the case did very little to attempt to solve the case. I do not know the man; he retired shortly after her death, but I would apologize to you on behalf of the department for the anguish you have suffered based on his incompetence."

Merita looked at Bailey. "We appreciate that very much," she said.

"I assume you know more," Bailey said, a tremble of emotion in her words.

"Yes, we do, and I'd like to share the information with you if you're ready."

Both Merita and Bailey nodded their assent.

"I was able to track down a woman who was a witness to the crime. She was able to give me a rough estimate of what had occurred and some information on Nessa's killers," Desi said. "She is an older woman who was sitting in a darkened bus bench waiting to go to work. She witnessed two young African American teens as they approached down the street and was wondering what no good they could be up to at that hour."

Desi looked at Bailey. "I think I am going to need a bottle of water too."

Bailey walked into the kitchen to get three bottles, handing one each to Desi and Braxton then taking the third back to her seat.

"The teens, JT and Tyrone, had been expelled from school for their behavior and were trying to become initiated into their local street gang so they could run drugs and make some money. They were given the order to do a carjacking to prove their value to the gang and were told they had to bring a Honda Accord to the gang leader."

Desi paused for a sip of water. "The boys had been walking around Memphis all night searching for a Honda Accord, smoking pot, probably drinking, and had given up and were on their way home when it was unfortunate your daughter arrived in the area. The traffic light changed and she was stopped when one of the boys stood in front of the car and the other approached the driver's side to confront Nessa."

"She should have just run them down," Bailey snarled.

"You know Nessa would never have done that, Bailey," Merita said.

Bailey just nodded her head in agreement.

Desi continued the story. "The boys were not experienced criminals and as JT was pulling Ms. Williams from the car, it started rolling. The door hit the arm he was holding the gun in and it startled him, and the gun discharged. Your daughter was only about a foot away from him and the shot hit her in the chest at point-blank range. The boys panicked and sped away in the car, crashing into a parked vehicle as they fled the scene."

Desi looked from Bailey to Merita to gauge their comprehension and found them both listening to her intently.

Merita was the first to ask a question. "How did you find out who the boys were?"

"The boys took the car to the gang leader and he had some others take the car and strip it before setting it on fire to destroy evidence, but there were fingerprints that were lifted from the car. I ran the prints through an analysis and it revealed Tyrone was one of the boys."

"That had never been done?" Bailey asked.

Desi shook her head no. "Once we had a name it was not hard to find him. He is in a maximum security prison in Nashville on death row for a gang-related murder."

"And the other boy, where is he?" Merita asked.

"He is dead, killed by another gang."

"How did you find that out?" Bailey asked.

"We went to Nashville to talk to Tyrone yesterday, and he gave us the whole story," Desi said.

"You did all that?" Bailey asked.

"Yes, we did," she answered.

"Actually, that's not completely true. Desi did most of it, I just drove her to Nashville," Braxton said.

Desi could see the tears welling in Bailey's eyes so she turned away to look at Merita. "I know this doesn't change much, but at least you know what happened and who was responsible."

"I thank you so very much for finally giving us some answers," Merita said. "It means so very much to us to know all of this."

"I just wish a proper investigation had been done and that you did not have to suffer this long waiting for answers," Desi said. "Are there any other questions you may have?"

"Just one," Bailey said. "Did she suffer?"

Desi had anticipated the question and had reviewed the medical examiner's report to verify her information. "No, I do not think so. The report stated the bullet ruptured an artery and she died very quickly."

"Thank you," Bailey said.

Desi and Braxton stood to leave. "If you have any other questions, just contact us," Desi said, and they left, leaving Merita and Bailey alone together.

"See you Monday, partner," Braxton said as they walked to their cars. "You did a great job in there, and I'm proud to be your partner."

"Thanks, have a great night."

Desi drove the short distance to her house and changed clothes before feeding and playing with Fubar. Her heart had desperately wanted to stay and offer comfort to Bailey, but she knew Merita and Bailey needed time together to start healing.

†

When Braxton and Desi had left, Merita looked at Bailey. "Nessa would be pleased that Desi is your new woman. She is amazing and would not have done this if she did not have very strong feelings for you."

"I know," Bailey said as her tears began to fall.

Merita took her in her arms. "Nessa is at peace. Now we have to move on with our lives now that we know what happened," Merita whispered to Bailey.

They cried together and talked for another half hour before Merita left for home. "I will see you soon," she promised as she entered her car and drove away.

Bailey watched her leave and looked over at Desi's house. The lights were on so she walked the short distance to her house and knocked on her door.

†

When Desi saw Bailey on her doorstep, she opened the door and welcomed her inside. Bailey fell into her arms, her body still quivering with emotion.

"It's going to be okay," Desi said as she held Bailey close.

"I know I just wanted to thank you for what you did."

"Nessa, you, and Merita deserved better than you got and I needed to right that," Desi said.

"Thank you," Bailey said and tenderly kissed her.

When they ended the kiss, Desi asked, "Are you going to work at the club?"

"Yes, I think I need to stay busy. Why?"

"I thought I might drop in a bit later for a nightcap," Desi said with a grin.

"I will look forward to it," Bailey said as she walked to the door and then turned to rush back for a final kiss goodbye. "See you soon," she said and went out the door.

†

When Bailey arrived at the club, she was pleasantly surprised to see Marie sitting at the bar. "What's up?" Bailey asked and walked behind the bar.

"Marie was getting bored and lonely, so she decided to come and emcee the shows tonight," she said.

Bailey loved her brother, and his alter ego Marie was just as mischievous.

"Admit it, you just couldn't stand to be away from all this eye candy," she teased.

Marie placed her hand over her ample bosom and said, "Well, I do declare you have seen through me once more, baby sister," and with a girlish giggle, Marie leaned over and kissed the cheek of a handsome young man sitting next to her.

"She's been behaving herself pretty well so far," Louise said as she wiped down the counter in front of Marie.

"But the night is still young," Marie said.

"Don't make me send you home for Sarah to babysit you. Remember our agreement," Louise warned.

"Yes, Mama Louise," she teased. "I did promise to be good."

"This I have got to see," Bailey said.

"So, how was your day?" Louise asked.

"Very interesting," Bailey answered and told them about the visit from Desi and Braxton.

Marie, ever the sensitive one, broke into tears as she told the story. "Damn, there goes my makeup," she said as she left the bar and headed to the dressing room for a touch-up.

"So, how are you feeling about all this?" Louise asked.

Bailey looked at her and shrugged her shoulders. "I don't really know how to describe how I feel. I must be suffering from a mild case of shock to be honest. I had no clue that Desi was even looking into Nessa's case."

"That just goes to further prove how much she thinks about you."

"Yeah, I guess it does," Bailey said, wearing a smile. "She's going to drop by later for a drink."

Louise smiled broadly. "That's fantastic."

Marie came tottering back to the bar and took her seat. "The girls are just about ready for the first show. They have been practicing so hard this week," she added.

"Are they going to perform the numbers they were rehearsing the other night?" Bailey asked.

"Yes, they are so excited. I just wish I could be up there with them," she said with a sigh.

"Soon enough," Bailey said and winked at Marie. "You will have some company at the bar later," she added.

"Oh really? Is that gorgeous woman of yours coming to see me?"

Bailey laughed, but ended smiling. "Yes, Desi said she was stopping by for a drink."

"Oh, girl, she is something else," Marie cooed.

The door opened and Marie and Bailey noticed Louise lit up like a neon sign as she watched someone enter the club. They turned to see Beth walking up.

"I do believe, baby sister, that you are not the only one falling in love these days," Marie said.

"Oh hush, you two," Louise said from across the bar, without denying anything.

"Hey gang," Beth said as she arrived at the bar. "How's it going?"

"Great night so far," Louise said.

Bailey picked up a dishpan. "I'm going to do some busing," she said and left to clear some tables.

"I, um, will go check to see if the girls need help with their makeup," Marie said.

Beth looked at Louise. "Do I smell funny or something?"

"No, darling, that is just their way of giving us a few moments of privacy, to do this," Louise said as she took Beth in her arms and kissed her new lover. "Hiya," she said after the kiss.

"Wow," Beth said. "I'm tempted to go out and walk back in so we can do that again."

"No worries, there will be many more to come," Louise said, her eyes glittering with excitement.

Bailey turned back toward the bar to witness the kiss and smiled to herself before placing her dishpan on a table to clear the bottles and glasses. She made her way around the club talking with regulars and new customers alike. When her pan was full, she returned to the bar where Beth and

Louise were now serving customers. She placed the glasses in the sink and stored the bottles in the back. She returned to find Beth washing the glasses. "I was going to do that."

"No problem, you can clear the rest of the tables if you want, and I will wash these," Beth said sweetly.

Bailey nodded her head and cleared the remaining tables as the crowd jumped and gyrated on the dance floor. The crowd was electrified as the lights began to flicker and the deejay faded out the song. She returned to the bar to empty her pan and was standing at the end of the bar when Marie stepped out on the stage to a roar of applause.

"Good evening, Club Fubar," Marie said, glowing with excitement.

"Good evening," responded the crowd.

"Before we get the show started for tonight, I want to thank you all for the beautiful card and well wishes. You have all helped me to get back on my feet quickly and I hope to be performing again soon."

"Hell yeah," someone yelled from the crowd.

"Thank you, honey-boy, see me after the show for your reward," she said and the crowd burst out in laughter. "Nikki and Charlise have agreed to stay on for a few more weeks and they and Victoria have worked really hard on this weekend's shows. So without further delay, give a warm welcome to the ladies of Club Fubar."

The lights dimmed as the curtain slowly opened and the silhouettes of Nikki, Charlise, and Victoria appeared in the shadows. The music started with a slow beat and when the song took off, the lights suddenly blazed and the performers came alive to the roar of the crowd.

Bailey did not see Desi slip into the club as her eyes were transfixed to the stage, watching the performance. She quickly became aware of her arrival when a pair of warm arms encircled her waist and she felt Desi's warm breath on her neck. The alluring scent of her perfume filled Bailey's senses as Desi held her close.

"Hey, you sexy beast," Desi said, stealing one of Tommy's lines and making Bailey chuckle.

"I'm glad you could make it," Bailey answered. "Do you want a seat at the bar?"

"No, ma'am, I am perfectly content right here unless it bothers you," Desi said.

"Not in the least," Bailey said as she enjoyed Desi's closeness. She could feel a thrumming of excitement running through her body.

Desi rested her head on Bailey's shoulder as they watched the show. "Is that Tommy on stage?"

"Yes. He begged Louise to let him emcee tonight's show."

"He looks really good," Desi said.

"Yeah, he does," Bailey said with a smile.

They watched the entire show standing like that and when it ended, Bailey turned to Desi. "Grab a seat and tell me what you want to drink before the rush arrives."

"A draft will be fine," Desi said as she took a stool at the end of the bar to be closest to Bailey.

She watched Bailey, Beth, and Louise dance around each other as they filled orders for the thirsty crowd. It appeared they had been working together for a long time as they quickly found their rhythm. When the rush died down, Bailey poured a Mountain Dew and joined Desi at the end of the bar. She wiped a bar towel across her brow and took a long drink. "That is so much easier with an extra person," she said.

"You all work well together," Desi said. "By the way, I have other news to share with you."

Bailey put her glass down and turned to Desi. "I'm listening."

"Braxton and I asked for and were granted a new assignment, at least on a temporary basis, but if we perform well, it could be permanent."

"What is it?"

"The boss was so impressed with our work on Nessa's case he asked if we could work on the cold case files that fill up nearly half a room. We will pick our cases, work strictly Monday through Friday if we choose and select our own hours instead of being constantly on call."

"That is fantastic news," Bailey said. "I am happy for both of you."

"It will be a good break for us and maybe we can close some of the cases that have been abandoned."

"Speaking of breaks and your new free weekend status, I wonder if I could ask a favor in the future."

"Sure, what can I do for you?"

Bailey nodded toward Louise and Beth. "We have a budding romance here and I thought it would be nice if they could have a free weekend from time to time, but I will need some help. I thought maybe I could convince you and Merita to join me."

"I would love that, but I must warn you I have no bartending skills at all."

"I can teach you anything you need to know," Bailey said with a wink.

Desi chuckled at the innuendo behind Bailey's words. "I'm sure you can," she said and kissed Bailey. "There is one thing I would ask though."

"And that would be?"

"Once the trial is over, that we also get some free weekends. I would love to take you to New Orleans to meet my parents and there are other places I would like to share with you."

"I have plenty of vacation time. I just need someone to share it with."

"I gratefully volunteer to fill all of your free time," Desi said with a grin.

"You, my dear, have yourself a deal."

After the final show, Louise came over to where Desi and Bailey were sitting. "I think we can handle things from here if you want to call it a night. I know you were up early for the extra run today and you are probably exhausted."

"You know, Louise, I'm not going to argue that tonight. I am whipped."

"Go home. I will see you tomorrow night."

"Thank you."

They walked to Desi's car together. "Do you have any plans tomorrow?" Bailey asked.

"No, not really, what do you have in mind?"

"I have an errand to run in the morning, but I think it is time for a cookout, to celebrate the closure of Nessa's case and your new assignment, if you think it's safe for you."

"That sounds wonderful to me. It's a group event, so it should be fine. What will we cook?"

"I think I will smoke a Boston butt, and we can make a farmers market run for some fresh vegetables."

"My mouth is watering already," Desi said. "What time do I need to be ready?"

"Ten. That will allow plenty of time to run my errands and get the butt cooking. I'll go back in and tell Louise to bring Beth and the boys. I thought I would invite Merita too."

"Sounds like it will be a blast."

"Okay, be safe and I will see you at ten."

Desi pulled away and Bailey walked back inside the club to invite the rest of the crew before climbing into her Jeep and driving home.

Chapter 12

Bailey woke early the next morning and went outside to set up the grill while her coffee brewed. If the weather cooperated, it would turn out to be a fine day she thought. A gentle breeze bathed her face as she filled the grill with charcoal and placed wood chips in the bucket to soak.

As she walked back inside to grab a cup of coffee, she planned her morning. She would shower and dress before going to the store for the butt, lighting the fire as she left for the store and then come back to give the butt a nice rub before placing it on the grill to slowly cook.

She dressed and poured a fresh travel mug with coffee before heading out to the butcher shop. To her delight, the breeze was still cool so she pulled back the top of her Jeep and climbed inside. Traffic was light as she drove to the shop.

Back in her kitchen, she unwrapped the butt and rinsed it with cool water, gently patting the meat dry with a paper towel before coating it with her favorite seasonings, gently rubbing the mixture into the fresh cut meat. She placed the butt on a cookie sheet and carried it out to the deck to open the grill. The coals had started nicely and she lifted the grate to rake the hot coals to one side before placing the meat opposite the hot coals. She added more charcoal and some mesquite chips before replacing the cover.

Bailey returned to her Jeep and stopped at a nearby flower shop to buy a bouquet of pink carnations, which she placed on the seat beside her. She drove down Poplar Avenue until she reached her destination, Memorial Gardens, and pulled into the cemetery. She drove to the small hill that held a solitary black headstone and parked.

"Good morning, my love," she said as she placed the flowers on the grave, removing the wilted bouquet from the previous week's visit. Bailey sat down beside the headstone and placed her hand on the stone, which felt warm from the early morning sun. "We got a lot of answers yesterday about what happened to you," Bailey said as she felt tears filling her eyes. She told the story that Desi had shared with them as tears rolled down her cheeks. "I wish I could have been with you, my love, maybe things would have been different," she said.

Bailey felt a cool breeze caress her right cheek and she imagined it was Nessa's touch. So many times in their relationship, Nessa had stroked her cheek in the exact same manner. "I will always love you," Nessa had told her while stroking her face. "I will always love you," Bailey had always replied.

She had not heard the approach of the car, and jumped when a warm hand rested on her shoulder. She turned to find Merita standing beside her. "I thought I might find you here this morning. Would you mind some company?"

Bailey wiped the tears from her face. "Not at all, pick out some grass," she said with a grin.

Merita kissed the top of the headstone and placed a single yellow rose on the grave beside Bailey's bouquet.

"Did you tell her about our visit last night?"

"Yes, I did," Bailey answered.

"I hope you have taken some comfort with the news," Merita said.

"Strangely enough, I have," Bailey admitted. "I know nothing will ever bring her back, but at least it is some measure of relief and closure to finally know what happened."

"Nessa will never leave your heart," Merita said as she placed her hand on Bailey's thigh. "The love you shared will forever be a part of you, but it's time to move on."

Bailey nodded her head in agreement.

"Desi has been sent to you to help you heal and learn to love again," Merita said. "Nessa would be very happy with your choosing Desi. I know that in my heart."

The odd breeze picked up again and seemed to circle around them at the gravesite. "Do you feel that?" Bailey asked.

Merita smiled. "Nessa wants us to know she is here with us. I feel it often when I visit. I think it is her way of holding us, to let us know everything is right in her world."

Just as quickly as it had begun, the breeze faded. "I think you are right."

They sat in silence for a few more minutes and then with a sigh, Bailey stood to leave. She offered a hand to Merita. "What are you doing this afternoon?"

"Nothing in particular," Merita said, accepting Bailey's hand and standing.

"I am having a cookout and I would love for you to join us."

"What time and what can I bring?"

"A good appetite," Bailey teased her. "I'm smoking a butt for some pulled pork, so we won't eat until late afternoon, but you can show up anytime. We will probably have some sandwiches at lunch to tide us over."

"I will see you around noon then. Are you sure there is nothing I can bring?"

"Nope, but if I can find some fresh fruit at the farmers market you can make us a nice fruit salad," Bailey said.

"You have a deal," Merita said as they walked back to their vehicles.

✝

Bailey smelled the cooking butt as soon as she pulled into her drive. A quick check found it cooking nicely. Then she walked inside and collected the fabric shopping bags she would place her produce in and drove to Desi's house.

Desi opened the door and Fubar ran up to Bailey, who picked her up for some attention. "Good morning, ladies," she said as she leaned in to kiss Desi. Fubar purred in her hands as she scratched under her chin. "Are you ready to go to the farmers market?"

"Yes, ma'am," Desi said. She walked to the kitchen to pick up her wallet, giving Bailey an excellent view of her legs in the

193

shorts she was wearing. She turned around and saw Bailey watching her with a smile. "Do you like what you see, Ms. Chambers?"

"Most definitely, Detective Dexter," Bailey teased back. "Very nice indeed, don't you think Fubar?"

The kitten meowed in response and Bailey put her back down on the floor. "Guard the house for Mama," she said to Fubar and they left the house.

"It looks like we have a great day for a cookout," Desi said. "Oh, my goodness, it that your grill I smell?"

"Yes, it is. I've had the butt on for about an hour now," Bailey said.

"It smells heavenly already," Desi said.

†

When they arrived at the farmers market, they met Beth and Louise already strolling down the aisles of produce. "Fancy meeting you two here," Louise said with a smile. "Good morning, ladies."

"Good morning. What have you bought already?" Bailey asked.

"Some more of the peas and beans we had last time," Louise said. "What else are you planning?"

"More okra, corn on the cob and Merita will make us a fruit salad so I thought some melons, strawberries, and pineapple. I think the Ripley tomatoes are in this week, so maybe some sandwiches for lunch?"

"We will bring some fresh bread and deli meat for the sandwiches and the boys are bringing drinks and paper goods," Louise said.

"Damn, my mouth is watering just thinking about it," Beth said.

"You better get used to eating good fresh food. We do this all summer long while it lasts," Louise told her.

"No worries, love, this is right up my alley," Beth answered with a warm smile.

"Let's go see what else we can find," Bailey said.

"Just a friendly word of advice, Desi, keep her away from the home-baked goods," Louise teased.

"Ha, that is going to be one of my first stops," Bailey said. "That woman's cookies are to die for."

"Well, we wouldn't know since you ate all of them last time," Louise teased.

Bailey blushed. "Yeah, I guess I did."

"So we will buy more this time," Desi said as she took Bailey's arm and pulled her forward.

"Welcome back," the baked goods vendor said with a warm smile when she saw Bailey approaching her booth. "I hope you enjoyed the cakes as much as the cookies."

"They were heavenly too," Bailey said as she searched the table for more of the cookies. "May I have three dozen of those cookies?"

"Yes, you may," the woman said. "I made some butter cookies you can sample while I package the others for you," she said and handed each of them a cookie.

"Oh, my goodness," Desi said as she bit into the cookie made with fresh Amish butter. "You better add a couple dozen of these too," she said.

"I agree," Bailey said.

"No problem," the merchant answered with a smile.

They were all loaded down with fresh goods when they left the market, Bailey carrying a large watermelon while the others carried bags full of produce and baked goods.

†

Merita was just pulling up when Bailey and Desi arrived and helped them carry the bags inside. "Louise and Beth stopped off to get some deli meats for sandwiches," Bailey said as they carried their purchases inside.

"That should give me time to go ahead and get this fruit sliced up so we can get the salad chilling," Merita said.

"Can I help you?" Desi asked Merita.

"You can cut up that watermelon while I clean and slice the rest of the fruit," Merita said thankful for the help.

"I'm going out to check the meat, but will be right back," Bailey said and left the kitchen.

She lifted the lid on the grill and added more wood chips to the coals. The aroma had her mouth watering as she walked back into the kitchen to find Merita and Desi working side by side, just as she and Nessa had in the past. For a second her heart ached with longing and then Desi turned to her with a beautiful smile.

"Will you bring us your garbage can for these rinds?" she asked.

"Certainly will," Bailey said and brought the can over to them.

"Thanks," Desi said, smiling, clearly enjoying herself.

The boys arrived next carrying a cooler with cold beer and sodas, which they placed on the covered deck. A round of kisses from the women welcomed Tommy, carrying a bag with paper plates and napkins into the kitchen. "Girl, don't you look divine," he said as he took a step back to look at Merita.

"Oh, you are still just sugary sweet," Merita said to him.

"No, I'm serious, retirement suits you well," he said.

"Well, thank you," Merita said with a blush.

"What y'all working on over there?" he asked.

"Desi and Merita are making a fruit salad for dinner, and I'm slicing some Ripley's to go with sandwiches when Louise and Beth arrive," Bailey said.

"Girlfriend, she looks so happy with Beth," Joe said.

"Yes, she does. I haven't seen her ever smile this much," Tommy added.

Charles and Tony sashayed in the door exclaiming, "Look who we found outside," as they carried in the bags Louise and Beth had brought.

"Welcome all," Bailey said and introduced Beth and Merita.

"Would someone please start making some sandwiches," Tommy said. "I'm starving."

"What would you like, your highness?" Charles asked.

"Oh no, you did not just call him that," Bailey said. "We will never hear the end of it now."

Tommy, taking her comment in stride, sat at the kitchen table and crossed his legs. "A sandwich fit for a Queen," he answered. "What else?"

"We bought shaved ham, turkey, cheeses, and lettuce," Louise said. "I hope you have mayo and mustard."

"You know I do," Bailey said, pointing to the refrigerator.

"What may we fix you then, your highness?" Louise asked as she started spreading out bread while Joe brought the condiments.

"Mm, ham and cheese with mayo and a slice of that tomato Bailey is slicing," he said.

"Do I need to cut your crusts off your sandwich, your highness?" Louise teased.

"No, girl, I like them left on," he camped.

"What kind of sandwich do you want Bailey?" Louise asked.

"Mayo, tomatoes and a little salt," Bailey said with a grin.

"Such a little country girl," Tommy teased, the flip-flop on his foot flying through the air as he swung his crossed leg.

"You are certainly feeling your oats today, brother," Bailey said as she took a seat beside Desi.

"Well, why wouldn't I. I am surrounded by a room full of beautiful women," he said.

"Braxton would be jealous," Desi joked.

"Well, why don't you invite him for dinner? There will be plenty food," Bailey said.

"Seriously?" Desi said.

"Yeah, I'm serious. Give him a call and tell him we will eat at five and bring his wife," Bailey said.

"All right, I'll give him a call in a few."

†

After consuming the pile of sandwiches, the others retired to the living room to watch a movie. "I'll join you in a minute. I want to check the meat."

"I'll go with you," Desi volunteered. "You save us room on the couch though, Tommy," she said, pointing at him.

"Yes, Detective," he said with a salute. "Come on, girls, you heard the woman," he said.

She and Desi walked out to the deck and Bailey lifted the lid. "That really does smell heavenly," Desi said. "I should have never doubted your cooking ability."

Bailey grinned at her as she picked up a thermometer and checked the meat. "Right on schedule," she said as she added more wood chips and charcoal. "I'm so glad you are here today," she said as she turned to face Desi.

"There is nowhere else I'd rather be," Desi said as she wrapped her arms around Bailey.

"I could think of a few more intimate places, but my couch will do for now," Bailey said with an impish grin.

"Do you want to give Braxton a call while we are out here? It's liable to be very noisy when we get back inside?"

Desi called her partner and he was delighted with the invitation and agreed to arrive around four to join the party.

"Excellent," Bailey said as they walked back to the house.

†

As anticipated, the boys were in full chorus as *Priscilla Queen of the Desert* was playing on the television. "See what I mean?" she asked Desi as they entered the room to take up their place on the couch.

Desi just chuckled as she snuggled in beside Bailey. She had seen the movie before, but never exactly like this. Tommy and the others knew every line and when the dancing started, they could not resist giving their own rendition to the roar of laughter from the women in the room.

When the movie ended, Joe searched for another movie while, Bailey and Louise went to the kitchen to start the vegetables. Desi, Merita, and Beth followed them.

†

Louise got the beans and peas cooking while Beth shucked the corn for boiling. "Will you make some tea?" Bailey asked Merita.

"What can I do?" Desi asked.

"You, my dear, can rinse and cut the okra while I go check the meat. Would anyone like an adult beverage on my way back in?" Bailey asked.

"Heck yeah," Joe yelled from the living room.

"Good, you can come help me then," Bailey hollered back at him.

Joe came trotting into the kitchen and followed Bailey out the door. Joe worked on serving cold beer to everyone while Bailey went to check the progress of the meat. Joe returned and handed Bailey a beer.

"There is a nice breeze blowing," she said as she watched the temperature rise on the thermometer. "Let's eat out on the deck," she suggested.

"Great idea, I'll get the boys and we can join you on the deck while you finish cooking," Joe said and disappeared into the house.

Bailey chuckled and turned on the stereo system. The boys were already in rare form and could not resist putting on a performance to the music on the system.

She passed them on her way back to the kitchen. "I will be right back," she said.

"What did you say to them?" Louise asked. "They all went flying outside."

"I just suggested we eat outside. There is a nice breeze blowing," Bailey said. "Add a little music and poof, we have an impromptu drag show," she said with a grin. "You know I can never get enough of the boys."

"We are just about done in here, so we will join you in a few minutes," Louise said.

Bailey looked over Desi's shoulder to see she had nearly finished slicing the okra. "Will you put that in a bowl and pour some buttermilk over it?" she asked.

"Yes, ma'am," Desi said.

Merita returned to the deck with Bailey and helped Joe pull out some chairs for the others. "Are you having a good time?" she asked.

"Oh yes, I think I love these boys almost as much as you," she said, wearing a huge smile.

"Good, I think we are stuck with them. At least two of them for sure," she said.

Charles and Tony danced wildly on the deck while Joe positioned Tommy in a comfortable lounger. Bailey and Merita joined them to watch the impending show.

A few minutes later, Desi, Louise, and Beth arrived from the kitchen. "Everything is in good shape. The corn is on a low boil and the okra will be ready when you are," Louise said.

"Excellent, I'll cook it when I take the meat off to cool," Bailey said.

Everyone settled down drinking their beers and listening to the music when Braxton and his wife pulled up. Desi went to greet them and brought them to the deck to meet the crowd.

"Everyone, this is my partner Braxton and his wife Donna," Desi announced.

They were warmly welcomed and Joe pulled two fresh beers from the cooler. "Thanks," Braxton told him and took the beer. He turned to look at Bailey. "What on earth are you cooking that smells so great?"

Bailey smiled at him. "I've been smoking a butt all day," she answered.

"If it tastes half as good as it smells we are in for a treat," he said to his wife.

"I don't think anyone will go hungry," Desi said.

"Thanks for inviting us," he said to Bailey.

"Thank you for coming."

"I wouldn't miss your cooking for anything," Braxton teased her.

"He has raved about your cooking ever since you sent the Alfredo to work with Desi," Donna added.

"No pressure there," Bailey said with a wink.

Braxton must have talked with Donna about the boys before they came. She did not flinch a muscle except to smile as the boys camped it up to the disco tunes and even got up to dance with Tony, not that he would have accepted no for an answer. She and Braxton both appeared comfortable with the crowd and quickly joined the laughter.

Bailey checked the time and thought the meat was ready to pull off the grill to cool while she cooked the okra. She went to the grill to check the temperature of the meat one last time and then inside to get a pan and a meat fork to remove the butt. Braxton joined her at the grill and carried the butt inside.

"Is there anything I can do to help?" he asked when he set the butt on the counter.

"Yeah, you can cut the butt into quarters so it will cool faster," Bailey said as she turned on a burner to cook the okra.

She smiled as she looked at the counter. Louise had already come inside and placed the beans, peas, and corn into a Crock-Pot set to keep them warm and had washed up the pots she used to cook them.

"Damn, this looks awesome," Braxton said as he sliced into the smoked meat. "It is so tender."

Braxton had finished cutting the meat, and was leaning up against the counter watching her cook. "I haven't seen okra cooked like that since my grandma was alive," he said.

"I will give you fair warning then. Get all you want on the first serving. It will go quickly once the boys get their hands on it."

When the first batch was cooked, Bailey tapped on the kitchen window and motioned for Louise to come inside. When she walked in Bailey said, "Bring a couple of the boys in and get the deck tables set up, if you would. We can serve from inside and take our plates out to the deck."

"Is that meat cool enough to touch yet?" she asked Braxton.

He checked it as she asked. "It's tolerable," he answered, "do you want me to pull it?"

"Yes, that would be great," Bailey said, and Braxton went to work.

Desi came into the kitchen. "Hey, babe, what can I help with?"

"You can find out what everyone wants to drink and get them set up," Bailey answered as she fished out a second batch of okra. "Then get folks started serving themselves."

"You got it," Desi said.

Joe arrived with drink orders and helped Desi make them as the others began serving their plates. Bailey finished the last batch of okra and placed it in the empty pan, and then she and Braxton fixed their plates and joined the others on the deck.

"I can see what he was talking about now," Donna said as she swallowed a bite of the pulled pork. "This is all fantastic."

"It was a group effort," Bailey said.

"This is the best butt I've ever had," Braxton said.

"There is barbecue or hot sauce if you want some," Bailey said.

"This meat is so good it doesn't need a thing," he bragged. "I also call dibs on any okra that is left too," he said with a grin.

"Where are your manners?" Donna scolded him.

"Bailey warned me in advance it would go fast, so I'm just staking my claim," he told her.

"Okay, but only if I get some," she said with a grin.

"I guess I could share with you, my love," he said sweetly to a chorus of "awwws."

"See, Tommy, that's true love when someone volunteers to share Bailey's okra," Joe said.

"I love you, my friend, but keep your eyes off my okra," Tommy answered.

The group broke into laughter and Bailey agreed to buy a larger amount next time.

They finished off the meal with large bowls of the chilled fruit salad and everyone was stuffed. "I am so glad I don't have to perform tonight after this meal," Tommy said.

Tony snapped his fingers and bobbed his head. "Girl, I am juiced up and ready to go," he said.

†

After pitching in to help clean up, the group dispersed. The boys, Louise, and Beth, returned home to prepare for an evening at the club. They had left a notice on the door that the club would open late to enable everyone to enjoy the evening at Bailey's, but now it was time to go to work. Merita begged an early evening too and was followed out by Braxton and Donna, carrying a plate of leftovers to hold him until tomorrow.

"Will you come by the club later?" Bailey asked as she held Desi in her arms.

"Maybe for a little while, but I am bushed, so I won't stay late. I swear I don't know how you all do it week in and week out."

"Lots of practice," Bailey said.

"Can you at least sleep in tomorrow and get some rest?"

"I will probably be comatose until noon," Bailey assured her. "Would you join me for a late lunch of leftovers?"

"I could be talked into that," Desi answered.

"It's a date then. If you get home and change your mind about coming out tonight, just send me a text so I won't be looking out for you," she said. "I understand if you need to be home with Fubar, especially since I have been with you all day."

"I will," Desi said as they walked to the door.

Bailey pulled her close for a final kiss and sighed when she let her go. "I miss you already."

"I will see you later," Desi said and slipped out the door.

†

Desi crashed into her favorite recliner and Fubar climbed up and lay down on her chest. Desi knew that reclined was a dangerous position for her to be in, but she could not force herself to move. The warmth of Fubar on her chest and the soft vibrations of her purring lulled Desi to sleep. When she awoke again it was half past eleven. She panicked and jumped to her feet to find her phone to quickly send a text to Bailey. *Sorry, crashed in the recliner, and just woke. Going to head off to bed. I will see you for lunch tomorrow.*

Bailey felt the vibration on her phone and looked down to see Desi's text. She smiled and returned the text. *No problem. Ready for a bed soon too. See you tomorrow. Sweet dreams.*

It had been a crazy busy night and it was probably for the best that Desi had fallen asleep. She had barely stopped moving since she had arrived and the crowd was still growing. Still, she regretted any missed opportunity to see Desi.

When Louise finally locked the door behind the last customers, she looked at Bailey. "Come on, you are going home too. You look dead on your feet. The boys and Beth will help clean up. You have been going full tilt since early this morning."

"You will get no argument from me," Bailey said.

Chapter 13

The next few weeks for Bailey passed quickly and she lived for the stolen moments with Desi, when they could spend precious time together. Her longing for Desi continued to grow with each passing day. Bailey realized, however, that the forced abstinence allowed them time to get to know one another beyond the physical act of making love. Bailey found the more time she spent with Desi, the deeper she truly fell in love with her.

Two weeks after the cookout, Bailey received a call from Desi while she was driving back to town. There had been a break in Tommy's case and she wanted Bailey's opinion.

"Hey, gorgeous woman," Bailey answered when she saw it was Desi calling.

"Hey, Bailey, how are you?"

"I'm better now that you have called."

"Aren't you just full of sweetness today?" Desi teased.

"I am always sweet when it comes to you," Bailey corrected.

"Yes, indeed you are," Desi agreed.

"What's up or have you just missed hearing my sexy voice?"

"I received a call today from ADA Bartlet, the prosecutor who is handling Tommy's case, and I wanted your opinion on something."

"Hang on just a minute I think I may need to pull over for this call."

Desi waited while Bailey slowed and managed to pull the rig onto the shoulder of the interstate.

"Okay, I'm ready," Bailey responded.

"Bartlet has met extensively with both defense lawyers for the men who attacked Tommy and they have discussed a plea bargain to prevent having to go to trial."

"Just what does that mean?" Bailey said.

"Basically that Whitlock would agree to plead guilty to assault instead of facing the hate crime charges and Doogan will be charged as an accomplice for his cooperation."

"Will they still do some prison time?" Bailey asked.

"Whitlock will be sentenced to a minimum of three years up to a maximum of seven. Doogan, because of his cooperation, will probably receive 364 days to two years."

"Why 364 days? That seems an odd number," Bailey asked.

Desi chuckled softly. "Anything under a full year's sentence can be served in a city or county jail without being processed into the prison system," she answered.

"That makes sense I guess. What is your opinion?"

"The scenario has its pros and cons," she said. "There would not be a public trial that could drag on for weeks."

"What else?" Bailey asked.

"They won't receive a sentence as lengthy as they would likely serve from going to trial and proven guilty."

"So what is your opinion?" Bailey repeated her question.

"If I were the vindictive type, I would go to trial just to ensure they receive the maximum sentence possible," she said. "On the other hand, a trial can be a stressful event to go through and there is always a chance something could go wrong and they are not convicted."

"Are you certain of the case you have built against them?"

"It's rock solid from an evidence point of view. The gamble is getting twelve jurors to agree."

"This is ultimately Tommy's decision to make correct?"

"Yes, I just wanted to run it by you before the ADA approaches him with the offer," Desi answered.

"Personally, I think the plea bargain is the better option. It is quicker and the thugs receive punishment for their crime. I don't think Tommy wants anyone to spend forever in prison."

"I agree with you," Desi said.

"What happens if he chooses to accept the bargain?"

"There would be a short hearing in front of the judge to review the bargain, accept or reject it and then sentence the two men, once all parties are in agreement."

"How fast can we get this done," Bailey asked."

"If we can get Tommy's approval, the ADA could schedule the hearing as soon as sometime next week," Desi answered.

"I'll be home in an hour. Will you meet me and we can go see Tommy together before I have to work at the club?"

"I will do better than that. I will call Bartlet and ask him to request a hearing date and give you an hour and a half so you can shower and change clothes. If Tommy decides against it, there is no problem in canceling the hearing request, but at least he will be in the queue."

"I will see you soon then," Bailey said, ending the call. She dialed Tommy's number to give him a head's up that she and Desi would be visiting.

†

Desi followed Bailey to Tommy and Joe's house. Tommy was sitting at the kitchen table waiting for them when they arrived.

"Where is everyone else?" Bailey asked, expecting to see Joe, Charles, and Tony.

"I sent them out to get us some dinner and to give us some privacy. They will come back in about thirty minutes," Tommy said.

Bailey nodded at him. "Good idea."

Desi switched into her professional mode and explained all the options to Tommy who listened intently to her every word. When she had finished, Tommy looked at Desi. "What would you do?"

"In my professional capacity, I cannot answer that, but in my personal opinion, I would go for the plea bargain agreement and put this behind you."

Then he looked at Bailey. "Your opinion, baby sis?" he asked her.

"Well, since the case doesn't include the death penalty for Whitlock, bastard that he is, I agree with Desi. Even a few years in prison will seem a lifetime for him."

"You said we could have the hearing Wednesday and been done with this forever," he said to clarify.

"Yes. ADA Bartlet has already got a two p.m. docket time for us on Wednesday if you agree, but we need to plan on being on hand all day in case schedules change," she warned.

"Let's do it then," Tommy said. "What do I need to do?"

Desi told him the ADA would have some paperwork he would need to sign and that he would need to be present to give his agreement to the judge when asked.

"I won't have to testify or anything?" he asked.

"No, just give your approval of the agreement and then the judge will hand down the sentences."

"Will they be in the courtroom?" he asked. She knew he was referring to Whitlock and Doogan.

"Yes, they have to be present to receive their sentences," she explained.

"Okay. Let's do this."

Desi nodded. "Okay. Bartlet will call you tomorrow to go in and sign the papers. Now, that's done, so what's for dinner?"

"Chinese and lots of it," he said with a grin.

Tommy was not joking about there being a lot of food. Desi looked at the bags the boys carried into the kitchen and wondered if they had bought one of each dish. An hour later, with less than half of the food consumed, Tommy opened the bag of fortune cookies and started passing them out.

They took turns reading them aloud until it was Desi's turn. When Bailey turned to question her, Desi only smiled and tucked the fortune in her pocket. "You will just have to find out later," Desi said with a grin.

†

Later that evening, Bailey glowed when the door to the club opened and Desi stepped through. "Hi there," she said when Desi took a seat at the bar. "What can I get you to drink?"

"What are you having?"

"The hard stuff, Coke on the rocks." Bailey grinned.

"I'll take one of those," she said.

The club was packed and the customers kept Bailey busy until the lights began to flicker to announce the start of the show. Tommy was returning to performing tonight, so it was a special night for everyone in the club.

Bailey took advantage of the preoccupied crowd to take a dishpan to collect bottles and glasses, which gave Desi and opportunity to talk to Louise in private. She motioned for Louise to come down to the end of the bar.

"I need your help tonight," she said.

"Sure, what's up?"

"The case is virtually over and I can't wait any longer to get Bailey in my bed," she said with a grin.

"Oh, so tonight's the night. Okay, what can I do?"

Desi slipped her a spare key to her house. "Give her this key, which I gave you in case I needed you to check on Fubar sometime and ask her to come wake me when she gets off work to take me to that breakfast she owes me."

"That sounds easy enough," Louise said with a conspiratorial grin.

"Thanks, Louise."

"My pleasure. I will tell her you called her cell after you left and I answered it when she was busing tables and I couldn't find her. Bailey will believe that. She always leaves her cell under the bar."

"That should work great. I'm going to stay for a little while and then go home to get ready."

Louise was about to burst with excitement as she walked away and obviously told Beth the plan. Beth looked over and gave her a thumb's-up. Desi put her finger to her lips to remind Beth to be silent and Beth nodded excitedly.

The show was a huge success, celebrating Marie's return to the stage. Several of the numbers focused on Marie's performance and particularly humorous were her performance of "Call Me Maybe," by Carley Rae Jepson, and Kasey Musgrove's, "Follow Your Arrow." In the latter performance, Nikki and Charlise entertained the crowd with a toy bow and arrow, shooting one another and then several customers with a suction-cupped arrow. The crowd roared with laughter and the tips were plentiful.

Desi had tears running down her face from laughing so hard and she turned to Bailey to find her watching her with a grin on her face.

"See what I grew up experiencing now?" she asked.

"The ladies were hysterical," Desi said as she finished her drink. "If you don't mind, I think I will head home now."

"No problem. You must be exhausted. Thanks for making it a great day," Bailey said.

Desi smiled, thinking of the plans she had for Bailey later. "My pleasure," she said. "See you later." With a wink to Louise, she left the club.

†

Desi took a long shower and dressed in a silky, black, two-piece outfit and then went to the kitchen to light candles and incense. She lit candles in the bedroom and slipped between the cool, clean sheets while she waited for Bailey to arrive. The comfort of the bed quickly took its toll on her and she slipped off to sleep.

†

After the final show, Bailey cleared more tables and when she returned, Louise played her role.

"Oh, there you are," she said, when Bailey walked behind the bar carrying the filled dishpan.

"Hey, what's up?" Bailey asked.

"Desi called and wants you to come by after the club closes to take her to that breakfast that you owe her." Louise played the part perfectly. She reached into her pocket, pulled out a set of keys, took one off, and handed it to Bailey. "She said to come in and wake her when you are ready. She is going to nap until you get there."

Bailey took the offered key and cocked her head at Louise. "What are you doing with a key to Desi's house?"

"Well, I *am* Fubar's Godmother you know. She gave me the key in case she ever needed me to go feed her or check on her if she was running late or got caught up at work."

Bailey bought it hook, line, and sinker as she finished unloading her pan and glanced at the clock. Only another half an hour and they would be closing, she thought with a grin.

Louise nudged her out of the way at the dishwashing sink. "You go. We can finish up here," she said.

"Are you sure?"

"Be gone with you now," she said. Bailey wasted no time leaving the club.

"You played that quite well, my love," Beth said with a quick kiss.

"Tommy's not the only performer in this family," she said and brushed her hair back in a flamboyant fashion with a comical grin.

†

Bailey felt odd sliding the key into Desi's door, but she was following her instructions. She stepped inside, locked the door behind her, and followed the glow of candlelight through the house to Desi's bedroom. She stopped in the doorway and leaned against the doorframe intoxicated by the sight of Desi lying in bed. Her dark hair fanned out across the pillow and her left leg had freed itself from the covers and was lying on top of the bed, giving Bailey a perfect view of her bare leg all the way to her hip.

Bailey felt a sigh escape her as she looked down at Desi's sleeping form. A longing to caress her smooth skin made her hands ache with desire.

Desi's eyes fluttered open to see Bailey leaning against her bedroom doorframe. She stretched seductively and wiped the hair from her face. "I guess I fell asleep waiting for you," she said.

"I was told I was to take you for breakfast," Bailey said with a grin as Desi moved to sit on the side of the bed.

Desi smiled up at her from the bed. "That was just a ploy to get you here," she admitted as she stood and walked to Bailey. "It's time," she said.

"It's time for what?" Bailey asked innocently.

"Time for you to open your heart to me," Desi said as her hand stroked down Bailey's face.

"What about—" Bailey started to say, but Desi placed her fingers over her lips to silence her.

"The case is all but done," Desi said. "We no longer have to wait to move our relationship forward if that is still want you want," she said as she leaned forward and kissed Bailey.

Bailey responded to Desi's kiss with equal passion as she realized the time had come for them to initiate a physical relationship. Her hands found their way under the silky fabric of her top. She stroked the soft skin of her back and as the kiss deepened she explored Desi's body. Bailey could feel the trembling of desire deep within Desi's body as her hands roamed further down to cup her buttocks. Desi moaned into her mouth when she gave them a soft squeeze and Bailey felt her heart begin to pound in her chest.

They backed slowly toward the bed as their tongues swirled and danced together. Bailey's hands moved upward to slide the top over Desi's head and drop it carefully to the floor. Her nipples were hardened to chiseled peaks as Bailey's eyes devoured her body. When her eyes rose to meet Desi's, Bailey saw the glitter of excitement, and desire in her eyes and smiled.

She gently lowered Desi to sit on the edge of the bed and as she knelt between her knees her fingertips flowed lightly across Desi's skin. Bailey leaned forward and buried her face in Desi's neck, nuzzling her skin, licking softly while inhaling the scent of her body.

Desi laid her head back, running her fingers through Bailey's hair, pulling her head firmly onto her neck. Bailey's hands covered her breasts, gently kneading her excited flesh. Her lips moved slowly down Desi's neck and across her collarbone as Desi's hands urged her lower.

Bailey wanted to take her time to enjoy Desi's body for the first time and fought her body's urge to move more swiftly.

Desi lifted Bailey's shirt over her head and tossed it onto the growing pile of clothes. Her nails raked lightly over Bailey's back, causing her to moan and sending delicious vibrations across her skin as Bailey's mouth covered her left breast. Standing, Bailey's sports bra followed her shirt and she kicked off her shoes. Lifting Desi to her feet, her hands gently eased Desi's silky bottoms down her hips and off her body. So much for restraint, she thought as Desi's hands eagerly unfastened her jeans and tugged them down her legs, followed quickly by her panties.

Desi pulled her onto the bed on top of her and their mouths and hands explored one another's body deep into the night until finally sated, they collapsed onto their backs. Desi carefully crept from the bed. "I will be right back," she said and disappeared into the bathroom.

When she returned several minutes later, Bailey also decided to give relief to her aching bladder and climbed from the bed. "My turn," she said with a grin.

Bailey drained her bladder and walked to the sink to wash her hands. Her eyes landed on the mirror and smiled back at her as she saw the fortune cookie Desi had received earlier taped carefully onto the mirror. The fortune read, "Tonight, all your dreams will come true." Bailey chuckled when she read the comment Desi had entered in bright red lipstick under the fortune: "They sure were," scrawled beneath it with a smiley face.

"So that was your fortune cookie message," Bailey said as she climbed back into the bed.

"Yes, ma'am," she said as she snuggled into Bailey's body. "You are more than I could have ever dreamed for," Desi said.

"Come here then and let's dream some more," Bailey said and kissed Desi passionately.

When they finally succumbed to sleep, Bailey's body wrapped around Desi's and they slept the morning away.

They finally woke around one and decided to shower and go for a much needed, late breakfast. Afterward, they returned to Desi's home where they spent most of the remaining weekend in bed.

When Monday morning came and they had to separate to go to their respective jobs, both women wore tremendous smiles.

†

Bailey was halfway to Nashville before the smile faded and it took a snarl of traffic to wipe the blissful smile from her face. It did not matter though, she thought. At the end of the day, she would end up in Desi's arms and everything would be right in the world.

†

"Oh, my Lord that looks good on you," Braxton said as Desi entered the room with a smile. "There's only one thing I

215

can think of that will put that kind of smile on someone's face," he said.

"What would that be, smart-ass?" she said.

"Love, love, love," he teased. "I take it the weekend went well?"

"It was fantastic," she said. "Beyond my wildest dreams."

Braxton smiled at the blushing Desi. "Let's get to work then," Braxton said.

Desi settled into work, continuing the project she had started the previous week. She was developing a spreadsheet, entering prime details from each of the cold cases from the last five years on the computer to organize the facts. She had three more cases to enter, and by the time lunch arrived, she had all the data entered. She printed out the spreadsheet and was busy reviewing the data while Braxton went to the deli to purchase sandwiches and sweet tea.

She was flipping page after page of the data sheet looking at items she had highlighted. Desi was shocked by the pattern she saw emerge from the combined data.

She looked up at Braxton when he returned with lunch. "You are not going to believe this," she said, her eyes wide with excitement.

"You solved them all while I was gone?" he said.

Desi waited for Braxton to take a seat and rocked back in her chair. "Not even close. We have a serial killer amongst us."

Chapter 14

Desi sat in her chair, staring at the printouts spread across the table in front of her. She could not believe what she was seeing. Surely she was reading something into the data that really was not there she thought, but as she and Braxton reviewed the spreadsheet, he slowly came to agreement with her.

"Damn, I think you are right. I count fifteen possibilities just in the first ten years," he said. "We need to go back farther," he said as they both turned to look at the wall of boxes that made up the cold cases of the unsolved murders in Memphis over the last twenty-plus years.

"It looks like August is pretty hot for unsolved murders as well as hot weather," Desi said. "At least one in August for every year," she said.

It had taken Desi nearly a week just to catalog the first ten years of their research onto a spreadsheet, and she was not looking forward to another week hunched over her computer screen. "You are going to have to help with this batch," she told Braxton, who flinched at the thought. "I know you are slower, however, we need to focus on this to get the entire spreadsheet done so we know exactly what we are looking at. This guy has obviously been around a while, and we need to find out just how long."

Desi made a copy of the blank spreadsheet while Braxton went to work arranging the boxes in chronological order. "I will get you set up on your computer, but I want you to check on something first," Desi said.

"What's that?" Braxton said, already breaking a sweat from moving the boxes.

"Our killer seems to be consistent with the month of August," Desi explained. "Go back, let's say to 1995, and check August to see if there is a case that will fit this profile," she said as she highlighted several key facts. "We need to try to find out when he started killing."

"What if I find a case in '95?" Braxton asked.

"Then we keep moving backward in time until we find a year with no August murders. Logically, that should give us at least a rough starting point, but just to be safe, let's go two years with no August hits."

"That alone may take me a full day," he said.

"It just might. Would you rather start entering data?"

"No, I will gladly take the cases," Braxton said as he opened a box from 2002 where they had left off. It did not take long to find the case both he and Desi feared would be there.

Desi began entering data on a new spreadsheet and contemplated whether they should ask for more assistance. However, she decided to wait until they had definitive information before asking for help. The last thing they wanted was a reputation for being premature in their analysis. They needed to have as much data as possible when they decided to approach Lieutenant Dawson, head of the detectives in their precinct, with their theory of a serial killer. Desi knew the first thing they would have to do once they could convince him of the possibility was to call the FBI into the case. It was already apparent from the first cases that the killer had abandoned his victims in multiple states, making it a federal offense.

Desi took a break to stretch and walked over to a calendar hanging on the wall. She walked back to her desk to check some data, and then turned to Braxton. "Hey," she said to gain his attention.

Braxton had just finished placing yet another box on the table and was rummaging through to find August cases. "What's up?"

"If the pattern holds true, like it looks like it just might, then we have less than four weeks before his next murder," she said, tapping at the calendar. "He usually strikes one to two days before or after the sixteenth."

"Are you thinking, what I'm thinking?" he asked.

Desi nodded. "I think so. We need to focus on the August cases. We can always go back to finish the rest of the cataloging."

"I'm so glad you can read my mind," Braxton said.

"You are like an open book to me," she teased back. "What year are you on now?"

"I'm just about to start on 1996," he said.

"I will take that one if you will work on 1995."

Braxton grunted but got up to locate the box he needed. By late afternoon, they had reviewed back to 1992, with all but one year 1993, having a murder to fit the profile. As they had agreed, they went back for another two years until they felt fairly certain that the killings began in 1992.

"It looks like '92 was the first year," Braxton said.

"Every August but 1993 had at least one case that fit the profile," she remarked. "I wonder what happened in August of that year."

"Maybe he was incarcerated," Braxton said.

In total, they had collected twenty-eight possible cases. Desi continued entering the data as Braxton took a few of the cases and began entering them at a much slower pace. At six, Desi's eyes were completely exhausted, and she found herself typing the same sentence repeatedly. She finally pushed back from her chair and said to Braxton, "I think it is time we call it a night."

Braxton rubbed his tired eyes and nodded his agreement. "We can finish up first thing in the morning and start analyzing the data."

They saved their files before shutting down their computers. Desi took a last look at the growing stack of files on the table, then reached for the light, and locked the door. With a deep sigh, she knew that even if they were successful in closing all twenty-eight, hundreds more remained for review. She walked out into the early evening and wondered if Bailey had made it home. She decided she would take her out to dinner.

†

Bailey had showered and dressed in shorts, a soft T-shirt, and sandals while she waited for Desi to return home. She had forgotten to tell her about their dinner invitation. She hoped Desi had not made other plans. She smiled when she saw her lover pull into the driveway and watched as she stepped out of the car.

"Welcome home, sweetheart," Bailey said as Desi walked into the kitchen and into Bailey's waiting arms. "Did you have a good day?"

"A long one, yes, and you?" she answered.

"Not bad. Did you have plans for dinner tonight?"

"I thought I might take you out. I am in no mood to cook," Desi answered.

"I forgot to tell you this morning that we have invitations to go to Joe and Tommy's for dinner. Charles and Tony are going back home to New Orleans, so he invited us over for a goodbye dinner."

"Anything we don't have to cook is fine with me," Desi said. "Do I have time to go change and feed Fubar?"

"Sure. I will pick you up in twenty minutes. Will that be enough time?"

"That will be perfect," Desi said and leaned in for another kiss. "I will see you soon."

Bailey watched as Desi returned to her car with a decidedly fresher bounce to her steps, and smiled.

†

When they arrived at Tommy and Joe's, a half hour later, the music met them at the door, and they entered the kitchen to find the four men in a flurry of activity. "Hey, boys," she said when none of them saw them enter.

"Hey, girlies," Tommy squealed when he saw them. "Grab a beer and get comfy, dinner will be served shortly," he said as he kissed each of them on the cheek.

Bailey went to the refrigerator and took out two bottles of cold beer, then returned to sit at the table beside Desi who took a sip and said, "I wonder if there is anything I can do?"

Bailey chuckled. "Your safest bet is to stay seated right where you are, out of the way," she teased. "Four queens in the kitchen are way more than enough to make spaghetti, salad, and garlic bread."

Thankfully, Desi heeded her advice and leaned back into Bailey's arms as they watched the men dance around each other like a Three Stooges movie. "See, you are safe and sound right here."

Dinner was a resounding success. What Desi had thought were slices of green pepper were actually slices of mild Greek peppers, the ones Bailey was so fond of which gave the spaghetti a slight kick. "Do you two put peppers in everything?" she teased.

Tommy dropped his fork onto his plate in shock. "Do you not like peppers?" he said as his face blanched.

"No, no, I love peppers. I have just never seen them in spaghetti. It's wonderful though," she said.

Tommy relaxed and picked up his fork. "That was close," he said.

"I'm sorry, I didn't mean to upset you," Desi said with embarrassment glowing on her face.

"Oh, no, dearie, I was just worried we had cooked a meal you didn't like," he said with a warm smile.

"Are you kidding? This family hasn't cooked anything yet that was less than fabulous," she said and watched his chest swell with pride.

Bailey smiled without speaking and kept eating. Desi was doing just fine without her intervention. She would have to learn to deal with the sensitivities of the boys in her new family all on her own.

"When are you two going back home?" Bailey asked.

"We are leaving in the morning. We will be back though, as long as the invite is still there," Tony said.

"Silly girl, you two are welcome here anytime," Joe said.

"This has been a very nice break for the two of us, and I hope we can return the favor in the future," Charles said.

"I think we are all due for a road trip to New Orleans," Bailey said.

"That would be really fun," Tommy said. "Especially now all this legal stuff is behind us."

"Even more of a reason to celebrate," Joe said as he placed his hand affectionately over Tommy's.

"Let's make it happen then," Bailey said and looked at Desi who had remained quiet during the conversation.

Desi just nodded, knowing she would have to explain things to Bailey later. If Memphis truly had a serial killer, her life was about to become very busy.

†

When Bailey and Desi made it back to Bailey's house for the night, they snuggled in bed, Desi curling into Bailey's body as Bailey softly stroked her hair. Bailey felt there was something bothering Desi.

"You have been unusually subdued tonight. Is everything okay?" she asked.

"I don't know," Desi said as her eyes lifted to Bailey. "I'm afraid I won't be able to go to New Orleans with you and the boys anytime soon," she answered with tears glittering in her eyes.

Bailey pulled her closer. "What is wrong?"

Desi turned in her arms to look up into Bailey's eyes. "I think I have uncovered something very nasty at work, and if I am right, my life is going to get very busy."

Desi told her about creating the spreadsheet and starting to see a pattern develop that may be indicative of a serial killer who had been killing in Memphis for twenty years undetected.

Bailey cupped her hand under Desi's chin. "That is incredible, and I am very proud of you. Don't worry about New Orleans. We can visit later. Right now you need to focus on work."

Desi was very appreciative of Bailey's understanding. She hoped the additional stress would not be damaging to their budding relationship. She smiled up at Bailey. "Have I told you lately how much I love you?"

Bailey grinned at her lover. "About an hour ago, but I never get tired of hearing it." She reached over and turned out the light, and they loved the night away.

†

After seeing Bailey off to work, Desi left for the precinct early, wanting to get straight back to the spreadsheet. She wanted to have the last cases entered, collated, and printed by the time Braxton arrived. She pushed open the door to their new office to find Braxton steadily typing away.

"Fancy seeing you here this early," she said.

"I couldn't sleep last night thinking about all this," he said. "I have been here since five, and am working on the last file."

"I will get us some fresh coffee while you finish. Then we can merge the files and see what we have," Desi said. A fresh pot had just finished brewing as she stepped into the break room. She quickly poured two cups and returned to Braxton.

When Braxton had finished the last case, he e-mailed his spreadsheet to Desi and watched as she collated the file, sorting out the files they were looking at, and then hit the print button. She looked up to see him watching with anticipation as the pages emerged from the printer.

"How many potential victims did we end up with?" he asked.

"Twenty-eight, just as we expected," she answered.

When the printer finished, Desi removed the two copies and they both sat back to review the data they had compiled.

They had agreed upon five criteria for inclusion into the possible list of victims, and all twenty-eight had met or exceeded the criteria. "This is incredible," Braxton said as he looked at the printout.

"Do you think we have enough to proceed?"

He looked up at Desi. "I have already called the boss. Dawson will be here by eight. If he agrees with us then we will need to meet with the chief as well."

"You can buy us breakfast then," Desi said as she saved the file and printed out a copy for the lieutenant.

They were so excited they could barely eat. At five to eight, they walked back to the precinct and waited on Dawson to arrive.

Dawson was a mountain of a man and had done his time in the streets, earning him the respect of every cop in the precinct. When he walked into their office, his body filled the doorway. Desi looked up and swallowed hard. She would have hated to be a criminal when he was active on the streets, she thought as he walked in to sit across from her.

"I hear you two have something very interesting," he said looking at her.

Desi looked at Braxton, who nodded for her to begin.

"When we started going through files, we thought it would be helpful to create a spreadsheet of all the data," she explained. "Not long after we started this project we started to see a pattern develop and we narrowed our search to specific criteria. These are our results," she said, sliding a copy of the report over to him.

Dawson took the pages and spent several minutes reviewing the data, nodding his head as he flipped from case to case. "This is amazing work," he said as he looked up at them.

"There is one other piece that concerns us and was the reason we abbreviated our search," Braxton said.

"What is that?" Dawson asked.

"The pattern that has developed shows a murder every year within two days before or after August sixteenth. That only gives us a few weeks to prevent another murder," Braxton said.

"I'll be right back," Dawson said and left the room.

Desi looked at Braxton. "Are we sick to be excited about the possibility of a serial killer?"

Braxton broke out laughing. "I asked myself the same thing last night. I look at it as getting justice for a lot of women in Memphis," he said.

"I like that point of view," Desi said with a grin.

When Dawson returned, he said, "Print out another copy and meet me at the chief's office in thirty minutes."

"Yes, sir," Braxton said and Desi started printing as Dawson left the office. "Have you ever been inside the chief's office?"

"No, this will be a first."

"Me too. Grab that copy and our files, and meet me out front. I'm going to brush my teeth and check my hair," she said.

"You look marvelous," Braxton said with a laugh as she left the office.

†

The reception area of the chief's office was opulent. Braxton introduced them to the chief's secretary who ushered them to his office. "He has been waiting on you with Lt. Dawson," she told them as they walked down a short hall.

Chief Bronson was a big man like Dawson and they stood when she and Braxton entered the office. Dawson introduced them and accepted a printed report from Braxton. "Detective Dexter, would you like to present your case?"

Desi had assumed Dawson would take over the presentation, but she cleared her throat and answered. "Yes, Lt. Dawson."

Twenty minutes later, Desi finished updating the chief on the case. He agreed with their assessment, specifically noting the limited time until the peak week of August coming up. He hit the intercom button on the phone. "Jennifer, will you get Rick Jordan, the Tennessee Bureau of Investigations Director on the phone for me please?"

"Yes, Chief," she answered.

"This is great police work," he said to Desi and Braxton. "I'm sure you know, though, that we have no choice but to turn this over to the Feds."

"Yes sir, we knew that would be necessary," Desi said.

"I will insist you be a part of working the case, if you are interested," he teased.

"Of course we are, sir," she said with a broad smile.

A few moments later, Jennifer rang in, "Director Jordan is holding on line one, sir."

"Thank you, Jennifer," he said and punched line one. "Rick, hey, how are you? Good, we are doing well here too. Look, I have something I think you will be interested in," he said. "Yes, two of our best and brightest have stumbled upon a probable serial killer who has been in operation for over twenty years."

He listened for a moment. "That's right, twenty years. They found him while working cold cases. Yes, that would be great. Of course, my folks will be available," he said with a wink to Desi. "Cooper, yes, she would be a great choice. Okay, we will look forward to meeting with them soon. Thanks, Rick."

The chief ended the call with a smile. Director Jordan has suggested a particular Special Agent from Virginia. He will contact the FBI to check her availability and call us back. The chief was excited to possibly have Special Agent Cooper assigned to the case, but withheld the information until he was positive she was available.

He returned to the report while they waited. "This is incredible work," he repeated.

The ticking of the clock on the wall echoed through the room as the group anxiously awaited a return call. Desi found herself holding her breath when the chief's phone rang and he smiled. She let it out and waited patiently until he ended the call.

Bronson grinned and said, "Special Agent Blair Cooper and a consultant will be arriving later tonight and will meet us here at eight tomorrow morning." He then turned to Dawson, "Do you know about Spooky Cooper?"

Dawson had a huge smile on his face. "Yes, I have read quite a lot about her these last few years."

"So you know enough not to call her Spooky?"

"Yes, sir, I do, and I will brief my team for tomorrow," he said.

"I will see you all in the morning then. Great work, folks," he said.

Dawson walked them out of the office. "I think it is time for me to buy you an early lunch. Where would you like to go, Desi?"

Desi looked at Braxton. "RG's sound good to you?"

"I will never turn down Italian, especially when it is free," he said with a chuckle.

Dawson looked at him with a deadly serious face. "Trust me, you will be earning this meal. I need to brief you on the special agent that will be arriving tomorrow, so this will be a working meal."

"Yes, sir," Braxton said.

"Leave your car and we will drop back by to pick it up later," Dawson said as they emerged from the building.

Chapter 15

In Virginia, FBI Director Carl Tolsen, picked up his phone, and dialed the number for Special Agent Cooper. When she picked up, he said, "I need you to come to my office. I have the perfect case for you and Tally."

"I'll be there in ten," she said.

†

Blair Cooper hung up the phone and got her briefcase together for a meeting with the director. Blair, was second generation FBI, following in the footsteps of her father Thomas, who was an FBI legend. Early in her career, when she worked under the tutelage of her father, he introduced her to his secret practice of utilizing a psychic on cases when traditional police work had failed. Unfortunately, a co-worker had overheard a conversation she had with her father's psychic after he retired and she was quickly nicknamed "Spooky," a name she despised as a form of ridicule.

However, her work spoke for itself and she gained the respect of the director by having the largest percentage of closure rates in the department. Director Tolsen continued to challenge her to improve the keen senses she had developed working with her father, and her recent success with a young psychic from north Georgia had won some highly needed positive praise for the department.

"What am I stepping into now?" she said as she picked up her bag and walked to the director's office.

†

She walked into the director's office and he greeted her with a smile. "I have something I think you will be very interested in, Blair," he said as he offered her a seat.

"Thanks, Director," she said as she took a seat and pulled out a notepad. "What did you have in mind?"

"I received a call from the TBI. Two Memphis PD detectives working cold cases think they have stumbled upon a serial killer that has been operating for twenty years."

"Twenty years is a long time to operate without being detected. How many possible victims are we talking about?"

"Twenty-eight, possibly more, but there is a catch," he warned. "The killer has killed during a specific time in August in almost every year since 1992," he said.

Blair's eyes flew to the calendar on his desk. "That's just a few weeks away."

"I want you and Ms. Rainwater to fly to Memphis to determine if we in fact do have a serial case," he said. He handed a piece of paper to her. "You are already booked on a flight to Memphis later tonight."

"Thank you sir," she said as she stood to leave.

"Good luck, and keep me posted."

"Yes, sir, I will call in as soon as we know something," she said and left the office.

†

Blair walked outside and dropped her sunglasses down to shade her eyes. She climbed behind the wheel of her SUV and pulled out her cell phone. When the person on the other end answered, she said, "Pack your bags we are going to Memphis. I'll see you in twenty minutes."

†

Desi, Braxton, and Dawson were secluded from the rest of the customers at a private table. After they had placed their orders,

230

Dawson looked at his two detectives. "Tomorrow you will have the pleasure of meeting Special Agent Blair Cooper, one of the FBI's best. She is second generation FBI, and her father is the legendary Thomas Cooper."

"I have heard about him. He was incredibly successful in profiling and bringing down some of the worst criminals of our time," Desi said.

"Yes, he was, and Blair is quickly filling his footsteps. She works with a very unusual partner that you need to be aware of though," he said. "Tomorrow before we start reviewing the data, I'm sure Special Agent Cooper will meet with you to discuss her partner before you actually meet her."

"Does he have two heads or gross deformities?" Braxton asked.

"No, you big goof, she is a psychic," Desi said, surprising Dawson.

"You're pulling my leg, right?" he asked.

Dawson seemed content to let Desi take over the conversation, so she continued. "No, a couple of years ago she met a young psychic from north Georgia and was able to solve a serial case with the psychic's help. However, there was a twist to the case, though, that most would not know."

Dawson looked intrigued while Braxton was still speechless. "Continue," Dawson said.

"Ms. Rainwater's mother is Native American and was swept off her feet as a young woman by a handsome traveling salesman who got her pregnant, and then disappeared. In actuality, he was returning home to Louisiana to purchase an engagement ring and was involved in a horrific accident." Desi paused, and took a drink of water. "The accident left him damaged goods, and he ended up being the serial killer they hunted. She was able to put two and two together when he kidnapped her, and in the end, she killed her own father."

"Wow," Braxton said.

"You have done your homework, Desi, I'm impressed," Dawson admitted.

"I'm sure there will be other information Agent Cooper shares with us, but that is basically all I know."

†

When they had finished their meal, Dawson took them back for their car. "You were both in early this morning, so I suggest you go home and get some rest. The next few weeks promise to be brutal," he added.

Braxton drove them back to the precinct. "Did you ever imagine we would be collaborating with the FBI on a case like this?" he asked.

"Not in my wildest dreams," Desi said as she looked out the window.

†

Bailey's run had gone well and she was approaching Memphis when Desi called. "Hey, baby," she said when she answered the phone.

"Hello, my love, are you almost home?"

"Very nearly, why do you ask?"

"I stopped by the butcher shop and bought two beautiful steaks I thought you might grill for us," Desi said.

"That sounds delicious. Will you take them to my place to get them soaking in the marinade I have in the fridge, and check my supply of charcoal?"

"I will indeed. What would you like to go with them?"

"A nice salad and some steamed veggies sounds good to me."

"I will handle that part if you will grill the steaks."

"Deal. I will see you as soon as I can get there."

"Be safe," Desi said and hung up.

Bailey looked at the time. It was odd that Desi was home this early in the day; she hoped nothing was wrong. She considered calling her back to find out and then realized if something had happened, Desi would have told her already.

†

Blair arrived home to find Tally packed and ready to go. She gave her a rundown on the case as she packed her bag and supplies for the trip.

"I have never been to Memphis," Tally said, "but I hear it can be a rough place to live."

"It was a beautiful town back in the day, but sadly most of the southern charm has left the city," Blair responded. "It's still a great place for Blues and barbecue. Maybe we will catch a glimpse of Elvis," she teased. "I hear he still walks the grounds of Graceland."

"Very funny," Tally said and punched her in the arm. "Are we going to grab a bite to eat on the way to the airport?"

"Yes, I thought we might. It will be late when we arrive in Memphis."

"Can we get Japanese?" Tally asked.

Blair chuckled. Tally had never eaten sushi until last year, and now she could not seem to get enough. "Japanese sounds great."

†

Bailey made it home safely and walked over to light the grill before she went inside. Desi was making a salad when she walked in through the kitchen.

"Welcome home," she said and stepped back from the sink to give Bailey a kiss. "Do you want to shower, change clothes, and meet me on the deck for a cold beer?"

"That sounds heavenly," Bailey admitted and left for the shower.

†

"I always hate this part," Tally said as she reached over and grabbed Blair's hand as the jet accelerated for takeoff.

"Relax. We will be in the air in a few seconds and you can curl up next to me for a nap," Blair said.

Tally smiled up at her. "I'd like that."

Once they were airborne, Blair lifted the armrest between them and allowed Tally to snuggle in next to her as she wrapped an arm around her. "I will wake you before we land," Blair said and kissed the top of Tally's head.

Tally enjoyed the warmth of Blair's body and slipped into sleep with Elvis and sushi on her mind. What a strange pairing she thought briefly, and then thought no more.

✝

Bailey closed the lid on the grill and returned to sit beside Desi. She took a drink from her beer and said, "So this FBI agent and her consultant friend are lesbians?"

"Yes, that's the rumor," Desi answered. "I hope you will have a chance to meet them while they are here."

Bailey smiled, happy to be included in Desi's world of work. "If the opportunity presents itself, invite them to dinner," Bailey said.

"I will," she said as she entwined her fingers with Bailey's. "I may not be around much these next few weeks."

"I know. I will miss you, but I understand how important this is for you. Would you mind if I brought Fubar to live here until the case is over?"

"I would appreciate that. She is so young, and I hate leaving her alone so much."

"I think we would enjoy one another's company while we wait for you to come home," Bailey admitted.

"Just don't spoil her too bad."

"Me? I would never think of doing that," Bailey said.

"Uh-hm, right," Desi said. "Is it time to start the vegetables?"

"That would be a good idea. The steaks will be ready soon."

"Do you want me to bring you another beer?"

"No thanks, I'm good," Bailey answered and watched Desi slip into the house.

✝

Blair looked down at Tally sleeping curled under her arm and felt the smile growing on her face. She gently shook Tally. "Honey, we are almost in Memphis," she whispered.

Tally's eyes fluttered open and she stretched before looking out the window at the city full of lights. She rubbed the sleep from her eyes and looked back at Blair. "Is that really a Pyramid I see?"

"Yes, it is. It's a large convention center on the banks of the Mississippi," she explained.

"The Big Muddy," Tally said with a note of sadness in her voice. The Mississippi River reminded Tally of difficult memories.

"Yes, the Big Muddy," Blair said and pulled Tally closer.

†

Blair was pleased to see a man from the rental company holding up a sign for them as they entered the baggage claim. "Good evening," he said warmly. "I have your vehicle waiting for you outside."

"Thank you," Blair said. "I can't wait to get to the hotel and hit the sack."

"I can understand," he said. "The paperwork is in the glove box, and if you point out your bags I will load them for you."

True to his word, the man loaded their bags, and Blair tipped him nicely for his service. "Thank you," she said as she climbed inside the SUV.

"The GPS is already programmed to your hotel," he said and closed the door behind her.

The traffic that time of night was light, and thirty minutes later, they checked into the hotel and were ready for bed.

"Will you go in first tomorrow?" Tally asked.

"Yes, that usually makes people a little more comfortable. Do you mind?"

"No, not at all, will you hold me until we fall asleep?"

Blair answered the question by wrapping her arms around Tally and kissing her deeply. Tally relaxed and laid her head on Blair's chest. Blair listened to her breathing slow and deepen as she fell asleep. "Sweet dreams, baby," she whispered and closed her eyes.

Chapter 16

"Good luck with your big day today," Bailey said then kissed Desi. "I am very proud of you."

Desi looked into Bailey's eyes. "Thank you. I don't know when I will be home, but I will call you later today if I can."

"I will go by after work and pick up Fubar and we'll be waiting for you."

"I'm jealous already. I know she will be snuggled up with you."

Bailey chuckled. "That's okay, love, we'll save plenty of snuggling for you."

"Be careful and I will see you soon," Desi told her as they walked to Bailey's Jeep. Desi watched her leave then walked home to feed Fubar and get ready for work. She was both excited and terrified about what this day would reveal, and how it was destined to change her life.

†

Desi drove to the precinct and rode to the chief's office with Braxton and Dawson. "Are you two ready to be plunged into the world of the FBI?" he asked.

"I think so," Braxton said timidly.

"We don't have much choice now," Desi said.

"You can always ask to be reassigned and let someone else work with the Feds," Dawson said.

"Hell no, sir, we have come this far, we need to ride it to the end," Desi said.

Dawson smiled. "That's more like it."

†

When they arrived at the chief's office, Desi noticed a young Native American woman sitting in the reception. She was wearing dark sunglasses and had a lock of white hair over her left eye. This has to be Tally Rainwater she thought as Jennifer waved them into the chief's office.

†

Blair Cooper sat next to Chief Bronson and Desi felt her eyes on her, sizing her up as she took a seat across from her. She smiled at her when their eyes met and the chief began the introductions.

"Good morning, and thanks for inviting us in to review this case with you. If the data reveals what we think may be a serial killer then we will be working closely for an indefinite amount of time," Blair said. "Before we get started, and you meet my partner, I wanted to give you some background on her." She took a sip of her coffee, and continued. "Tally Rainwater has the gift of second sight. Some people call her a psychic, but make no mistake, she is not the kind of psychic you meet on a telephone hotline," she said very seriously. "While some in law enforcement scoff at the prospect of using psychics, I have personally witnessed her abilities, and the results that have come from her talents. If either of you have any concerns about working with a psychic, I would invite you to leave now." She looked at Braxton and then at Desi. Neither made a twitch to leave.

"Very well," she said with a smile. "There are a couple of things I need to make you aware of for your comfort and safety. Tally was born with two different colored eyes that some call Demon Eyes, but let me assure you, there is nothing evil about her." She paused briefly. "Tally's mother is full-blooded Cherokee and claims the source of her second sight was revealed when her eye color changed as an infant, but her abilities didn't fully appear until the summer she turned twelve, when she was near fatally struck by lightning."

"Wow," Desi said.

"People have a tendency to react strangely to her eyes so Tally typically wears dark sunglasses to hide them, and to also protect them. The damage from the lightning strike made her eyes very sensitive to light." Blair took another drink and looked at Desi and Braxton. "Lightning also serves as a conductor of her abilities. When a storm is about, Tally may seem to be in a trance, or appear to be suffering some form of seizure. I want you to know she is completely safe from harm and you do not have to render emergency assistance. I tell you this because as a team, we will be traveling together and you need to be aware. Are there any questions?"

"No ma'am," Desi said, and Braxton shook his head.

"Very well. Chief, will you invite Tally to join us?"

Bronson called Jennifer and asked her to bring Tally into his office.

Tally Rainwater took a seat beside Blair who introduced the others. She remained quiet and shyly nodded her acknowledgment of each person with a soft smile.

"Now, I understand you have some data you would like us to review," Blair said. She sat back as Desi presented the data she had shared with Dawson and Bronson. "It does sound like you are on to something here. Can we review the case files?" she asked.

"Yes, you can," Desi said. "They are back at our office."

"Chief, if you will excuse us, we will get to work," Blair said and shook his hand. "Detective Dexter, would you care to ride with us?" she offered.

"Sure," Desi said and the group left the office.

†

When they were safely inside the SUV, Blair looked at Desi in the rearview mirror. "It is apparent you have been the lead in putting this information together. Good work."

Desi was quick to say, "Braxton and I work as a team, but yes, I was the first to notice a pattern develop. It took us almost a week to put the data together from the cold case files."

"Your work on the spreadsheet was brilliant," Tally said, her soft voice surprising Desi.

"Thank you," Desi said, slightly embarrassed.

"Is there anything that you haven't shared with us yet?" Blair asked.

"No other facts, but I am desperately trying to determine what is so special to him about August, that week to be exact," she admitted.

"Yes, that will be crucial to the hunt," Blair said. "We will discover that together."

†

They reached the precinct and Desi got them set up in their office. Dawson came in briefly to welcome them and said, "If there are any additional resources we can provide, please do not hesitate to ask."

"Thank you, Lt. Dawson," she said.

When he left the room, Braxton picked up the box of files and placed them on the table.

"I would like the file of the first victim to review," Blair said. "Can you retrieve a large map of the city and post it on that wall?" she asked Braxton as she pointed to an empty wall.

"Yes ma'am," he said and left the room.

Then she turned to Desi. "Will you go back to your spreadsheet and bring up all the locations of the dump sites?"

"That shouldn't be a problem."

"I would assume you have a large dry erase board we can use as well," Blair said.

"Sure, I can get one delivered," Desi said.

"That would be great," Blair said.

Desi left the room to request the dry erase board, and then returned to her computer.

Blair picked up the file on Dorothy Smith, and began to read the file.

Desi noticed Tally studying the list of names from the printout for several minutes, and then she picked up the spreadsheet and removed her sunglasses.

When one of the other detectives brought in a dry erase board on wheels, Blair walked over to it and wrote down question one. "Why August?" she wrote in bright green print.

†

Lisa Evans, a victim from a previous serial murder case, acted as Tally's spirit guide. She asked to remain to assist Tally with the spiritual realm after the case and had become an invaluable asset.

Tally scanned the list of names in the left-hand column of the spreadsheet until her eyes focused only on one name,

Melissa Spears. She closed her eyes and concentrated on the name as she used her subconscious to call Lisa to her.

"This is very interesting," Lisa said inside Tally's mind.

"I hope you have been listening," Tally said.

"Yes, I have since you invited me back this morning," Lisa answered.

"The name Melissa Spears pulls me. Is she here?"

"Give me time, and I will see if I can find her."

"Hurry," Tally said and opened her eyes.

Tally opened the file on Melissa Spears. Identified as the potential second victim, Melissa, abducted on August 15 and found murdered on August 16, 1994. Melissa had been twenty-four when she was murdered. Tally opened the envelope containing photographs, and the face of a beautiful, young, brown-haired woman smiled back at her in the first photograph. The file stated Melissa was a third-grade teacher, reported missing by her mother when she did not return home from school. She continued to look through the photographs and found it odd that Melissa was clutching a small brown teddy bear in her dead hands.

Tally went back to the file to search for any mention of the teddy bear. Other than a brief mention in the crime scene inventory there was no further mention of it in the investigation.

Blair, seated at the opposite end of the table, smiled as she watched Tally pick up a pen to scribble a note on a pad of paper. She knew her lover had discovered something that had caught her interest.

"Got it," Braxton said as he walked back into the room carrying the map, shattering Blair's concentration.

"We need pushpins, preferably colored ones," she told him. He put the map on the table and went to his desk drawer to remove a container.

"Here we go."

"I want you to hang the map on the wall, and then use the pushpins to locate each of the dump sites. How is your handwriting?" she asked.

"Horrific," Desi said as she approached carrying another printout.

"Okay, so Braxton can pinpoint the locations. I want you to note each site by date and initials of the victims," Blair said. "We have to start from scratch," she said as she went back to her file.

†

Elizabeth Beach was born in Memphis in 1937. She grew into a beautiful blond-haired woman, and by the time she reached Humes High School, she was the object of many young boys' desire. She was the captain of the cheerleading squad, and her claim to fame into adulthood was that she briefly dated Elvis Presley, who graduated two years before her. She went on to date, and later wed, the quarterback of the football team, Mark Beach.

Like most women of her era, Elizabeth was beyond a mere fan of Elvis; she was obsessed with everything Elvis. Much to her husband's dislike, she even named their firstborn Aaron, Presley's middle name.

Baby Aaron was even born with dark wavy hair, and after he became a toddler, his mother dressed him up as Elvis for Halloween for another six years. This only intensified Mark's hatred of Elvis and he became less than a model father to Aaron.

He had taken a position as a police officer after high school, and when his storybook marriage turned into a nightmare, he began drinking heavily. His addiction soon caused him to lose his career with the police department. By the time Aaron reached his teens, his father was miserable in a security guard position and began to take his frustrations out on his wife and child in the form of physical abuse.

Aaron had idolized his father until this time in his life, and he showed little emotion when his father was killed in a failed robbery attempt. Fatherless as a young teen, Aaron clung to his mother and became obsessed with gaining her approval. He was a brilliant student, excelling in all of his classes, but his lack of social skills quickly gave him the reputation for being a nerd by the time he entered high school.

He was a beautiful boy and his mother doted on him, sometimes fantasizing he was Elvis's son even though there was no denying his paternity. Aaron learned of this fantasy and imagined what life would have been as the son of the King of Rock and Roll.

Elizabeth had indoctrinated him thoroughly with frequent viewings of every movie Elvis had ever starred in. By his fifteenth year, Aaron could do a fantastic job of impersonating his idol. Even with his good looks, Aaron's dismal lack of social skills prevented him from having the courage to date girls in high school, which suited Elizabeth just fine. She did not want to share her baby with any of those free-spirited young women who would tarnish her baby with the evil music they called disco. So every Friday and Saturday night, they would pop popcorn and share a marathon of Elvis movies.

Their home was a shrine to Elvis, every wall having photographs or some other type of memorabilia plastered across them. For his birthday when he turned seventeen, Elizabeth managed to buy tickets to see Elvis in concert. They had patiently waited in line for two hours to receive an autographed picture, which she framed with the ticket stubs to add to their shrine.

Later that year, the announcement of his death on August 16, 1977, at his beloved Graceland, sent his two most adoring fans into a spiraling train wreck of emotions. The nation mourned the loss of an icon, along with Elvis fans across the world.

Elizabeth Beach would never be the same after that day, and though he tried his best to please his mother, Aaron failed to bring her out of a deep depression. The highlight of their lives post-Elvis was the annual candlelight vigil held outside the gates of Graceland every year on the date of his death where thousands of adoring fans gathered to worship him and celebrate his life.

Fifteen years later, Aaron watched as a golden casket holding his brokenhearted mother disappeared into the ground on a cold January afternoon.

✝

Tally made a few more notes then closed the file on Melissa Spears, after returning the envelope of photographs to an inside pocket. She read over her notes then watched Braxton as he placed each pushpin on the map. Desi danced around him to write the date and initials of each of the victims as Blair had requested. She was staring at the map when she felt a familiar tingling in her head, and she knew Lisa had returned.

"Have you had any luck?" she asked Lisa.

"Yes, I have found her, but she is not ready to speak. She has lost herself in the darkness and it may take a while for her to remember how to speak," she explained.

"I understand," Tally said. *"Please let me know when she is ready."*

"I will," Lisa said.

"Desi," Tally said.

Desi turned away from the map and looked at Tally. She looked directly into her odd eyes and was glad Blair had forewarned them. "Do you need something, Ms. Rainwater?" she asked.

Tally smiled at her warmly. "Please call me Tally. I was wondering if any of the other victims had a stuffed animal at the crime scene."

Blair looked up when she heard the question and waited for Desi's answer.

"There was something in one of the files," Desi said as she walked back to study her list. "Give me a few minutes to see if I can remember which one."

Blair looked at Tally with a question in her eyes, but Tally held up her hand, motioning for her to wait.

Desi was nervous and fumbled with her list as she tried to remember which file she was looking for. She did not want to fail on the first test. When her brain calmed down so she could think clearly, she found the name and walked to the table to pull out a file.

She opened the file for Brenda Wilson from 1996 and pulled out one of the crime scene photos. Desi smiled when she saw the tiny red devil in Wilson's left hand. She handed the photo to Tally. "Brenda Wilson, 1996. Her body was left in a city park just off Beale Street and no one saw anything, which is surprising given the number of people there all during the night."

"Do you have something?" Blair asked.

Tally opened the file from Melissa Spears and pulled out a picture placing it beside the picture of Brenda Wilson. "Maybe a signature item," she said.

Blair smiled at her and walked over to the dry erase board. She picked up the green pen and wrote, Possible Signatures and under that, "stuffed animals or other items left on the body."

Tally looked at Desi. "There was no mention of a teddy bear in the report other than the crime scene inventory. Is there anything in the report of the doll?"

Desi took a seat and opened the case file reading it thoroughly. She found no mention of the devil doll. "Nothing. Not even mentioned in the inventory. It seems to have been completely overlooked."

Braxton had finished placing the pushpins on the map and walked over to join them. Blair looked up at them with a glitter of excitement in her eyes. "You finish labeling the map," she told Desi, "then join us back here. I want to go through all of the crime scene photos to see if other items were left on other victims." She took a sip of water. "Look for anything that just doesn't look like it belongs."

Desi went back to the map as Braxton pulled out a file to start searching. A few minutes later, Dawson came through the door carrying a large bag and a gallon of tea. Desi looked at the clock to find that it was nearly two, and none of them had given any thought to food. "You all need a break and some brain fuel," he said. "Braxton will you get us some plates and plastic cups?" he said.

"Yes, sir," Braxton said.

Blair cleared a spot on the table and Dawson set the bag down and started pulling out sandwiches and chips from the deli.

"Thank you for reminding us to eat," she said.

"No problem. How's it going?" he asked, glancing at the board.

"Slowly, as expected, and we are finding more questions than answers for now, but it's a start. Your detectives have saved us a lot of time by pulling these files together."

"They are two of our finest," he said with pride. "Enjoy your break and let me know if you need anything."

"We will, thanks," Blair said.

Desi settled on a turkey club and ate slowly as she stared at the map, trying to determine if it would show them anything.

Blair caught her staring at the map and softly knocked on the table to get her attention. "Food first," she said with a warm smile. "There will be plenty time later for staring at the map."

"Sorry, there just seems to be something that should be obvious to us," she said and returned to her sandwich.

"When the time is right, it will show itself," Blair assured her. "Patience is a virtue in this game."

"Aw hell, we're screwed then," Braxton said and elbowed Desi, who blushed.

"We all enjoy quick results, but they are far and few between when covering this much material," Blair said.

Desi had placed her cell on the table and she jumped when the vibration from a text message came through. She picked it up, smiling when she saw it was a text from Bailey. Bailey would be home early and wanted to know if she wanted to invite her new work pals home for a home-cooked Italian dinner at eight.

She looked up at Blair with a bit of trepidation. "Do you and Tally have dinner plans tonight?" she asked.

"No, not that I am aware of," Blair said.

"Would you be interested in some home-cooked Italian?"

Blair looked at Tally who smiled and nodded her head. "That sounds wonderful."

"Will we be finished here by eight?"

"We will be brain dead before then," Blair said, and cracked a smile. "Eight would be perfect."

"You will really enjoy Bailey's cooking," Braxton said.

Desi looked at him and said, "You and Donna are invited too."

"We will have to take a rain check tonight. It's our date night and she already has plans, but please tell Bailey I will take any leftovers she might have."

It was Desi's turn to chuckle. "I will be sure to tell her that," she said and texted Bailey. *Two extras for dinner, do I need to pick up anything?*

Two bottles of wine please.

No problem, see you soon. Love you.

Love you too.

Desi put her cell away and cleared the trash from the table.

"Let's try to wrap up the file review by six, if that meets with everyone's approval," Blair said. "We all need a good meal and a full night's rest."

Desi nodded and went back to work on the map, getting all the locations labeled within another twenty minutes. She was eager to dive back into the files. She took the 1997 case of Susan Wright and began studying the report and the crime scene photos. There was nothing left on the body, but something in the coroner's report caught her eye. In the back pocket of the jeans she had worn was a flyer about the candlelight vigil at Graceland, but the flyer was from 1994. "That's odd," she said aloud.

"What is it?" Blair asked.

"It was not on the body, but the coroner's report said there was a flyer for the candlelight vigil that is held every year at Graceland in her jeans pocket. It was dated August, 1994, but she was murdered in 1997."

Blair stood up and noted the flyer on the board.

"What is the candlelight vigil for?" Tally asked.

"Oh, you have lived a sheltered life, my dear," Blair said sweetly. "Every year on August sixteenth, thousands of people flock to Graceland to memorialize the death of Elvis."

"Holy shit," Desi said as a lightbulb came on in her head.

Blair looked at Desi and thought about what she had said about the vigil. "Yes, I think you are spot-on."

"Will someone please fill me in so I can stop feeling like a dunce?" Braxton said as Blair turned and walked back to the board.

"I think, Detective Braxton, we have just uncovered what is so special about that week," she said.

"The dates are all within Elvis Week in Memphis," Desi said.

"Great job, Desi," Blair said as she held out the green marker. "Would you like the honor of writing down the possible answer to our first question?"

Desi flew from her seat to accept the marker and walked to the board. Underneath the question "Why August?" she wrote, "Elvis Week," in bold letters.

"Okay, let's see what else we can find," Blair said as she handed Desi another file.

Two hours later they had written several more items on the board. Braxton had found a case where a lit candle was burning in a victim's hand, while Blair found a necklace with a picture of Elvis on a victim. Tally found the final piece of evidence from the records when she located a carved wooden heart left in the right hand of the victim of 2002. Even more interesting was a dark red spot on the back of the carving that looked suspiciously like dried blood.

Blair added the carving to the list. "We need to get our hands on that carving to see if that indeed was blood. Is there any mention of it in the report?" Blair looked up at Braxton with excitement burning in her eyes. "Braxton will you locate the box this file was in and see if you can find that heart?"

Braxton returned to the stack of boxes while Desi walked over to her laptop and ran a search for Elvis songs. When she looked up smiling, she found both Blair and Tally watching her.

"What did you find?" Blair asked. "I can tell by that grin you've found something."

"I pulled up a list of his music. The 'Teddy Bear' should have been obvious. That was one of his biggest hits. He also had songs called 'Wooden Heart' and 'Devil in Disguise.'"

"I think that confirms that our boy is definitely a huge Elvis fan," Blair said with a grin.

"Just like millions of other people," Tally said to dampen the moment.

"No luck on the heart," Braxton said. "I looked through that box and the others from the year before and after with no luck." It was obvious he was disappointed in his lack of results.

"That would have been way too easy; to find an article with the killer's blood and DNA, even if it was his," Blair said. "Still, we have had an amazing day." She checked her watch to see that it was five thirty. "Let's call it quits for tonight. Good work, team," she said.

Desi wrote down Bailey's address and handed it to Blair after Braxton left. "We will see you at eight. I put my cell number with the address in case you get lost."

"Never fear, we have a GPS," Blair said as they walked to the parking lot together.

✝

Desi was excited about the events of the day and drove past the wine shop. She made a right turn to circle the block, and went inside to find the wine she had selected before. The young man who had waited on her previously was behind the counter and quickly guided her to the right section.

"You must have enjoyed the wine," he said as he rang up her purchase.

"Yes, it was lovely, thank you for suggesting it," she said.

"My pleasure, ma'am," he said, handing her the change. "Come back soon," he said, and Desi waved at him as she walked to the door.

When she arrived home, she placed the wine in the freezer to chill then walked to her bedroom to shower and dress in something more comfortable. The house seemed eerily quiet until she remembered Bailey had come to take Fubar to her house. Funny how she had gotten used to the little fur ball meeting her at the door so quickly, she thought as she stripped out of her clothes to enter the shower.

†

"Not a bad start to the case," Blair remarked as she drove back to the hotel.

Tally smiled up at her. "I just wish Melissa was in shape to talk. I think she could be very helpful in giving us some answers."

"Do you think a more recent victim would be in better shape?"

"That's a possibility we may have to pursue, but for some reason, her name stood out for me," Tally said.

Blair smiled and reached over to take her hand. "Stick with your gut instinct then, you are usually right."

"You really seem impressed with Desi," Tally said.

Blair chanced a look over at her lover and saw a worried frown. "She appears to be intelligent and has a keen sense about her."

"I think she's a bit intimidated by you," Tally said.

"I know. I felt that too, that's why I'm glad we could join Desi and her partner for dinner. I hope it will put her at ease."

"Her partner? Desi is gay?" Tally said.

Blair could not help but chuckle at Tally. "Remind me to polish your gaydar antennae when we get to the hotel. Yes, she is a lesbian."

Tally huffed and crossed her arms across her chest in a pout. "I don't have gaydar," she growled.

"And you don't need it. I'm the only woman you need to be concerned with," Blair teased, bringing a smile to Tally's face.

When they reached their room, Blair asked, "Do you want to shower together?"

"No, you go ahead. I'm going to just chill for a few minutes if that's okay."

Blair smiled at her. "No problem at all. Relax, and I will be out shortly."

Tally sat in a comfortable chair and laid her head back to relax. She closed her eyes, and into the darkness, she called for Lisa.

"Are you there, my friend?"

Tally could feel the buzz of the tingling sensation grow behind her eyes that alerted her to Lisa's presence.

"Yes, I am here, Tally."

"Have you paid attention to today's events?"

"Yes, I have, and I am happy to report some progress with Melissa, but she is not quite ready for your questions. Hopefully soon though," Lisa said.

"That is very good news. We sure could use a description or name of the person who killed her."

"He seems the very despicable type from what I heard today. I hope you can catch him soon."

"Me too, Lisa, thanks for your help."

"You're welcome. I'll do what I can with Melissa to help bring her along."

"Thanks. Let me know when you feel she is ready."

"I will, Tally," Lisa, replied. "Enjoy your evening and get some rest."

"Yes, Mom," Tally teased, but Lisa was gone.

Blair walked out of the bathroom towel drying her hair, and for an instant, thought Tally was asleep until she lifted her head at the sound of her approach. "Mmm, you smell nice," she said, looking up at Blair.

"Thanks, I feel a lot better too."

Blair slipped into Tally's lap and the towel she had wrapped around her body came open. "You're looking mighty tasty too, ma'am," Tally said as she leaned forward to run her tongue across Blair's erect nipple.

"Eat first and then we will come back for dessert," Blair said as she ran her fingers through Tally's hair.

"You know I like doing things in reverse order," Tally said with a grin.

Blair smiled at her. "Yes, dear, I know, but we have a dinner date, remember?"

"Yes, yes, I know," Tally said. "Food first." She ran her fingers down Blair's arm. "I talked with Lisa, but Melissa is still in no shape to talk yet. Hopefully she will be by tomorrow."

"It would be nice to get some information about her killer," Blair said. "I guess that will come in due time."

"Do you think we will catch him?"

"With you on my team, how could we not?" Blair said and kissed the top of her head.

"Thanks for the vote of confidence. Now, madame," she said with a smile, "if you will kindly remove thyself from my lap, I will go shower so we can feed that stomach of yours."

Blair stood, pulled Tally up from the chair, and kissed her before she made her way to the shower, then turned to find something comfortable to wear for the evening. Settling on jeans and an oxford, she dressed quickly and went to finish in the bathroom while Tally showered.

Chapter 17

Desi dressed and walked the short distance to Bailey's. She found her in the kitchen, the front of her shirt covered in flour as she finished making the pasta. The sauce was simmering on the stove. "It smells fantastic in here," she said as she walked over to Bailey and kissed her. "I have to admit though, you look comical with all that flour on you," she teased.

"I had a bit of an accident with the flour," Bailey admitted.

"Oh really," Desi smirked.

"Do I have time for a quick shower?"

"Sure go ahead, I will get the wine ready, while you are gone."

Bailey reached over and turned the heat down on the sauce. "Don't let it scorch, and put a big pot of water on to boil for me please," she said.

"You got it, boss," Desi said.

"I'll be back shortly then," Bailey said and kissed Desi.

†

Bailey finished dressing and walked back into the kitchen to see Desi standing on her tiptoes to stir the sauce. "Is my sauce safe?"

"Yes, my dear, I have been tending it well," Desi said as she turned to face Bailey. She had Fubar tucked under her left arm.

"I bet she was glad to see you," Bailey said as she scratched under the kitten's neck.

"She hasn't stopped purring since I picked her up."

Bailey walked to the stove to check the water and added a pinch of salt and a dollop of olive oil. "She has found her way into the bay window in the front of the house and took a long nap in the sunshine earlier."

"She seems perfectly content here," Desi said.

"Just like her mama, I hope."

"Yes, most definitely," Desi said as she placed Fubar on the floor and wrapped her arms around Bailey's neck.

Chuckling, Bailey was leaning down to kiss Desi when she heard a knock at the door. "Would you like to go welcome our guests?"

Desi answered by taking her hand as they walked to the front door. Bailey opened the door and guided Blair and Tally inside. Blair made it safely into the room but Fubar ran to see what the excitement was all about and tangled up in Tally's feet. She stumbled forward directly into Bailey's arms.

Bailey caught her, preventing a fall, and felt a tingling sensation from Tally's hands as she struggled to right herself. "Easy there," she said and looked into Tally's unique eyes.

"Fubar, that is no way to treat our guests," Desi said as she swooped up the kitten. "Are you okay, Tally?"

Her eyes locked with Bailey's and it took several seconds for her to respond. "Yes, I'm so clumsy, but I didn't see the kitten until it was too late," she said as she let go of Bailey's arms.

"I'm sorry, I should have taken her to another room," Desi said.

"Nonsense, this is her home," Tally said with a smile as she reached for Fubar.

Bailey, still frozen in her tracks, snapped back to reality and closed the door behind them. She had no clue what had just transpired, but felt that she and Tally had just shared a moment of some sort.

"Okay, let's try this again. My name is Bailey, and welcome to our home. This fur ball is Fubar," she said, pointing to the kitten. Bailey shook hands with Blair and Tally.

"That's an odd name," Tally said.

"You can tell that story while I pour the wine," Bailey said. She entered the kitchen as Desi told the story of Fubar.

"So your family owns a gay club and your brother is a female impersonator?" Tally asked as Bailey handed her a glass of wine.

"Yes. Louise, my cousin, owns the club and Tommy and I work weekends to help out."

"I would love to see a show," Tally said as she looked hopefully to Blair.

Bailey and Desi looked at her too. "I'm sure we could work that into our schedule," Blair said.

"Come by this weekend, and your drinks will be on the house," Bailey said. "Are you three hungry?"

"Starving," Blair said with a smile, and Bailey grinned back at her.

"I will start the pasta and bread, if you want to migrate to the kitchen."

"Just follow that heavenly smell," Desi said. "Is there anything I can help with?"

"You can set the table. Other than that I think I have everything under control," she said as she placed the pasta into the boiling water.

"Braxton said to tell you he calls dibs on any leftovers," she told her.

"He is such a hound," Bailey said with a smile as she began slicing the chicken breasts.

"I am jealous of a woman who can cook from scratch," Blair said as she leaned against the counter, watching Bailey.

"I love to cook when I have the time," Bailey said with a smile. "It also helps to have people who enjoy a good meal to cook for."

"What do you do?" Blair asked.

"I drive a route for FedEx from Memphis to Nashville," she said.

"One of the big rigs?" Blair asked.

"Yes. I generally drive a tandem set of trailers on a daily turn and burn."

"Turn and burn?" Blair asked.

Bailey smiled. "I drive to Nashville, drop the two trailers, pick up two others to go back to Memphis."

"Ah, I see now. That must be very enjoyable," she said.

Bailey smiled at her comment. "I enjoy the freedom of being out on the road, and I get to see a lot of things I couldn't see sitting behind a desk all day."

"I can see the advantage of that," Blair said.

"How long have you worked with the FBI?"

"It feels like all my life. Father was an agent until he retired, so I spent a lot of time with him as I grew up. I've been on the government payroll for ten years though, to answer your question."

"That must be a really exciting career choice."

"Never a dull moment," Blair said and took a sip of her wine. "This wine is delicious."

"You can thank Desi for that. She is the wine buyer in this family."

"A very good selection," Blair told Desi.

"I have made a good friend of a competent young man at the wine shop," Desi admitted.

Desi went to the refrigerator, took out a pitcher of tea, and poured Bailey a glass for dinner. "Would anyone else like tea with their meal?"

"Yes, please," Tally said. "It's hard to find good tea on the road."

"I think I will stick with the wine," Blair said and Desi refilled her glass.

"You can pull out the salad," Bailey said. "The pasta will be done in just a few. Bring the plates over to me and I will serve from the stove if you two don't mind."

"Not at all," Blair said.

Desi took the bowl of chilled salad to the table and returned for dressing. She smiled when she found bottles of ranch and blue cheese to complement Bailey's standard honey mustard.

The garlic bread finished toasting and Bailey pulled it from the oven to slice it into generous helpings. After straining the pasta, she placed generous portions on their plates, added the chicken, and then the Alfredo sauce.

"This looks wonderful," Tally said.

"It tastes even better," Blair said after swallowing a bite.

"There is plenty, so eat all you want," Bailey said.

They shared the meal with light conversation and Blair surprised herself with a smaller second portion. "Braxton was absolutely right about your cooking. This is the best meal I've had in a while."

"I will second that," Tally said with a shy smile to Bailey.

Bailey had caught Tally sneaking looks at her throughout the meal, and she was dying to ask her what she saw when they touched at the door. Bailey was convinced the psychic had seen something while they were in contact. Finally, her curiosity got the best of her. She took a drink and asked, "Tally, may I ask you a question?"

Tally looked up at her without blinking. "You want to know what I saw when we touched?"

Almost embarrassed, Bailey said, "Yes, if you are willing to tell."

Tally smiled at her. "I only see the past or present. I do not see the future. When you caught me to keep me from falling, I saw a beautiful woman who was special to you. I believe her name was Nessa." Tally paused for a moment. "She was taken from you by violence. I also saw a young man, who I believe is your brother, who was severely beaten. I hope he is well now."

Bailey's mouth hung open. She was sure Desi had not told either of them about Nessa or Tommy, and the shocked look on Desi's face confirmed that. She managed to close her mouth and swallow hard before speaking.

"Nessa was my partner, and, yes, she was murdered in a carjacking two years ago. Desi and Braxton opened up her case and managed to solve it for us recently. The man you saw beaten is Tommy. He is well physically, but I feel he has not completely healed emotionally. That was when Desi and I met."

Blair smiled at the still gaping Desi. "Now do you see why she is a joy to work with?"

"That is incredible," she finally managed to utter.

Blair reached over to hold Tally's hand. "She is a remarkable woman."

"How did you know her name?"

"That is very personal to you, but if you wish I will share the information," she said to Bailey.

"Please, I need to know," Bailey said.

"I saw you dreaming of her and when you woke, you called her name."

During the last two years, there were many nights when she woke, just as Tally described.

"I'm sorry but I have to ask one more question."

"Go ahead," Tally said.

"Can you speak with her?"

Tally lowered her eyes for a second and Bailey was afraid she had offended her. "I'm afraid not, she is no longer in the darkness. Her spirit has moved on recently."

Desi could see the tears in Bailey's eyes, but she could not tell if they were from sadness or joy. She hoped they were of the latter. Reaching over she placed a comforting hand on Bailey's arm.

Tally's eyes flicked to Desi and then back to Bailey. "She loved you very much, and would be pleased to see you happy."

"Thank you," Bailey said.

"You are very welcome," Tally answered.

"Does it always work like that for you? By touch I mean," Desi asked.

"Touching the person or often an item that belonged to them; I'm sure Blair also told you about the visions I have when there is lightning in the air."

"Yes, she did," Desi said. "Incredible."

"I want to thank you both for inviting us into your home," Tally said. "A lot of people get freaked out by my abilities, but you have made me feel welcome."

"You are welcome to come as often as you can while you are in Memphis. I have enjoyed having you for guests."

"She can cook a pretty mean steak too," Desi said.

"Hopefully we will have a chance to find out," Blair said.

"Will you be working Saturday?" Bailey asked.

"That depends on the how the case develops, but probably," Blair answered.

"I have to work at the club at eight, but I could cook before I go to work," she offered.

"My new friend, you have yourself a deal," Blair answered. "May we help you clean up before we go back to the hotel?"

"Absolutely not, I made the mess, so I will clean it myself."

"That really was a fantastic meal, but I'm afraid we need to call it a night to get some rest," she said.

"Thank you for joining us tonight." Desi looked at Tally. "Maybe after dinner Saturday we can go to the club to see the early show. It starts at ten doesn't it, Bailey?"

"Yes, it does, and we would love to have you at the club."

Tally's strange eyes sparkled when she answered Desi. "I would really like that."

They walked their guests to the door. "I will see you in the morning," Desi said.

"It was a pleasure to meet you, Bailey," Blair said. "Desi is a lucky woman."

Bailey chuckled. "I think I'm the lucky one to have her in my life."

†

Working together, they had the kitchen cleaned in record time, including a container of leftovers for Braxton. When they undressed for bed, Bailey reached down to pick up Fubar and place her on the bed.

Desi understood that tonight had been an emotional night for Bailey, and when Bailey laid her head on her chest with tears freely flowing, she held her, and stroked her softly until she cried herself to sleep. Desi could find no words to soothe the ache Bailey must have been feeling.

†

After making love Tally lay wrapped in Blair's arms, listening to her steady heartbeat. "Do you think I was too honest with Bailey tonight?"

Blair kissed the top of her head. "No, I think Bailey needed to hear what you saw. Your words may be cathartic in her healing process."

"She has had a difficult few years. She seems like such a sweet person," Tally said as her fingers traced circles on Blair's stomach.

"Hopefully her luck is changing. Bailey certainly seems smitten with Desi."

"I thought their little touches and quick glances at one another at the dinner table were precious. I'm not sure they realized they were even doing them."

"Young love," Blair said with a heavy sigh.

"Are you happy with me?" Tally asked.

Blair repositioned her body so she could look into Tally's eyes. "I have never been happier in my life. I love every second we spend together."

"I'm sorry, I must be feeling a little insecure," she said.

"We all have moments like that, but please don't doubt my love for you. You are the best thing to ever happen to me."

"Thank you for loving me the way that you do," Tally said and snuggled back into Blair's body.

†

Aaron Beach drove the short distance to his job. After his mother's death, he had little ambition in life and took a job at the security firm where his father had worked. It was easy work; he drove around several businesses on a routine schedule. Sometimes it would be an hour or more before he saw another person. He had very little supervision from his boss and was able to travel to other parts of town without detection to scout for his next project.

He was in an excellent mood tonight. His boss had told him the firm won the contract to work as foot patrols during the candlelight vigil at Graceland, keeping adoring fans from trespassing on the property or vandalizing Elvis's shrine. He drove past Graceland and smiled as the eternal flame on the grave made shadows dance in the night.

When Aaron drove back to the warehouse on his route, he spotted a secluded driveway that led to a small park area overlooking the river, which he thought may have great possibility for his plans. He smiled and slowly circled the warehouse, his spotlight searching for any sign of trespassers. His light sometimes scared up a raccoon or possum that was looking for an easy meal, and once in the winter, he encountered a homeless man that ended up floating in the Big Muddy after Aaron finished dealing with his infringement onto his territory. The word must have circulated, because even in the worst of weather, the bums did not dare to take shelter on his property.

Chapter 18

For the next week, the team put in long hours as they slowly pieced together the evidence they had to work with. Tally's frustration mounted each day. Melissa was still no closer to speaking than the day Lisa had found her and Lisa was having difficulty finding a more recent victim.

†

On Wednesday, Braxton made an appearance at the courthouse for the hearing on Tommy's case. They had decided that it would be best if he made the appearance while Desi continued working with Blair and Tally. She had no doubt she could have maintained a professional demeanor, but there was no need for her to be present. Bailey understood the reason for her absence and that was all she needed.

When Braxton returned from the hearing, he pulled Desi into the break room to share the results.

"Buster got the 364 days we had assumed he would get, but Harold got the full three years," he told her.

Desi gave him a high-five for the great news. "How did Tommy hold up?"

"He did a great job and it was over quickly."

"That's fantastic," she said as they walked back into the office.

†

Bailey kept her promise to grill steaks on Saturday, and Tally was as excited as a kid at Christmas when she met Joe and Tommy, then watched their performance. She even went onstage to tip both of them in appreciation of their performances. Her face wrinkled into a pout when Blair reminded her that they had work to accomplish the next day, but quickly relaxed when she hugged Bailey and Desi goodnight.

†

Braxton growled in frustration as he stared at the board. He felt like there was something that was waiting to jump out at him, but he was having difficulty finding what it was. Finally, he stood up and announced, "I need a Starbucks. Does anyone else want something?"

Blair had sensed the growing frustration in the room. "I think we will all join you. We need a break from this room."

They walked to the parking lot and climbed into Braxton's car. The group spent an hour sitting in the cool shade outside of the coffee shop before Braxton pointed toward the river. "A storm is moving in for the afternoon," he said with a curious look at Tally. "I think we should go back to the precinct before that hits."

There was no argument from the group as a distant rumble of thunder reached their ears. The winds from the west had picked up, and Braxton thought they would be lucky to be inside before the first drops of rain fell. He was correct. They had just returned to the office when the skies opened, pelting the roof of the precinct with heavy rains.

Blair, Braxton, and Desi returned to their notes while Tally sat back in her chair with her eyes closed. Braxton looked up to watch her. He thought it was a bit macabre that she was clutching the small teddy bear that had taken been from the dead hand of Melissa Spears. He fought off a cold shiver that ran down his spine and returned to his notes.

†

Tally could feel the electricity building in the air and knew the lightning would arrive soon. She closed her eyes and opened her mind, hoping the approaching storm would bring a vision that would jump-start their stagnant case. Everyone in the room needed some fresh information to focus on and soon, as time was rapidly ticking away.

Her grip on the teddy bear tightened as she heard the crack of thunder close by and felt the tingling behind her eyes.

"Is Jasmine Bryan here?" Tally spoke into the darkness *in her mind.*

Tally waited in hopes that the most recent suspected victim would appear. Although she was not one of the August victims, the team felt certain that the killer was one and the same. Minutes passed as lightning struck all around the building, as if it were seeking her out. Many times since her childhood, Tally had worried that she would die from another bolt of lightning, thinking the strike from her childhood acted as a lightning rod for future strikes.

Her concentration on this morbid thought clouded her vision and she did not see the movement deep in the shadows. She called out again. *"Jasmine Bryan, are you here with us in the dark?"*

Lisa showed up at the sound of Tally's voice. "Keep calling her. I feel something happening."

"Jasmine, if you can hear me, I only want to talk to you."

This time Tally could clearly see movement in the darkness, and her heart raced as the outline of a figure formed in the darkness.

"Why are you calling for me?" a beautiful dark-skinned woman asked.

"Because I need your help," Tally said.

Jasmine continued to approach the sound of Tally's voice, which brought her to Lisa. *"You are not speaking to me,"* she said.

"No, her name is Tally, a friend who helps us find our way in the dark," Lisa explained. *"She is a psychic that helps bring those who have harmed us to justice."*

"No one can help me now," Jasmine said mournfully. *"I am just another lost soul."*

"Tally can help you find your way, but she has to have your help. When your killer is found, you can pass through the darkness and be at peace."

"How do you know this?" Jasmine asked with doubt.

"Because she found and punished the man who killed me," Lisa answered.

"Then why are you still here if you are free?"

"Because I chose to stay as Tally's spirit guide, to help her when I can find the lost souls who can help her bring their killers' evil to an end."

Jasmine looked at her with curiosity. *"What does she want?"*

Tally began speaking to Jasmine. "You can tell me about the man who killed you. We think he has killed many and is ready to kill again. You may be able to help us, and keep him from killing any other innocent women."

Jasmine spoke slowly, but with confidence. "He is a security guard. He had been in the club many times, but I never knew his name. The uniform he was wearing that night said Johnston's so I assume that is the company he worked for."

"Can you tell me what he looks like?"

"He was a decent-looking man for his age. I bet he was quite the looker in his younger days."

"How old do you think he is?"

"Late forties, maybe fifty with some gray hair in his black waves. He has dark, smiling eyes."

"Is he white?"

"Yes he is, not a big man though. He wasn't much taller than me, but he was strong."

"That is very good information, Jasmine. Can you help me with something else?"

"If I can," she agreed.

"Help Lisa. See if you can find anyone else killed by this man and see if they have more information we can use. This has to be done quickly; he is due to strike again very soon."

"I will do what I can. Thank you," she said with a bashful smile.

"I will do everything I can to catch him. If you can think of anything else or find anyone who knows more, let Lisa know, and she can contact me."

"I will, I promise," Jasmine said, and the vision faded.

Tally sat up straight in her chair, placing the bear on the table, and began to write. Her excitement drew the team's attention to her and Blair held a finger to her lips. They waited until Tally finished writing and she looked up at them. "I need a drink."

"Water, soda, or coffee," Braxton said.

"Water please."

Desi rushed to the break room for a bottle of water for Tally, twisting the cap off as she returned to the office.

"Jasmine arrived and has provided some information," Tally said after swallowing a long drink of water. "If it is the same killer, our man is probably in his early fifties now, has black curly hair with some light gray in it, and dark eyes. White, medium height, slim build, but strong." Tally took another drink and looked at Blair. "The best part yet is that he is some sort of security guard. She remembered him from the club where she worked. The uniform he wore said Johnston's."

"That's one of the oldest and largest security companies in Memphis," Braxton said. "They probably have a couple thousand employees."

"That's your next assignment. Get us a meeting with whoever we need to talk to about their personnel files," Blair said. "I will call Dawson and get him started on a warrant."

Desi looked at Tally with a huge grin growing on her face. "Great job."

"Thanks," Tally said, pleased that she was finally able to contribute to the efforts of the team.

"What can we do?" Desi asked.

"Go for food. We are bound to have a long night," Blair said.

Desi looked out the window at the raging storm then looked back at Tally. "You stay. No need for both of us to be out in this."

Tally smiled. "I won't argue with you this time," she said as rain lashed the windows.

Desi walked back into the break room and tugged on an all-weather coat before heading into the rain.

†

Bailey frowned as she saw the darkened skies off in the distance and resolved herself to the fact she would hit rain before she made it back to Memphis. She had made good time on the day's run, and had hoped to be home early, but now she would be lucky to make it home before dark.

The flash of lightning across the road miles ahead of her reminded her of Tally, and she wondered how the young psychic would fare in the approaching storm.

Bailey slowed when she saw a school bus coming down the entrance ramp and downshifted the rig further to allow the bus to merge into the flow of traffic. The faces of several young boys pressed against the back windows of the bus, and they pumped their fists up and down to give the sign they wanted her to blow her air horn. Bailey smiled and pulled on the cord to send two blasts of the horn into the heated air, much to the delight of the boys. The exuberance they displayed made her day and she smiled back at them as they waved.

Then time seemed to slow as a horrifying image filled Bailey's vision. The rear axle on the bus snapped and sparks flew up from the pavement as the frame dropped, causing the rear of the bus to begin to fishtail across the highway, careening dangerously to one side as inertia threatened to topple the yellow monster. The driver worked frantically to gain control over the bus. Bailey realized a split second later that she had a deadly decision to make, to hit either the ditch or barrel into a bus full of children.

The bus was sliding sideways blocking both lanes and any hope for a safe escape path for Bailey. Her foot hit the brake and she frantically downshifted as she steered hard to the right. Her rig barreled through the guardrail, barely missing the front of the bus, and plummeted into a ditch. Bailey closed her eyes, preparing her mind for the pain that was sure to come as her body ricocheted around the cab of the truck, barely restrained by the seat belt. She heard and felt the shattering of bones, as a rush of hot liquid filled her eyes and throat when she opened her mouth to scream. The last memory she had was watching the front wheel still spinning as the truck came to rest on its side in a muddy field, and then the darkness came to claim her.

†

Desi had returned with food and they had nearly finished devouring the subs when Tally screamed and clutched at her head. Blair was the first one to her side, kneeling down beside a violently trembling Tally.

"What's wrong?" she asked.

Tally was shaking so badly she could not respond for several long seconds. Braxton had pulled out his cell and was preparing to dial 911 when she looked up at Desi. Her face was void of any semblance of color as she locked eyes with Desi. "Call Bailey," she croaked and then fainted.

Blair was barely able to prevent her from tumbling out of the chair until Braxton stepped in to assist in leaning her back in the chair. "I have her," he told Blair. "You need to help Desi," he said as he looked at his partner whose face was ashen and she was beginning to hyperventilate.

Blair swiveled to Desi. "Easy now," she said. "Slow your breathing," she coached and reached for Desi's drink. "Take a sip," she said.

"What the fuck?" Braxton said as he held Tally upright. Blair could see the panic in his eyes.

"I have no clue," Blair said.

Chapter 19

Miraculously, the bus driver was able to manhandle the bus to a stop halfway onto the shoulder of the road. He breathed a sigh of relief until he looked to his right to see the overturned truck lying in the muddy field. He turned to find the children shaken but safe and looked at the closest adult who had volunteered to chaperone the trip. Her face was ashen with fright but she was unhurt. "Can you get the kids off the bus safely?"

She nodded and he sprang to action, prying the jammed door open and rushing toward the truck. He heard a siren in the distance and saw a state patrol car screaming down the shoulder of the road.

Two other truckers had jumped from the cabs of their trucks to give aid to a fellow driver while a third directed traffic slowly beyond the damaged school bus. The bus driver was the first to arrive at Bailey's truck. He carefully climbed onto the overturned truck and peered inside the window. There was blood everywhere and he had to force back the urge to turn and empty his stomach. He heard a cell phone ringing inside the cab but could not locate the phone with his eyes.

Another driver, also a FedEx driver, climbed up beside the bus driver and peered into the cracked back window. "Screw this," he said and kicked the window into the cab of the truck. "Oh shit, it's Bailey," the bus driver heard him say.

The state policeman raced over to the truck. "How is the driver?" he yelled up to the men.

"It's bad, there is blood everywhere," the bus driver said as he burst into tears.

Bailey groaned and tried to move her body, causing her severe pain.

"She's alive," the trucker shouted when he heard her groan.

The state policeman keyed his shoulder microphone. "Dispatch, we need Life Flight on I-40, near mile marker 32," he said calmly.

"Affirmative," was the response from the dispatcher. "Contacting them now."

The officer turned at the sound of footsteps and saw a man in scrubs running toward him. "I'm an ER physician from Memphis," he said as he raced past the patrolman. The doctor scrambled up the back of the truck, and the bus driver jumped down into the thick mud.

He walked over to the policeman, who asked, "What happened here?"

"The rear axle on the bus collapsed and she took to the ditch to keep from hitting the bus," the man said as his eyes turned to the children who were anxiously watching the action.

"Can you call your supervisor and get another bus to pick up the children?" the officer asked.

"Yes, I will do that," he said and starting walking toward the bus.

"Have the adults walk the kids down the shoulder a bit, but keep them safely away from the road. I don't want them to see what might be happening here," he said as he nodded toward the truck.

✝

"Her name is Bailey," the truck driver said as the young doctor slowly climbed inside the truck to examine the woman. The seat belt held her body suspended in the overturned truck, but he was hesitant to move her or release the belt until more help arrived.

"Thanks, what is your name?"

"I'm Mark," he answered.

"Daniel," the doctor said as he moved closer to Bailey. "Your friend is injured, but we're going to make sure she's going to be all right, so hang with me," he said calmly.

Bailey's right femur had torn through her pants and her left arm was obviously broken. A deep gash across the front of her head was gushing blood, and there were several other smaller cuts across her body. "How fond of that shirt are you?" he asked.

Mark stripped off his uniform shirt and Daniel folded and placed it over the cut on her forehead. "Can you reach in here, Mark?"

"Yes, I think so."

"Hold this in place as firmly as you can, but don't move her head," he said.

Mark leaned inside the truck and followed his instructions.

Daniel still had a stethoscope wrapped around his neck and used it to check Bailey's heart rate. "Good, strong heartbeat," he said.

The officer climbed up behind Mark and spoke into the cab. "Life Flight is on the way. How is she?"

"Several broken bones and a nasty cut on her head as far as I can see," he said.

"Paramedics are rolling too, so you will have some help soon. What can I do?"

"You can see if you can get the cab door open," Daniel said. "It will make it easier to remove her if we can get the door open."

"I'm on it," he said as they heard more sirens approaching.

Lucas, the patrolman, managed to pull the door open and then used all of his weight to spring the door to break the hinge, pinning it against the side fender of the truck.

Daniel used his eyes and his hands to examine Bailey for other injuries. He could not feel any other broken bones, but as his hands moved down her left side she groaned in pain. He gently pulled her shirt open and saw the ugly bruising just below her left breast. He feared a broken rib, or that the force of the impact had ruptured a vital organ, causing internal bleeding. He silently prayed the helicopter would arrive soon.

Bailey felt his touch and briefly opened her pain-filled eyes.

"Hey there, Bailey, I'm Daniel," he said softly. "Can you lift your right hand?"

It was a struggle, but she managed to lift her hand. "That's great, how about your left foot. Can you wiggle it?"

She had movement, but Daniel knew she could possibly have some spinal damage. "Hang in there, Bailey," he said but she had already lost consciousness again.

The paramedics had arrived and were rushing to carry equipment to the scene. The policeman carefully jumped down and a paramedic took his place. The paramedic looked into the cab, and said, "Hey, Doc."

Daniel looked up to see Rusty, a paramedic he saw often at the Methodist Emergency Room. "I'm glad to see you. We need a collar and I'll set up an IV if you will pass me the supplies."

A cell phone began ringing from the area of the crushed dash. Mark looked at it and then Daniel. "Ignore it for now." He looked at Rusty. "We are also going to need a backboard and a pressure wrap on her head. Life Flight is on the way."

Rusty nodded his head and turned briefly to speak to his partner, giving him instructions on the items he needed. Then he returned to Bailey and began securing her neck with a cervical collar.

Daniel started the IV and lifted the bag of fluids to Mark. "Can you handle holding this?"

Mark shifted to wrap his forearm carefully around the blood-soaked shirt and took the bag in his hand.

"Good job," Daniel said. Mark was sweating profusely and all the color had drained from his face. "Are you doing okay?"

Mark nodded. The position he was in was painful and the coppery smell of the blood in the truck's cabin assaulted his senses, but he would not give up on Bailey.

They heard the thump, thump, thump of the rotors of the approaching helicopter and Daniel let out a short sigh of relief. It would take many more trained hands to get Bailey on the backboard safely. Rusty handed the pressure wrap to Daniel to address the wound on Bailey's head.

"You can let go of her head now, Mark," Daniel whispered as he placed a hand on his forearm. "You did well. Keep holding the IV bag though," he said. Daniel knew Mark was suffering from a mild case of shock and would need some treatment of his own once Bailey was safely on her way.

Rusty held her head gently in place while Daniel placed a thick bundle of sterile pads over the wound and began wrapping gauze tightly around her head to maintain pressure on the wound to stifle the bleeding.

The helicopter landed on the highway in front of the bus and the team rushed to the site with additional equipment. A nurse climbed up beside Mark and peered into the truck. "Hey guys," she said. "What do we have here?"

"A badly broken right leg and left arm, head wound, and possible broken ribs. I would also have her checked for ruptures on her left side. She has a lot of tenderness there."

"Are we ready to try for a backboard?" she asked.

"I think so," Daniel said and nodded to Mark. "Still good?" he asked.

"Yes, I can do this," he said.

With careful precision the team was able to position the backboard beneath Bailey's body. When they were all in their assigned positions, Mark released the seat belt, and Bailey slipped into their waiting hands.

Bailey's limp body was strapped onto the backboard. The team then slowly removed her body from the cab of the truck, into the hands of the Life Flight team who carefully loaded her into the helicopter and took flight for Memphis.

Daniel and Rusty walked with Mark between them to the back of the ambulance. They guided Mark to sit on the bench and treated him with first aid for the shock he was experiencing.

"I need to call this in," he said. "Bailey's family needs to know," he said.

Daniel thought about the cell phone ringing in the truck and asked the state trooper to retrieve it for him and then handed Mark his personal phone. "Can you dial?"

Mark nodded his head and took Daniel's phone to contact his supervisor. "I need to speak to him please," Daniel said before he hung up.

Daniel took the phone and introduced himself. "We need an extra driver. Mark is okay, but he is in no shape to drive the rest of the way. You should be proud of the way he performed." Daniel listened for a few seconds. "Yes, I plan to stay with him for a while. Okay, thanks," he said and ended the call.

Tony Valentine was the driver supervisor who had received Mark's phone call. He immediately dispatched a team of drivers to the location and an emergency crew to handle the wreckage and freight. He pulled up Bailey's personnel file and opened it to locate her emergency contact. "Louise Chambers," he said and dialed the number.

†

Desi was on the verge of panic when they were finally able to resuscitate Tally. "What has happened?" Blair asked her lover.

"Bailey has been hurt, but I don't know how badly," Tally said.

Desi crashed back into her seat and picked up her phone as Braxton raced from the room.

Braxton went to a desk in the forward office and dialed the dispatcher to find out if there had been an emergency on I-40 involving a semi-tractor. He quickly learned about the bus malfunction and the truck that barely veered in time to save the lives of twenty children. She also told him Life Flight was bringing the driver to Methodist but she did not know the condition of the driver.

Desi kept getting Bailey's voice mail. Tears were running down her face as Braxton returned to the room. "There was an accident; Bailey is being transported by Life Flight to Methodist. I don't know about injuries," he said as he took her in his arms in a comforting embrace. "She saved the lives of twenty children by ditching the truck," he whispered to her.

†

Valentine dialed the number for Louise, who answered on the third ring.

"Hello," she answered.

"Is this Louise Chambers?" he asked.

"Yes, who is this?"

"I'm sorry. Tony Valentine from FedEx. You are on the list as Bailey Chambers's emergency contact," he explained.

The blood in Louise's veins ran cold and she gripped the phone so tightly her knuckles turned white. "What has happened?"

"Bailey was involved in a traffic accident on I-40 and is being transported by Life Flight to Methodist," he said. "She has serious injuries, but I'm sorry that's all I know. May I come and get you?" he asked.

"No, no, I'm okay. Thank you for calling."

"I'm sorry for bringing you bad news. I will be praying for Bailey," he said.

"Thank you," Louise said and ended the call before he could say more. "Beth, Beth," she shouted as she dialed Tommy at work. Beth entered the room as Tommy picked up the call. "Tommy, there has been an accident. No, I do not know how bad Bailey is hurt yet. Get Joe and meet us at Methodist. Since you will have to go by the club to get there, put a closed for the night sign on the door. I'm afraid we are in for a long night." She listened for a second. "Okay, you boys be careful."

"Oh, my God, I was just watching that on the news," Beth said as she wrapped Louise in her arms. "She will be okay."

"Let's go," Louise said.

"I'm driving," Beth said as she took the keys from Louise.

†

Chief Bronson arrived amid the chaos in the room and looked around. "What on earth is going on?" he asked.

"Desi's friend has been in an accident," Blair said. "She is being delivered to Methodist by Life Flight."

Bronson looked at the warrant he held in his hand, to Desi, and then at Blair. "I will take Desi to Methodist. You three stay on task with this warrant," he said, handing it to Blair.

"But—" Braxton started to say.

"I will make sure Desi is taken care of, I promise," he said.

"He's right. Go, I will be okay."

"I'll call you as soon as I can," Braxton said and hugged her again. "If you hear anything before, call me."

"I will," Desi said. "Find him."

"We will," he answered and ushered Blair and Tally from the room.

†

The helicopter landed on the roof, met by a team of specialists who barked out orders as Bailey disappeared into a large elevator.

Nurses went into action, cutting her uniform off as X-ray techs took images of her body and phlebotomists drew blood. A portable CT scanner wheeled into the room while the specialists gathered in the hallway.

"If the CT is negative, I want her prepped for surgery so we can address the broken limbs," an orthopedist said.

"We have to ensure she has no internal bleeding first," another doctor said.

"Agreed," the surgeon said. "I will go prep in two. Bring her up as fast as you can," he said and ripped the films of Bailey's arm and leg from the viewer.

A nurse removed the pressure bandage and cleansed Bailey's forehead with Betadine solution then shaved her hair to allow a doctor to stitch the wound on her head.

When the test results revealed no spinal damage or brain trauma, the staff removed the cervical collar and Bailey was unstrapped from the backboard. "Can we clean her and tape the ribs before surgery?" a nurse asked.

"Yes," the ER physician said and left the room to walk to the nurses station. "Has anyone from her family arrived?"

"They are in the private waiting room," the charge nurse reported as he started down the hall.

✝

The lights on the chief's car did an adequate job of clearing traffic in front of them and they made it to the hospital as the helicopter was leaving the roof. Desi looked up to watch it fly as the power of the rotors blew leaves from the Bradford Pear trees surrounding the hospital.

The rain that had given them a few moments respite to arrive at the hospital now returned with full force and the rumble of thunder echoed in the distance.

"Let's go," the chief said as he took her arm and they rushed inside the emergency room.

They met Louise and Beth at the nurses station. Louise turned to see Desi and wrapped her in her arms. "Bailey is a strong woman, and she will be just fine," she reminded her.

Desi introduced the chief to Louise and Beth and they walked to the private waiting room where Louise poured them a cup of coffee.

Unable to sit, Desi stood at the window staring at the raindrops sliding down the windowpane. She heard a phone ring and turned to see the chief on the phone.

"I see," he said. "Yes, I will be right there."

He ended the call and looked at Desi. "I'm sorry, but I have to go. Please keep me informed on how Ms. Chambers is doing."

"I understand," Desi said. "Thank you for bringing me to the hospital."

"Jennifer said you might want to see the news. It seems your friend is quite the hero," he said with a smile and left the room.

Beth reached for the remote and turned on the television. A reporter was on the scene and the camera panned to show Bailey's truck, then a school bus, and in the distance a large huddle of small children. "A horrifying disaster was averted today by the heroic sacrifice of one brave woman," the reporter stated. "These children standing behind me," she said with a wave to the crowd, "were saved from certain injury, or worse, when FedEx driver Bailey Chambers ditched her truck to prevent a horrific crash when the rear axle of the bus broke, disabling the vehicle."

Desi sank onto the couch beside Louise as she stared in disbelief at the television.

Tommy and Joe arrived moments later. Their hugs and tears interrupted by the arrival of a doctor.

"Good evening," he said. "I'm Dr. Will Hatfield, Ms. Chambers's primary ER physician," he said.

The group quickly introduced themselves and he took a seat next to Desi. "Ms. Chambers has suffered some serious injuries and is on her way to surgery to repair some broken bones, but she does not have any life threatening issues. She has a broken leg and arm, a few broken ribs, and a serious gash on her head. She will be with us for several days, but she will be all right in a few weeks."

Desi let the breath she was holding release and her body began to tremble. "She's going to be all right," she repeated.

"Sore as hell and will probably need some extensive physical therapy, but once she's out of surgery she will be on the road to recovery," he repeated.

"Oh, thank God," Tommy said as he collapsed into Joe's arms.

"I will be on duty for the rest of the night, and when the surgeon has finished, we will bring you more news. Let me know if there is anything we can do for you," he said. When no one else spoke, he nodded and left the room.

Desi placed her head on Louise's shoulder. Wrapped beneath her warm arm, she surprised them all by falling asleep.

"Her body is shutting down as a coping mechanism," Louise told the group. "Right now let's just let her sleep."

The hours ticked by slowly as they waited for more news on Bailey's condition.

†

Braxton drove the team out to Johnston's for the meeting. "How did you know about Bailey?" he asked Tally.

"I'm not sure, but I felt she was in pain," Tally answered.

"Do you want to drop us off and go to the hospital?" Blair asked.

"Hell no, Desi would kick my ass," he said with a grin. "I will go later, after we are done."

"You can take us all and hopefully we will have good news to share," Blair told him.

"We can only hope," Braxton said and pulled into a parking spot.

†

Desi slept for three hours and then shot straight up on the couch after waking from a nightmare. She looked confused for a moment as she looked around at the faces watching her closely. "Damn, I wasn't dreaming," she said embarrassed.

"No news yet," Louise said after looking up at the clock. It had been three long hours of waiting. She looked over at Tommy and Joe. "Would you two go get us some food?"

Joe grinned at her. "More of those yummy cheeseburgers we had before?"

"Yes, that sounds good," Louise said, reaching for money.

"I've got this," Joe said as he pulled Tommy to his feet. "Come on, lover boy, you can help."

†

Kay Palmer, head of the Human Resource Department at Johnston's, welcomed the group into her office. She sat behind her large desk reading over the warrant then handed it over to Thomas Walker, president of the company. He read the warrant and said, "Give them whatever they need," and left the room.

"So who are we looking for?" she asked Braxton.

"Caucasian, late forties to mid-fifties, dark hair and eyes," he said.

"This is going to take some time," Kay said. "Would you like to grab a bite to eat and return in an hour or so?"

"Sorry, ma'am, but we have to remain here," Braxton said.

"Would you at least like some coffee then?"

"Coffee would be great," he said with a warm smile.

She picked up her phone and requested coffee be delivered to her office. They sipped on coffee and waited while Kay's fingers flew across her keyboard as she searched and sorted the thousands of files on her network.

Two hours later, Braxton stood and stretched. "I'm going to step out and call Desi," he said to Blair. "I will be right back." Blair nodded.

Braxton slipped out the door and leaned against the wall as he pulled out his cell. He took a deep breath, found Desi's number and pushed send.

"Hey, Braxton," Desi said when she answered the call.

"Any news yet?" he asked.

"Bailey is still in surgery, but the doctors say she will be okay. She has a broken leg, arm, ribs, and a head wound, but she's going to be okay," she repeated.

"How are you?"

"I'm okay. The boys just left to get some food."

"Good, you need to eat something."

"How is it going on your end?"

"We are waiting too while the HR Director creates a list for us. She warned it could take hours."

"So we are both just sitting and waiting," Desi said.

"Yeah," Braxton said and she could hear the smile in his voice. "Something neither one of us is good at," he teased.

"Keep me posted," Desi said.

"You too. We could be here a while. Then we are coming to see you," he said.

"Okay, thanks, partner. Good luck."

"See you soon, Desi."

Braxton walked back inside the office to sit beside Tally, and continue the wait.

"How is Bailey?" she asked.

"She is in surgery to repair some broken bones and has a head wound, but she's going to be all right," Braxton said, echoing Desi's sentiment.

"Good," Tally said. "That's very good news."

†

The boys returned with bags full of greasy delight and large cups of soda. Desi took a drink feeling her throat was parched and looked at the greasy burger with suspicion.

"I know how these look, but trust me, they are fantastic," Joe said. "We feasted on these when Tommy was in the hospital."

Desi was about to comment when the door opened, and two men entered. She recognized Dr. Hatfield, who smiled at her as they entered.

"This is Dr. Monroe, who performed most of the surgery on Ms. Chambers," he said as the two men took seats across from them.

"Ms. Chambers did well in surgery and is being monitored in recovery at this moment. In a short while she will be transferred to the Intensive Care Unit for observation and pain management tonight."

"Is she critical?" Louise said.

"Her condition is guarded, just until we can rule out any undetected head trauma, but we fully expect her to move into a private room tomorrow."

"Can we see her?" Desi asked.

"I would recommend moving up to the ICU waiting room on the fourth floor. She will be transferred as soon as they are ready for her upstairs. Once they have her settled I'm sure you can visit for short periods of time."

"Thank you both," Louise said as they stood to leave.

"Our pleasure. We hear she is quite the hero," Dr. Monroe said. "The lobby is swarming with media, so I would steer clear of that area. We will address them soon to give them an update with your permission. Memphis needs a hero right now."

"That will be fine," Louise said.

They finished their meals quickly and rode an elevator to the fourth floor. They checked in at the nurses' station and then resumed their vigil in the family waiting room.

†

Two hours and thirty minutes after they arrived, Kay was able to produce a spreadsheet of the sixty men that fit their profile. Forty-nine of them were still active employees, but they would have to evaluate every one of them to rule them out.

Braxton thanked her and they left the office.

"Are you ready to go to the hospital?" Blair asked as they climbed inside the car.

"Yes, if that's okay," he answered.

"Let's go," she said.

†

Desi jumped to her feet when the door opened and a nurse entered the room. "Hello, I'm Brianna and I will be Ms. Chambers's nurse tonight. She has been transferred, and I can let one of you in for a visit at a time. So who is first?"

Everyone looked at Desi.

288

"I guess that means you're the lucky one. Before you all visit, I want you to know she has every machine possible attached to her and there is still a bit of swelling from surgery, so prepare yourselves." She looked at Desi. "Are you ready?"

"Yes, please," she said and followed the nurse from the room.

"Ten minutes and then let someone else visit," Brianna said as she pulled the curtain to allow Desi to enter.

Desi's breath caught in her throat as she looked at Bailey. She approached the bed and carefully placed her hand in Bailey's as she studied the monitors and tubes leading from the bed. "You have given us quite the scare, Ms. Chambers," she whispered as she leaned in to kiss Bailey's bruised cheek.

Bailey's eyes fluttered open and she struggled to focus on Desi. "We are going to have to stop meeting like this," she said weakly.

"I always heard a hospital was a great place to pick up hot chicks," Desi teased.

"I'm not feeling too hot right now, but I will take a rain check," Bailey said. "Where am I?"

"You are at Methodist in ICU so they can keep an eye on you tonight," Desi explained.

"I look like a plaster factory," she said as her eyes scanned her leg and broken arm.

"They had to call for another delivery of plaster, or so I heard," Desi teased. "The docs say you are going to be fine."

Bailey squeezed her hand. "I love you."

"I love you too, and I will be in and out as long as they will let us visit."

"Okay, but I can't promise I'll be awake," Bailey said.

"Oh baby, you don't have to stay awake for us. Rest and regain your strength," she said.

Bailey smiled at her. "Send in Louise, if you will," she said. "I love you."

"I will see you later," Desi said and kissed her softly.

Desi walked back to the waiting room and looked at Louise. "She wants to see you next."

Louise nodded and left the room.

†

Louise followed Desi's instructions to the room and found Bailey struggling to stay awake. "Hey, baby girl," she said when she entered the room.

"Louise, I am very tired and will be asleep soon. I want you to take care of Desi if something happens to me," she said.

"You are going to be just fine," Louise said.

"But if it goes bad for some reason, promise me you will use the money you have invested for me to take care of Desi. Promise me."

"I promise you, Bailey, but you are going to be fine."

"Thank you," Bailey said and closed her eyes.

Louise looked at the heart monitor to see the steady, strong pulse and realized Bailey had drifted off to sleep. She left the room and returned to the waiting area.

†

There was a man Louise did not recognize when she entered the waiting room. "Louise, this is Tony Valentine from FedEx," Tommy said.

"Pleased to meet you, and thank you for calling to let me know what had happened," she said.

"I'm going in," Tommy said.

Louise nodded and said, "She's sleeping."

"How is she doing?" Tony asked.

"She's stable and will be okay," Louise said.

Tony handed her a business card. "I want you to call me at any time if you or Bailey need anything," he said. "Please also let her know the whole crew is proud of what she did."

"I will," Louise said. "Thank you again."

Tony left the room and Louise sat beside Desi. "She fell asleep and is resting."

When the door opened next, Braxton, Blair, and Tally stepped into the room. "How is she?" he asked.

"She's going to be okay," Desi said. "She will be in ICU tonight and transferred to a private room tomorrow, if all goes as planned."

"That sounds very positive," Blair said.

Tally walked over and reached out her hand to Desi. "Bailey is a strong woman and will be just fine."

"How did you know?" Desi asked.

"I don't know. I guess we were still connected a bit," Tally said. "I just knew she was hurt."

"Have you all eaten?" Blair asked.

"Yes, the boys brought us up some cheeseburgers a little while ago," Louise said.

"Would you mind if we stayed for a little while?" Braxton asked.

"Of course not, you are like family to us. All of you," she added to include Tally and Blair. "Can I send Joe after some food for you?"

"A cheeseburger does sound good."

"Three cheeseburger specials coming right up," Joe said.

Beth went with him to help carry the food.

"How did it go with the warrant?" Desi asked.

Braxton looked at Blair, who said, "We have a list of sixty names to rule out."

"Damn, I was hoping it would be much less. That's going to take a long time to work through."

"Not with the three of us working on it together tomorrow," Blair said.

"Four you mean?" Desi said.

"No, you need to be here for Bailey, and for you," Blair said. "We can handle this without you."

"Thanks," she said, secretly relieved she was not expected to work tomorrow.

"No worries, we will save some work for you," Blair said as Joe and Beth returned with the food.

While they devoured their meal, Tommy returned to the room looking rather pale and plopped down beside Joe. "What's wrong?" Joe asked.

"I've never thought of Bailey as being fragile, but she looks so frail hooked up to all those machines."

"Trust me, big brother, there is nothing fragile, frail, or weak about Bailey," Desi said. "She is only resting."

"I will take your word on that," Tommy said with a grin.

†

Aaron looked at his calendar as he dressed for work. "Only a couple more days, Elvis, before I send you a fresh one," he said. "I will find a real beauty for you this year, I promise."

His promise increased the excitement pulsing through his veins and he found pulling on his pants a nearly unbearable experience. For a moment, he dreamed of the possibility of taking one tonight, to ease his pain, but that was against the rules, his rules, and he would have to wait. "Only a couple more days," he repeated and walked to his car to drive to work.

†

The sound of the clock ticking rang in Tally's ears, amplified until it was almost unbearable for her keen senses. "I'm sorry, but I need to get out of this room," she said and walked out into the hallway.

"Is she okay?" Desi asked.

"Yes, she is just supersensitive in this weather," Blair answered. "I think I'll take her back to the hotel. Will you call if you need anything or if anything changes here?"

"Of course I will." She looked at Braxton and said, "You need to go home too and get some rest. There's a bad man out there that needs catching."

Braxton started to speak but Desi interrupted him. "I'll be fine. I don't think I'll have any luck sending the others home, so I will have plenty of company tonight."

"We aren't going anywhere, Braxton," Louise confirmed. "Go. We will call if necessary."

"Okay. I'll take Blair and Tally back to their car and call it a night." He stood and walked over to Desi, taking her in his arms for a bear hug. "Don't forget to take care of you."

"I won't," Desi said as she walked him to the door. "I will talk with you tomorrow."

When she returned from the door, four pairs of eyes were watching her. "What?"

"You are an amazing woman," Louise said. "Visiting time comes again in five minutes, and after that I think we all need to try to get some rest. It's going to be a long night."

Desi nodded and walked over to the window. She watched Braxton, Blair, and Tally enter his car and drive away as the rain continued to fall. A flash of lightning lit up the outline of the hospital followed closely by a clash of thunder. She remembered earlier in the day when Tally trembled, frozen in the clutches of a vision when the storm arrived. She worried the young woman would get very little rest tonight if the storm continued to rage.

Louise walked over to Desi, placing a hand on her shoulder. "You first," she said.

†

Desi stood beside Bailey's bed, holding her hand. She looked so peaceful. Some color had returned to her face, and she slept, the dreamless sleep induced by the pain medications dripping slowly into her veins.

Tears flowed slowly down her cheeks. "I couldn't bear the thought of losing you," she whispered.

"I don't plan on going anywhere soon," Bailey said, "so you don't have to worry."

"I thought you were sleeping."

"I was until I felt your hand in mine. I knew it was you. I want you to know how much I love you, Desi," Bailey said with a lopsided grin.

"I love you too."

"I know, and we will be together for a long time."

Desi continued to cry. "Why are you crying, baby girl?" Bailey asked.

"I don't know," Desi said as she brushed away the tears.

"Hey, I was thinking something. Do you think you can get two weeks off after the case is done?"

"I would think so, why?"

"I think it is time for us to spend some time at a coast somewhere. Do you think you can push a wheelchair?"

Desi smiled. "I will push you anywhere you want to go."

"That's my girl," Bailey said with a smile. "You decide when, and I'll decide where."

"Deal," Desi said and smiled.

"I should go so the others can see you."

"Desi," Bailey said. "Get some rest. I know you won't go home, but at least get some sleep."

"I will," Desi said and leaned over the bed to kiss her. "I love you."

"Love you too."

†

Blair tucked Tally into bed. She was exhausted, both physically and emotionally, and drifted right into sleep. The adrenaline running through her veins had her wired, and Blair knew sleep would not come for her for several hours, so she booted up her laptop.

She pulled the list of names from her notepad and began running searches of the men on the list.

Three hours later, she felt a hand on her shoulder and looked up to see Tally standing naked beside her. "Why are you still up?"

"Too much energy to sleep," Blair said as she powered down the laptop.

"I have a nicer method for burning off the energy," Tally said and offered Blair her hand to lead her to the bed.

Chapter 20

Braxton tossed and turned until finally at four o'clock he climbed from bed to shower and dress for work. He stopped by a local fast-food joint and ordered six ham and egg biscuits and six containers of orange juice then drove to the hospital. When he walked into the waiting room, they were all asleep. He stood watching, questioning if he should just leave when Desi woke.

"Hey," she whispered and sat upright. Her head was in Louise's lap while she slept, and her movement woke Louise and Beth. "What time is it?"

"Almost six," Braxton answered. "I thought I would bring breakfast."

"That is very sweet of you," Desi said as Tommy and Joe stirred.

"Do I smell biscuits or am I dreaming?" Tommy said.

"You smell biscuits," Braxton said as he placed the bag on the table and began unloading them. "I hope everyone likes ham and egg."

Beth stood and stretched. "I will put on a fresh pot of coffee."

"How is Bailey?" he asked.

"She is doing well. The doctor will complete rounds about eight, and we will learn then if she can be moved," Desi answered.

"That's good news," he answered as he handed her a biscuit.

†

The nurses on the second floor began preparing room 224 for an arrival from ICU. All night long, the hospital had received flowers, cards, and letters for Bailey Chambers from well-wishers. Hospital policy prevented them in ICU so they kept them in store. Now they were busy placing the cards and letters around the room with at least a dozen bouquets of flowers and balloons to fill her room.

Merita had arrived to add a bouquet of yellow daisies, and helped the nurses prepare Bailey's room.

†

Dr. Monroe arrived at eight thirty to announce that Bailey's condition had remained stable and that she would be moving to room 224 within the next fifteen minutes. He suggested they move to the waiting room on that floor to wait for her arrival and promised to have the nurses let them know when she arrived.

The group cleaned the waiting room then rode the elevator down to the second floor. Merita waited for them in the family waiting room. She smiled up at Desi.

"Oh my goodness, I completely forgot to call you," Desi said as she rushed over to hug Merita.

"That's okay, I heard it on the news and knew she was in good hands," Merita said as she hugged her.

†

Braxton made it to the precinct by seven thirty to find Blair and Tally already at work. Blair had made a copy of the list, which she handed to him. Several names were marked through on the list. "I'm down to thirty-six possibilities," she said. "Let's get it down to a dozen or less before today is through."

He stared at the list. "Did you sleep at all last night?"

Blair looked over at Tally with a smile. "I got enough," she said with a wide grin.

Braxton returned her grin as he sat down at his computer. "I'll start from the bottom and work up," he said.

Tally was sitting at the table very quietly, and Braxton assumed she was seeking out other victims.

Lisa was there with Jasmine, and Tally was indeed communicating with the spirits.

"We are working on a list of names for potential suspects. Blair is printing photographs of those that have records. Do you think you would be able to identify him if you looked with my eyes?" she asked Jasmine.

"Yes, I think so, but can we do that?"

"Possible yes, but I have never done this, so it may take several tries," Tally said. "I will prepare myself until the time comes. Thank you both."

"Will it be dangerous for you or painful?" Lisa asked.

"I don't know, but the risk is worth the attempt."

†

Bailey was escorted into her new room by several of the nurses working on the second floor. Brenda, who was her primary care nurse, smiled as Bailey was wheeled into the room. "Welcome home," she said.

Bailey looked around the room filled with cards, letters, and flowers. "Is this someone else's room?"

"No, these are all for you. More keep coming every hour."

"Incredible," Bailey said as her eyes landed on the bouquet of daisies. She smiled, knowing exactly who they were from. She looked around to see Merita in the doorway.

"Hello," she said.

"I'm glad to see you," Bailey said.

"The others are in the waiting room. I just went to use the restroom. I will go get them," Merita said.

"Thank you for being here," Bailey said.

Merita turned to her with a smile. "You are a daughter to me," she said and turned away to retrieve the others, just as Desi and the rest of Bailey's family stepped inside the room. "Wow," she said. "It looks like you are one popular lady."

Joe and Tommy were checking out the letters and cards. "I think every kid on that bus made you a card or wrote a letter," Tommy said.

"We've gotten bits and pieces of the story," Louise said. "Can you tell us what happened?"

"I was cruising back to Memphis with hopes I could beat the storm. I saw a school bus attempting to merge into traffic and slowed to let them enter in front of me." Bailey paused for a second to collect the memory. "A couple of boys were in the back window and signaled me for a blast on the air horn, so I gave them a couple. A few seconds later, the road was filled with sparks flying all over the place as the rear axle of the bus broke and was dragging the asphalt." A look of pain crossed Bailey's face. "The driver was struggling to keep the top-heavy bus upright as it started to fishtail into the other lane. My rig was barreling right toward the center of the bus." She swallowed hard before continuing. "I had no other choice but to ditch the truck. Ramming that bus full of kids was not an option. After that, I really can't tell you much, until I woke to see you looking at me," she said to Desi.

"No wonder they are calling you a hero," Joe said.

"I'm no hero," Bailey said as she took Desi's hand in hers.

"From the looks of this room, I beg to differ with you," Louise said. "You are a hero to these kids, their families and more."

Bailey was too tired and sore to argue with Louise. Besides it was pointless, she never won an argument with her cousin.

The door opened and Brenda returned carrying a green Sharpie pen. "Okay, who's going to be first?" she asked. "That's a whole lot of white plaster."

Tommy bounced up and down like an excited kid as he reached for the pen. "Me, please let me go first."

"Okay, but nothing obscene," Louise warned.

"Well, I would never," Tommy said, feigning hurt.

They took turns signing and making drawings on Bailey's casts. Desi was the last to take up the Sharpie and drew a big heart on Bailey's left arm with I love you written beneath it. "That way you will always know, even if I am not by your side."

"I know it right here," Bailey said, pointing to her heart.

"Aw, isn't that just the sweetest thing," Joe said as he wiped away tears.

"Oh stop, you silly queen, before you get the rest of us started," Louise said and punched his arm.

The room filled with laughter and Bailey cringed at the pain from her broken ribs. "Please everyone, stop laughing, you're killing me here," she said, grabbing at her ribs.

"Sorry, Bailey," Tommy said.

"It's okay, Tommy," Bailey said. "I know at least five of you have been here all night long. I wish you would go home, and get some rest, now that I'm in a permanent room," she said.

The group started to groan in protest. "I'm captive here. Even if I could leave I doubt they would let me," she told them.

"I will stay with her today," Merita volunteered. "She needs to rest and not be entertained by you clowns," she teased the boys.

"Okay," Desi finally consented. "Can I have a minute alone with Bailey before we go?"

They all said goodbye to Bailey and followed Merita from the room.

"Now that I have you all to myself, be warned, I am spending the night with you tonight," she said.

Bailey smiled up at her. "I will reserve this spot just for you," she said, patting the right side of the bed. "But now you need to go home, feed Fubar, take a shower, and get some decent sleep."

"I will be back."

"I know you will," Bailey said as Desi leaned down and kissed her.

✝

"That's the last of them," Blair said as she added a mug shot to the pile. "The others will have to come from their driver's license."

"I'm almost afraid to ask, but how many?" Braxton said.

"Eight, four with records," Blair answered.

Tally had been silent as she sat at the table across the room. "If I can have those photos, I want to try something," she said.

"What do you have in mind?" Blair asked.

"I want to bring Jasmine in through my eyes so she can see if she recognizes him," Tally said.

301

"Is there no other way?" Blair said, worried about the danger to Tally.

"None that I can think of at the moment," she answered.

"Is it dangerous for Tally?" Braxton asked.

"We don't know for sure. She has never tried it before," Blair said.

"Can we at least talk to the supervisor of these men before we go to that extreme, see if he can lead us to our suspect?" he asked.

Blair considered his request and finally said, "That's a good idea. See if you can set it up for this afternoon."

Braxton went to his phone to make the call. Blair joined Tally. "We need to try one more avenue, before we risk letting her view through your eyes."

Tally nodded in agreement. "I will be ready if we need to try."

"I know you will," Blair said as she pulled her into her arms. "We will get him."

Braxton returned to the room. "We can meet him in an hour."

"Will you print out the DMV photos in case we need them?" Blair asked. "I want to drop Tally off at the hotel to rest, and I will be back."

"I'll be ready," Braxton said as they left the room.

He printed off the photographs and added them to the pile of mug shots. He called Dawson and gave him an update.

"How is Desi holding up?" Dawson asked.

"She was good when I saw her this morning," Braxton said. "I will give her a call later. I'm hoping she's at home getting some rest."

"Tell her she and Bailey are in my thoughts," Dawson said.

"I will, boss. Thanks."

✝

Desi slipped the key into Bailey's back door and Fubar was immediately there as she entered. "Hey, little girl," she said as she bent down to scoop up the kitten. "We didn't forget you," she said as she scratched under the kitten's neck. "Your other mama is a little banged up, but she will be fine," she said as she walked into the kitchen to fill the food and water bowls.

She left Fubar in the kitchen eating and walked to the bathroom, stripping out of her clothes for a long, hot shower.

After a refreshing shower, Desi dried and climbed into the bed after setting the alarm on her phone. She would sleep for a few hours then stop by her place to pack a bag before returning to the hospital. For a brief second she considered calling Braxton, but decided the call would have to wait as her head hit the pillow and she was down for the count.

✝

Herman Franks was the head supervisor of the security drivers at Johnston. Braxton explained to him briefly what type of information they were looking to gain on the eight men in question before placing the photographs in front of him.

Herman studied the photographs for a brief moment then pulled one of the DMV photographs from the pile. "This one died a year ago in a car crash," he said. "These three," he said, pointing to three pictures, "are some of my most reliable guards and will be working tonight." He cocked his head to the side at the next photograph. "This one will also be at work tonight. Aaron is an odd duck, but his old man worked here after he got himself fired from Memphis PD for drinking on the job. He died while working for the company, so I felt we owed the kid a chance. He's been reliable and is quick to volunteer for extra shifts."

"What do you mean by odd?" Blair asked.

"Not a real social fellow; keeps to himself when he has to come in for training or a meeting."

"That doesn't sound all that odd," Blair said.

"He once told one of the men he was Elvis Presley's son," he said, shaking his head. "Weird thing, though, he does look a lot like Elvis." He smiled and continued. "The boys nicknamed him The King and Aaron loved it, having no idea he was the butt of their jokes. Whenever someone called him The King, he would smile and say 'Thank ya, thank ya very much,' in his best impersonation of Elvis."

"Now we are getting somewhere," Blair said.

†

At the hotel, Tally was reclined on the bed and had almost drifted to sleep when she felt the buzzing in her head begin, stronger than usual. She could feel the movement behind her eyes and she opened her mind to Lisa.

"I am here," she said.

"We have good news," Lisa said. Melissa has spoken one word. That word was a name. Aaron. He was the man that killed her."

"That is fantastic news," Tally said. "Thank you."

"Good luck," Lisa whispered and was gone.

Tally rushed to find her cell phone to call Blair. She found the number and pressed send. The phone rang several times, but there was no answer. Tally ended the call and hit redial, still without answer.

"Oh, Blair, where are you?" she cried.

†

Blair reached for her phone to call Tally when they were leaving the security supervisor's office and realized she did not have her phone. When they reached Braxton's car, the phone was sitting on the floorboard blinking furiously. She picked it up to find that Tally had called twice, just minutes ago. She hit the redial button and waited for Tally to pick up.

"Blair, I know his name," Tally said when she answered.

"What? How?" she asked.

"Melissa finally spoke one word. Aaron. That is the name of the man who killed her."

"Excellent job, we will swing by to pick you up in twenty minutes."

†

Aaron was finishing his dinner when he heard a strange noise. It took a few seconds for him to realize it was the sound of his phone. It rang so infrequently he had almost forgotten the sound. He picked up the phone. "Hello."

"The FBI came by to ask questions about you and some of the other guards," a voice said.

"Who is this?"

"That doesn't matter. Be wary of what you do tonight," the voice said. Aaron heard a click as the call ended.

His stomach boiled and he barely made it to the bathroom before his body purged its contents. Aaron retched when he had no more to purge. The chill of fear ran through his veins. He had always known this day would come, but he did not expect it now.

He ran to his bedroom and threw together a bag, stuffing a pistol and two extra sets of clothes in it. A garment bag also hung in his closet and he smiled as his fingers wrapped around the handle. He had cash stuffed in an envelope that he tossed into the bag on his way to the kitchen. He took a set of keys to his mother's old Cadillac from the hook by the door, and ran to the garage where it had been stored since her death. He was glad that once a month he took the car out for a drive, and it now awaited him fully fueled and ready to go.

He backed the car from the garage and pulled his car inside so no one would realize there had been a second vehicle at first glance. His mother's name was still on the registration of the Cadillac, and he was praying it would take some time for the FBI to figure that one out. He smiled to himself as he pulled away from his home, pleased that he may have fooled the FBI, if only temporarily. Aaron glanced in the rearview at the place he had called home, certain he would never see it again.

†

Blair turned to Braxton who was behind the wheel and said, "We were right. Aaron Beach is the killer. Melissa finally spoke one word and that was Aaron, the name of her killer."

"What now?"

"We collect Tally from the hotel then request a meeting with Dawson, and the chief to determine our next course of action."

"Do you want to call or should I?" he asked.

"You drive, and I'll make the calls."

Before they reached the hotel, Blair had called Dawson to give him a report and to request a meeting with the chief immediately. Dawson said he would call him then call her back with the time. They were pulling into the drive at the hotel when he phone rang. Blair listened for a minute then said, "Yes, we can be there in twenty minutes."

Tally ran out to meet them and climbed into the backseat. "Where to?" Braxton asked.

"The chief's office," Blair said.

†

Desi was in the shower when Braxton called to tell her the news, but she did not see that he had called when she holstered her phone to head back to the hospital.

"No answer," he said as they walked into city hall to meet with the chief of police. "I will try again later."

They rode the elevator up and when they reached the chief's office, Jennifer waved them through.

"Welcome," Bronson said as he showed them to their seats. "I take it from the urgency of this meeting that you have good news to share."

"That we do, sir," Blair said. "We believe we know who the killer is."

"You have my attention, Agent Cooper," he said and leaned forward in his chair.

"With Tally's help, we were able to get a description of the suspect and a lead on where he worked. After reviewing personnel records and speaking with supervisory staff, we think we have narrowed the field down to one suspect. A man named Aaron Beach."

"Beach, you say, I knew his old man. He got washed out for drinking on the job and if my memory serves me right, he got killed in a holdup," Bronson said.

"Your memory serves you well, Chief. He is one and the same."

"Is it time for me to request a search warrant and one for his arrest?" he asked.

"Yes, that would be great. I would like to get into his place as soon as we can. Braxton already has people keeping an eye out for him so we can get a tail on him until we can arrest him."

Bronson looked at the clock. It was almost six. "It may take a couple of hours, but I will get you those warrants tonight," he promised. "Great work, folks. Why don't you grab some dinner and I'll have Dawson call you when I have the warrants ready."

"Yes, sir, thank you," Blair said.

"Thank you all," Bronson said.

Braxton led them out of the office. "Would you mind if we went to the hospital now to share the good news with Desi?"

"I was hoping you would take us there. I'm hungry for cheeseburgers," Blair said with a grin.

†

When Desi arrived, Merita decided to go home to give them time together. "Thank you for keeping an eye on Bailey today, I hope she wasn't too much trouble," she said with a wink.

"No, she was fine, slept on and off most of the day, but did eat pretty well at lunch. Dinner should be arriving soon."

"May I come back tomorrow to sit with you?" she asked Bailey.

"I would love that, and I will try to stay awake tomorrow."

"I didn't mind. To be honest, I think I slipped off a few times too for a quick nap," she confessed.

"Be careful going home, and I will see you tomorrow," Bailey said.

Merita leaned down to kiss her, then hugged and kissed Desi. "Call me if you need me."

"I will. Thanks, Merita," she said.

Desi sat down on the edge of the bed and softly stroked Bailey's cheek. "I brought my jammies," she said.

"Good. I think we might cause a stir if you sleep in the buff."

"Could be fun though," Desi said with a wicked grin. "Have you heard from Louise, and the boys?"

"She called earlier and I convinced her to open the club tonight. It wasn't easy, but I assured her a gorgeous detective was going to keep me out of trouble tonight." She grinned. "If I know my brother, he will come sashaying through the door at any moment."

"I bet you are right."

"He called earlier. Tony and Charles are on their way back up. When he told them about the accident, they volunteered to come back to help Louise out at the club, and to keep me in line."

"It will be good to see them again," Desi said.

The door opened as Bailey's dinner tray arrived. The woman placed it on the rolling table and left. Desi lifted the lid and made a face. "Turkey and dressing?" she asked.

"I think that is what I chose. It was that or meatloaf, and I just couldn't stomach meatloaf."

Braxton had stepped inside the door as the woman left and heard the exchange. "Would a cheeseburger taste better?" he asked as they entered the room.

"Oh, hell yeah," Bailey said. "You are a godsend, Braxton."

"You are on a regular diet correct?" Desi asked.

"Yes, ma'am."

"Bring on those cheeseburgers then," Desi said as she removed the tray from the table.

"How did it go today?" she asked Braxton.

Braxton looked at Blair, who nodded and said, "Go ahead."

"We think we know who our suspect is," he said.

"Are you serious?" Desi asked.

They settled into seats as Braxton told her about the events of the day. "So, we are waiting on a call from Dawson to tell us the warrants are ready to be picked up."

"So you are going to pay him a visit tonight?" Desi asked, her eyes twinkling with excitement.

"That's the plan," Blair said. "He is supposed to be at work at seven."

Bailey saw the excitement in Desi's eyes as they talked about the case. "Why don't you go with them?" she said.

Desi's head whipped around to look at her. It was obvious how torn she was between wanting to stay with Bailey and being a part of the entry team on the biggest case of her life.

"No, I can't," she said.

"Why can't you?"

"Because I want to be here with you," Desi said.

"I can stay with Bailey," Tally said. "You really don't need me to search his place."

Everyone in the room turned to look at her.

"Desi should be there. This case would not be alive without her," she explained. "She deserves to be there."

"See. What will it take, three, maybe four hours?" Bailey said.

"They do have valid points. We could have you back here by midnight if all goes as planned," Blair said.

"Are you sure you wouldn't mind?" she asked Bailey.

"Nope. You need to catch the bad guy, Desi, that's who you are."

Just as they finished eating, Joe and Tommy walked into the room. "I do believe we are missing a party, Tommy boy," Joe said. He sniffed the air. "They had cheeseburgers too, and didn't save us one."

"I will gladly go get you boys cheeseburgers," Desi said.

"No, darling, we have perfectly good legs. Does anyone need anything?" Tommy said.

Bailey looked at him. "If they have some of those delicious brownies, grab some, and a carton of milk, please."

"Anyone else?" he asked.

No one else had any requests, so he and Joe exited the room.

They had barely closed the door when Braxton's phone rang. Everyone looked at him with excitement as he answered the call. "Braxton," he said and listened to the caller for several seconds. "Yes sir, we will meet you at the precinct in fifteen," he said. He ended the call and looked at Desi. "It's a go."

"I will be back as soon as possible," Desi said and kissed Bailey. "Thank you."

"Be careful, and I will see you when you return," Bailey said as they left the room.

"I hope you like brownies," Bailey said to Tally.

"Is it dark outside?" Tally teased.

†

They arrived at the precinct in record time and assumed they would pick up the warrants from Dawson and be on their way, but he had other plans. He met them out front, warrants in hand, and told Desi, "Scoot over, I'm coming along."

"Glad to have you aboard, sir," Braxton said.

"I wouldn't miss this for the world. I have been on pins and needles since you called tonight. This is the most exciting case we have had in Memphis for a long time," he added with an excited grin. "So what's the plan?"

Blair turned to face him. "We have an entry team on alert and ready to go. We will have them enter and sweep the house before we go in to complete a detailed search."

"Is the suspect at home?" Dawson asked.

"Doesn't appear to be from the reports we have gotten so far. He is on schedule to work tonight, but has not shown up for duty. Braxton put an alert out on his vehicle to notify us if he is spotted. We don't want to give him any reason to bolt."

Braxton followed the directions to the house and turned off his headlights as he pulled up behind a blacked-out van sitting a block from the target. He turned off the interior lighting and nodded to Blair.

Braxton tapped on the rear door of the van and stepped backward. A man stepped out of the van, and saw Braxton. "Hey, you sumbitch, how you doing, Braxton?" the man said, slapping Braxton on the back.

"Good, Jones, have you met our lieutenant yet?" Braxton said, nodding to Dawson.

"No sir, begging your pardon," Jones said.

"No problem," Dawson said, extending his hand as Braxton introduced Desi and Blair.

"The FBI, wow, pleased to meet you," he said.

"Do you have any updates for us? Braxton asked.

"Not even a mouse moving inside the place. The vehicle is in the garage but there does not seem to be anyone at home. We have a sniper in position, but I don't think we'll be in need of his services tonight."

"Whenever your entry team is ready, we have the warrant in place," Braxton said.

"We are all over it," Jones said. He keyed the microphone on his shoulder. "Team One, it's a go, be slow and thorough."

Within seconds the team moved into action. Desi heard a deep male voice announce "Memphis PD," and when there was no answer at the door, a battering ram blew it open. The team rushed through single file and scattered throughout the house. Desi could see their shadows dancing on the walls of the house as they searched the house, room by room.

"All clear, Jones," the team leader reported, "Lights coming on and ready for Team Two," he announced.

"It's your turn to dance," Jones told them. "The house is all yours."

"Let's do this," Blair said and they followed her as she entered the house.

Desi felt a bead of perspiration slide down her back beneath the Kevlar vest that was standard entry procedure. She entered the house behind Braxton and immediately felt the eeriness of the place. The walls were covered with photographs of Elvis as well as other memorabilia. To describe it as a shrine was a severe understatement. "This is a serious obsession," she whispered, even though others were speaking at full volume.

"You can say that again," Dawson said.

"Okay, let's fan out," Blair said as she broke off to the right into a bedroom. It was obviously a woman's room, but there was no record of a marriage for Aaron Beach and from the supervisor's report, she doubted he had a live-in girlfriend. A glance at a photograph on the bedside table answered her question. A photograph of Beach and his mother smiled up at her.

The other photographs on the walls were of a young boy, many times dressed in the type of jumpsuits Elvis had worn during his performances, carrying a trick or treat bag or bucket. "She started on him at a young age," Blair spoke aloud.

Desi pulled on a pair of latex gloves as she entered the second bedroom. The stale odor of perspiration assaulted her as she stepped into the room. She willed her mind to forget what other smells she could be experiencing as she focused on her task. She opened a door to a closet with a solid row of uniforms and a smaller row of casual clothing. The back of the closet held a variety of leather, or maybe pleather, jumpsuits. She shivered as she backed out of the closet. The small bed was made with military precision, and other than the odor, the room was spotless. She walked to the table beside the bed and carefully opened the drawer. She could not believe what her eyes were seeing.

"Blair, guys, I think you need to see this," Desi said.

They rushed into the room to see what had caught her attention. Desi had found trophies, a brilliant find, and Blair whistled loudly. There were two stacks of drivers' licenses bound together with rubber bands. She looked at Desi. "Remove them touching as little as possible, take the bands off, and spread them on the bed," she instructed. "Braxton, will you call in a crime scene crew please?"

"Sure thing," he said and left the room.

Dawson and Blair watched as Desi unbundled and spread thirty-three drivers' licenses across the bed. Desi looked at the faces as she placed them on the bed, many of them matching photos of victims from the cold case files. "This has to be the killer. There are many of our victims here. I do not know exactly how many, but most of them for sure."

"My list is in the car in my notepad," Blair said.

"I'll go get it," Dawson said.

"This is the one. I feel it in my bones. We have to find him, and soon. The window opens tomorrow," Blair said.

"Crime scene is on their way," Braxton said. "Where did Dawson go?"

"To get the victim list from the car," Desi said.

Dawson returned, and passed Blair her notebook. She took out a pen and began calling out names to Desi, placing a checkmark beside victims whose licenses were on the bed. All but one name was checked when they finished the list.

"Okay, does anyone disagree that this is our guy?" Blair asked.

"No, I think this is definitely him," Braxton said. The others nodded.

"Let's toss this place and see if we can determine where he may be hiding. I don't think he will be returning here, especially if he has gotten wind somehow we are on to him," Blair said.

"Lt. Dawson, can you get DMV records to see if there is another vehicle registered to this address? Has anyone found any mention of a mother's name?"

"It's Elizabeth," Braxton said. "I saw it on an old power bill."

"I will see what I can do," Dawson said and walked outside to make some calls.

†

Tommy and Joe returned to the room to find the others gone. "Where did everyone go?"

"To handle some police business, but they will be back later," Bailey said.

"I guess we will have to eat these brownies by ourselves then," Joe said as he handed one to Tally then to Bailey. "Milk anyone?"

"Is it cold?" Bailey asked.

Tommy smiled at her. "It's icy cold."

"Awesome," Bailey said as she struggled to open her brownie.

"Here, I will help you with that," Tally said and moved to the bed to assist Bailey.

Bailey watched with eagerness as Tally removed the plastic from a large brownie and opened a carton of milk for her. "Do you want this in a cup?"

"No, I'm good, thanks," Bailey answered. "How many brownies did you buy?" she said as Tommy kept pulling them out of the bag.

"A dozen," he said with a grin.

Bailey took a bite and moaned. "Damn these are good."

"What's on the tube tonight?" Tommy asked.

"I don't know," Bailey said between bites of brownie. She handed him the remote. "Here you can surf."

Tommy pulled up the television guide channel and burst out laughing. Bailey looked up at the screen, and smiled at her brother. "Okay, but you absolutely cannot make me laugh."

"Good luck with that," Joe said as Tommy changed the channel to *Mama Mia*.

Tally looked up at the television. "I haven't seen this one."

"It's hilarious," Bailey said.

Tally pulled a spare pillow from behind her in the chair. "In that case you better take this and pad those ribs."

That was all it took to send the boys into a fit of contagious laughter. It hurt like hell, but Bailey was just glad to be there to share the moment.

†

Aaron was well aware of the seedy side of Memphis and knew the perfect spot to rent a room for a couple of days. He checked in and paid for two days with cash. The man took his money, handed him a room key, and did not bother getting any information from him. Perhaps he knew any information he would get would be false anyhow so he never bothered.

He opened the door to the room and the heat hit him in the face. Aaron walked in, tossed his bag on the bed then dropped the thermostat as low as it would go. He seriously doubted the room would cool off much based on the condition of the antiquated air-conditioning unit, and for a moment, he considered finding a better room.

Aaron sensed time was running low for him and the police would probably track him down soon. His only hope was he could get one more for Elvis before they caught up with him. He just had to survive one more night and then his hunt would begin. He would take her from the vigil, and after that, he decided, nothing else mattered. He returned to the car for the garment bag, and placed it carefully in the closet, then drove through a fast-food drive-through for food. Aaron had no idea how long it would take the police to realize there was another vehicle involved, so he decided he would do his best to conceal the car while keeping it as safe as possible in this part of town.

He pulled the car into a mechanic's shop the security company used and parked the car in the lot. He talked to one of the mechanics and told him about a fictitious engine malady he wanted them to check out. He knew the garage was about to close for the day, which was all part of his plan.

"No problem, I will be back tomorrow to check on it," he said, taking his bag of food and walking back to the motel. Locked behind the garage's chain-link fence would keep it safe from the street thugs, who would strip everything off the old gal, and would keep it away from the prying eyes of the police if they were looking for him.

†

"Jackpot," Dawson said when he walked back into the house. The crime scene techs had arrived and were processing the house. He located Blair, Desi, and Braxton in the master bedroom. "Elizabeth Beach has a yellow 1975 Cadillac still registered in her name," he informed them.

"That's what we need to be looking for then," Desi said.

Blair gave the crime scene lead technician instructions for processing the house, and the group drove back to the precinct to drop Dawson off and to pick up Blair's vehicle.

"Get some rest tonight. Tomorrow is going to be hectic searching for Beach unless we get lucky," Dawson told them, then climbed from the car.

"If you will drop us at the SUV, I will take Desi to the hospital and collect Tally," Blair said. "Let's plan on meeting at six tomorrow," she told Braxton as he pulled into the parking lot.

"See you then," he said and watched until they climbed inside the vehicle before pulling away.

Blair started the ignition and turned to Desi. "I don't know about you, but I'm exhausted. Somehow I don't think I will be sleeping much tonight though."

"I know the feeling. We have to find him tomorrow," Desi said.

"Yes we do," Blair said as she pulled onto the street.

†

"He's our man," Blair said as they entered Bailey's hospital room.

"Did you catch him?" Bailey said.

Desi smiled at her lover. "Not yet, sweetie, but we know who he is now, and even more about him so it is just a matter of time before we catch him."

"Tomorrow is the candlelight vigil, isn't it?" Bailey asked.

Desi was amazed that Bailey would remember those facts after everything she had been through the last twenty-four hours. "Yes, it is, love, we think he will strike again tomorrow and we are gambling it will be at the vigil."

"So tomorrow is going to be a very long day. If you will excuse us, Tally and I are going to try to get a few hours of sleep," Blair said.

"See you at six," Desi said and walked them to the door. When she turned back around to Bailey, she was scooting over in the bed. "Let me get my jammies on and I will be right there."

Desi stepped into the bathroom with her bag, brushed her teeth and hair before dressing in a pair of pajamas. She turned off the light and slipped into the bed beside Bailey.

"Welcome back," Bailey said as she kissed the top of Desi's head. "Just mind all the tubes and plaster," she teased.

"I am so exhausted, I probably won't move a muscle," Desi said as she snuggled into Bailey's warmth.

Bailey turned the television off and dimmed the lights. "Rest then, you have a bad guy to catch tomorrow."

"Yes, dear," Desi said as her hand slipped under the hospital gown to feel the warm, soft skin of Bailey's midsection. Her fingers traced slow circles on her stomach and then fell still.

Bailey looked down and saw Desi had fallen asleep. She smiled and held her lover snuggly until she slipped off to meet her in dreamland.

Chapter 21

Desi snuck from the bed to take a shower and dress for work, leaving Bailey sleeping soundly. When she crept back into the room, Bailey was awake and smiled at her.

"I know I won't see you for a long while, but call if you can to let me know how the hunt is going. Tony, from the FedEx office, brought me a new smartphone since my screen was cracked in the crash, but the number is the same."

"I will call as often as I can. Keep your fingers crossed we can find him before he strikes."

Bailey chuckled softly. "I will cross everything I can."

Desi looked at her for several seconds. "I love you so much."

"I know, and I love you. Be safe out there and watch your back," Bailey said.

Desi looked at the clock and knew Braxton would be waiting downstairs for her. She hated to leave Bailey, but she had a very important job to complete. "I will. See you as soon as I can get back."

"See you soon, my love," Bailey said and watched Desi leave the room.

Merita stepped off the elevator as Desi approached. "Good morning," she said with a pleasant smile.

"Good morning. Thanks for staying with Bailey today. Tommy and Joe will be here after work," Desi said.

"Don't worry, we will keep her out of trouble," Merita said. "You on the other hand, need to be very careful today and find that wicked man."

"I will," Desi said and stepped into the elevator.

†

Braxton was sitting out front waiting for her as she anticipated. He looked like he had not slept much and smiled when he looked up to see her approach.

"Hey, you look really tired," she said as she slipped into the passenger seat.

"My mind just won't shut down. We have to catch him today."

"Any news from the precinct?" she asked.

"No luck finding him or the caddy," he said. "Every available unit is on the hunt."

Desi knew the frustrating part was just beginning. They knew who the suspect was and probably what his plans were, but they did not know where he was hiding. Desi was running low on patience and from the look on his face Braxton was too.

"What is the game plan for today?" she asked.

Braxton pulled onto the street. "We will take a tour around the grounds of Graceland and make a strategic plan for surveying the area tonight. Dawson has pulled in another twenty officers to be in plainclothes to mill through the crowd."

"Should we dress down too, look a bit less like Five-0?" she teased.

"That probably wouldn't be a bad idea," he said. "I think Blair plans to rest for a few hours after lunch to prepare for a potentially long night, so I will drop you home if that's okay?"

"That would be perfect," she said as he pulled the car into the drive-through at Starbucks. "We are going to get him today right?"

"Yes, we are," Braxton said. "Tonight the hunter will be hunted and captured."

†

After a short briefing, Braxton, Desi, Tally, and Blair drove to Graceland. Braxton had managed to locate a map of the property and they selected several sites that would have a good view of the crowd. It was only ten, but the crowd had already begun to form. Desi knew the police would barricade the street to block traffic, and it would overflow with thousands of people, making their search the proverbial needle in a haystack.

Blair bought them lunch before they returned to the precinct for the final briefing. Once they all were confident of their plan, they dispersed to get a few hours of sleep, shower, and dress in more casual attire before meeting back at the precinct to ride to Graceland together.

Desi called to check on Bailey as Braxton drove her home. When she stepped inside Bailey's, she scooped up Fubar, checked that she had food and fresh water before walking to the bedroom. The room felt so empty without Bailey. She stripped out of her clothes and snuggled into Bailey's pillow, enjoying the scent of her lover as her eyes closed and she drifted. She slept for three hours before a dream woke her with a start. She was chasing someone through the darkness. She woke when a figure stopped to point a gun at her. Coated in sweat, her body tangled in the sheets, she looked up to see Fubar's green eyes watching her closely.

"Hey, baby," she said as she began petting the now purring kitten. "Mama hasn't gone crazy. I was just having a dream."

Fubar blinked her eyes and rubbed her head into Desi's hand. She enjoyed a few minutes with the kitten before climbing from the bed for a hot shower. She dressed in a loose-fitting pullover, jeans, and boots for the evening. Even though they would be in plainclothes, they still had to follow protocol to wear a Kevlar vest beneath their shirts. It would be hot in the muggy August night, but if attacked, the protection could make the difference between serious injury and possible death. She strapped on the vest with a deep sigh, and with a final kiss to Fubar, she walked out to ride with Braxton.

†

Aaron slept in until almost ten then showered before going to check on the car. The mechanic met him when he walked onto the lot. "I've checked her out and can't find anything wrong with her," he said.

"Maybe it was just my imagination then," he said. "What do I owe you?"

"Nothing this trip," the mechanic said, slapping him on the back.

"Thanks, man," he said and slipped in behind the wheel. He still had several hours until sundown when the car would be less obvious to the eyes that were probably searching for him by now, so he pulled into a parking garage, to hide the car then hit the streets to find and eat a leisurely lunch.

†

Desi felt the tension in the squad room as soon as she walked in. The final briefing with the plain-clothes officers had just ended, and they were on their way to Graceland. Blair had decided to give them a lead of an hour before they

323

would drive as close to Graceland as they could get. Braxton would drop Blair and Tally at a predetermined site. Then he and Desi would park at a reserved site to take up their positions. They completed a final radio check, and Desi stepped out to call Bailey.

"Hey baby, we are about to head out. I just wanted to say I love you and hope to see you soon," she said when Bailey answered. She could hear Joe and Tommy chattering in the background. "I hear your evening bodyguards in the background," she teased.

"I know. I have to get out of here soon before they blow up from eating cheeseburgers," Bailey said. There was a pause. "Be careful and hurry back to me," Bailey said.

Desi could hear the emotion in her voice as Bailey spoke.

"Keep my spot warm," she said, "I'll be there as soon as I can."

"I love you and am so proud of you," she said.

"Thank you, that means the world to me. I have to go, baby, love you," Desi said to end the call.

✝

Braxton dropped Blair and Tally as close to the crowd as he could then turned the vehicle to find the parking spot reserved for him.

He and Desi left the vehicle and began walking toward the crowd. Desi spotted numerous men walking through the crowd wearing the Johnston uniform and thought how ironic it would be if Beach showed up in uniform to blend in with the rest of his co-workers. She scanned each face in search of their suspect, and she scanned the crowd for the plainclothes force that was present. None of them jumped out at her as undercover police. She smiled to herself. They were doing their jobs very well.

When she looked to the left, she saw a man and woman, posing as local news reporters, scanning the growing crowd with a facial recognition unit disguised as a news camera. All three units owned by Memphis PD would be working the crowd tonight to help them find the needle.

"Stay close, Desi," Braxton said as they moved into the crowd. Full darkness was upon them. It would be easy to become lost in the crowd lit only by the thousands of small candles and the few streetlamps in the area.

"Team Two, this is Dawson," Desi received in her ear. "I have just heard from a patrol unit that they have discovered Elizabeth Beach's yellow caddy parked in a lot about a half mile from Graceland. Be advised Beach is in the crowd or on his way."

"Affirmative," Desi said and gave Braxton a thumb's-up. "Blair, did you copy?"

"Yes, we did," Blair said. "Keep your eyes sharp."

"He's getting close," Tally said.

Blair turned to look at her lover and noticed she had gooseflesh on her arms. The temperature was still hovering around ninety degrees and the humidity was high, so she knew Tally's chill was not weather related.

"Can you tell where he is or in what direction?" she asked Tally.

"Not yet," Tally answered.

"Keep trying," Blair said.

†

An hour earlier, Aaron had finished a hearty meal before retrieving the caddy to return to the motel and begin his preparations. The two days of beard growth disappeared down the bathroom sink and he took a hot shower. He used a blow-dryer to give more volume to his wavy hair. When he was ready to leave the motel, he pulled on his clothes, dropped a pair of oversized Ray ban sunglasses over his eyes, and stepped out to the fading afternoon light.

He drove to Graceland as the twilight faded into night and parked the car in a pay lot. His bag and remaining money were safely stored in the trunk awaiting his getaway, but deep down Aaron felt he would never make it back to the car. His dreams had told of this moment and he accepted his capture was imminent.

The crowd was rapidly growing thicker as he approached Graceland; he walked with a group of middle-age women into the center of activity. He looked at the group and decided none of them was the one. He needed someone young and spectacular for his final gift to Elvis. He milled among the crowd in search of her.

†

Desi was amazed by the wide variety of people amassed at Graceland from the old to the very young; some of them not even born while Elvis lived. She searched every face she passed in the crowd. When a speaker came over a public announcement system, she stopped in the crowd to listen. She was standing next to a brown-haired woman, eyes fixed on the gates of Graceland, where the speaker was welcoming them to the vigil. Next to her was a man in a white leather jumpsuit, like the ones Elvis wore in concert. She remembered thinking the man had to be melting inside the costume. When her attention turned back to the speaker, the man impersonating Elvis attempted to strike up a conversation with the woman. When she dismissed his advances, he placed a hand on her arm and whispered something into her ear.

✝

"Bingo," Braxton heard someone say in his ear. "We have him. Beach is disguised as Elvis and is wearing a white leather jumpsuit at five o'clock to the front gate, toward the back of the crowd."

Braxton scanned the crowd searching for Beach. To his horror, he found him standing almost directly next to Desi. There was a woman he appeared to be talking to standing between them. Desi appeared to have missed the announcement of the identification over the noise of the crowd. Braxton called for her on the radio.

"Leave me alone," the woman said as she pulled her arm free of the man.

"Hey, buddy, leave the lady alone," Desi said as she quickly flashed her badge at him.

His body froze in surprise and when Desi looked closer, she realized she was within arm's reach of the suspect. Her eyes grew wide with surprise. Beach realized too that she had recognized him and shoved the woman into Desi and took off at a full run through the crowd, pushing everyone out of his way.

Desi steadied the woman on her feet and triggered her microphone. "Suspect in white leather jumpsuit, running south at the back of the crowd," she announced as she pursued him on foot. A strange thought came to her mind as she ran through the crowd. She wished she had opted for her trainers instead of the leather boots that now weighed down her feet.

The suspect was twenty feet ahead of her and picking up speed as he ran. Desi jumped over a body he had pushed out of his way and when her feet touched ground, she glanced to her left to see a dark figure slicing through the crowd.

Beach stumbled when his feet tangled with a bag someone had brought with them for the evening. That was just enough time for the dark shadow to launch himself at Beach to tackle him to the ground.

Desi was close enough to hear the groan of pain emitted when Beach hit the ground with Braxton's two hundred pounds of muscle forcing him flat on the asphalt. Braxton acted quickly, pulling one of Beach's arms behind his back to snap a handcuff on it before Beach comprehended what was going on. That only took seconds and the struggle was on. For a smaller man, Beach gave Braxton a challenge and it wasn't until Desi grabbed his left arm to assist that they were able to slip the other cuff onto his wrist.

"Suspect down and in custody," Desi announced over the radio as Braxton pulled him to his feet and began marching him toward Braxton's car. Desi stepped forward and heard a crunching sound. She looked down at her right foot to find she had stepped on the Ray bans Beach had been wearing. "Oops," she said as she bent down to retrieve the glasses.

Unaware of what was going on, the crowd parted to allow them to pass through without hesitation. When they cleared the crowd, Tally and Blair joined them on the path to the car.

"Call for a unit," Braxton said.

Desi stepped away from the crowd to use the radio to call for a patrol unit to take Beach to the police station.

When a cruiser arrived, Braxton read him his Miranda rights with several witnesses present. Beach remained silent, refusing to speak or acknowledge the comprehension of his rights. Braxton shrugged and placed Beach safely inside the cruiser for transport.

"Let's follow him back to the precinct," Blair said.

"Thanks Team One, suspect in transport," Braxton's voice came over the radio. "Dismissed."

†

The patrol officers escorted Beach into an interrogation room and remained with him until the others arrived. Dawson turned to the chief who was wearing a huge smile. "Do you have any issue with Blair conducting the interview?"

"Not at all," Bronson said.

Blair nodded to him as she approached the room. Desi, Braxton, Dawson, and Bronson were in a small observation room to watch and listen to what transpired in the room. They listened as Blair began speaking, informing Beach of his rights again and then described the charges against him. Beach stared at her, remaining mute as she paced back and forth in front of him.

Desi watched for several more minutes and Beach still refused to speak. He motioned with his hands he wanted to write something, so Blair pushed a notepad and pencil over to him. Desi did not need to see the note to know that he had written, "I want a lawyer" in bold print. Blair picked up the pad and held it up toward the window for all to read then left the room.

†

Tally could not stand the sight of the man so when they reached the precinct, she returned to the office they had been working in and sat staring at the board and the long list of names that had been printed on it. It only took seconds for her head to start buzzing.

329

"So you have him in custody?" Lisa asked.

"Yes, he is being interrogated now," Tally said.

"Do you not wish to participate in the interview?" Lisa asked.

Tally took a deep breath and released a sigh. "I can't stand to look at him. The man's aura reeks of vileness," she explained.

"I will pass the news on to his victims," Lisa said. "Great job, Tally."

"We couldn't have done it without your help," she told Lisa. "Thank you."

"My pleasure," Lisa said as the sound of her voice faded away.

Desi found Tally sitting at the table, still staring at the board. She walked over to her and sat beside her. "Are you okay?" she asked.

"I'm okay, I just don't want to be near him," Tally said.

Desi placed a hand on her shoulder. "I can completely understand. Would you like some coffee?"

"I'd love some," Tally said and they walked to the break room together for a fresh cup.

✝

"There is not much else we can do now but see if we can get him a lawyer," Blair said. "Can he be placed under suicide watch in solitary for tonight?" she asked Dawson.

"Yes, we'll have him searched and processed before we place him in a cell. There is not much we can do about a lawyer until morning," Dawson said.

Bronson turned to face the group. "Great job, folks," he said. "I suggest we go home and get a well- earned night of sleep then reconvene in the morning. Nine o'clock okay with everyone?" he asked.

"It will take us all day to wrap up the reports," Blair said. "I really don't expect Beach to do any talking, do you?" she asked Bronson.

"No, I think he's going to clam up and not utter a word."

"So we need to get all the case reports airtight for when it goes to trial. It will be a very lopsided event if he refuses to participate," she said.

They met Desi and Tally in the office and made their departures. "Tell Bailey we are thinking about her and we will be by to see her soon," Blair told Desi on the way to their cars.

"Thanks, I will," she said as she climbed into Braxton's car. "Will you pick me up in the morning? I still have a set of clothes at the hospital."

"Of course I will, Desi." He started the car. "Is there anything you need before we get to the hospital?"

"No, I think I'm good. I'm too tired to even think about celebrating," Desi said.

Braxton looked over at her. "I don't think the enormity of what we have done has sunk in yet."

"I feel numb, Braxton, do you think that is normal?"

"I would never accuse you of being normal, Desi, but we just arrested the biggest suspect this area has seen since the West Memphis Three."

"Yeah, that's right," Desi said in a voice vacant of emotion.

Braxton was concerned about the lack of elation he felt Desi should be experiencing. He worried she was experiencing a mild case of shock. If she did not appear better tomorrow, he would take her for examination himself, he thought as he drove to the hospital.

"See you tomorrow, partner," she said with a small smile when she got out of the car.

"Get some rest," he called after her.

†

When she reached Bailey's room, the lights were down and Bailey slept peacefully. There was no one left to send home, so she quietly slipped into the bathroom to change clothes before crawling into Bailey's arms. Bailey shifted on the bed to allow her room, but did not wake. Desi placed her head on Bailey's shoulder and fell almost immediately to sleep.

Chapter 22

The next three days passed in a blur for Desi. The team had worked long hours to wrap up the reports and evidence against Beach. Blair informed the team that the morning after his arrest, a court-appointed defense attorney took on the case on his behalf; however, Beach held strong to his commitment of silence. The lawyer reported that when he met with Beach, he gestured for a notepad, and wrote, "No trial, plead guilty and let's be done with this."

Bailey was healing quickly and discharged on the third day after the capture. Blair and Tally had also completed their assignments but decided to stay through the weekend before flying home on Sunday.

On Friday, the mayor held a ceremony on behalf of Desi and Braxton's work on the case, calling their dedication to justice heroic and presented them both with plaques for their achievements. Both Tally and Blair had chosen to defer the recognition to the local heroes, wishing instead to maintain low profiles for future cases.

That night at Club Fubar, another celebration included Blair and Tally, introduced as the newest family to the club. Charles and Tony had arrived from New Orleans and were sharing Bailey-sitting duty during the day. With Tommy and Joe's help, they planned a gala celebration and show in honor of the heroes.

On Saturday, from the seat of her wheelchair Bailey grilled up another round of steaks in a more private setting for Desi, Braxton, Donna, Blair, and Tally.

As they sat around enjoying the food and the growing friendship, Blair remarked. "It was a lot of fun working with you two. Are you sure you don't want to go back to Virginia with us?"

"I think we have about as much as we can handle right here," Desi said. "It is a tempting offer, though."

"The invite is always open if either of you change your minds," Blair said.

Bailey took a sip of tea as she studied Blair from across the table. "Will we see you two after tonight?" she asked.

"Since there is no trial, we will go back to Virginia, but I'm certain Beach will get the death penalty. I seriously doubt he will make any effort to appeal either. You can bet we will be back when he is executed to serve as witnesses."

"Any idea how long that will take?" Bailey said.

"Not really. It can be as short as six months to years depending on the schedules and elapsed appeal rights."

Bailey smiled and said, "You don't have to wait until then to come for a visit. You are welcome anytime."

Tally grinned back at her. "The road travels both ways you know."

"How well I know. We may have to take a little ride to Virginia," Bailey said to Desi.

"I'd like that, sweetheart."

†

After their guests had departed, Bailey and Desi were lying in bed. "You will get your arm cast off in a week or so right?" she asked Bailey.

"Yes, in two weeks. I might even get a walking cast for my leg then too. Why do you ask?"

"Braxton and Donna leave for their cruise in two weeks, and I thought that would be an excellent time for us to get away as well."

Bailey smiled at her lover. "You get the time off, and I will start making reservations Monday."

"Why not tomorrow," Desi teased.

"Because, my dear, tomorrow will be the first day we have had alone together in ages and I plan to keep you right here until noon at the earliest."

"Good luck with that. You will be starving by nine o'clock."

"You can make us breakfast in bed then," Bailey teased back.

Desi broke out in laughter and looked at Bailey. "I love you, Bailey Chambers."

"I love you too, gorgeous woman," Bailey said and pulled her in for a kiss

Epilogue

Bailey and Desi did get to spend two beautiful, love-filled weeks on the Gulf in Florida. Their mornings were spent drinking coffee and sharing breakfast on the balcony, overlooking the emerald-green water. On several occasions, they witnessed aerial shows by a pair of dolphins swimming along the shore. The afternoons were for lounging in the room or sunning by the pool, and when the sun began to dip, Desi would assist Bailey to a bench by the beach to watch the beautiful fall sunsets. Bailey would hold Desi in her arms until the sun sank below the horizon and then end the day with a soft kiss.

On the last day of their vacation, Bailey moped around and finally flopped down on the bed while Desi packed their bags. "What's the matter, my love?" she finally asked.

"Our two weeks together have gone by way too fast. I wish we could stay another month."

Desi stopped packing and sat beside Bailey. "I agree. So I have booked us two more weeks in February," she said and kissed Bailey. "That will get us through the holidays and by then I'm sure we will both be ready for another break."

Bailey smiled at her. "Have I told you how much I love you today?"

"Several times, but I never tire of hearing it," Desi said as she kissed her again.

Bailey pulled her in for a deeper kiss and then looked into Desi's smiling eyes. "I love you more with each passing breath."

"What more could a girl ask for?" Desi said as she ruffled Bailey's hair. "You know, I really like this gray patch," she said as her fingers played in the gray hairs that had returned after the wound on her head had healed. "It makes you look very distinguished and handsome."

"I guess I won't be dying my hair after all," Bailey said with a smile.

†

When they returned to Memphis, Bailey began physical therapy. Every morning promptly at eight, Louise would show up to drive her to her therapy sessions and then drop her off at work. They had arranged for Bailey to do deskwork and training while she was recuperating from her injuries and the tediousness of the work gave her incentive to work harder in therapy to get back on the road. The therapist declared it miraculous when three months after the accident, Bailey resumed driving her run.

†

Their lives had returned to a normal flow. Bailey made her runs four days a week and worked at the club on the weekends while Desi and Braxton worked the cold case files. The chief surprised them by advancing them both a detective grade after their success with the Killer King case. They were successful in closing several more of the cases, but none that had been as exciting. Still, Desi enjoyed being away from the immediate horrors on the street and felt she could actually put her education and sharp eye for detail to better use on the cold cases.

Blair had called to check in with her several times, each time trying to lure her away from Memphis to come work

337

with her at the FBI. "Maybe one day, but not today," Desi had told her and it soon became a joke between them. Blair would call and immediately ask, "Is today the day?" which would always get a chuckle from Desi.

She and Bailey had discussed the option of moving to Virginia, but had agreed that home for them was Memphis.

†

Nearly a year later, Braxton returned to the office after a summons to Dawson's office and placed a notice of execution memorandum on her desk. "Are you ready for a trip to Knoxville?"

"Most definitely," she said. "I will drop Blair an e-mail and give her the particulars."

"Dawson has already arranged two rooms for us to spend the night. Do you think Bailey and Donna could come along?"

"I don't see why not. They can hang around the hotel and then we can get a nice dinner on the river after the deed is done."

"Let's make it happen," Braxton said.

†

Three weeks later they were in the lobby of a Hampton Inn talking with Tally and Blair. They had been busy working several cases since they left Memphis, but none nearly as exciting as the "Killer King," as Beach had been nicknamed. There were so many missing details of why he had done what he did to at least thirty-two people, but Beach was determined to go to his grave with his evil secrets. Aaron Beach had surprised them all by not speaking another word since the time of his arrest. Blair told them that the warden had described him as a model prisoner—quiet, trouble free—but he still would not turn his back on Aaron Beach.

†

Desi had never witnessed an execution before and she felt a bit morbid about being excited about another human's death, but she felt by being there it would provide some closure for her and all the women Beach had murdered. Before they left Memphis she had mentioned her apprehensions to Braxton, who assured her that unlike his victims, Beach would suffer a pain-free death.

†

When the time approached for them to drive to the prison, Tally opted to stay behind with Bailey and Donna. "That place is filled with evil and death," she had said. Desi could understand her reasoning when she thought of the nightmares and visions Tally dealt with throughout her young life.

†

The warden personally greeted them and escorted them into the witness theater to observe Beach's execution. "You all did a great deed in removing this one from the streets," he said as they took their seats. "Memphis should be very proud of the work you did."

At fifteen minutes to six, a door opened and Aaron Beach was led into a small plexiglass-walled room the prison called the tank. Desi knew the glass was tinted and he could not see through it, but she felt his cold eyes were looking directly into her soul. She felt a shiver rush through her body and shook her shoulders trying to shed the eerie feeling.

Blair had witnessed her reaction and leaned over to ask, "Are you okay?"

"Yes, I'm just thankful this will be the last time I ever lay eyes on him," she whispered back.

His body was strapped onto the restraint table and an IV line started in his left arm that would serve as the portal for the lethal dose of medications that would end his life. A prison chaplain offered the sacrament of Last Rites to Beach, which he refused, also declining an opportunity to make any final statements.

The clock on the wall echoed through the theater as it ticked the final sixty seconds of Aaron Beach's life away. The first plunger of medications began to fall, filling his veins with a rapid-acting sedative and when the second plunger began to lower, Beach sang out a verse from Elvis Presley's hit, "Blue Suede Shoes."

Those were the last words spoken in this world by Aaron Beach as the sedative performed its intended purpose and he was rendered unconscious. Desi watched as the machine injected two final doses of medication into his veins. The prison medical director watched the heart monitor until it had remained flat-lined for five minutes then pronounced him dead.

Desi was not surprised when someone, another witness, spoke aloud, "The King has left the building," when Aaron Beach was pronounced. Several other witnesses chuckled at the snarky remark.

She watched as Beach's lifeless body was taken from the room on a gurney. For a brief moment, Desi felt sadness wash over her as she realized Beach would have no one to claim his body and would end up as a pile of ashes in a state-owned crematorium.

They stood in line to sign the perfunctory witness statements attesting to his death and then walked back out to the car.

"You know, I was holding on to a glimmer of hope that Beach would break his silence to share at least some information," Desi said, obviously disappointed.

Blair smiled at her. "I think in a way he did," Blair said. "That verse from 'Blue Suede Shoes' in his last worldly moment confirmed his complete obsession with Elvis Presley. Everything he did, he did willingly as a sacrifice to the man he worshipped as an idol in hopes of gaining his favor."

"I don't think he will be meeting Elvis in the afterlife," Braxton said as he drove them back to the hotel.

"The King has left the building," Desi repeated in the backseat. "Yes, he has," she added with a smile.

†

They drove in silence and when they arrived at the hotel, Braxton turned off the engine and turned to the backseat to look at Desi. "I want us to agree on one thing before we go any further," he said.

"What would that be?" she asked.

"That we put all of the ugliness from this case to bed once and for all. Beach was a focus in our lives for long enough and now we need to move forward."

"I agree," Desi said. "We have more important people to focus on," she said with a grin.

"Absolutely," Blair said, "so let's go get them and have a wonderful night on the river."

The End

About the Author

Ali Spooner

Ali Spooner is a native of Florida, currently living and working in Memphis, TN. Home for Ali is Pensacola, Florida where she has a partner of twenty years, one son and a grandchild that has her wrapped completely around her little finger. Her other children are all four legged, three dogs and two cats, and my dearest companion in Memphis, Rascal, a rescued tiger kitten named after my favorite country group.

A true daughter of the South, Ali enjoy spinning stories about the South, the strong, but gentle women and creatures that make it a wondrous place to live.

As an "Indie" author, Ali has been writing for many years as a hobby, and after a cancer diagnosis in 2010, she decided to take a leap and start self-publishing and has published over a dozen stories. Ali's characters range from cowgirls and psychics, to a healthy dose of supernatural beings. She has written stand-alone titles and series. Ali frequently writes several stories at a time, depending on which characters are bouncing around loudest in her head.

Ali is an avid reader and her other hobbies include photography, outdoor activities and watching college sports.

Other Books from Affinity eBook Press

Alane Hotchkin- Beginning of the End What happens when life doesn't go exactly as you planned and you must protect others from your own fate? Escaping a horrific childhood, Nikki longed to find happily ever after in adulthood. What she found was Hell. Or did it find her? Finding the courage to break the cycle of betrayal, she opens her heart one last time. Alex lived a childhood others dreamed of. Her father never once denied the young rebel a thing. All her life she dreamed of protecting others; to follow in her father's footsteps. Soon though she learned sex and fists made the most powerful of weapons. Alex controls the women in her life through fear and sex, will breaking the cycle be too much to overcome? Will loving Nikki be enough to change her, or is Alex beyond help?

Alex would give Nikki the world, but at what price? When a person's tightly controlled reality snaps what then…? This is the Beginning of the End for one of them and the ultimate sacrifice for the other. But who is who in this game of life?

Galveston 1900: Swept Away- Linda Crist On September 7-8, 1900, the island of Galveston, Texas, was destroyed by a hurricane, or 'tropical cyclone', as it was called in those days. This story is a fictional account of Mattie and Rachel, two women who lived there, and their lives during the time of the 'great storm'. Forced to flee from her family at a young age, Rachel Travis finds a home and livelihood on the island of Galveston. Independent, friendly, and yet often lonely, only one other person knows the dark secret that haunts her. Madeline "Mattie" Crockett is trapped in a loveless marriage, convinced that her fate is sealed. She never dares to dream of true happiness, until Rachel Travis comes walking into her life.   As emotions come to light, the storm of Mattie's marriage converges with the very real hurricane. Can they survive, and build the life they both dream of?

This second edition of one of Linda Crist's best-loved novels maintains the original story, while incorporating some reader-pleasing passages that were cut from the first edition. As an added bonus, the short story "Something to Celebrate" is included at the end of the novel, detailing further adventures of Rachel and Mattie.

Rapture: Sins of the Sinners- A. C. Henley & Fran Heckrotte
A serial killer is targeting young lesbians throughout the state of Texas.Texas Ranger Cochetta Lovejoy is assigned to the case. Convinced she knows who is committing the murders, Ranger Lovejoy is willing to do whatever it takes to put the perpetrator behind bars--even if it means stretching the limits of the law by manipulating the judicial system. Detective Agnes Kelly-Elliott is one of Ft. Worth Police Department's finest investigators.   When Ranger Lovejoy appears on the crime scene of a recent murder, Agnes fears a dark secret that, if revealed, could destroy her family ties, and end her career. This is a dark, gritty, graphic tale of desire gone awry, and flawed characters looking for redemption in all the wrong places.

Till There Was You- S. Anne Gardner Julia is a woman used to power and is not afraid to use it or impose her will to get her way. She appears to have the world but a part of her is empty and cold as a frozen tundra. Julia rides in the mornings to clear her head and to make plans for what she is about to set in motion. Theodora, known as Teddy, is trying to put together a marriage filled with uncertainties. She felt once upon a time that she would have a great love but that has eluded her. One morning these two women meet and from the first instance, it is explosive. The attraction is undeniable, the fears very real and the end without question will change them both forever.

Denial- Jackie Kennedy Time spent in Somalia has Doctor Celeste Cameron accustomed to living and working in a war zone. Coming back home to America, Celeste is glad to see the end of the peril she has been in—or so she thinks. Danger seems to follow Celeste and she finds it in the shape of Amy. What Celeste feels for Amy scares her more than anything she has faced in war zones. Amy has the same feelings, but is in denial and vows to marry Josh, Celeste's twin brother, no matter what. When fate brings them together again, will they give in to their mutual attraction or will they once again deny what they feel.

In Name Only - JM Dragon - Sequel to The Fix-it Girl Can an agreement forged out of necessity actually work?

'55 Ford - Erin O'Reilly Andrea McBride, the author of four books, wants to find someone to restore an old '55 Ford truck that she inherited in a real estate purchase. She will only settle for the best and finds RJ Whittaker who many proclaim to be the best restorer among millions.

An Affair of Love- S. Anne Gardner From a dark past, a forbidden love, a secret comes. Among the confusion and the chaos of an unwanted reality, two women find something they neither want nor can deny.

Desert Heat - Dannie Marsden For Luce Diamond, an undercover policewoman, her life is in shambles. Her longtime lover left her and an automobile accident that resulted in a child's death haunts her.

Taming the Wolff - Del Robertson ONLY ONE WOMAN...HAS THE POWER...TO TAME THE WOLFF...

Private Dancer - TJ Vertigo Reece Corbett grew up on the mean streets on New York City, abused, used and in trouble with the law. Faith Ashford grew up wealthy, with all the creature comforts that money provides. When they meet fireworks begin.

Miriam and Esther - Sherry Barker Miriam thought her life would play out in the bustling metropolis of Dallas, but after a life-changing accident, she moves to the small town of Cool Lake, Texas to get her head on straight and regain her senses.

McKee - A.C. Henley Private Investigator Quinlan McKee has returned to Los Angeles after a three-year absence, only to find herself embroiled in a world of child slavery and police corruption.

Nocturne - JD Glass From acclaimed author, JD Glass, and featuring some of her most loved characters. Nocturnes is a collection of events and adventures, from the sensual dreamscape of the deepest love, to the brooding intensity of desire.

E-Books, Print, Free e-books

Visit our website for more publications available online.

http://www.affinityebooks.com

Published by Affinity E-Book Press NZ LTD

Canterbury, New Zealand

Registered Company 2517228